SHARDS

A NOBLEBRIGHT
FANTASY ANTHOLOGY

Edited by C. J. Brightley and Robert McCowen

ISBN 9781723792021

Published in the United Sates of America by Spring Song Press, LLC. www.springsongpress.com

Cover design by Kerry Hynds of Aero Gallerie.

B. MORRIS ALLEN
J.E. BATES
JADE BLACK
GUSTAVO BONDONI
BOKERAH BRUMLEY
STEPHEN CASE
R. K. DUNCAN
M.C. DWYER
CHLOE GARNER
KELLY A. HARMON
PETE ALEX HARRIS
BEN HOWELS
TOM JOLLY
BRANDON M. LINDSAY
ALICE LOWEECEY
JASON J. MCCUISTON
ALEX MCGILVERY
VILLE MERILÄINEN
JENNIFER R. POVEY
HOLLY LYN WALRATH
PAT WOODS
RICHARD ZWICKER

AND EDITED BY

C. J. BRIGHTLEY

AND ROBERT MCCOWEN

Contents

# Acknowledgments

Many thanks go to the talented authors who contributed to this anthology and to all authors who infuse their works with noblebright ideals.

Robert McCowen assisted with every phase of editing this anthology from story selection to copyediting. I'm immensely grateful for his insight and attention to detail.

And of course, the greatest thanks go to you, dear reader, for believing in noblebright fantasy.

C. J. Brightley
cjbrightley.com
springsongpress.com

Foreword

Noblebright fantasy offers hope in the darkest moments. In noblebright fantasy, flawed (yet realistic) characters can choose to be kind, honest, and principled even when it hurts. Redemption is possible, and good characters can make a difference.

Noblebright fantasy is fantasy for our time. It isn't utopian fantasy—we all know the world can be dark. Instead, noblebright fantasy offers glimpses of what it looks like to oppose that darkness with courage, integrity, love, and sacrifice, and how those choices can make the world a little brighter.

For more information, please visit Noblebright.org and SpringSongPress.com.

C. J. Brightley
Spring Song Press
SpringSongPress.com

P.S. - Please subscribe to the Spring Song Press newsletter!

Smoke Wraiths

Ville Meriläinen

Flames gorged on the woods like locusts on summer grain, and the Hanged Man fled from them. Not for fear, no, but because the smoke wraiths had taken his fire and he needed it back before the grand pyre turned him to ash. If he died empty, momma warned, he'd return as one of them.

"Come back, you bastards!" he yelled. The wraiths laughed with the sound of crashing trees and exploding sap. They had taken from him what was most precious and exposed it for all the world to see, and now the mountain burned with the love once hidden in the Hanged Man's heart. That's what fire was, no? All the poets momma was so fond of seemed to agree, and so the Hanged Man had thought he might one day marry a beautiful girl and have a child of his own despite his uncomeliness. He was so full of love everything he touched burned to cinders.

"Come *back*! You can't take what is mine!" he screamed. The smoke wraiths mocked him by making a tree come crashing down and break into a swarm of glowing fireflies. They hated him for housing fire, and now that they were free, they dragged it along with their tails and turned it against its master. They made the air blistering and taste of pain, which was contradictory with his state. Hurting and breathing were discomforts of the living, and the Hanged Man was definitely dead. His hands would only cool once he was ready to kiss the dirt, momma used to say, and though the force of his heartbeat after the tree nearly fell on him would've made him want to argue, momma always knew best.

Tears wet his ash-stained cheeks, but he'd cried enough to know crying didn't bring anyone back. So he kept running, and when the smoke wraiths laughed, he screamed louder. Maybe they were taking him home, to where the yellow flowers grew and where the house sat by a mountain lake. The Hanged Man hadn't been there since the first time they'd escaped and he'd needed momma's help, and when he saw the river falling down the mountainside ahead, a little sadness seeped into the fear pulsing in his veins.

The smoke wraiths brought his precious fire to the path, where it waited for him like a bully, but he knew how to deal with those and that was by going around. The Hanged Man scratched his legs and arms climbing the rock face, but he couldn't go any closer to where the worst blaze was when there was none of it left inside him.

Halfway up the crag, there came a voice from above that made the Hanged Man stiffen and stop. Beneath the jeering of the wraiths someone cried for help, and though he was scarcely in any position to give it, the desperation in the voice broke his stupor and made him climb faster. His arms were bloodied by the time he reached level ground, and the sight waiting there made him groan. The blaze was as strong here as below, chewing up firs and licking berry bushes.

The voice cried again, and the Hanged Man ran. His skin had turned a shiny pink and hard as scales long ago and didn't feel much, but the higher he'd climbed, the less scar tissue and deadened nerves guarded him from heat. The thought crossed his mind the weeper didn't have *any* such boons, and dead or alive, it had to be him or the smoke wraiths to help whoever was trapped in the hellscape. Heaven knew the wraiths weren't about to help anyone.

The Hanged Man found a young girl hanging onto a rock jutting out of the river. The sight of him made her shriek with fright.

"Don't be scared," the Hanged Man said, but then thought the girl must've never seen a dead man walking before. "It's only me, the boy from the mountains."

The girl kept crying, and he racked his brain for the name momma had given him. He hadn't been a boy for a long time, and she was surely too young to know him by this moniker.

He couldn't recall it, but then thought it probably didn't matter. He wasn't trying to make a friend, but to help someone, and so he waded as far into the water as he dared, reached out a hand and said, "I know a place away from the fire. Let me take you there."

The girl traced a look along the shiny skin of his arm up to his scarred, smiling face, and shook her head with a whimper. "Come, come," the Hanged Man coaxed. "It's not a nice place, but it's nicer than this."

The girl shrieked when a branch broke off and fell in the river with a great splash. It floated past her, cracking and steaming, and she let go of the rock. Her legs reached the bottom of the shallow pass, but the current was strong and swept her off her feet. The Hanged Man jumped in and fished out the girl, who coughed out water when he climbed out cradling her.

"Are you hurt?" he asked, watching the cloth of her skirt touch his palm. It didn't smolder, to his shared relief and dismay.

The girl shook her head. She shivered, strange though it was, but the Hanged Man couldn't tell how cold the river had been. He pondered whether it'd be safest to wade upstream along it, but the many branches drooping over the stream sold him against it.

She still coughed, though there was no more water coming out. Even as he started to run, the Hanged Man made a choice. Whether or not the smoke wraiths were going to momma's house, that's where he'd go. He'd been given the chance to help someone, and of all the many things momma used to say, there was one thing she made sure the Hanged Man never forgot: You could squander a great many chances in your life, but you never, *never*, let the chance to help someone slip you by.

So, as gently as he could, the Hanged Man pressed the girl against his chest with both hands and said, "Don't you worry. I know where you'll be safe."

It was tough scaling the cliffs with one arm wrapped around the child, but breathing soon got easier. When the Hanged Man finally reached the mountain meadow, the sun burned as red as the woodland, hanging low above the lake behind the charred remains of the house. Smoke rose to cloud the evening as a great pall, but it was only smoke and the wraiths were gone from it. The flowers around the house came abloom with the sunset, and even with the acrid smell clinging to him, their scent was sweet and funereal.

The Hanged Man watched the town burning in the distance, at the foot of the mountain past the woods, when the girl roused him with a sniffle. She, too, watched the town, but not with the Hanged Man's melancholy. Hers was a mask of loss and terror, and the Hanged Man recognized it as one he'd worn long ago. It came to him this girl must've lost her own momma tonight, and through his scorched lids pushed tears of sympathy.

"You may put me down now," the girl said. Her voice was dull with heartbreak, but its tones were soft and deliberate. Her dress was fine, and so must've been her house and heritage.

For a long time, she sat still, arms wrapped around her knees, and wept. The fire never calmed, but she did. When night fell to curtain the flames, as deep and dark as though it had become one with the smoke, she turned from the ruins.

"I feel hollow," she said, a newly-made orphan of eleven at most. "Like all the tears have carved me empty. I feel I should still cry, but more refuse to fall."

"Tears don't bring anyone back," the Hanged Man said. The callousness of his words became apparent only when the girl whimpered.

She was quiet another while, then stood. Moonlight turned her blonde hair silvery when she straightened her dress, took a last deep breath, and faced the Hanged Man with an air of solemnity. She donned a cordial mask in place of the weeper's, the way fine folk did when they were abashed for showing emotion, but her grip was tight, desperate, as though she clung onto him the same way as to the rock in the river. It chilled and saddened the Hanged Man at once; if a child ever needed a reason to show sorrow, those reasons were far lesser than this.

"Thank you," she said. "I would surely have perished without you. My name is Lucy, and I think I know who you are, but only by reputation. May I ask for your name?"

Her sudden calmness sent the chill deeper—until the Hanged Man realized that, though she had survived, she had lost one life and her habits were all she had left of it. He responded to her strain by straightening his back as he searched his memories. Of all the things momma said, hearing his name had never been his fondest. She only used it when she was mad, but there was another one that came to him at once, and it had only ever been spoken lovingly.

"Jacob," he said firmly, claiming as his own the name of momma's favorite of the poets who'd shared her bed for a time. He bowed deep and kissed her hand, the way she'd seen men with silken jackets do when they greeted a lady. "My name is Jacob, and I'm very pleased to meet you, Lucy."

Lucy returned a tight smile that cracked the mask. "If only we'd met under kinder stars. To think I'd planned to surprise my parents only this morning with berries I picked myself, and tonight I would mourn them." She let go of his hand, then held the blackened end of the noose around his neck and furled her brow. "But prithee, Jacob, would you tell me why you wear such a strange necklace?"

The Hanged Man grunted, took the rope from her. Fiddling it between his fingers, he said, "I'm not sure how to put this, but, do you think there's anything odd about me?"

Lucy averted her eyes and sucked on her lip. "I would not want to be rude towards someone who rescued me, but yes, since you ask, I do notice some… unusual features."

"What I mean is I'm dead."

A sound of surprise fled the girl, and her gaze shot up to meet his. "If you are joking, I'm afraid the humor is lost on me."

The Hanged Man shook his head. "I'm not like you. Did it burn, holding my hand just then?"

"Of course not."

"It should, and it don't because the townsfolk hanged me. See, this," he tapped the charred end of the rope, "this is what the smoke wraiths did. They escaped when I died and pulled out my fire with them, and now they want me to burn with the town so they can make me one of them." He turned to scream at the house over his shoulder, startling the girl. "And I know you're in there, so don't think I'm not coming for you!"

"There's no one there," Lucy said. She'd taken a step closer to the edge, away from him. "Is this your house, Jacob?" she asked. Her voice had lost its softness and become tenser.

"It was momma's. They got out once before here, but she put them back in me. Knew they'd be better inside than out making misery for everyone." His mouth bent into a mournful arch. "But she's not around no more to do it again. Momma burned to trap the smoke, and the wind took her ashes long ago."

Lucy looked as though about to respond, but her unvoiced reply trailed off into an inquisitive hum. The Hanged Man turned to find smoke erupting from the house. It hid away the flowers, fell past them like a grey waterfall, rose to the sky to envelope everything around them. Lucy started to cough, and the Hanged Man picked her up. The open doorway loomed ahead, a portal into the very world from where the smoke flowed.

"Think I'm scared? Think I'm not coming in?" the Hanged Man yelled. A rumbling cackle rolled over them, and stole the verve of his defiance. He advanced with a step as sure as he could muster, but the girl wrapped her arms around his throat and sniffled.

"Please, Jacob. Don't go in there."

The Hanged Man met her frightened look. For a moment, her fancy manners and grown-up way of talking had made him forget how small she was, and remembering it made him feel a little braver, if only for the want to protect her. Maybe he'd never found a wife, but in her he might find a daughter.

"I won't be long. They're cornered now. You can wait here and I'll be out before—"

She gripped him so tight he choked and gagged. "I don't want you going at all."

"I have to." He gently stroked her hair. "It's the only way I get my fire back."

Lucy whimpered, but loosened her grip enough for the Hanged Man to breathe. "I'm not staying here."

"Then I'll take care of you. I promise."

The smoke wraiths laughed at him. The Hanged Man gritted his teeth and stomped into the house.

Lucy began to cough harder as soon as they crossed the threshold. There shouldn't have been anything left to burn, but the house was ablaze like the woods below. Smoke billowed everywhere like upside down ocean waves, and the wraiths were there in multitudes, hanging onto every strand and tendril that wove itself around the Hanged Man's feet.

Now that they were within his reach, he wasn't sure what to do. Momma had bound them with her own flame, but he couldn't touch them. The Hanged Man's attention snapped up from the loose tendrils when a voice spoke out.

"Look at you, boy. You ain't got a lick of sense in that head."

The Hanged Man's mouth fell open. Momma stood before him, at the foot of the stairs right where he'd scooped up her ashes, arms akimbo and as livid as ever. He nearly dropped Lucy from the surprise, and momma tossed up a hand at that. "What're you thinking, chasing smoke with someone like her? I thought I raised you better."

"You did, momma!" cried the Hanged Man. "I had a chance to help her and I did!"

Momma folded her arms and scowled. "Ain't no wonder no nice daughter ever took a shine to a fool like you. Poor girl ain't like us. She can't breathe in here."

The Hanged Man brought a hand to Lucy's mouth, met momma's scowl with a mortified look, and spun on his heels to get the girl out. He found no door behind him, and when he completed his circle to beg for momma's help, found no momma either. Even as he looked, the house collapsed around him, but not on him; he was left in the middle of the smoky plain like before, but now there was nothing but grey emptiness, nowhere for him to take Lucy.

The Hanged Man prodded her, tried to shake her, but the girl's eyes stayed closed. He cried her name, shook her again, but she did not revive.

At his misery, the smoke wraiths laughed.

"That does it, you bastards!" the Hanged Man screamed, so long and loud his lungs ran empty. "You think this is funny? Huh? You think a dead little girl is funny?"

They laughed and laughed at the way his voice cracked, but that only inflamed his rage further. With his lungs empty, the Hanged Man sucked in a deep breath, inhaling so much smoke his head felt dizzy and his stomach sick. He kept sucking it in, until his lungs were too full to breathe in any more, and then he screamed again.

No smoke came out, only went in. The Hanged Man kept at it until he collapsed to his knees. By then, the laughter was gone and so was the smoke. It swirled inside him, made his bones vibrate with its cackling and movement.

When the Hanged Man could again see the sky and the yellow flowers surrounding him, Lucy's dress began to smolder where he touched it.

The Hanged Man watched lifeless smoke rise from the cloth, smelled how her flesh began to cook against his hands. He'd gotten his fire back, but at a cost much too dear. He shuddered with a sob, began to cry. Tears wouldn't bring anyone back, never did, but that was all he could do.

The Hanged Man stood. Fire had died from the woods when he'd eaten the smoke and the wraiths, and he started down the charcoal path to take Lucy back home. He wanted her ashes to rest with her family, and his with hers. Returning to the folds of the living meant nothing if he would be alone.

By the time he reached the village her bones had burned and he carried an armful of ash. He let it scatter on the ground, beneath the tree where they'd tried to hang him. Tears left darker dots on the small mound, as useless as all the way here.

He knelt down, and as he did, crying made him hiccup. A tiny cloud of smoke fled the prison of his lungs, but the Hanged Man caught it in his fist. When he opened it, the smoke had nowhere to go. His touch was fire again, and smoke was ever a slave to flame. It danced and swayed as if on the wind, and as he watched it, a thought formed in the Hanged Man's head.

In the smoke had been a memory of momma, even though she hadn't died empty. It had become her where her ashes had fallen, and ash wasn't so much a slave as something fire didn't want…

"Smoke wraith," the Hanged Man said, trying his hardest not to let it know his eagerness. "You became momma in the house. Could you now become Lucy?"

The smoke wraith laughed in a spectral voice, and when the Hanged Man got so mad he was about to eat it off his palm, the wraith took Lucy's form.

The Hanged Man gasped, and the smoke dispersed. He held his breath until what remained resumed dancing, and said, "If I freed some more of you, would you help me shape her ashes?"

The smoke became Lucy again, and the Hanged Man breathed out more. He brought both his hands to the mound of ash, where the smoke settled in. He feared too much of her had spilled through his fingers, but then a breeze picked up and the smoke clung to it. Whorls of ash filled the air around him and gathered around Lucy's growing grey body.

The figurine of ash and smoke was perfect, but it didn't move. The Hanged Man watched it solemnly, but then realized that even if he could bring her back, she would want her parents to be with her. Now that he knew what to do, he also had a chance to help them. Maybe they weren't all that nice to him, but that didn't mean it was his place to pass the chance to help someone.

He breathed out more smoke, and again it hunted the scattered ash on the breeze. When Lucy's parents rested beside her, the Hanged Man still didn't know how to give them life, but thought they'd want their friends with them if he found a way. The more smoke he eased out, the better he felt, and the clearer was the crackle of fire in his heart when the wraiths weren't laughing inside him. It wasn't long until all the villagers lay side by side on the ground.

The Hanged Man looked at them, and while he thought, he became aware of how loud the crackling was. He pondered upon it for a long while, how much stronger it was than before. Sometimes, when he'd looked at the baker's daughter or the stabler's wife, it had grown nearly as strong.

He went to Lucy's shifting body, and when the crackle became as loud as in the inferno's heart, he knew it was the sound of the love he burned with, the love that had taken their lives and which neither smoke nor ash could return.

"Smoke wraiths," he said, "if I gave you some of the fire you stole, would you try to run again? Only this time, I want you to lift these ashes with you."

The smoke wraiths cried with glee, and the Hanged Man touched each puppet in turn. Each wraith claimed some of his flame, but now reached deeper than before. The more he gave, the greyer his skin became, until ash began to flake off with the breeze. When only Lucy remained without a spark, he said, "Smoke wraith, I will give you everything I have left, on one condition."

The wraith waited with patience he hadn't yet seen.

"You must take Lucy wherever she wants to go. She'll bear far too much love for a place this small. She needs to find someone who cares as fiercely as she will." The girl's lids dotted darker when the Hanged Man leaned over her. "But don't you ever let her burn the one she chooses. You hear me?"

The smoke wraith laughed, but now the Hanged Man liked what he heard. It was how he imagined Lucy would sound, if he ever heard her laughing.

Color seeped into the girl's ashes as it faded from the Hanged Man's, and when she was whole again, he was ready to crumble. Wind swept through the village and carried off the Hanged Man with it. When the villagers rose and looked around at the ruins of their home, all that remained of him was a blonde girl's hair turned ashen grey from his touch.

About the Author

Ville Meriläinen is a Finnish university student by day, author of little tragedies by night. His short fiction has won the Writers of the Future award, and has appeared in various journals and anthologies, including Pseudopod, The Death of All Things, *and* Disturbed Digest.

BRIGHT CARVER

PETE ALEX HARRIS

This broken scrap, this splintered, imperfect chunk of pine log would do. Simone knew it would do, though she did not yet know what it would do *for*.

She held it up in front of her face and turned it about. She could hardly lift it, but in a few days she'd have whittled away most of its bulk, leaving something elegant she could lift with one hand. She would begin just as soon as she saw what must remain.

It was her first time entering the great contest. She had spent years in study, her fingers a lacework of tiny scars and splinters in the rough skin. Her hands smelled of smoke and sweat and greasy, cheap food, and always the sap and resin of her life's work. She couldn't read books, but she could read wood. Usually.

This time it was a struggle to find the core of the piece: the overlap between what was inside the wood and what was inside her. Perhaps she was trying to make it do too much, matter too much. Maybe for her first attempt at the contest she should make something simple, like a curled fox or a comical goose. She wouldn't win anyway.

Simone carried the log out of her father's hut, out from the looming shadow of the castle walls, carried it away some distance to see it in sunlight. Forget the contest. Let the piece be its own thing. She set it down on its widest end and walked around it. Then she upturned it, balanced it on the other end with care and sat cross-legged, her hands hanging loose over her knees, staring into it.

Yes.

Back at the hut, she sawed and chiseled away most of the cracked front side of the log, shaped a base at the narrower end, thinned out the middle, left the wide end with two curved lobes, like arms or wings. A figure, standing, arms stretched out, raised forward around the curve of the woodgrain, slightly above shoulder height. Enough material below to support them while detail was added, to be cut away later or perhaps become long sleeves hanging.

And there she stopped, unable to see the figure's face. The pose of the figure was incomplete in her imagination without knowing how the head would sit, where it was looking, whether it was smiling or scowling. For days she sat with it between her household chores, while other carvers shaved and sanded and engraved their pieces. Her father eventually noticed.

"You need to get to work on that, if you want to enter it. I won't have my child bring an unfinished carving to show the lords. For shame. Trim it, shape it, get some paint on it. Nobody expects it to be a winner, but if people know you started and couldn't finish, they'll not respect you, girl. They'll not respect me."

"I'll finish. There's time. I just don't see it yet. I don't know what it's trying to say."

"You are a worry, Simone. Don't put so much of yourself into it. There's only disappointment in that."

"I know."

He'd said so many times before. He'd made winning carvings, three times, and none of them had been his personal favorites. He'd seen his best work passed over without remark and thrown in the fire. It was just the way the contest worked.

But when Simone got back to work on her carving, even without feeling any particular inspiration, she somehow put herself into it. The head that took shape was her head, her face. Except unlike her, hunched and frowning in concentration, the figure's head was raised, chin up, eyes open, confident and serene.

The rest followed. A flowing dress with long sleeves, hands relaxed, palms inward, one leg with the knee slightly forward; a figure in motion. Imperfections in the wood made the dress ragged. Simone followed the raggedness where it wanted to go, shredding the hem in tatters. This wasn't a proud lady in finery, nor a poor artisan's daughter like herself. It was something of both. It felt new.

"It's beautiful," said her mother, doubtfully, glancing at the back wall of the hut. That glance carried a lot of weight—the weight of the stone castle wall that seemed to press her down even by thinking of it. That glance meant: they won't like it.

"I'm nearly happy with it," said Simone, trying to reassure and encourage her mother, although rightly it should have been the other way 'round, "and I know it won't be chosen. There was little chance of that anyway, so don't worry for me. I want only to do a good job of it, for my first contest. It's not quite finished, but I don't know what it needs. Or what I need it to be. Some last touch."

Her father looked up from his own work. "It won't win, but that's not my worry. The lords for the most part don't care about the carvings. They throw most of them in the fire, and for all I know they throw the rest in a cupboard and never look at them again. We may please them or bore them, and it's all one. But we mustn't anger them."

"I'm not trying to anger anyone."

"You're not trying to please them, either."

"I'm not trying to *bore* them."

"I'd rather you did. This carving doesn't flatter them. It's ragged and proud. They don't want to see pride in anyone else, and they don't want to be reminded of how ragged their own is. You've done good work. But it will go to waste. They'll scorn it."

"Let them."

Wastefulness and scorn were soaked into the traditions of the castle and dried in like an indelible stain. The contest may have once been about the lords' taste and the craftsmen's aspiration to better themselves, but that was dried up too. Now it was a yearly ritual, written down in a book. Carvings were displayed, three must be chosen, the rest must be burned. Which three hardly mattered. Sometimes Simone wondered what would happen if one year only two carvings were presented. Would the lord pick up some other third object to make the required total, a wooden spoon from the festive table, or anything, and never even notice?

Then she wondered what they would burn if no carvings remained. That's what convinced her the tradition had to be continued. Tradition was safe, her mother always said. But then she'd glance at the wall, not saying out loud what it was that tradition kept them safe from.

Her father wasn't done with her. "At least get some paint on it. Some bright ochre for the dress, green for the eyes?"

"I like the colours of the wood. Cream, orange, pink."

"That's not our way. It looks all wrong. Like you're spiting me for all I've taught you."

"It's not about you. It's mine. Shall I varnish it, then? Or beeswax it to a nice shine? That'll help it burn, won't it? It's not going to win, and that's nearly all you've ever taught me: I can't win. We don't get to really win anything."

"Of all the nonsense. I never did tell you such a thing!"

"You showed me!"

She snatched her carving up and ran out into the dark, past the lights of cooking fires and candles, down the zig-zagging dirt path of the carvers' village and away from the castle, to where she'd first stared at the log that had been hiding her inspiration.

It was too dark out here to look at anything but the sky. Smoky brown light above the castle walls, which she turned away from to gaze at the stars, pure sparks of white and pink fire that were never snuffed out.

She came back much later, took some dry leftovers for her supper, and sat up by the warm ashes of the fire, feeding it shavings of wood as she worked, brief flares of light to see by. She adorned the figure's dress and sleeves with ambiguous curves: feathers or flames. She shaved the wood so thin that the light glowed through it. Out to the ends of the sleeves, she used the orange-red of the wood to heighten the flame effect. She cut away more of the dress, made the definition of the legs stronger, the calf muscles tensed and ready to leap.

She couldn't make something that would win on merit, because no idea of merit was written down in the rituals. She wouldn't make something that could win by seeking approval, or flattering. She wouldn't *ever* make a comical goose.

Whatever she made would burn, so she made something that would own the fire.

ABOUT THE AUTHOR

Pete Alex Harris is a mostly SFF and Weird writer, with three self-published novels and a few short stories in various genres. You can find him on Twitter as @ScavengerEthic.

The Raven's Venture

Brandon M. Lindsay

Dain lifted another timber to his shoulder as a watcher on the wall called down for the main gate to be opened.

Dain glanced over at the gate while he shifted the heavy timber into a slightly more comfortable position, but only for a moment. He could feel the eyes of the vilkath on him, and he didn't want the man to think he was dragging his feet. Once he was sure the timber was balanced properly, Dain walked briskly over to where the other timbers were stacked, the late afternoon sun beating down on his bare back.

The hinges of the main gate squealed loudly as the doors opened, momentarily drowning out the constant sound of the other prisoners scraping their planes over roughly cut logs. A troop of six horsemen rode through the gate and into the prison's main yard. Dain could tell a couple of them were injured by the way they swayed in their saddles. They were soldiers, most of them wearing long purple tabards over shirts of chain mail. A few had smears of blood on them.

One of the riders, however, was finely dressed. His loose black trousers were tucked into supple black leather boots. A black brocade jacket, belted and quartered at the waist, hung past his stirrups. The man's right arm was bound in a sling sewn directly onto the jacket and made of the same brocade; it was likely that the injured arm was not expected to heal. Other scars marred his face. One eye was nearly swollen shut with scar tissue, and a small divot broke the fine line of his jaw.

A few of the other prisoners paused, but only long enough to take in the man's appearance. "The Raven," one whispered in awe.

Despite his disfiguring injuries, the man in black—the Raven, if the other prisoner had guessed right—moved with the confidence and grace of a warrior in his prime as he slid out of his saddle. Twin sheathes crossed his back, but only one carried a sword—the one within reach of his still-functional left hand. While the other riders ignored all the prisoners even as they handed their reins over to them, the Raven's attention instantly gravitated to Dain, taking in his tall, muscled form in a glance. His gaze lingered a bit longer on Dain's own scars, the tallies cut into his chest and stomach, signaling him as a Marked.

Each of those tallies represented a life Dain had taken.

Though he may have once been Dain the Marked, one of the greatest assassins in the empire, he was now merely Dain the Prisoner, sentenced here by his own order for killing out of vengeance—something the Order of the Marked had no tolerance for. Though Dain didn't move to cover the scars, he did lower his eyes. Like any good prisoner would.

"Back to work, prisoner." The vilkath, glaring at Dain, spoke with a threatening tone, but he wasn't standing anywhere near him. With his wooden club gripped firmly in both hands, the vilkath was standing near Orahn, who straddled a log, running a scrub plane over it. Orahn was a few years older than Dain, thin, and with his milky eyes, mostly blind. To the dom, who ran the prison, Orahn was a burden, not worth the food he ate.

To the vilkath, however, he was very useful. The vilkath knew that Dain had taken to the blind man, and he used that affection to keep Dain in line.

And it worked. Dain quickened his pace to gather another timber. On his way back, he glanced over at the man in black. That man was still staring at Dain. He didn't bother to hide his fascination. Likely he had never seen a Marked before. Few people had and lived to tell about it.

"Ah, honored guests!" The dom, a short, fat man, trundled down the hill from his residence, entourage in tow. "I am sorry for making you wait!" Dain noticed that the dom was wearing his least-stained silks and his narrow beard was freshly oiled. He had probably heard that his guests seemed to be important, and he wanted to look his best, even if he had to make them wait.

Trailing behind the dom were a pair of prisoners serving as his personal servants, a handful of soldiers, and the sorcerer. The sorcerer, with his head shaved save for a dark blond topknot folded over and pinned to itself, wore a brown woolen robe that trailed in the dust but never seemed to get dirty. His wholly green eyes seemed inhuman as they fixed on the visitors.

Although Dain didn't slow in his work, he watched out of the corner of his eye, just as he was sure the other prisoners in the yard did. Visitors were rare here at the prison, especially since it was so far removed from the rest of the empire. Even the vilkath was watching, trying and failing to be surreptitious as he occasionally prodded someone with his club while blinking at the visitors.

"You must be the dom of this... place." The Raven looked at the prison camp around him, disdainful even if his tone and expression didn't show it. His own dignity and poise did the job well enough.

"At your service." The dom bowed his head as he took in the condition of his guests. "Did you have some trouble recently?"

The Raven nodded. "We did, not too far from here. A league to the north, near a large pillar of rock, not far from the road. Perhaps you already know of this particular source of trouble?"

The dom chuckled nervously and waved for them to follow him. "Won't you please come up to my house, honored guests? I think it best if we speak of this matter privately. Over wine and food, of course."

Once they had disappeared beyond the gate to the dom's residence, the vilkath barked, "All right, prisoners! That's enough for today. Get some sleep tonight, because we're starting early tomorrow." It was still early, not quite sunset, but of course no one would complain. It wasn't often that the vilkath gave them an entire night off.

Dain didn't have to wonder why he had. Almost immediately, the vilkath stalked over to the gate to the dom's residence, likely wanting to be by his side should the dom need anything. And of course, watch what was going on with the visitors.

Dain forced himself to stop thinking about them. He was just a prisoner. Visitors had nothing to do with him.

He walked over to Orahn and helped him up off of the log. "How's your back today?"

Orahn smiled, milky eyes fixed on nothing in particular as he clung to Dain's arm. "As good as new."

Dain chuckled as he led Orahn to the mess hall. He knew Orahn was in pain, but Orahn never complained. Orahn's strength was not physical, but it was still strength of a sort, strength that none of the other prisoners seemed to have. Dain took comfort in it, and had ever since Dain's first day here, when out of all the prisoners only Orahn had bothered to talk to him. Orahn's strength was, perhaps, the only comfort Dain could claim in this place.

And it was a comfort that others openly resented. As he waited in line to get his bowl of slop and heel of stale bread, Dain could feel their eyes on him. He bent his head and said quietly, "Today I think it best if we don't eat in the mess hall."

Orahn merely nodded.

A handful of others huddled in small groups in one of the large rooms where the prisoners slept, eating silently while sitting on the hard dirt floor. Dain and Orahn didn't speak either. All that could be heard was the scraping of fingers along the insides of wooden bowls. When he and Orahn were finished, Dain took their bowls back to the mess hall.

"Tell me the story of your wolf amulet," Orahn said as soon as Dain returned. He had heard the story more than a dozen times, but he never tired of it.

Dain smiled and sat at the foot of the tattered rag Orahn used for sleeping, folding his legs. "It began at the forest's edge," he said, sweeping his hand out as if to paint the scene. Orahn couldn't see much, but he could see a little, enough to tell Dain's theatrics. His eyes widened, already enchanted.

"Just outside my village," Dain continued. "I was just a boy then. Ten years old." He lifted his hands, spreading all ten fingers before him. "And small for my age. My friend Aythen was just a year older than me, but he was strong. I looked to him as an older brother.

"It was midday, and we were swinging on vines and falling into the river, laughing and playing as children do, when Aythen saw smoke rising up from the village, and I heard the horses."

Orahn seized Dain's wrist tightly. "Was it raiders?"

"Aye. Raiders from the Shawek tribes. Aythen and I, we watched helplessly as the Shawek burned down our huts and cut down our people with their curved swords..."

Orahn smiled reassuringly and patted Dain on the arm. Truth was, the wounds from that day, the wounds in Dain's spirit, felt fresh, or just barely scabbed over. And telling the story was like ripping those scabs off. Every time.

Still. He wouldn't deny it to his friend.

Orahn leaned forward, milky eyes intent. "Then what happened?"

"The raiders dragged some more people out of the huts by the hair into the tall grasses that surrounded the village. We recognized the people. They were our families. The raiders..." Dain paused to breathe. "They held their swords over the heads of our people and then... brought them down."

Dain took a deep breath before he continued. "As I said, Aythen was like a brother to me. He told me, 'Go, hide! I will see our families avenged!' Then he grabbed a stone so large he almost couldn't carry it."

"He went into the village then, did he?"

Dain smiled again and shook his head. "Not before I tried to stop him. I grabbed him by the arm and told him we should both run away. But he insisted. So I took the wolf amulet, the one carved from white driftwood by my mother's hand, and said, "Take this! And may it keep you safe!' He put it round his neck and said, 'I'll only need it for a moment. Wait here and I'll bring it back to you!' Then he ran towards the village, whooping and shaking the stone over his head like a fool."

Orahn chuckled and waited patiently for Dain to continue.

Dain took a deep breath before he spoke again. Everything up to that point was true, but he couldn't tell the truth of what had happened afterward. The smoking ruins of huts. The Shawek wagons, hauling away food and cloth and screaming captives. The shards of pottery that were all that was left of his people—shards that mirrored the soul of the boy that was left behind.

Dain didn't speak of the fact that he never saw anyone from his village ever again, that he had been alone among its ruins and near starvation when a man of the Marked came upon him and saved him. The first time Dain had told the story, the pain was still fresh, even after all these years, so he had changed the ending. After seeing the hopeful grin on Orahn's face after the first telling, Dain couldn't tell the truth of what happened in the subsequent tellings and see that hope wiped from Orahn's face. He believed that was what kept the blind man going in this terrible place.

"But Aythen never got his vengeance," Dain said quietly. "He found that our families had only been wounded, not killed. And as if a guardian wolf spirit had possessed him,

Aythen threw the rock with all his strength straight at the Shawek leader's head." Dain tapped his own head with a finger. "Killing him straight away. The other raiders cried, 'If this is the strength of their youngest, we must flee for our very lives!' And the Shawek rode away in shame."

Orahn closed his eyes and lay back with a content smile. "And then?"

"And then," Dain said, "Aythen was declared protector of our people, and a banner of a wolf was made for him. I wanted to follow in his footsteps and become a great warrior, so I joined the Marked." Lies, all of it—save for that last little detail.

Dain had joined the Mark not because of Aythen's success, but because of his failure. Aythen had been no great warrior. Like the others, he was a victim of Shawek cruelty and had become a slave or worse.

Dain had wanted vengeance and had gotten it. Three of the marks on his stomach were for Shawek warlords. Dain had never learned if one of them was the one who had raided his village, but it didn't matter. Those men had been guilty of equal crimes and worse. The scales of justice were balanced.

Orahn's chest rose and fell steadily. Dain rested a hand on the man's arm gently, so as not to wake him, and lay down on his own sleeping rag on the hard-packed floor. As he closed his eyes, he wondered if Orahn knew just how much of Dain's story was true and how much was not.

Dain was wakened by the sharp jab of a wooden club to his back.

He twisted around, blinking sleepily, to see the vilkath glaring down at him. Two guards stood behind him, one of whom carried a shuttered lantern. A few of the other prisoners stirred at the presence of light in their quarters, but quickly stilled when they saw who carried it.

"Up, prisoner," said the vilkath. "The dom's calling for you."

Dain immediately stood to obey, sparing a quick glance for Orahn, who still slept.

For summer, the night was brisk. The sand of the yard was cool under Dain's bare feet as he followed the vilkath past the visitors' picketed horses and up the rocky path to the dom's house. A white-plastered timber palisade twice as tall as a man encircled the house and the guard barracks. The palisade wasn't designed to repel a siege, merely for keeping out rambunctious prisoners, and so wasn't thick enough to warrant a walkway. To Dain's eyes, it was more of a fancy fence than a wall.

The only entry was a simple gap in the stockade. On either side stood a swordsman, and behind each of them, an archer. More archers stood on raised platforms at intervals along the inside of the palisade, peering at him over the sharpened ends of the timbers. All of them eyed him warily. None of them would hesitate to put an arrow through his heart. No one trusted a Marked. Especially not guards.

The vilkath stopped at the gate and seethed as he gestured Dain in with five guards for escort. Likely he was just the errand boy, and he hadn't been called into the dom's residence as Dain had.

Wooden posts carved and whitewashed to look like pillars propped up a stone tile facade facing the gate. The house itself was made of wood, but the dom obviously didn't want people to know that. Three of the armed strangers sat on wooden chairs under the facade, smoking pipes. They were the injured ones, but their injuries had been patched up, and the way that they lounged suggested they didn't even feel their wounds anymore. Their eyes passed over him like they would for any other prisoner, barely even registering a man, but one man's eyes lingered a moment on the scars on Dain's stomach.

The guards led him into the receiving hall, staying close behind him with their hands to their weapons, where the remnants of a small feast were laid out on the dining table. The dom, his sorcerer, and the remainder of the guests—the Raven included—sat around the table.

The dom slapped his napkin down with a flush-faced grin, rattling dishes. "There he is! The poor fool you asked about." The dom stood, a bit wobbly. Much of his feasting had likely involved wine. "Go on. Take a look at him."

The Raven gestured for his men to leave. Once they had, he stood and walked closer, inspecting Dain from head to toe. "If the marks tell the truth, he must be a formidable killer." He turned to the dom. "How long has he been here?"

The dom stumped back to his chair with a frown. "Since the rains, I believe."

"And he hasn't tried to escape?"

A challenging smile spread across the dom's wide face as he leaned toward the Raven. "He's as docile as they come." He said the words slowly, weighting them with significance. But what that significance was, Dain couldn't fathom. Something was happening between these two men, and for some reason Dain had been dragged into the middle of it.

But it wasn't as if there were anything he could do. He was a prisoner, after all.

The Raven nodded as he considered. He pointed at the collar around Dain's neck. "How does this work?"

"It works very well." The dom's grin widened as he walked over to Dain. He hooked his fingers around the thick circle of seamless bronze. "It's called a leach collar. Once a prisoner steps outside the walls, the spell on the collar activates. Hollow spikes fold inward, piercing the neck. Blood drains out until they either die or come back. And the farther a prisoner gets, the deeper they dig in. If someone gets far enough away ..." With his hands, the dom mimed a head popping off its shoulders and chuckled.

The Raven didn't laugh, but he nodded and frowned in serious interest. A few long moments passed before he spoke. "All right, then."

The dom's eyebrows lifted in disbelief. "All right? You said all right. Are you sure that's what you mean? All right?"

Dain fixed his eyes on a point on the wall rather than watch the exchange. What was going on here? What was the Raven agreeing to? Dain felt that decisions were being made for him and about him, which, admittedly, was nothing new. Such decisions were made on a regular basis by the dom.

But this was different. There was no contempt in the dom's eyes, as there usually was whenever he gave orders. There was eagerness. Almost hunger.

For what?

The sorcerer, who had remained sitting at the table as still as stone since the moment Dain arrived, rose fluidly to his feet and clasped his ringed fingers in front of himself. Whereas the dom's smile was eager, the sorcerer's was malicious. Dain hated the sorcerer when he smiled. Something horrible always happened when he did.

Usually that something horrible happened to a prisoner.

Pupil-less eyes, green shot through with veins of white, like polished orbs of marble, fixed themselves on Dain. "May I suggest, dom," the sorcerer said, "that we inquire about the prisoner's understanding of the situation? If he already knows too much," he nodded his head significantly at the Raven, "it could... complicate things."

Suspicion passed over the dom's expression as he glanced between Dain and the Raven. Then he flipped his hand disinterestedly. "Question the prisoner, if you think it prudent."

"At your leave, dom." The sorcerer bowed, then crossed the room, robes rustling. With each of the sorcerer's slippered steps, the lamps, which had been producing a warm orange light, began to glow an otherworldly green.

The sorcerer seized Dain's head in his long-fingered grasp. Though the sorcerer spoke quietly, his voice seemed to shout at him from all directions. *"Do you know this man in black?"*

The force of the sorcerer's voice made the whole world shudder. Dain gasped in pain. "By reputation only," he said through gritted teeth. As he spoke, the pain eased slightly. "He's the Raven, is he not? Everyone has heard of the one-armed warrior."

If the stories were true, the Raven had only become stronger at the loss of his arm, worth twenty men in battle. As a leader, he was even more formidable, pushing back the relentless tribal invaders and bringing the war to their lands, even wiping out some of the tribal armies to a man. No one in the empire was more renowned than the Raven.

The sorcerer's voice pounded into Dain's skull again. *"Have you met him before this day?"*

"I've never seen this man before." The pain eased a little more.

"No communication? No letters or messengers?"

"In here?" The pain flared. "No! No, I haven't! Never!"

After a long, agonizing moment, the sorcerer released him and stepped away. Dain fell to his knees, covered in sweat, chest heaving. The pain vanished so completely that Dain wondered if he had imagined it. He rose to his feet and did his best to compose himself.

"Well?" asked the dom.

The sorcerer's smile was gone. He looked... disappointed. "He's telling the truth."

"You're certain?"

The sorcerer folded his hands before and regarded Dain with his unearthly stare. "*He* is certain. Which, in this, is what would matter. Is it not?"

"So it is, so it is." The dom motioned to the collar around Dain's neck. "Do what you need to do."

The sorcerer stepped closer to pinch the collar between his thumb and forefinger. Like a fine-chained necklace that had been unclasped, the collar fell away from Dain's neck, but when he looked down, the collar had regained its ring shape, completely whole and solid again.

Holding the collar in front of himself, the sorcerer bowed to the dom, topknot dropping past his forehead. Without another glance at Dain or the Raven, he left through the heavy curtains at the back of the room.

Dain reached up to rub his neck in amazement. The collar truly was gone.

The dom grunted. "Don't get too used to it, prisoner. Once you've finished your task and returned, the collar goes back on."

Dain frowned. "My... task, dom?"

The dom slapped Dain on the shoulder, who flinched at the too-familiar gesture. "Yes, prisoner. You see, our good guests had some trouble with a demon up the road, and we decided you're the man to take care of it."

In the morning, Dain was prodded through the main gate by the vilkath, backed by half a dozen archers, their arrows nocked and drawn. At the order of the dom, a guard trotted out to hand Dain a sword before rushing back. Behind the archers stood the Raven's entourage, some with knowing grins on their faces. A couple chuckled under their breath. Presumably at their good luck, and at Dain's bad luck. No one liked taking care of demons, but everyone liked having them taken care of. Only the Raven watched Dain without expression. As if curious to see how he would act.

The Raven didn't have long to observe. Both steel-reinforced doors slammed shut, followed by the sound of the bar sliding into place. They would only open to him again if he came back with the demon's head.

Dain rolled his shoulders to loosen them and tossed the sword, still in its scabbard, to the roadside. He didn't need it. It would be more of an encumbrance than a tool. He was no mere soldier. He was a Marked.

Dain reached the main road after just a brief jog. It stretched north and south, between pine-covered hills on either side. In the south lay all the cities of the empire. Civilization.

To the north was the demon... and not much else. Wildlife trails, a small lake. Nothing of strategic value. Nothing that would interest a troop of men led by the empire's greatest warrior.

So why had they come? To kill the demon? Then why did they turn tail and ask the dom to take care of it? No, that didn't make sense.

None of it did.

Dain glanced up at the cloud-spattered sky as a few drops of rain dampened his hair. Rain was rare this time of year. He turned his mind from the motivations of the Raven; he might as well ponder why the rain chose that moment to fall. Neither would change what Dain had to do. He started walking north, scratched at his neck, and froze.

He had no collar.

He was free. He could leave the dom's prison behind and no one, not even the sorcerer, would come looking for him. Not with the demon still on the loose.

He looked south. While the Shawek had taken massive losses in their war with the empire, especially from the forces led by the Raven himself, there were always more Shawek to kill, more vengeance to be had.

But without Dain's protection, Orahn wouldn't last the week. To the dom, Orahn wasn't worth the food he ate. If he didn't kill Orahn himself, then the vilkath would, or any of Dain's many enemies would. Dain's presence, and the threat that his presence implied, were the only things that had kept Orahn alive all this time.

So what will it be? Dain asked himself. *A life spent fighting for the dead? Or a life fighting for those who still lived?* Free or prisoner, Dain would still have his war. All that remained was deciding why he fought it.

He chuckled, shaking his head. He already knew the answer, even before he asked the question. Killing for the dead was all he had before. It had been an empty life, one barely worth living. Protecting someone precious to him, however... that was a good life. *A true life.* Even if he had to live it from behind prison walls.

He would walk free one day—with Orahn at his side. But that day had not yet come.

Today, Dain would kill a demon. Or die in the attempt.

A man leaned against a giant finger of granite jutting out of the hillside, arms folded. Or at least he looked like a man, from a distance. He wore brown leather trousers and a wide-brimmed gray leather hat. The form-fitting jacket he wore was a mottled yellow. But as Dain passed out of the poplar thicket at the base of the hill, he realized it wasn't a jacket at all. It was the man's bare skin.

The demon lifted his head and removed his hat at Dain's approach. His head was hairless and the same mottled yellow as the rest of him. Instead of eyebrows, bony ridges protruded over completely silver eyes. They looked as if molten metal had been poured into his sockets and hardened there.

The demon grinned as it studied him. "So. They sent a Marked for me to play with, did they?" With a long-fingered hand, the demon gestured casually to a pile of bodies not far from where Dain stood. All of them wore the same colors as the Raven's men. "This pleases me. The last toys they gave me broke so easily."

Dain wasted no time on banter, instead sprinting up the hill. The demon crouched, pointed teeth bared in a mad grin.

As Dain reached the demon, he thrust his bare foot in the scree and kicked it up at the demon's face. In the same motion, Dain brought a fist down to hammer the demon's knee in order to break it. The demon, anticipating the blow, folded his knee to dodge, but the fragments of loose stone sprayed at his face caught him off guard. The demon spun in rage, howling.

Dain took that moment to knife punch the demon's kidney. It nearly broke Dain's fingers—it was like punching the trunk of an oak. The demon spun back around to face him, claws extended. Dain rolled out of the way just in time. The demon's claws raked through scree and bedrock alike.

Stronger than it looks, Dain realized, smiling. He would use that strength against the demon. Such was the way of the Marked.

An idea formed in his head. Slowly, Dain circled around the demon until the granite, several tons of stone towering up out of the hill's crest at an angle, was at Dain's back.

"I fear that when this is all over," Dain said, "you will have left quite a scar." He tapped his finger against his stomach, next to all the tallies marking his kills. "So if you could aim here from now on, that would save me some trouble."

Shrieking and wild-eyed, the demon leapt forward, claws extended.

At the last moment, Dain ducked out of the way.

The demon's hands punched *into* the stone--just as Dain had hoped they would. Cracks spiderwebbed out from where the demon's hands were trapped. The granite groaned.

Dain threw himself down the hill as massive shards of stone came crashing down, drowning out the demon's terrified screams with a sound like thunder.

An hour later, Dain stomped up to the main gate surrounding the prison grounds. Several people stood atop the wall, peering between the merlons as they waited for Dain's return. Among them were several of the dom's guards, the dom himself, and the Raven and his men.

The Raven was the first to spot him. Once he did, all the others turned and stared at Dain in disbelief. Apparently, none of them had expected him to survive.

"Ah, prisoner! So you've decided to return," the dom said. He didn't seem particularly overjoyed at this, frowning down at Dain. "Do you have the demon's head?"

"There wasn't much left, dom," Dain called up. "Only these." He raised his fists. In each one, he held an ichor-smeared silver orb. The demon's eyes.

The dom blanched, then disappeared from sight. So did the Raven and his men. The dom's men stared down at Dain, terrified, as if only now realizing what kind of man was in their custody.

Dain heard the dom's and the Raven's voices pitched low and intense. They seemed to be arguing about something, but Dain couldn't tell what.

"Wait right there!" called the Raven, his head only appearing for a moment. A few minutes later, the oaken double doors groaned open, revealing the Raven and his men, all ahorse.

There were two more saddled horses. One was riderless, reins held by the Raven. On the other horse sat Orahn, a contented smile on his face.

Orahn wore no collar.

"Don't say a word, now," the Raven said, holding the reins to Dain once close enough. "No questions. Just get on your horse and let's ride out of here."

Dain tossed away the eyeballs and did as he was told, vaulting wordlessly into the saddle. He didn't know what was happening, but Orahn had his collar off and was outside the walls.

As they rounded the first bend, Dain looked over his shoulder, watching as the trees began to obscure the wall. Soon, the prison entirely fell from sight.

When they reached the main road, they turned south.

"You're probably wondering what happened back there," the Raven said then.

Dain nodded, silent despite all the questions he wanted to ask.

"Your good friend, the dom," the Raven said in a dry tone, "seemed to think that any prisoner would flee, given the chance. No matter what the prisoner believed. No matter what the prisoner cherished." The Raven shrugged. "So I made him a little wager. I said if you killed the demon and came back, both you and your friend here could leave as free men."

Dain scratched at his neck, frowning in thought. "I can think of nothing that would persuade the dom to accept such a wager."

With a wide grin, Orahn heeled his mount forward to join them. "Tell him the stakes, Raven."

Dain's glance flicked from Orahn to the Raven.

The Raven was silent for some time, his eyes fixed on the road ahead. Finally, he spoke again. "I told the dom that if you didn't come back, I would stay in your place."

Dain gaped. "Why would you do such a thing?"

The Raven shrugged. "I knew you would come back." He met Dain's eyes then. "Besides, I had something that belonged to you. And seeing how poorly your luck had turned, I thought you could use it more than me." He pulled something out of his saddle bag and tossed it.

Dain snatched it out of the air and stared at it. When he realized what it was, tears filled his eyes.

A wolf's head amulet, carved from white driftwood by his mother's own hand.

"I knew you would come back for your friend," said the Raven, "because that's what I would do."

About the Author

Brandon M. Lindsay grew up in the Seattle area, and now lives in Tokyo, Japan. He received a degree in philosophy from the University of Washington in Seattle.

To date, he has released the novella Spear Mother, *the novelette* Dark Tree, *and* The Clans: Tales of the Fourth World, *as well as several short stories in various anthologies. His website is https://brandonmlindsay.com/.*

A Trail of Breadcrumbs

Alice Loweecey

The reek of unwashed drunks replaced the stink of fish guts as Jade left Market Street for the Copperhead district. Despite the assault on her senses, Jade breathed easier. This was home.

She stepped over two of the tavern's regulars, snoring against the Alt-World Collision siren. A junior Copperhead nodded to her as he nailed a sign above the drunks' heads:

Pre-Shock Documents Discovered!

Copperhead and Sorcerer Joint Lecture!

Humans Only—No Constructs Allowed

Be Prepared for the Next Collision!

"Can't earn bounty money listening to old men flap their yaps," Jade said to the unconscious man crushing her shoulder.

She reached her front door and maneuvered the key out of her pocket. The criminal's inert heels preceded her into a room clouded with pings and whorls of magic. She waved a clear space in front of her eyes to see the other half of her team exactly where he promised he wouldn't be.

"Windbag, either you get yourself off the floor or I dump this moron onto your precious conjuring circle." Jade hefted the trussed-up thief higher on her sore shoulder.

The Greatest Sorcerer in Nine Kingdoms—at least, according to his promotional flyers—looked up from the innards of his robot minion.

"For the ten-thousandth time, my name is Windham. Park your criminal somewhere else. Sparky needs an enema." His right hand wormed inside the coiled wires and magic-infused circuits of his creation. Despite that, no dirt or oil stained the sorcerer's black trousers and crimson shirt. Not a strand of his long black hair had escaped its tie of cobra skin.

The multicolored circle surrounding the two glowed and swirled as the sorcerer muttered words in three different languages. The robot's body spasmed.

Jade turned away. "I'd bet the second greatest sorcerer has minions who handle robot maintenance." She swept two spell books from the worktable and dropped her captive in their place. The unconscious man's head bounced off the pitted oak surface.

Jade checked herself for bloodstains and scuffs. Two clumps of mud marred her red leather pants. Her leaf-patterned boots and tailored linen shirt passed inspection. Only then did she untie the gag in her captive's mouth. "Don't want you choking on your own puke before I get the reward for turning you in to the Copperheads." She pried open his eyelids. The pupils reacted as they should to the afternoon sunlight flooding that half of the workroom. Her fingers flaked dried mud out of his orange-and-green hair as she felt for the lump. "No broken skin and no cracks in his skull. I am a magician with a cudgel."

Windham's voice, distant with concentration: "There. Got it." He snapped the robot's front panel together. "Close your eyes. I'm going to give Sparky a boost."

Jade clapped her hands over her face as blue-white light eclipsed the sunshine. "Showoff."

After several seconds of muted thunder and trapped lightning, he said, "All right."

Spots of conjure-light blurred Jade's vision as Windham crossed to her side of the room. "Who's dirtying up my worktable this time?" He retrieved the spell books from the floor and placed them on one of the chairs. "Hideous hair."

Jade shook out her leather jacket despite her protesting shoulder. "Pete Pumpkineater. One of the gang that's been knifing the upperclass. Caught up to him in the traveling kids' show that performs pre-Shock fairy tales."

Windham looked down his crooked nose at Jade. It was no great feat, since she was half a head shorter than him. "Well?"

"Fine. Thank you, Windbag, for calling up the ghost of his last victim. Without your matchless skills, I'd still be slogging from town to town wasting my time and our money on bribes."

The sorcerer didn't rise to her bait. His sleek black eyebrows furrowed as he ran spotless hands over the unconscious criminal. "This is a glamour."

"You sure? Hey, you're forgetting your part of our deal: you clean me up. Can you take care of this, too?" She pulled her shirt off her right shoulder. "Sir Hideous-Hair got one hit with a wooden stage sword before I clubbed him."

Windham splayed one hand over Jade's bruised skin. "Contusion. Muscle tear. Burst capillaries."

"Windham, just fix what's broken, please."

He whispered two sentences Jade couldn't understand. Heat enveloped her shoulder. Her skin hissed and popped like a roasting duck.

"There." The sorcerer snapped his fingers twice. "Good as new, along with your reconnoitering clothes."

Jade worked her shoulder, testing the repair. "Thanks. Whaddya mean Pumpkin-boy here is wearing a glamour?"

"It's quite good, but not as skillful as one of mine. However, I can see a longer nose and differently shaped ears beneath his current visage."

"I'll be a Copperhead's floozy. Can you take it off?"

Windham snorted. "Don't insult me." He spread his four-knuckled fingers over the captive's face. The fingertips, elongated by himself to prove his mastery of post-Shock surgical architecture, hummed a B-flat chord. As the notes increased in volume, the unconscious man's body shimmered. The chord changed. Mist rose. Green and orange, white and brown, it swirled around all three of them. Windham clapped his hands and it vanished like a popped soap bubble.

Jade gasped.

Windham's gaze snapped in Jade's direction. Her tan had abandoned her face, her freckles like a bruise on her cheekbones. Her embellished outfit no longer made her appear deceptively cute. Now she looked like a child dressing up in her big sister's clothes.

The once-multicolored captive groaned. Now his face was also freckled and only brownish mud patterned his straw-blond hair. His real nose hooked down to hover over his thin lips.

"His hair is still a mess," Windham said.

Jade didn't reply. Windham looked from Jade to the captive and back again. Something about both their ears nagged at him.

The blond on the oak table couldn't move much more than his head, what with Jade's red leather thongs cutting grooves in his wrists and ankles. His baby-blue eyes pried themselves open and stared at Jade.

"Squirrel?" His lips cracked, his voice sounding more froglike than human.

In one smooth movement, Jade stepped up to the table and cold-cocked him with her left fist. "You thief. You liar. You bastard." Her voice ratcheted higher with each phrase. She turned her back on the blond and strode to the sorcerer's potions shelf. Each hand grasped an empty beaker.

"Wait—" Windham stretched out a hand.

Jade hurled the beakers to the stone floor.

The *tap-tip-tap-tip* of Sparky's footflaps cut through Jade's deep, ragged breaths. The robot's left hand retracted and a vacuum nozzle slid into place. Whisper-silent suction made narrow trails in the shards around Jade's feet. Still without speaking, Sparky *tap-tipped* over to the tin bucket in the far corner and ejected the beaker remnants.

Jade spoke through clenched teeth. "So the Greatest Sorcerer in Nine Kingdoms mucked up a simple finding spell."

"What do you mean?" Windham stayed by the table, staring at the object of his partner's wrath.

Jade turned on one booted heel and stalked back to the table. Windham jumped out of her way. She scooped up the former Pumpkin-head and returned him to her shoulder. On her way out the door, she said, "Remember my older brothers? The ones you said must've got caught in an alt-world intersect because there was no trace of them? This fetid sack on my shoulder is Birch, brother number four."

Thirty-six hours later, Jade returned to the narrow house she and the sorcerer shared. Her anger and weariness eased a trifle at the sight of their home. Back when she was the petted little sister of the king's assassin squad, her brothers would have broken the backs of anyone who dared to bring her here to the capital's underbelly.

That was before the alt-world collisions became more frequent. Before sorcerers like Windham became the power behind the Copperheads, because arresting criminals who could move through walls wasn't part of Copperhead training.

Before Jade's brothers went on a special Collision-exploration mission for the king and never returned. Jade waited for weeks. They always returned. They always conquered the bad guy and saved the kingdom and made her proud. Not that last time. When the mercenaries came for her, Jade had to adapt or die. Good thing Birch and Ash had secretly taught her everything she needed to know, just in case.

Everything except the little facts that their stellar careers had been a perfect front for their real talents: lies, murder, and thievery. Birch the murderer in his fairy-tale glamour proved that.

The relief of homecoming vanished. Jade slammed and locked the door behind her.

"Sparks? Windbag?" She stepped farther into the multipurpose central room. From her new angle she could see glimmering light outlining Windham's closed bedroom door. "At least I don't have to wake you up." She turned the doorknob. "Windbag, I—"

Jade froze in the doorway. Sparky stood behind Windham's oversized bed, his magic-tempered alloy glowing in a counterfeit of candlelight. Schmaltzy music played from his lipless mouth opening. Both Windham and his companion were indeed very much awake.

Jade turned her back and studied the map of the Nine Kingdoms on the wall as Windham and his partner finished their business. She recited the Sorcerers' Guild's price list for Extra-Large Constructs for Farming, Towing, Hauling, and Building, then the price list for robots like Sparky. The noises petered out halfway through her mental map of barren post-Shock subsidence zone locations.

"Hey, Jade."

Jade faced the bed again, and vaguely recognized the woman as a bartender from a pub two streets over. She combed her fingers through her long brown hair, and smirked. "I had some information your partner wanted. We came to a mutually agreeable bargain."

Windham wagged his eyebrows at Jade. "Bribes and brute force aren't the only paths to knowledge."

Jade grimaced as the music changed to something worse. "Would you please turn Sparky off?"

The sorcerer snapped his fingers and the robot closed its mouth. "Pennie, do please give my partner your news."

The bartender plopped her feet in Windham's lap. "You have one more part of our deal to fulfill." While he massaged them, she said to Jade, "Heard you're after the theater gang. Mm, yes, just like that on my arch. The sister of one of their road crew lives portside way. She's our fish supplier. She told me that Bad Wolf was Pumpkineater's second-in-command."

Jade kicked the footboard. "Windham, I'll be back in a few days. Tell our pet Copperhead to get the money ready."

Windham's right hand flailed at Jade. "We have to talk."

"Talking is useless. I'm off to get us money for more potions and spell books and wine."

"Jade, stop."

The air around her congealed. She breathed ice; blinked through fog. "Wind... you..."

"Pennie, give me a moment, please." Windham climbed out of bed. He reached through the translucent jelly and grasped Jade's rigid shoulders. "Tell me about your brothers."

"Un... magic me." At the last word, her mouth worked free of the spell. "I hate it when you play with me like this."

"Listen to me. I never said I was Hoodin himself. Your brothers found a more powerful sorcerer than me." He shook her slightly. "Don't tell me you believed my advertising?"

"Guess I did." Her rigid smile made him flinch. "Unmagic me, now."

The air snapped clear. Jade turned her back on the room. As she reached the door, Windham said, "You need to hear what else I learned today."

"Go play with your new friend. I'm done here."

Jade applauded at the end of 'Little Red Riding Hood' along with the crowd of kids and their parents. She'd disguised herself as a cook with brown pants and shirt, plus old leather shoes and an apron. Illustrations from dozens of ancient fairy tales covered the inside of the white canvas tent. Once the show began, she'd stared only at the Big Bad Wolf, listened only to his voice. If it was one of her brothers, the glamour was impeccable. For the first time she regretted her lack of magical powers. Knife-throwing, close combat, and subterfuge skills couldn't undo a glamour.

"I'm living in my own fairy tale," she muttered. "That one with the twelve vanished brothers and the sister who goes looking for them." She glanced around the tent again, searching for that particular story. There—the one where an angry magician turned the brothers into swans.

As she snuck around the dressing-room trailer after the show, she listened for the Big Bad Wolf's voice. She reached the corner without getting a clear read on it, and she paused to re-attune her ears to the outside of the trailer. When she heard nothing, she reached out to balance herself on the neck of the gigantic Construct horse hitched to the trailer's front.

A hand gripped her wrist and yanked her around the corner. Her arm wrenched almost out of its socket but she didn't make a sound. She planted her feet and broke the grip at its weak point, where thumb met index finger.

Another pair of arms grabbed her in a bear hug from behind. She wasted two seconds trying to wriggle out of it, then tried to crush her assailant's instep.

"Be quiet or we'll knock you out."

She didn't recognize the voice and shammed passive. The one who'd spoken carried her into a different trailer. More footsteps thumped on the three steps up to the trailer door. Four pairs of feet total, she thought. What a day to be in disguise. Besides her fists and feet, she'd have to get to the knives in the kitchen area.

Mr. Bear Hug dumped her in a creaky wooden chair and clamped down on her shoulders so hard she heard her bones creak. More work for Windbag later. The other three loomed over her.

"The children wouldn't be happy to see you like this," Jade said with as much scorn as she could pour into her voice. "The Big Bad Wolf, the Woodsman, Prince Charming, and—" she looked up— "Puss in Boots."

They kept up the silent and menacing act. Jade played along, waiting for Puss to shift his hold.

The wolf caved first. "We want you to break Pete out of jail."

"Already spent the reward; sorry."

"We'll pay you."

"I've got an ongoing gig. Makes it awkward." She attempted to move; no luck.

The Wolf clamped his hands onto her forearms. With his fur-painted face inches from hers, he said, "We're not asking."

Jade grinned through his bruising grip. "And I'm not selling."

Prince Charming said, "You think you're going to turn us into the Copperheads for the reward."

"And here I thought the handsome prince was always dumber than a sack of potatoes."

The four actors glanced at each other. The Wolf and Puss in Boots released her. Jade sprang out of the chair.

Their faces started to change. Multiple colors of mist rose from their exposed skin, giving off light like sun through fog. When it cleared, four different men surrounded her.

"Hey, Squirrel," Prince Charming said.

Jade only faltered a moment. She'd been prepared for this. "Drop dead, Ash."

"Squirrel, listen—"

"I'm not your adoring little sister anymore, Ash. I work for the Copperheads and will be collecting four fat pouches of reward money for all of you."

"No!" Puss in Boots—who turned out to be Oak, her oldest brother—swung her around by her shoulders. "We can't get stuck in jail."

"How sad for you. Guess you shouldn't have dropped off the nine corners of the world and become murdering thieves."

"Squir—Jade, that's not it," Cedar said.

"Tell it to the hag who prints the Wanted sheets for the Copperheads." Her cool voice hid the tearing fury in her gut. Her own brothers, once handpicked by a king, now the lowest kind of criminal.

She eyed the nearest window: Too far. The chimney. Too small. The door… just right.

Jade shifted onto the balls of her feet. "Don't bother looking over your shoulders, gentlemen. One by one I'll be coming for you. You'll never see me. Just ask Birch when you land in the cells with him."

On her last word she spun on one foot and kicked Ash in the stomach. Her left fist split Cedar's lips. Her right hand chopped Oak's windpipe. She leaped around Larch's clutching hands and dived shoulder-first through the door. A backflip onto the grass and she took off into the woods.

A few minutes later she slowed to get a handle on the anger boiling in her head.

A moment later, Windham stepped into her path from behind a cluster of dogwoods. Jade checked an automatic swing.

"Nine Holy Hells, Windham!" She looked over her shoulder. "Hide us."

The sorcerer muttered and drew a circle with his hands. "Done. What did your brothers say to you?"

Several replies choked themselves trying to escape her throat. "How long have you known?"

"A day or so. Since you brought the first one home." He looked past her. "They're not coming out."

"They told me it isn't what I think and that they can't go to jail. I left."

"I expected as much."

"That's why you didn't bother to see if I needed a little help?"

A shrug. "You can take care of yourself. That's why we set up this partnership." He glanced past her again. "They have resumed their glamours and are returning to the stage area."

"Doesn't matter. I know where to find them. We won't have to worry about your magic needs or the wine cellar for quite a while."

He shook his head. "You don't understand. There's a reason they've changed."

Jade leaned against the biggest dogwood, its abundance of pink blossoms caressing her face. "Yeah?"

"I was right. Well, partially right. People have disappeared in alt-world collisions." When she didn't reply, he said, "They come back... changed."

Jade left the district's Copperhead Hut by the back door. A few blocks' walk, a couple of purchases, and she'd be home to cook breakfast. The spring morning held the promise of rain, mud, and overflowing sewers. Nothing new about that.

The street vendors' voices crashed into each other as they hawked fresh fish, smoked hams, shoes, wool, wine, beer, and—for the daring—poppy juice and False Snow. Jade inspected the fish.

"Come home."

Jade looked right and left, but she saw no one. The bodiless voice didn't exactly sound like Windbag's but that was probably the spell's fault. She bargained for a minute and got the one-pound fish for two-thirds of the asking price.

Windham was playing poker with Sparky when she returned.

"Nice voice-throwing spell," she said as she slapped the trout on the cutting board.

"What?" Windham spread his hand on the small card table. "Full house."

Sparky revealed his own cards. "Straight flush."

Jade could've sworn she heard glee in its toneless metallic voice. To hide her face, she lit the stove before bending over the fish with a fillet knife.

Windham threw down his cards. "I'll turn you into a pre-Shock telephone that communicates with the dead."

Sparky gathered up the cards. "You require my services as a factotum."

"It's my own fault for adding extra magic to your circuitry." He appeared at Jade's side, oiling the cast-iron frying pan. "Excellent fish."

Jade looked sideways at him. "I had to bargain fast. Why'd you tell me to come home?"

"Is that what you meant earlier? What are you talking about?"

She salted the fillets. "I'm talking about you projecting your voice to me while I stood at the fish stall. Did you finally get the hang of astral projection as well as teleportation?"

He added hot peppers to the pan. "The only spell I worked this morning had to do with the cracked dinner plates you've been nagging me about."

"That's what I like about you: you're practical." She added onion to the pan and stirred it. "If it wasn't your voice, then something's haunting me."

The sorcerer stepped back a few paces. His inner eyelids slid over his silver eyes. After staring at her for several seconds, he said, "No. There is no residue in your aura."

Jade shrugged. "I'm heading back to the traveling theater after breakfast. Can you glamour me into a wrinkled old seamstress?"

Before he could answer, the Collision siren started wailing. Sparky's arms retracted into his torso and a panel in the back of his head opened. His feet sprouted grappling hooks, anchoring him to the floor. Screams from the connecting houses on either side filled the quiet morning, cutting across the ululating din. In the street outside their closed door, women shouted the names of their children and men called for rope and nails to tie things down.

Sparky began to recite numbers. Proximity metrics, Windham had called them. Atmospheric pressure and dimensional bulging, too.

Jade ignored the statistics. "Windham, get your beakers and bottles. I've got the cupboard locks." She blew out the cooking flame. "Close the bookshelf doors."

"I'm on it. Get the wine."

"Already there," she called from the pantry.

Sparky's mouth opening added a smaller siren to the cacophony from the one on the corner. "Proximity. Proximity. Proximity."

Jade ran into the center of the room. "Come on, Windham!" She yanked out a red leather cord and strapped her wrist to Sparky's left leg.

Windham skidded across the floor to the robot's right leg and did the same with his cobraskin hair tie. The sirens cut off.

In the silence, Sparky said, "Alt world data detected. Thought patterns, thirty percent. Electrical discharge, twenty-three percent. Biometrics, ninety-eight percent."

"Sparks, the collision hasn't hit us yet," Jade said.

"Collision imminent. Fourteen point eight seconds. Data is from collision five point two years prior to this date."

Windham grabbed Jade's free wrist, spat on it, and whispered six words. A miniature Jade rose from the spot.

"But... that's how I used to look," Jade said. "Fancy dress and jewels. Before I hooked up with you and the Copperheads."

The house shook. Something crashed in Windham's bedroom. A high-pitched screech came at them like the whistle of an approaching train. Through slitted eyes, Jade saw a different house, different street, different sun overlap the workroom. Strange faces stared through them, mouths open like they were screaming, hands covering their ears.

Sparky's voice, distorted and wavery, kept the count. "Collision time ten seconds. Eleven seconds. Twelve seconds. Collision peak."

Their door crashed open. Five people tumbled into the room. Jade couldn't tell if they were from this world or the alt.

"Collision ebb." Sparky's voice. "Twelve seconds to separation. Eleven seconds. Ten seconds."

The figures crawled toward them over the rippling floor.

"Windham! Do somethi—"

The first alt-worlder grabbed Jade by the waist and yanked. Her red cord snapped free of its anchor. Sparky's voice jittered and faded.

"Three seconds. Two sec—"

The sirens stopped. Jade's ears pounded. She blinked several times.

The ceiling was different. Painted wood instead of smoke-darkened beams. Her hands felt the edge of a carpet.

"Squirrel!" Pete Pumpkineater—no, Jade remembered, Birch—pulled her upright by both arms.

She jumped away and assumed fighting stance. "What did you do? If you think kidnapping me means I'll give up on turning you in, you're stupider than I remembered."

Birch laughed. "Squirrel, you can call us all the names you want. We're home. You're home."

"Home?" She looked around. The room resembled something from a half-forgotten dream. "Home is mine and Windham's place. I don't know how you did this, but you're headed for Copperhead cells. Especially you." She nodded at Birch.

Ash and Oak exchanged looks. Birch nodded. "Show her."

Ash took a small glass jar from his pocket and tipped a pinch of green powder from it into his hand. He spoke to it and flung both hands in a circle. Within it, like a pre-Shock relic, a miniature of the Nine Kingdoms appeared. Ash manipulated his fingers like Windham always did, and the Nine Kingdoms resolved into Jade's house. Another finger manipulation and she was staring at the workroom. Sparky's legs were just unhooking from the floor. Windham untied the other half of her red thong and looked up. He mirrored Ash's actions. A similar circle surrounded him and Sparky.

"Tell her," Birch said.

Windham's voice came through both circles thinner, but still honey-rich. "Jade, this is what I was trying to tell you. Your brothers weren't caught in an alt-world collision. You were."

Jade stared.

"Sparky didn't pick it up because I didn't have complete information for him before today. Not that we could've done anything about it until the next collision in our kingdom." He smiled. For the first time, Jade saw sadness in it.

"The collision changed you, Squirrel," Ash said, still concentrating on the circle-window. "You used to be timid and sweet. We had to force you to learn self-defense back then."

Jade stared at herself, her weapons, her fighting clothes.

Birch said, "When you vanished around the time of an intersect, Ash got leave from the King to develop his sorcerer skills. It took him three years to become powerful enough to track you down, and even then we had to wait for another intersection to jump across to find you."

Oak said, "We joined that theater troupe because they traveled all Nine Kingdoms. We never expected you to get so tough, Squirrel. We heard you were working for the Copperheads, so we figured the best way to get your attention was to go criminal."

"You killed innocent people," Jade said.

"Actually, no," Birch said. "We only killed the ones who were nasty pieces of work. Ash could see through their classy fronts."

"So you see, Jade," Windham said, "Now you're back in the correct world—for you."

Jade shook her head. Slowly at first, then faster and faster, till her braid slapped against her cheeks. "Hoodin's Wand, Windbag, you don't believe these low-lifes? Make that circle bigger, and I'll toss them through it. The Copperheads have reward money with our names on it." When he didn't move, she said, "Please, Windham."

"Goodbye, Jade," Windham said. "I will miss you."

"No!" Jade leapt for the circle.

It winked out.

Ash and Birch each put a hand on Jade's shoulders. "Little sister, perky Squirrel, you're home now. We'll help you relearn who you really are. Everything will be just like before."

Jade looked at the five men she'd thought were criminals. Her hands longed to punch the smiles off their faces.

A door behind Birch opened and another man entered. He carried a fancy green dress and a pair of soft-looking leather shoes, clothes almost as rich as the ones he wore.

"My darling." He embraced her. "I've waited five years for your return."

She returned his embrace. Strategy. Never let the enemy think they've surprised you.

"Your brothers promised me they'd find you. Gentlemen," he said, keeping one arm around Jade, "the King is ready to return you to your proper places. Except you, Ash. He told me to say that if your alternate-world intersect plan went as predicted, you would become his chief sorcerer."

Ash grinned. Oak and Birch pounded his back.

Jade smiled at the man holding her. He obviously had the king's confidence. Perfect for her. She accepted the useless dress and shoes from him. She'd disguised herself as a lady before. Easy to do so again.

"I'll go and change. Ash, may I speak with you for a moment?"

"You sound more like yourself already," Ash said. He fell into step with her. "We've missed you, little one."

"I have a favor to ask." She called on all her undercover skills and smiled with girlish charm. "Would you teach me a little bit of sorcery?"

He stopped. "But why? You're the Prime Minister's betrothed. You don't have any need for it."

Jade's charm never flinched. "I'm so impressed by what you've done that I want to do a little good with it myself." She raised her eyes to his, making them large and earnest. "Maybe even finding lost children. I want to make people as happy as you have, now that I'm home."

Ash returned her smile. "Squirrel, I missed your sweet nature. Of course I'll teach you. Run along now and change."

Jade closed herself into a dressing room and dropped the demure mask like a rotten apple. Hoodin's Wand, men were idiots. She fingered the dress with distaste.

"Windbag," she whispered, "you won't get rid of me that easily. When I get back, I'll challenge you for the title of Greatest Sorcerer in Nine Kingdoms."

She unbraided her hair and pulled her remaining red leather cords from her pocket. It took only a minute to tie them under her long black hair and fluff the rest of it out to conceal them. Changing her face to this Squirrel everyone thought she was took a little longer, but she did it.

She opened the door with a bright smile on her face and plans for magic in her heart. "Here I am."

About the Author

Alice Loweecey has eight ex-nun PI mysteries published through Midnight Ink and Henery Press, and a horror novel under a pen name. She has short stories published with Occult Detective Quarterly, Astounding Outpost, *and others.*

THE LASTING HILLS

STEPHEN CASE

In the Abbey, they sing of Claire and the World Tree. They sing of the planting of the seed and of the shards of stone above the sky. The oldest of the Sisters move in the candlelight, their limbs like branches of gnarled wood, knotted against the storms of decades. The knights among them keep their silence. Above, bronze eyes watch like lanterns.

The song dies into whispers.

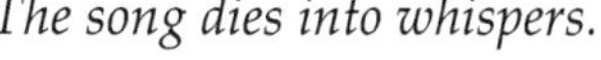

Claire stared at the stone doorway without moving, unable to shake the feeling it was watching her. It seemed a cold and attentive creature rising up out of the jagged hillside, though it was only a spare arch of weathered granite.

Claire had been searching for it for days.

If there were trees, it would be easier. Imagine a crumbling stone arch nestled between the towering trunks of her oaks back at the Abbey. The trees there would have whispered assurances. They would have given Claire some sign.

These hills were dead though. The only voice belonged to the wind.

She pulled the last of the hard bread from the satchel at her side. There was no reason to ration it now that she had found the doorway. She would either turn away, retracing her steps and not stopping until she reached the Abbey, or she would walk through. The hint of trail she had followed this far passed through the archway and continued uninterrupted up the slope beyond.

"Just walk through," the fledgling had said, immediately before it had lunged at her and leapt into the sky. "The only magic is your lack of hesitation."

Claire came across the fledgling on her third night in the hills, tangled in a treetop snare. She had waited under a copse of whip-elder a full hour, watching the young dragon as she watched the doorway now. He was smaller than the creatures she had seen among her trees at the Abbey, but his eyes were baleful crescent moons.

He told her he would teach her the way into the Aeries if she released him.

"Not that you would last long once you arrived," he said. "But you wouldn't last long in the mountains either."

"I am looking for someone."

"Obviously." He strained against the ropes entangling him. "If he's a human, you won't find him."

"How do I know you won't kill me after I cut you down?"

He had tried. But he was either injured or she was lucky or both, and after that first swipe of beak and burst of flame he was gone.

Now she stood at the doorway.

Do it, she told herself. *If you don't, you will always wonder whether Baiden was beyond it. Whether he lives.*

She stepped through.

A chill moved across her, clinging and wet like water, but she found herself not upon the path beyond the doorway but instead in a warm, dry chamber of curving rock. Eyes opened in what for a moment she took to be a rockslide half-filling the chamber.

"Humans devoured upon entry," said a voice like gravel. "In violation of treaty."

It did not help to scream. She had seen dragons before. She reined her panic and spoke. "Am I in violation of a treaty, or is it a violation of a treaty to eat humans?"

The wide mouth opened and paused. "I do not think it matters."

"It matters to me."

The eyes narrowed. "Then you should not have come to the Aeries!"

"I'm looking for someone."

The dragon's eyes narrowed until they were twin slits of orange. "Did Tryggslygga send you? Do not lie. I will know if you are lying."

"A captured fledgling told me the way."

"Extortion!" The voice was deafening.

"Hold, Hydrygglysga!" A human figure stepped out of a side tunnel and held up an arm. "At least find out who it is she seeks."

The voice was unmistakable, as was the face when it turned toward her. Claire had last seen him the night the dragons came to the Abbey, when he left her side to go to the aid of his brother knights. They had been killed, and Baiden had been carried off. Now he had a bemused, unreadable expression on his face.

Her voice had not failed speaking to the dragon, but it did now. "You were gone," she began, and then tried again. "Mother Superior said you would be dead, but I had to—"

"To find me? In gods' names, why?"

"Because . . ."

Because you trusted me, she wanted to say. *Because you would not leave me behind when the dragons came to my trees. Because anyone else would have.*

The dragon groaned like rocks splintering. "Is she under your protection, Baiden, or shall I end her?"

"My protection, Hydrygglysga. She is a friend."

It groaned again and slid away, back up the chamber.

"This way," Baiden told her. "The chambers above are cooler, and some have been cut to human proportions."

"You're not dead," Claire said.

"Not yet."

"And that one obeyed you."

"For now."

Baiden's armor was gone. He wore a simple loose-fitting white tunic, which seemed suited for the heat of the caverns. His face looked less lined, somehow younger than Claire remembered.

"Where are we?"

There was no apparent source of illumination, but the stones in the chamber were suffused with an orange-yellow glow. Higher, they became bluish and cooler as Claire and the knight climbed a spiraling passage.

"These are the Aeries," Baiden said, "the home of the dragons."

"We're in caves? In the mountains?"

He shook his head. "They are mountains, but I do not believe they are the mountains of the north, where we campaigned."

"Then where?"

"I'll try to show you."

They climbed in silence, and Claire worked to order her thoughts. She had left the Abbey with no plan other than a sense of responsibility toward this knight. Baiden had used her, had lied to her to learn about the Abbey and its grove, but on the final night, he alone had insisted she be included and witness the meeting between the sisters and the dragons among the trees.

And he had remained beside her as long as he could.

"How were you down there?" Claire suddenly asked. "At the door? How did you know I would be there?"

"Tryggslygga, the fledgling you mentioned, came through just before." Baiden chuckled. "He said a human woman had threatened to abandon him to the huntsmen unless he told her the way to the Aeries. That caught my attention. I asked him what she looked like. Dragons are not much for remembering human features, but I only knew one girl who might be stubborn enough to try to find me. So I waited near the gate."

They reached a doorway that opened into low chambers, still of stone. There was furniture here, and rugs hung from the walls. "Despite what Hydrygglysga said, there have been human visitors to the Aeries, though not for some time. I am the only one at the moment. These chambers are maintained for our usage."

Claire walked into the rooms. But for the pale blue glow they might have been in the catacombs of the Abbey. Brighter light poured in from a doorway at the far end.

"What is that light?" she asked, pointing.

"You might want to take my hand."

"Why?"

"Beyond that arch is a glass chamber on the mountain's surface. You are seeing light from outside."

Claire ignored his hand. "Is it night? It looks like moonlight."

At the threshold she paused. It was a glass chamber, as he had said, small and with a vaulted ceiling and chairs set about a small table. Snowy slopes fell away steeply beyond the glass. A dark, starry sky filled the view.

"How is it night here?" she asked.

"It is always night here."

She looked at him in confusion, and he pointed upward.

Above hung an unfamiliar moon. It was impossibly large, filling the view like a second sky. It was impossibly colored as well. Not cool and grey but cold and blue, with spirals of white.

Claire stared up at it for a long time without speaking.

"It was the same for me," Baiden said. "There are no words."

"What is it?" she finally whispered.

"We are on a stone suspended in the sky, Claire. What you see is the shape of our world. Somewhere on that white and blue ball above us is the doorway you stepped through."

Claire did not sleep well that night. She had become accustomed to nights on the road, so it was not being outside the Abbey's walls that troubled her. In many ways these chambers seemed like coming home. She had a room to herself, with Baiden in another down the corridor. It was quiet, and if there were indeed dragons in caverns all around them, they made no sounds.

What troubled Claire was the feeling of falling. She would be on the edge of sleep when the impossible moon would rise up before her and she would feel herself falling upward toward it. This happened again and again until she finally slipped into the linen tunic that had been left for her in the chamber and walked back to the crystal chamber.

The huge moon still hung above, unmoved, though now it was dark, visible only as an absence against the darker sky. Somehow this made it easier to watch, and she stared at it for what may have been hours. Cold seeped in through the walls.

Finally an orange glow appeared on the edge of the dark circle above. Claire watched as it grew, as though someone was pouring molten gold onto the edge of a pan, until it gathered itself into a brilliant star and lifted away.

"The sun." She breathed a reverent curse she had heard other novices use.

"It is lovely," came a voice by her side. She spun, thinking Baiden had approached silently. There was no one, but the voice came again. "You desire breakfast?"

"Where are you?"

"I am here." The air rippled and two wings unfurled from nothing. It was like a dragon, but smaller and more lithe. It lacked the leathery hide of the fledgling. Its four wings were gossamer. "No alarm or intrusion intended. Some find our appearance unsettling."

Claire laughed, deciding she would take additional impossibilities as they came, and the shades of the creature's wings brightened.

"Breakfast would be lovely," she told it.

The creature brought a tray from somewhere loaded with a tea service and steaming bowls smelling of honey. Claire questioned it while she ate but the creature either did not hear or did not understand. After a time it moved on, saying it needed to wake the knight. Minutes later Baiden wandered into the chamber and took the second bowl from the tray.

"I saw an angel," Claire told him, "and the sunrise."

Baiden nodded. "That is what I call them too. They maintain these quarters, and I am sure they do other things in the Aeries as well. There is much I still don't understand."

"Why are you here?" The teapot held something that tasted of mint. "Are you a prisoner?"

"We knights were trying to do the same thing as the senior sisters at your Abbey. We were trying to re-forge or renew the old alliances. There were legends of humans, of soldiers, who had passed into the Aeries centuries ago, just as there were rumors that your order kept ancient congress with dragons. We needed to confirm that, and we needed to make a contact of our own." He shrugged. "The initial meeting didn't go as planned. It is harder than we realized to keep hostilities at bay. But they didn't kill me."

"And here you are."

Baiden smiled wryly. "The first man to reach the Aeries since the King's departure."

"And the first woman?" Claire asked.

He shook his head. "There has never been a woman here."

Claire set down her cup. "I thought you needed help. I thought—somehow—that it was my fault, and I needed to know you weren't dead. Now I do. I can go home."

"Do you want to?"

She glanced upward at the huge globe in the sky, shading now again toward blue and white. "Of course I do. I belong with my sisters."

"I can talk with Myrdrylaggsyl. The dragons will meet in council in a day or two. But I don't know that they would allow it. They don't like people finding their way in."

His tone was guarded, and for the first time she was touched by fear, as slow and cold as the shards of stones around them.

Claire waited in the chambers of the Aeries. The rooms were spacious and comfortable though silent and cold. Time took on an unchanging quality in keeping with the silent skies beyond the crystal windows. Baiden left to meet with the dragons, and Claire found herself falling back into the rhythms of prayer and silence of her life in the Abbey, rhythms that had lapsed during her time on the road.

"Are there trees here, Baiden?" Claire asked when he returned to their chambers.

"What?"

"Plants. Trees. Anything. All this stone and glass. It feels dead."

"I don't know. I can try to find out."

The voice of an angel sounded at her shoulder. "There is the World Tree." The creature remained invisible. Claire asked what it meant. "At the mountain's summit," it said. "Climb upward."

Claire looked at Baiden, who shook his head. "I try not to wander these chambers on my own. It's easy to get lost."

But Claire was already moving toward the entrance. Beyond, the rock held the orange tint of the cave where Claire had first entered. She followed a wide corridor until she found a flight of stairs heading upward. This brought her to an even wider corridor with a high, arched ceiling, which ended at a spiraling staircase. Here the stones in the walls began to glow a faint purple. Baiden hurried to catch up to her, grumbling under his breath.

They saw no dragons. Instead they saw shafts of light and shadow Baiden said were more angels.

"How long have the dragons lived here?" she asked him as they climbed.

"I don't know," the knight answered. "Hundreds of years, I think. Before the Absent King departed, certainly. We do not know much of their history or the role they played in the War of Departure. We cannot say which side they'll be on when the King returns."

"You believe he will?"

Claire did not realize how the question sounded until it was out of her mouth. The belief in the return of the Absent King was in the prayers the sisters chanted at the Abbey at sunrise, noon, and sunset, but it felt strange to hear Baiden speak of it here and in terms of history. The King's return was something Claire felt in her bones, like the knowledge of death, not something discussed in common conversation or in terms of political alliance.

"There are signs," he said, "but there always are. Maybe it is nothing more than the fact that we can't last much longer unless he does." Claire remembered things he had told her in the Abbey about the campaigns in the mountains. "At least, that's the way it looked when I left."

"We pray, in the Abbey." Claire did not slow her upward climb. "I always thought the legends had truth to them whether they were real or not. I wasn't sure even the sisters believed his return would be more than metaphorical, a symbol of the spiritual awakening we all seek. The King is not dead then?"

"Oh, he died. I've seen the Tomb myself, at the center of the Plain of Ice. But I don't want to believe we have been fighting a rearguard action for seven hundred years on account of a metaphor."

Claire slowed. There was a ribbon of brown running through the wall to their left. "This is a root." The wood twisted like a rope through a split in the rock, and she passed her fingers along it. "Listen."

She quieted as Sister Mauro had taught her, listening for the life of the root within the stones. She expected a whisper, a murmur, as though of something moving listlessly in sleep. It was the way trees spoke to her, even in high summer and their days of greatest wakefulness. She did not expect a shout, a song, a resonance bursting up and out of the grey shards in which the root waited.

The power of it must have shown on her face. Baiden stepped forward and took her arm. "Are you all right?"

She found her voice and nodded, her head spinning. "Keep climbing," was all she could say.

The roots grew thicker as they climbed. The stairway ended in a dark slope, a surface running like molten stone now hardened. In the pale purple light of the walls it took her a moment to realize it was the trunk of a tree emerging from the floor. The staircase ended in a chamber with a ceiling like the surface of the gate Claire had passed through to the Aeries. The trunk of the tree formed one wall. Above them that wall rose into a starry darkness.

It was difficult to see the shape of the tree above. The trunk before them was so wide it would have dwarfed even the immense oaks of the Abbey. It curved away on either side like the walls of a city. Above, beyond the shimmering ceiling, it reared as a tree in winter, a shape against the stars. She could see no hint of leaves among its upper branches, which from their distance may have been miles away and fathoms long.

"I had no idea this was here," Baiden breathed.

"It is the World Tree," Claire said. There were other names that the root had pressed into her mind, but this was closest to the handle of speech. "Do the dragons speak of it?"

Baiden shook his head.

Around them the shifting quality of light, as though the tree did indeed have branches with sunlight slanting through them, indicated the presence of angels.

"Did the angels plant it?" he asked. "Do they tend it?"

Claire laughed softly. The root had spoken. It had told her that she had been summoned. She had not stumbled into the Aeries because of luck and the loose tongue of a fledgling or because of the stirrings in her heart Baiden's face had awakened. Rather, she realized now that all of those things had been the aspects of a summoning.

The tree had brought her here.

"No one planted it," she whispered. "The angels hewed these caverns when dragons were dust and when men were not yet even a whisper in the forests. But they hewed them because the tree was already here, growing in silence."

Baiden stared at her.

The wood of the trunk was smooth as glass but warm to her touch. She knelt beside it as she had at the foot of the oaks in her grove in the Abbey. A voice was waiting beneath the wood. It had spoken through the root, but it was gathering itself to speak again now.

She braced herself.

"Catch me," she said to Baiden.

"What?"

"If I fall. Catch me."

She reached out and touched the trunk.

Claire woke back in her chamber with silver light from the room at the end of the corridor shining on the stone ceiling above her. Baiden was there, speaking softly to an angel. Claire found she could see it more clearly now, the outline of wings and the triple-faced head rotating slowly upon an ivory neck.

She sat up.

"The dragons," she said. "Their council."

Baiden made a hushing noise as though she were a child. It made her bristle, and she spoke again, louder.

"They are meeting now in the chambers below," he admitted.

"The tree's message. I have to deliver it."

She tossed the thin covers back and then gasped and pulled them back when she realized her legs were bare.

Baiden glanced away. "You were drenched with sweat when I carried you back. Like you had a fever. The angels said to take your cloak. They told me to bathe you with cool water."

"You . . .?"

"They were here too."

She forced the thought of his hands out of her mind and tried to make her voice firm. "Get my clothes. We need to see the dragons."

"They will not like being interrupted. I've been warned—"

"My clothes."

When he left the room, she tried to gather her thoughts. She felt she had absorbed a lifetime of knowledge from the touch of the tree. But how much of anyone's lifetime did they recall at any single moment?

The tree was indescribably old.

"We need to go now," she told Baiden when he returned.

"You shouldn't go anywhere. Not yet. You are still weak."

"Turn around."

He did, and she forced herself out of the bed and into her clothes. She was weak, but she would not lean on him. When he turned, she squared her shoulders and hoped he couldn't see her trembling.

"Now. Take me to the dragons."

He led her back into the caves. Despite her efforts she was leaning on his arm before they had gone far. Shimmers in the air around them told her they did not walk alone, that the angels were gathering as they descended.

They stopped in a wide chamber with rows of stalactites hanging down like staggered teeth. There was a huge iron door in the rock before them, perfectly round and nearly as high as the trees Claire had warded at the Abbey.

"The dragons keep congress in the chamber beyond," Baiden whispered. "It would be unwise to enter without permission."

Claire had to extend her hand above her head to reach the lower edge of the iron portal. She rested her fingers on the warm metal and recalled the command of passage the tree had revealed. With a faint groan of metal on metal, the plates forming the portal rolled away to reveal a huge conical chamber beyond and hundreds of rows of craning grey and green and bronze necks.

And wide, golden eyes.

Heat billowed outward, and the wall of angels around them glistened.

Claire turned to Baiden. "Help me over the threshold."

"They will kill you."

"Not before they listen."

He groaned and went to a knee before her. "Let me hold your foot and I will—"

It was like climbing a tree. She placed one foot on his back, the other on his shoulder, and pulled herself up over the dragon's threshold. Baiden stared for a moment at the place where she had disappeared and cursed. Then he reached up to pull himself over the threshold.

"You will die in this heat, Baiden," a dragon said to him when he had dropped to a space of stone beside Claire. It was not a threat. "No humans come here."

"We did not mean to offend, Trggysklydyk."

"Names are not spoken in this chamber, human," the dragon rumbled. "Here we are one, as in the oldest days."

The dragon addressing them was only the nearest of the legions crowded into the vast chamber. Another, larger, moved forward and arched its neck above them.

"Your presence is not permitted in the exchange, human." Its eyes were narrowed. "But you opened the doors. And you are not burned."

It waited.

Claire spoke. "I have touched the tree. The tree in whose roots you shelter."

Several of the dragons hissed at these words.

"It has a message." She paused. "No. That implies consciousness and will. Rather, I read the story of the years beneath its bark, and I must share what I learned with those who are allies of the Absent King."

The dragon before them blinked its eyes slowly.

"Say rather we are not enemies," it said.

"Tell them," Baiden whispered.

"The tree will bear fruit."

The breath of the dragons flared around them. Baiden threw himself in front of Claire to shield her from the sudden flames.

"Peace!" one of the dragons bellowed.

The thousands of eyes were wide and bright upon them.

"I speak . . ." Claire hesitated. Baiden did not move away. He still gripped her shoulders. "I touch trees and know their history, know what they have seen and felt. The story of this tree, hung in the sky, the World Tree, is too large for me."

Several of the dragons bowed their heads low. "We are the serpents in its roots," they murmured.

The bronze dragon shifted its eyes to Baiden. "Do you speak for her?" it asked. "Do you confirm her words in the name of the truce that keeps you here as token and emissary?"

Baiden glanced at Claire and nodded. "I do."

"We hear," the dragon said. They waited.

Claire pulled away from Baiden's protective embrace and spoke. "The tree is bearing fruit. I don't know how many. I don't know how often." In her mind Claire saw the images the tree had carried, a jeweled weight growing in branches bare in the cold emptiness of starlight.

"Never in our memory," the dragons whispered as one.

"One must be plucked," Claire said. "One must be planted."

"Where?" they asked. They were spread out before her in the chamber like a field of fire and scales, of wide bronze eyes in a thicket of steel.

She licked her lips, chapped and dry in the heat of the chamber. "Before the Tomb of the Absent King."

Baiden was pacing. They were in the room Claire was beginning to consider a solarium, though the sun through its panes held only the empty heat of stars on a winter night.

"Years," he said, through gritted teeth. "It took years to orchestrate this exchange, years to allow a single knight passage into the Aeries. And you have unraveled it in a single meeting. Do you know how long I waited to have an audience with the dragons?" Claire watched him passively. "I was here for months."

She shook her head. "That's not possible. You disappeared—were taken—only days before I found you."

He waved a hand with irritation. "Time is different here."

For a moment Claire was again frightened. She had an image of a return to the world below where the Abbey was only a ruin and her trees had been dead for centuries.

Claire glanced at the white and blue moon hanging above the solarium's windows, the moon she knew was actually her own world. Whatever had impelled her here, whatever hope and uncertainty she had held—and looking at Baiden now it seemed as though that wild, witless hope would never be realized—had given way to a deeper certainty and purpose.

The tree had spoken.

Baiden was watching her. She met his eyes.

"How do we get the fruit?" she asked.

He rubbed a hand along his chin. "Besides everything else, that is one thing I don't understand. We can't get topside of the Aeries, as the cold would kill us. A dragon might be able to, but asking one would be—"

"Hydrygglysga awaits you on the stairs," whispered a voice of chimes at Claire's elbow.

"We will not have to ask," Claire said.

The dragon's bulk filled the faintly blue stairway. The light of the rocks reflecting off his grey scales gave him the look of a creature carved of ice.

"No dragon in living memory has climbed the World Tree." It was a bearded dragon, with horns like silver foam sprouting above its eyebrows and chin. "Not since Arrllgryllmndyll the Very First. Not since we carved ourselves burrows in its roots above the world."

Claire bowed low and remained silent.

"We spoke for hours of what you told us," the dragon continued. "We would have spoken for days. It is our way to speak and to speak and to speak. To remember, and seldom to act." The smoke that rose from the dragon's lips when it spoke smelled of cinnamon. "Of what it means, there was much discussion. Of what comes of remembering the old alliances of our youth now in the weariness of our age and of bringing Man once again into the Aeries."

Its eyes rolled to fix for a moment on Baiden.

"But the tree has spoken." The dragon's ivory claws clicked on the chipped stone steps. "There can be no action until we know for certain. Until we see if there is indeed fruit in the branches of heaven." Its long lips curled. "So say the youngest among us. And so I am chosen to make the climb."

"Hydrygglysga," Baiden said, "you will die."

The dragon showed its teeth. "Never speak of death to a dragon."

Hydrygglysga moved fluidly through the tunnels. In what seemed like moments they stood where the flesh of the tree rose up from the ground like a river of wood. The rock over their heads ended, and through the shimmering barrier that kept the cold at bay, they looked up at the vastness of the tree.

Its bulk ran from the stones at their feet into the blackness of the sky like a giant's causeway, like the highway of the gods. At the end of a year's journey upward, so it seemed from this vantage, it divided into branches that passed between the clustered stars. If it bore any fruit besides those stars, it was impossible to tell at this distance.

"I climb," Hydrygglysga said, "like the first serpent in the first tree." Without a glance at Baiden or Claire, the dragon moved up the wooden face before them, passing through the shimmer above their heads.

"Its fire will die in the cold," Baiden said.

They watched the dragon climb. It should have flown, as the dragons had settled into the branches of Claire's oaks on the night that now seemed long ago, but there was no air to push against in the emptiness above the Aeries. The dragon was as much now a serpent as any wingless snake on the world beneath. They watched until Hydrygglysga was only a small, icy sheen on the curve of the wood, impossibly high above them.

Claire found she was gripping Baiden's hand. They stood at the foot of the tree like two children in a forest.

When Hydrygglysga fell, it fell with an impossible slowness. Claire saw its shape appear again against the bulk of the tree above them. There was no cushion of wind for its wings to brace themselves against.

Baiden pulled her backward, but the force of the impact still made the rocks tremble around them. Hydrygglysga shattered like glass, shards of scales and bones ricocheting off the tree and stones of the surface.

All Claire could think of in that moment was the fruit. She pulled away, ran to where the tree rose to the surface, and began climbing. Then she was beyond the barrier, on the surface, with the ice of the emptiness piercing her skin like spikes. Her legs trembled. The dragon was broken, but it gripped a fruit in one of its splintered iron claws.

It was perhaps a dozen yards away.

Claire forced her body over stones that seemed knives beneath her feet. There was nothing in her lungs, and her skin burned. It was difficult to see.

When she reached it, she knelt to take hold of the fruit. It was shaped like the pit of the stone-pears Sister Mauro used to grow in the Abbey's hothouse, but it was the color of ice. She touched its hull, impossibly smooth and cold, and pulled it from beneath the dragon's claw.

She could not breathe. The cold was too intense, and there was a rushing sound, a rising pressure, behind her ears.

Claire closed her eyes.

Baiden's arms surprised her, encircling her and the fruit, pulling her upright and half-carrying, half-dragging her back toward the opening to the cave. He stumbled, nearly throwing her back down to the corridor below.

Warm air billowed around them like steam from a bath. Claire lay on the stone floor, sucking deep shuddering breaths. Baiden lay on the rocks beside her, calling her a fool.

Claire turned toward him, wrapped her arms around him, and buried her face in his neck. They lay like that, harboring each other's heat, with the tree's cold fruit nestled between them like a dead child, until Claire found the strength to rise.

"They have a passage," Baiden explained. He had come from his final meeting with the dragons in the chambers below. "It is an old one that has not been used in years, but it will take us to the Tomb."

Claire was in their chambers, gathering her few supplies, folding and stashing them in the satchel she had carried with her from the Abbey. There were thin, silky robes that had appeared in her room each morning, but she was leaving them behind, trading them once again for the rough fabric of her habit. "Thank you, Baiden," she told him. "I know I have made your mission difficult."

"You have ended it." She looked at him, trying to read his face. "The dragons feel that with Hydrygglysga's sacrifice and their aid in passage, they have fulfilled their old obligations. There will be no more ambassadors of man in the Aeries."

"I'm sorry."

Baiden shrugged. "I did not want to remain here forever."

"Where will you go?"

"I'm coming with you."

Claire shook her head. "You have no responsibility to me. I came after you because I didn't understand what had happened that night. I don't know what I wanted or hoped to accomplish." She felt foolish telling him this. "But I satisfied myself you were safe, and I ended up putting you in greater danger. Once I plant this seed, I will return to the Abbey."

"And that is well. But I am coming with you to take the fruit to the Tomb. Then I will see you home."

She shook her head again. "I'm not a girl. I found my way through the wilderness to the Aeries. I can find my way home."

"The Tomb of the Absent King is much farther than you wandered, Claire. It is in the mountains, where it is always winter. It will take you months to return."

She was tired of arguing. She could not forbid him to follow her back, and she admitted he deserved to see the fruit planted—just as he had once insisted she see the dragons roosting in her oak trees. She glanced through the chambers to the glass-walled room that looked out over the emptiness and up toward the world above. Angels whispered around her, but she did not understand what they were saying. They had crowded the room since she had carried the fruit down.

"All right, Baiden," she said. "I will be glad for the company."

They stepped from an arch of stone to a plain of ice. The last wisp of dragon-heat behind them died and was gone, and a brilliant, frigid whiteness with specks of snow hit them full on. Claire gasped.

"Here," Baiden said.

He wore one of the blue fur-trimmed robes the knights had worn when they first came to the Abbey, and he wrapped it around Claire now. Together they stepped from the stone arch of the passage onto snowy ground.

"Where are we?"

"This is the Plain of Ice," Baiden said. "When winter dies and the King returns, this is where he will build his city." He pointed toward a line of mountains in the distance. "We are on the edge of the plain, but if we walk that direction we will find the Tomb."

"You've been here before?"

He nodded. They began to walk, the wind whipping at the edges of the robe and snatching Baiden's words from his mouth. "Each season. The remaining companies make their way to the Plain and camp within sight of the Tomb."

She was thinking about the ground. If it was frozen, how would she plant the fruit? And how would anything grow in this bleak wasteland? "It's always winter here?"

He nodded grimly. "For nearly seven hundred years. Since the King's departure."

Claire cradled the seed.

They walked. The wind did not vary, and it seemed they moved no closer to the mountains that ringed the plain. The landscape itself was featureless, holding only low ragged grasses in the places where wind had swept it of snow.

"There." Baiden pointed.

There was a low foundation on the horizon, nothing more, but Baiden hurried them toward it. As they drew closer, Claire saw it was a platform of stones, rough and featureless. A ring of rusty swords formed a broken perimeter, their blades sunk nearly to the hilt in the frozen soil of the plain. Some were so old they were mere shards of steel, stripped of any design or ornamentation by the wind and snow and years.

"There will be torches and wood inside," Baiden said, gesturing to a stairway that led down beneath the platform.

"Wait a moment." Claire knelt, her knees cold against the snow. In the Abbey, they kept vigil for the Absent King's return. They read words attributed to him in the sacred texts and the epistles to his stewards. She never thought she would make a pilgrimage to the place where the armies of the north awaited his return. Now, for a moment, she repeated one of those prayers.

May we wait in hope. May your return bring peace.

Baiden waited.

"I'm ready," she said, rising.

The room beneath the platform was small, but the stones were well-laid and blocked the wind, and there was wood piled against the nearest wall.

"I have only been inside this chamber once," Baiden said, lighting a torch that hung from a bracket on the wall. "When I was knighted. We are all knighted at the grave itself." He pointed.

The Tomb was here, a grey stone ark in the room's center. Baiden took the torch and led her to it. The only carving or ornamentation in the entire chamber was the stone lid.

"It's him," she whispered.

The spare illuminations depicting the King that decorated the margins of texts in the Abbey showed only an idealized representation: wide eyes, full lips, flowing hair. The graven image on the lid of the Tomb was different. It was real. It showed a man in the fullness of power and strength and wisdom. The margins were worked with leaves, the carvings sharp enough they might have been cut that morning, so fresh it seemed stone shavings should still litter the flagstones around them.

"He's in there? His body?" Claire found her hands were shaking. She was afraid to touch the stone.

"He is gone, Claire." His words were heavy. "We believe the Tomb is empty. No one has ever looked within."

Claire felt cold. The songs and scriptures from her years in the Abbey seemed suddenly far away, like the memory of games played in childhood. She imagined bones moldering in the stone sepulcher, rotting like all the legends she was taught of his departure and return, their forms falling away like his armies that had been failing now for centuries. "What if he's just dead," she heard herself asking, "and he's in there and everything about him has always been a false hope?"

"Claire." Baiden smiled. "We have come from the dragons' Aeries. Among shards of stone in the sky. Where the World Tree grows. What is the return of a dead king to that?"

Claire smiled too, but it was around an ache that suddenly blossomed and spread from her chest into her arms and legs.

"We take an oath when we are knighted," Baiden continued. The torchlight made his features look angular, fitting together like a broken puzzle. "We are pledged to the chief things of the ancient mountains, to the precious things of the lasting hills."

"What does it mean?"

Baiden shrugged. "That we endure. That we hope. That we prefer to live as though he will return."

Claire turned from the Tomb and felt for the seed against her in its sling. At the top of the stairs, snow was falling. She brushed away what had accumulated until she reached the earth beneath, cold and hard as rock.

"We need fire," she said when Baiden joined her. "The ground is frozen. We need to build a fire to thaw it."

He nodded and went back into the chamber. When he emerged, he was carrying a load of wood. "We might get visitors," he grunted, dropping the wood. "Patrols do not come through the plain often, other then when we make the annual pilgrimage. But some might see the fire."

Claire nodded.

He placed wood where she indicated and before long had kindled a low, dull flame. It grew as she watched. She listened to the wood hiss and wondered about stories it held. Were it part of a living tree, something stunted and twisted growing in the blasting winds of the mountains lining the plain, she could have felt its story. It would have been one of snow and wind and spring thaws bringing water thick and slow as sap. It would be a story of trees that grew over hundreds of years, clinging to the margins of the rocks, carving out slices of brown and green in the silence. But now they were burning.

The stories were falling to ash.

Claire watched the fire through the night. Baiden prepared a meal with food they had brought from the Aeries, and she watched him as well. Then she turned from the fire to watch the stars. The World Tree was up there, growing in an impossible margin between sky and earth. She could not see the rock on which they had somehow perched, the rock in which dragons even now were burrowed like vipers. Maybe there were a thousand stones like that, scattered in the space above the earth, passing overhead unseen each evening. Maybe there were entire forests in the sky, immense trees rooted to drifting shards of granite.

Claire stirred the fire. She would keep it burning all night. Then perhaps the ground would be warm enough to plant the seed.

She could not shake her new certainty that the King was dead and long decayed in the Tomb behind them. The World Tree would not have sent its fruit to die in a frozen waste but rather to shelter the growing city of the King's return. But it was only a tree, and it was old.

"Do you have a sword there in the ring?" she asked, when Baiden returned with more logs for the fire.

He glanced outward to where the weathered hilts stood like tiny crosses. "No. Not yet." He shifted his own blade across his shoulders. "When I am dead, they will burn me on the plain, outside the Tomb, and then they will leave my sword to stand watch."

"Waiting for the King."

He watched her. "It is a tired hope, Claire. But it is the only hope we have."

"Why?" She rose to her feet and felt for a moment like her trees on the night the dragons had come, angry and swept by storms. "What will happen if the armies march south? Abandon these passes? You have been in the sky, Baiden. You have met with dragons beneath the World Tree. You don't need to waste your life in a wilderness of stone and ice. For how long? How many years? Why?"

"So we will be here when he—"

She cut him off with a gesture. "He's dead, Baiden. I've seen his Tomb. He lived and he died, and now we write songs about him. Whatever kingdom he had is over and dead."

She watched his face, hoping to find something. She wanted to see anger, perhaps, or sadness. But it was as blank as the plain they waited within.

"I have met with the dragons, yes, Claire." His voice stumbled on her name. "But you have spoken with the World Tree itself. What did it say?"

"It didn't say." Claire turned her face away. "It showed."

"What did it show?"

She pulled the seed from where it lay heavy against her chest. Its surface was now the color of iron, with lines and whorls that hinted at the grain of wood but held no meaning, no structure, apart from bundled, waiting life. "Ages and ages of the world," she said.

She paused, trying to find words for the images she had felt through the weathered and ancient bark.

"Silence and watchfulness," she added. "Waiting."

"For what?"

Claire sighed and lowered herself to a sitting position again, cradling the seed in her lap. "For this," she muttered. "For a planting. For a new tree below."

"For you, Claire." He sat beside her but faced the opposite direction, his back to the fire and his face to the Tomb. "We may have waited hundreds of years in vain, but if we had not . . ." The grin came again, but this time it was sharper, as though cut by a knife. "If we had not, the Tomb and the Plain would have been lost. This place would have been scoured by ice generations ago. There would have been nowhere to plant the seed."

"We could have planted it farther south then. The tree would have showed us somewhere else to go."

"But then it would not be here."

"You want a miracle."

"You are holding one, Claire."

She pushed the seed into his hands and walked away from the fire, out beyond the circle of corroded swords.

Baiden made no move to stop her.

In the morning the fire was dead, and Baiden stomped and spread the ashes until they were cool enough to touch. Claire had walked alone across the plain until the sun appeared on the horizon, a smear of light through the grey clouds. The only memories that came to her were memories of the Abbey, the faces of the nuns, as weathered and ancient as trees themselves, waiting and hopeful. Now she crouched as Baiden used his hands to scoop a hole out of the wet, warm dirt beneath the ash.

"How deep?" he asked.

"That's fine."

He backed away, and she placed the seed in the hole, where it settled like a stone in mud. "What now?"

She was already pushing dirt and ashes back over it. "Now we let sun and soil and time do its work."

"There is not…" He paused. "A sacrifice to be made? Some magic to be worked? A song or prayer?"

"Every seed is a song, Baiden." She leaned over the mounded dirt until her brow was stained with ash. "Every planting is a prayer."

She stood and held out her hand. He took it.

"I will take you home," he told her.

Claire thought of the long walls of the Abbey, of the mossy stones and hills of clustered trees. She thought of a life of patience and watchfulness.

She thought of stone shards in the sky.

She nodded.

They left the plain together. Behind them, the warm dirt did not stir.

ABOUT THE AUTHOR

Stephen Case gets paid for teaching people about space, which is pretty much the coolest thing ever. He also occasionally gets paid for writing stories about space (and other things), which have appeared in Beneath Ceaseless Skies, Daily Science Fiction, *Orson Scott Card's* Intergalactic Medicine Show, Shimmer, *and elsewhere. His novel,* First Fleet, *is a science fiction horror epic (think H. P. Lovecraft meets Battlestar Galactica) published by Retrofit Publishing and available on Amazon. Stephen holds a PhD in the history and philosophy of science and will talk for inordinate amounts of time about nineteenth-century British astronomy. He lives with his wife, four children, and two illegal backyard chickens in an undisclosed suburb of Chicago. His website is https://stephenrcase.wordpress.com/.*

Pale Reflection

Gustavo Bondoni

The pool was perfectly smooth, reflecting everything in its surface. I could see the sky above, with clouds drifting lazily across. I could see the mountains in the distance, the same mountains that rose majestically from the plains in front of me.

But the sky on the other side of the pool was burning. The mountains were bare of snow. When I leaned in to see how I looked in the pond, I could barely recognize the creature that gazed back at me: her hair was torn and ragged, her face dirty. Her eyes were wide with surprise, and they bulged in the pale gaunt face.

I pulled away with a gasp.

"I told you not to look into that thing," Wati scolded. "Now you know why."

"But... what is it?"

"Just a reflection."

"No," I said, running my hand through the silky, well-tended hair that I'd brushed just that morning. "I don't look that way. The sky doesn't look that way."

"It shows us what we might be."

"I could never be that way."

"Sometimes it's impossible to control what you become," Wati replied. "Now go wash this," she handed me a basket full of potatoes, "in the stream, and stay away from that pool. We'll stay here tonight."

I obeyed. It wasn't the place of a twelve-year-old girl to question her teacher's orders, but all through the afternoon, as I prepared the food, I stole glimpses of the water. The sky above was deep blue, but the pool reflected brownish-orange. As night fell, I expected it to go dark, but it didn't: it just lay there, below the inky black sky, glowing its unnatural shade. I wondered if the people there were looking through and wondering what the millions of tiny white points in our sky might mean.

Wati caught me looking. She turned towards me. Her dark, wrinkled face held more concern than irritation. "What are you thinking?"

"Are they suffering?"

She pondered this for a moment. "No one really knows whether they're even really there. Some say that those pools simply show us the sickness in our own mind."

"And what do you think?"

Wati sighed. Clearly she'd expected to deflect the question. "I think there are people there. And yes, I think they're suffering."

"Can we help them?"

"We can't even reach them. If you jump into that pond, all you'll achieve is to be very wet. Oh, and I will punish you, too."

"All right."

The next day we moved on, but Wati remembered my concern when we arrived at the Circle of People. As soon as we'd found a good patch of healthy grass beside the stream, she called me over.

"Do you still want to know about the reflections? More than I can tell you?"

I nodded.

"Then you need to find a man called Huayra. He can tell you more." I turned to go. "Be back in time to eat," Wati called to my retreating back. I pretended not to hear her, but she knew me well enough to understand that I would do nothing to cause her concern.

My first stop was at the Hall of Sages, the tent of woven leaves that served to house any of the People's oldest men and women if they should happen to be present. I knew that Wati was close to the age in which she would be invited to the hall… in just a few more moons, I would have to find a different woman to teach me.

But that was a worry for another time. I stepped inside and was greeted by a man who, it was reputed, had lived for more than a thousand moons. His eyesight was as sharp as ever.

"Hello, little one. Still running in the Hall of Sages, I see. Perhaps you think that, if you run into one of us and break us in two, a space will be created for your mistress. I'm sorry to inform you that it doesn't work that way." He said it with a warm smile. This man was my great-grandfather on my mother's side, and his sharp observations about my shortcomings had been a constant in my childhood. I'd learned to listen to what he said: his words usually contained wisdom.

"I'm sorry. It's just that I'm looking for someone, and I thought one of the sages could help me to find him. You know everyone."

He chuckled drily. "I certainly don't know everyone, and I'm likely the oldest of the sages here."

"I'm looking for a man named Huayra."

My aged relative mulled this over for a moment. "The name is not familiar to me, but perhaps he has only recently earned it."

I wasn't expecting that answer. "Might you be wrong? I was told to consult him on a matter of lore."

"It is very possible that I might be wrong. But perhaps I can still be of assistance. The name sounds Tehuelche to my ears. Perhaps you should ask among the People of the south."

As there were no other sages present, I took his advice. The People of the south had a sector of the Circle of People to themselves, as befitted all visiting travelers, and they welcomed me with smiles when they realized that I knew the ritualized words to seek permission to enter. The words were almost never used, and the young, in particular were notorious for being ignorant of them. They admitted to having a man called Huayra in their midst… but also warned that he might not be what I was expecting.

I told them that I would accept what came, and they were pleased with that. They told me to choose a good patch and wait and they would fetch him. I sat cross-legged on the grass with my back to their camp—it would have been impolite to watch them while they searched for the man—and enjoyed the feel of the cool breeze on my bare arms.

"Hello, I'm Huayra."

Someone lowered himself onto the ground in front of me, and I saw that he was barely older than I was. Fifteen perhaps.

"I'm sorry. I may have made an error. I was looking for a loremaster. You seem to be a boy."

"I have earned my name," he replied sullenly. "And each person has their own lore."

"But I seek deep lore. I will go back."

"You've come all this way. Why don't you ask your question?"

I sighed but managed to avoid rolling my eyes. I think. "I wanted to know about the pools that reflect the burning sky."

"Did you ask your teacher about it?" he replied. His expression had suddenly turned serious, but it still failed to make him look older.

"I did. She says she doesn't know anything. I think she's afraid that I will learn things I shouldn't."

"So you came to me against her wishes?"

"No. She told me to seek you out."

"Ah." He sat there, thinking as the minutes stretched out. I couldn't get up, couldn't leave; I was a guest in this camp, and interrupting him or abandoning him would be worse than rude. "Your teacher is a wise woman."

I tried to suppress the sudden surge of pride. "She will be a sage soon."

"She will be a welcome addition to their ranks. But, what did you do to earn her trust and make her allow you to come speak to one she doesn't know about dark mysteries?"

It was my turn to think. I was no longer focused on Huayra's age. His words had convinced me that he'd earned his name and his right to teach about lore. The answer to his question was the important thing: failure to convince would end the interview.

"I... I think she believed me when I said I wanted to help them."

"Help who?" His look had grown intense.

"The girl in the reflection. She looked poor, and sad, and hungry. I think she was me."

"So you want to help yourself?"

I thought some more, and then I shook my head. "She looked like me. But she wasn't me. She had no hope, just fear."

"You saw all of this through a reflection?"

"I..." Again I had to stop to think about what I knew. "I'm not sure. I think so. I felt her fear, and her hunger, so strongly."

He held my gaze for a long time. I wanted to look away, but didn't want to offend him, so I sat there, trying not to blink. He had regular features and dark skin, even for one of the People, but his eyes were pale brown, nearly grey, with a dark ring around the center of the iris. His brow was furrowed, as if he was deep in thought. Finally, he spoke. "Are you sure you want to know what you saw?"

"Of course. I wouldn't be here if I didn't."

He sighed. "All right. The first thing you need to know is that not everyone sees what you did. Most people just see a regular pool and get a sense of unease. Some see strange colors.

Some see the landscape. A very tiny number see the inhabitants of the reflection."

"How tiny?"

"You are only the third anyone has ever heard of. The first was a sage called Sarga. He disappeared a few years ago. People say that the pools finally got him."

"There's more than one pool?"

"Hundreds."

"How come I never saw one before?"

"I don't know. Perhaps you were too young to realize what it was you were seeing. Or possibly your elders kept you far from the viewing pools."

"Why would they do that?" I asked.

"Many people prefer to shield children from uncomfortable knowledge. I know in my case, I only found my first pool because I wandered off the path and encountered one that was hidden from the adults." He smiled. "Even the best-meaning teacher can't keep you safe from something he can't see."

I suddenly realized why I'd been sent to speak to him. "You are the other. The third one who can see the inhabitants."

He nodded. "Many people thought I was lying to them. They wanted to send me out beyond the Circle for a season."

I gasped. Being sent beyond the Circle—banned from any contact with the People and forced to live as well as one could in harmony with the land, but without the benefit of the People's support and wisdom—was the worst punishment that could be administered to an individual. Even a short span, such as a season, was impossible for me to imagine.

"Yes. They thought I was being willful and disrespectful. They said I was trying to use the People's fear of the ghost pools to—"

I interrupted. "Ghost pools?"

"That's what they're called, yes. They thought I was just trying to call attention to myself. They wanted to exile me."

"And what did you do?"

"I told them that I could prove that I wasn't lying. That I could see things in the pool that they couldn't."

"How?" I was enthralled. Somehow, despite only having learned of the existence of the pools mere days before, I knew that they were linked to my future.

"Simple. There are more people in the pools than just our reflection. Pale strangers who have no parallel on our own side. Sometimes they throw things into the water, and only the ripples appear on our end. I explained this to my elders and they agreed that, if I could predict when the ripples would appear, they would believe me. Then it was just a question of doing so. I was telling the absolute truth, and after some hours, in which I never missed on a single prediction, they absolved me."

"And they gave you your name."

He nodded.

"But how did you know they were going to throw things into the water? What if none of the pale people had been there?"

He laughed. "There is one particular pool, more of a lake than a pool, actually, where there are always strangers present. I think, along the banks of that one lake, that there are more of the strangers than there are of the people anywhere in the mountains."

"Now I don't believe you. I only saw myself."

"Then you should come with me. I can show you the place. I think it's important that you discover whether you can see the pale people or not."

"Important to who?"

"Perhaps to no one other than to you. Perhaps to the whole world. I don't know."

I would never be allowed to go anywhere with him. I needed to find a new teacher, a woman, to take me under her wing. But I didn't want to leave the Tehuelche camp empty-handed. "You still haven't answered the question I came here to ask," I said. "What are the pools?"

"Sarga's theory was that the reflections show our world as it might be, or as it might have been. I never met the man, but we've conserved his lore."

"And what do you think?"

He paused, weighing me with his eyes. "I think what we're seeing actually exists. And I also think that Sarga managed to find a way across."

"Can we help them if we cross over?"

"I don't know," Huayra replied.

I left after that and didn't see him again for three years.

My new teacher, Beuna was her name, had been delighted to take on the pupil of the newly-created sage Wati. In fact, her expectations of me were so high that I felt I had to be a terrible disappointment. But if that was so, she never let on during the three years she taught me the ways of the water and the forests.

On the eve of my fifteenth birthday, she called me over from where I was scrubbing our wooden plates and motioned that I should sit beside her. She gave me a sad look.

"I'm afraid the time has come for us to part ways."

"Why? Have I been a disappointment?" I felt the tears brimming in the corners of my eyes and fought against them furiously. If this were going to be the end, if I were to be cast off, then I would attempt to keep my dignity.

She laughed. "Of course not. You have been the best student I've ever had, better than I had any right to expect. You have a sense for the paths, for the forests and for the mountains that, with time, will surpass my own. You are already far ahead of me when it comes to the streams."

"Then what is the problem?"

"There is no problem." She looked longingly up at the mountains to the west. "Except for time. The moons stop for nobody, and you have no name."

"I will earn it when my moment comes. I'm still young to have a name."

"Young in years and moons," she nodded. "Perhaps. But not young in knowledge. And you were allowed to me on the condition that I keep you only as long as you needed. To my shame, I have kept you a few moons longer than that... but one can excuse a woman her folly. I like having you with me." Beuna sighed. "But it's time."

I said nothing. My travels with this woman, to see the mountains, to gather herbs, to learn about the grasses and the flowers and the trees, had taught me not to respond too quickly when she paused. Beuna spoke as if she were untangling a vine she had selected for cord. The movements, slow and methodical, could not be hurried, but would eventually reach their destination.

"Before we set off from the Circle of the People on the day Wati ascended to her sagehood, she and I had a long talk about you."

I nodded, letting her proceed at her own rate.

"We both agreed that you were the most gifted girl we'd ever seen, but that your destiny doesn't lie with the lore of the forest or of herbs."

It was a slap in the face. "Then why make me spend my entire life learning about them?" I asked.

"So that you can bring a different perspective to your true calling," she replied.

"What new calling? I have none!"

"Are you certain? What would you say if I told you that you can have a new teacher?"

I thought about the women I knew. "There are no teachers I'd rather have."

"Not even Huayra?"

I opened my mouth to reply, but no sound emerged. The memory of that girl who wore an emaciated version of my own face looking up at me, framed by a red sky, came back to me. In the intervening years, I'd stolen glances into ghost pools when no one was looking... or, perhaps, when I *thought* that no one was looking. Teachers could be quite observant, even when they were invisible.

Beuna smiled sadly. "And that is all the response I really need. Your silence speaks more than an ocean of words. This is truly what you want."

"But..." She was right, I couldn't deny it. And yet, it was impossible. I knew it as well as she did. "But he is a man!"

"Of course he is. So what?"

I had no answer to that. Normally, men taught men and women taught women. It was how our society worked. Each of the sexes had a different relationship to the land and brought something unique to the People. They only mixed when they got married and started their own family.

"Listen. You are a grown girl, and you have good sense. Huayra is an honorable man, wise beyond his years. Some say that his wisdom stems from the things he's seen, things that no other has experienced in years. We don't foresee any problems."

I hadn't been thinking of that, but now that she mentioned it, I blushed. A teacher and a student spent days and months together in the wilderness with no witnesses to what they did.

"So, what do you say? Can you deny that this is what you want?"

I shook my head, not trusting myself to speak coherently. The inside of my head was filled with contradictions, all trying to get out. Finally, I collected myself enough to be able to ask a safe question: "When?"

"At the full moon. We are expected at the Circle of People in three nights. They will test you, you know. Huayra's people. They'll want to be certain that you're not just some nameless girl looking to seduce an important man and get a name she hasn't earned."

"Don't worry. I'll speak to them." I knew it wouldn't be a problem.

"Why is the sky that color?" I asked.

Huayra looked into the pool and studied the orange, brown hue of the reflected image. "I think they set it on fire."

"How can they live?"

"With great difficulty."

We were alone in this pool. By that, I meant that there were no additional people in the reflection other than the two we'd grown to know best: the emaciated version of me that always seemed so sad and the scarred and enraged image of the reflection of Huayra who was always talking, gesticulating violently as we watched.

"He is angry today," I said.

Huayra, the real one, the flesh and blood eighteen-year-old at my side, shook his head. "He's not angry. He is sad."

"He looks angry."

"He has no other way to show his grief."

I nodded. In this, I had to defer to him: he was the one who could sense the other man's feelings in detail.

But that was the only thing in which I deferred. Unlike Wati and Beuna, he didn't pretend to be my better in any kind of lore. As soon as he ascertained that we could both see the other people in the reflections—the pale ones with hair that ran the gamut from the lightest yellow to the darkest black and dark rings beneath their eyes—he admitted that what he had to teach I could see for myself.

"Then why do you want a pupil?" I asked.

"Because four eyes see more than two. Because two minds think more than one. Because I don't want to be alone with these truths any longer."

The final admission, so selfish, was the one that made me want to stay. I might not be able to help those pitiful waifs—myself included—on the other side of the reflection, but I could stand beside the only other person who could understand what I saw there. Yes, I understood his loneliness.

We had wandered for miles, from pool to pool, studying the reflection in each. We'd found ghosts in some, nothing in most. And now, after telling me that their sky was burning, Huayra turned to me. "I will show you my biggest secret. I haven't even told the Tehuelche elders about this. They might believe me. I think they believe everything I tell them now. But they could never understand." He held my gaze. "Only you can truly understand."

It took us three days to reach our destination. One moment, we were making our way through the twilight between trees that must have stood for as many years as I had hairs on my head. The next, we were standing on the shore of the largest lake I'd ever seen. The far side was lost in the evening mist.

"Is this..."

"Yes. This is Nahuel Huapi," Huayra said.

It was the lake of our people's legends. Every member of the people was expected to come drink from its waters once in their lives. Most waited until they were old enough to appreciate its serene majesty, but some, notably the Tehuelche and Mapuche people lived right along its banks. Huayra would have grown up here.

Anyone from my own branch of the people would have envied the forested hills and broad expanse of water, rippling in the distance. The very meaning of our spiritual lives centered, to a great degree, on this lake, its islands and the petrified wood on its shores.

The water of the lake burned bright orange. Brighter than the reflections in any other pool I'd seen so far.

I sat down hard on the rocky beach.

"And now you know why I never told anyone," Huayra said.

It took me nearly a day to recover from the shock of seeing something so holy for the first time only to discover that it had been defiled, ruined and poisoned by... I didn't know what it was. For some reason, the explanation that my people had always expounded, that some lakes were filled with spirits, simply didn't resonate with me.

Why were the spirits in some lakes and not in others? Shouldn't spirits that preferred to live under the surface be evenly distributed, each happy in its own pool? And what was their purpose in showing the images they did? Were the spirits actually us? If not, why did they look like us? And if so, who were the other people who appeared?

It just didn't make sense to me.

Perhaps I was not meant to know.

"Are you certain you want to go back to the lake?" Huayra asked.

"Yes. I need to do this."

"No, you don't. You can live your life in any other way. Out in the desert, there are no lakes, no ghosts that look like you. I know you have a great feeling for the land. You can do well in the desert."

"I need to see the lake again. I..." I paused, trying to articulate what I was feeling. "I need to understand what's happening."

"I'm not sure that's possible."

"Neither am I, but I want to be certain before I give up." I didn't tell him that I had no intention of giving up. I think he already knew that. He didn't have any intention of giving up either. Though he was careful not to encourage me or to transform my own feelings into obsession, I could tell that he felt just as strongly about it as I did. He wouldn't stop until he knew what was happening.

Or, perhaps, the spirits would take him like they had his predecessor, before any answers were forthcoming. I suspected that they'd eventually take me, too.

Despite my determination, I staggered back when I saw the lake again. It seemed even worse than before.

"Let's try some other day," Huayra said.

"No. I can do this."

He looked away and immediately aroused my suspicion.

"Tell me," I said.

"This isn't the worst part. There's more."

"Tell me," I repeated.

"If you think you're strong enough, it's better to show you." He led me along a trail that followed the water's edge. Sometimes the trail was merely a rocky beach, at others, it was clear that the People kept a path clear between the trees. After walking along it for half a day, the lake narrowed enough that I could have thrown a stone across it.

"Look now."

I did. At first, I couldn't tell what he wanted me to see. The tired face of my own double—always there when I looked into any ghost pool—stared back from my feet.

"Not there. Look across the lake. In the reflection."

A teeming multitude stood there. Some were looking over the lake, others jumping in and disappearing into the water, causing tiny ripples on our side. Many were eating strange food and discarding the material that covered it into the water, where it disappeared. On that single stretch of lake across from me I saw more people than the entire population of the lakes and the mountains. Probably more than the desert, too.

"Who are they?"

"I don't know. But they're always there, standing beside the lake, doing nothing but looking and eating under that orange sky."

"Why do they look that way? So pale and strange. They don't look like the people at all."

"They're spirits. They could be much stranger than they are."

"No. Look at me. I mean at my reflection. And your double, there. We both look normal. Sick, but normal."

I felt my double's emotions. I had learned to discern them: a tiny backdrop of some feeling that I wasn't experiencing myself, but that tinged the way I saw the world anyway. Normally, what came through were very basic sensations: fear, hunger, sadness.

This time, I felt contempt and I looked sharply down, wondering what had triggered it. My double, that emaciated and broken imitation, never felt contempt for anything, yet, as she glared across the water, that was what these images, well-fed and seemingly complacent, inspired in her.

"Does the lake get narrower further ahead? I want to have a closer look at the people on the other side."

"Follow me."

A short while later, I was studying them again. The disgust flowing into my mind was now tinged with fear, clearly the girl on the other side who so resembled me didn't like to be this close to the others.

I stared at them for a long time. Once I was able to see beyond the unnatural pallor of their skin, the interlopers seemed to be healthy. But looking closer, I saw signs that, everything might not be as it seemed.

The first thing that caught my eye was the sheen of sweat that covered their faces. It was a warm day, but neither Huayra or I was perspiring too much. Perhaps it was warmer where they were… but a single glance at the girl who resembled me showed that she, as well as Huayra's reflection, was weathering the temperature in a far better state.

And then there was the size. I was used to looking at the People. We always had enough to eat, but only when injury meant that we had to stay in one place for long periods did we begin to gain weight. The pale people on the other shore all seemed to be carrying the same weight as a long-prone member of our people. They were soft where we were angular.

But the thing that seemed most terrible, the thing that worried me most about them is that they never, ever looked up. They looked at each other, and at their friends frolicking in the frigid water and at objects I couldn't see in the reflection, but never, ever up at the sky.

"What are those things behind them?" I asked.

"I don't know. They look like mountains or big rocks, but if you watch, you'll see that they have openings. Sometimes those pale people come in and out of the openings."

He was right, even as I watched, a group of women emerged from the darkness within. I shuddered. These were evidently big tents made of stone, and the people on the wrong side of the reflection had knocked down everything else to put them where they were. There was not, as far as I could tell, a single tree standing on the far shore.

How could people destroy trees to put up their houses? There was plenty of room to put up a tent between the trees or in clearings. Even the rocky shore, if dealt with intelligently, would provide enough space for a shelter.

I looked at the same shore on our side of the reflection. Tall pines and leafy trees covered the land and there was no sign of human presence except for one place where the trail—likely the continuation of the one we were following—emerged from the forest onto the shore.

My eyes then went to the reflection and I realized that, perhaps, I was being hasty. Maybe the trees had not been removed to make way for the dwellings. Maybe the sky itself had killed all the trees. There were certainly few enough of them visible when I looked into any ghost pool. Perhaps the orange light was as poisonous to them as it seemed to me.

Along these same lines, I thought that the stone tents might be necessary to shelter them from the same light.

But if that were so, why did my alter-ego feel such contempt when she looked at them?

I spent two days on that beach, just studying the people in the reflection. They were so vivid, so obviously alive, that I often found myself trying to spot them on our own side of the surface. They *had* to be there.

But they weren't. There was nothing but trees where they would have been. The desolation on their side had no parallel on mine.

As I studied the pale people lining the bank aimlessly, I began to feel that they were of no importance, merely phantoms or ideas, and that the only people on the other side who mattered were actually the reflections of Huayra and myself. I extended that to include anyone else who was a reflection of a person from this side. Though better fed and seemingly happier—or at least less unhappy—the others were... well, they were just too pale to matter. Perhaps they really were ghosts and the pools were aptly named.

We walked around the lake, looking at the sky and the people—no stretch was devoid of them, seemingly doing nothing—for nearly half a moon. The most interesting thing was to see how the sky in the reflection changed color as the sun crossed the heavens and how the hues of the reflected sky went from orange to brown to yellow and back again. I never once witnessed a blue sky on the other side.

As we circumnavigated the enormous lake, my reflection never left me, always at my feet, always looking back at me whenever I looked down. At some points on the shore, the emotions coming in from my mirror image felt almost overpowering. I could feel her fear, her hunger, the cold in the night as if it was my own. I sometimes had to concentrate on the warm feeling of recently-eaten food in my stomach or the feeling of safety that came with being embraced by nature in the land of our people. At other times, it was just the vague echo of a feeling, like a scent passing on the wind.

It took me days to understand why this happened but, finally, I did. "The island. Can we go there?"

Huayra took a long time to answer. "That depends."

"On what?"

"On the reason you want to be there."

"I think we'll be able to feel what our doubles on the other side are feeling more clearly on the island. Whenever we get close to it, I almost feel as if the girl on the other side is me."

He looked uncomfortable. "I don't sense any difference." He looked out across the water that separated us from the wooded spit of land in the center of the lake. I was afraid that he'd dismiss my words as unimportant, my feelings as something that were driven more by wishful thinking than by any connection to reality. Then, he surprised me by doing exactly the same thing that Wati or Beuna would have done. He sighed. "We should find out if the feeling gets stronger on the island."

"You don't want to take me there." It was clear from his expression.

"That island it the most sacred place in the entire world. It is where the People were forged. One representative from each clan heard the voice of the world telling them how to cooperate and how to live their lives in harmony with each other and with the land."

I knew the story. Every child—male or female—heard it countless times before they were allowed to take a teacher. I felt myself go faint. "That's the island? *The* island."

He nodded.

"Oh." No wonder he didn't want to take me there. I hadn't even earned my name yet. "Maybe we shouldn't go there."

"No. We have to. It will be all right." He didn't sound certain, but I didn't press him to desist. We had to go there... It was the only place where I felt that I might learn the secrets of the burning sky."

So we began to gather fallen branches to build a raft.

"Are you all right?"

I looked up. I was lying on my back on the rocky shore with Huayra's concerned face blocking most of the sky. "Yes, I think so. What happened?"

"You looked around, then you screamed and fell. You barely made it off the raft."

I remembered. I had suddenly felt cold and weak, but mainly afraid. More fearful than I'd ever felt before.

"I think I'm all right now." I took his proffered hand and made it unsteadily to my feet. Then, without stopping to think about it, I approached the water's edge and looked down. My beaten, weathered reflection looked back at me.

Then it hit me. A storm of violent emotions: fear, confusion, hunger. The biting cold. They all washed over me and I let them flow past as I watched the reflection in the water.

The girl in the water's expression softened, as if she were feeling the exact opposite of what was happening to me. While I struggled to overcome the muddle of negative feelings coming my way, she seemed to relax and take solace in… something.

"Look at her," Huayra said. "It's almost as if you are calming her down."

Could that be it? Could she be receiving my own feelings as clearly as I was receiving hers? That would mean… I had no idea what it might mean.

Why are you following me around?

I heard the words inside my head. The language was unusual, mellifluous and soft, but somehow alien. I looked to Huayra, but he was just looking out across the lake trying to ignore the orange reflection.

"I…" Huayra turned to look at me and I motioned for him to stay away and stay quiet. "I'm not following you."

Yes. You are. I came to the island to get away from you. I had to fight the tourists to do it and hoard every centavo for weeks, and here you are.

I had no idea what that meant.

"Are you the girl in the lake?"

I felt the bitterness and heard the laughter. *No. You're the girl in the lake. I'm just a girl who is going crazier day by day. Now, I'm hearing voices. Just what I needed.*

Huayra was looking at me curiously. I stepped away from the shore and turned in his direction.

"Can you hear your reflection?"

"No. I can't feel him too well, either. Why? Do you sense something different?"

"As different as night and day. It's like she's living in my mind now. I know what she's thinking. I can feel her cold and her hunger. I can even tell that she needs to pee."

"That sounds awful."

"Why? We all have to pee sometimes."

He swatted my arm. "Be serious. Is she there now, listening to our conversation?"

I thought about it, casting my thoughts deep into my consciousness. "I don't think so. I think I need to be looking into the lake and seeing her there for it to work. Kind of like the way we used to get the feelings."

He gave me a dour look. "I envy you."

"Just a second ago you were saying it sounded awful."

"It probably is. Ugh. But you have just surpassed your teacher. I can't get any thoughts from my end. Do you realize what that means? You can take a name."

I was stunned. Taking a name wasn't a solemn ritual among the People. All it took was for your teacher to proclaim you ready to have one. Most people earned them in their seventeenth year. I had no idea what name to choose.

Near panic, I asked: "Do I have to choose the name now?"

He laughed. "Of course not. Or at least I don't think so. I'm new at this teacher business."

We stood silently for some moments neither knowing what to do.

"So what now?" he asked, finally.

"I want to see what she is."

"How does she feel… you know, inside your head?"

"She feels like me. Or at least like me when I'm hungry and scared."

"Do you think she's real?"

That was the question we always asked ourselves. Were the reflections, the emotions, the orange sky, there in reality, or were we somehow wrong in the head?

"*She* thinks she's real."

Huayra laughed ruefully. "That doesn't answer the question." He meant to say: we still don't know if we're insane.

"There's only one way to find out more." I walked back to the shore and found myself staring back at me. Now, after years of seeing her, I had no trouble recognizing myself in the image. "Hello again," I said.

Hello. It was a tentative, worried response.

"I am one of the people. I live… I live in a great open space full of mountains and lakes and desert, and I'd like to know something."

What?

"The sky. Is it orange where you live, or is that just the way we see it?"

Sadness flooded the connection between us.

They say they're trying to fix it. The Americans and the Europeans and the Chinese. But others say that it can't be fixed, that we've ruined the world forever.

I paused as comprehension dawned. "*People* did this?"

Of course.

But how could that be? I thought of the teachings I'd received, the ones that were intertwined with my earliest memories of my mother and father. The simple things like never making a fire where it could spread or more complex concepts like never killing animals we didn't need for food. How to save water in the desert. The true measure of a member of the People who'd earned a name as that, if you passed the same way as he or she had a few hours later, you wouldn't be able to tell that they'd been there. How could *people* destroy the sky?

"How?"

I received the mental equivalent of a shrug. My reflection didn't know.

I think it is because of all the cities.

"What is a city?"

Bariloche is a city. It's a place where there are lots of people and buildings. Do you really not know what a city is?

"There are no cities here."

Now our bond transmitted confusion.

Where do all the people live?

"In our tents, the way we always have."

Not our people. Not the Indians. The Europeans. Where do they live?

"What is a European?"

Frustration.

People from across the sea. They came here and took the land.

I sat down, an action which broke my line of sight to the surface and caused my connection to the woman on the other side to fade. The concept of land being taken was a new one to me, and I wanted to think about it without causing my reflection any more anger.

Why would anyone try to take land? What would you do with land? You couldn't eat it. You couldn't carry it around with you. Did that mean that they stayed on the land all the time, just to be sure no one took it back? I didn't understand.

After that, I avoided looking into the lake. I told Huayra about what I'd heard and we tried to understand it together. Huayra was angry, but I could only feel sadness and a huge sense of loss. An entire world, surely as big as our own, poisoned.

I cried all night. Huayra held me and tried to console me, but he fell asleep before I did.

Three days later, I felt strong enough to talk to her again. But she was sick. I could feel it when she looked into my eyes. A deep, gnawing illness that went beyond hunger. She looked much worse than usual.

I'm dying.

"I can tell."

Will you die, too?

It was a strange question. I felt like I was already dying. But no, under all that pain that wasn't mine, a strong heart beat and a healthy body held my spirit firmly. "No. I don't think so."

Will I live on inside you?

Stronger than the pain, much clearer than the anger, was the girl's fear. The sense that she was desperate to hear anything that might give her hope. Hope that I couldn't give her. "I don't know."

Will you sit with me?

"Yes."

And I sat. She held on for half a day. I could see the effort she was making to avoid falling back onto the shore and to keep her eyes locked on mine. All she wanted was to be with someone during those last moments.

In that period, I only spoke to her once more. There was something I needed to know.

"Do you have a name?" I asked her.

The reply was weak. *Yes. I'm called Sofía.*

"That's an unusual name."

Weak amusement came across.

It's very common here.

The effort exhausted her and I thought she might not be able to recover, but she held out for a few more hours. I could feel the strain of keeping herself alert through our connection.

Eventually, Sofía died. I felt it like sundown, a slow receding of the feeling in her mind. Then she was gone forever.

The moons passed one after the other. I took my own place as a teacher and watched my children grow and learn to live as I had.

When my years advanced, I never lived in the place of the sages, despite invitations from every one of the people who I met. I lived on the island, watching the lake. Only a few years after my reflection disappeared, I noticed that there were fewer of the pale ones ringing the shore. Eventually, some years later, they all disappeared. I wondered if they had simply stopped coming, but in my heart of hearts, I knew the truth: they would never come again. There were no more people on the other side. The orange sky that had turned fiery red would never allow it. Their stone tents fell into themselves.

I moved away from the lake and fifty more years I wandered the hills and forests. Only when my ninetieth year rolled around did I return to the island. The raft was rowed by my great granddaughter, a young woman already. She helped me onto the rocky shore and gave me her hand to help me sit.

"Why have we come here?" she asked.

"I came here to die. This is the right place for it."

She just nodded, and I felt pride. She knew how to live, what the cycles of life demanded.

I looked into the lake, searching for a face I knew I would never see again. And, as always, the shores were empty. Trees were again growing where none had been.

Finally, I looked at the sky and wondered whether my eyes were finally giving out. I expected to see the same orange tint I'd left fifty years before, but instead, the sky was as blue as the one above my head. Only a raft of orange clouds that drifted in to the reflection convinced me that I wasn't seeing a faithful representation of the sky of my own land.

I smiled to see that the world on the other side was healing, saddened only that I would not be alive long enough to see how it ended.

As I had when I was a young woman, I felt death within me. This time, there was no young body to convince me that I would live. My time would soon come.

But I would die content. When I chose my name, I promised to the girl I took it from that I would return it to her when I no longer needed it.

I would keep my promise. I asked to be buried here, right where she fell. Only the surface of the lake would separate, forever, one Sofía from the other.

About the Author

Gustavo Bondoni is an Argentine novelist and short story writer who writes primarily in English. His debut novel, Siege, *was published in 2016, and his second,* Outside, *in 2017. He has nearly two hundred short stories published in fourteen countries. They have been translated into seven languages. His writing has appeared in Pearson's Texas STAAR English Test cycle,* The New York Review of Science Fiction, Perihelion SF, The Best of Every Day Fiction *and many others. His website is www.gustavobondoni.com.*

The Binder

Pat Woods

"It was my grandmother's," said the old woman. "She used it pretty much every day, as did my mother." She handed Senn the shattered fragments of a clay mixing bowl with the same reverence as if they had been the shards of a queen's tiara. "I want it to go to my Rowen too, after I'm gone, you know."

Senn nodded. She knew. Had this been a recent purchase or some cheap pygg pot, old Kayla would've tossed it away without a second thought. For an heirloom like this, however, Kayla, just like all the other folk of Tortala, went to the Binder.

She examined the pieces, laying them out on the mat of soft grey felt that covered her work bench. "You're sure you got all of them?"

Kayla nodded. "Oh, yes. I know how important that is."

"How did it happen?"

"It just slipped out of my hands as I was lifting it down off the shelf." Kayla sighed. "I suppose my hands aren't as sure as they used to be. Happens to us all, in the end, though you young folk never think it will."

Senn smiled. "I haven't thought of myself as young in a long time, Kayla."

"Nonsense. You could still bear a couple of young'uns, if you married again." The old woman gave Senn a knowing look. "And I did hear that a certain farmer had been seen around your shop quite a lot lately..."

Senn just about managed to keep her sigh internal. "Heft's cows kept pushing his fences down, and he wanted me to do something about strengthening them. There's nothing more to it than that." This wasn't entirely true, she knew, but what romantic interest there was between herself and the farmer was wholly one-sided.

"Heft's a good man, well-off and not hard to look at, apart from those ears," Kayla said. "Mind you, his mother had the same ones, that whole family had tabs like jug handles." Senn let the old woman ramble on about Tortalan genealogies as she examined the broken bowl, only paying attention again at the words "...and you not having anyone since your Olven passed away, what three years back?"

"Four," Senn said softly.

"Well, exactly. It's not good for a woman of your age to be alone."

It was a privilege of the elderly, Senn reflected, that they could gossip about you in your presence and say to your face what others only said behind your back. Speculation as to whether or not she would take another husband was a popular topic, she knew, particularly amongst Tortala's older bachelors.

"And the bowl just broke on the counter?" she asked.

"What? Oh, yes, I'd almost set it down when it slipped out of my hands. None of the pieces went on the floor, and most of them are quite big."

"That makes my job easier," Senn said. "If you call around the same time tomorrow, I should have it fixed for you."

"That's so good of you, Senn," said Kayla, who then paused. "And...how much would..."

"Don't worry about it." Kayla wasn't a wealthy woman, and Senn wouldn't have felt right taking what few spare coins she'd been saving for a rainy day.

"Oh, come now, you must take something..."

"Really, there's no need..."

That went on a little longer before Kayla went on her way, quite content, Senn knew, to pay nothing at all. It wouldn't work out that way, of course. The old woman would undoubtedly bake Senn a pie or a few loaves of bread, and her daughter Rowen would drop off a "spare" shawl she'd made. That was how things generally went with those who needed Senn's gift but couldn't quite afford to pay her in bronze or silver.

She spent some time arranging the pottery fragments, figuring out where each piece fitted into the whole. Kayla had been lucky; it wasn't a bad break. She wouldn't be able to finish it that night, but she could make a start. Senn picked up two of the larger fragments and, ensuring they were properly aligned, spoke the Binding.

It was an old magic, passed down through family bloodlines from a time so far in the distant past that it was legendary rather than historical. A Binding joined two objects together so that no common force could separate them. Though the magic waned over time, anything bound in this was essentially immune to everyday wear and tear. On a good day, Senn could manage half-a-dozen Bindings, though this left her with a headache and the same tiredness her body would feel after a day of hiking in the hills north of the village.

Senn managed to bind two more pieces of the bowl together, and join a third piece to these. Though it still lay in several fragments, the parts Senn had bound looked as though they had never been broken. By then, she needed to sit down and rest, sipping gratefully from a cup of water as the sweat cooled on her brow and pooled at the small of her back. Her muscles ached, and she knew she was done for the day.

She locked up her little shop, where she made and repaired simple items of jewellery by way of supplementing the income she earned from her Bindings. Senn slept in the back room, which had just about enough space for a bed and a stand-up wash basin. There was nothing to cook with, but that wasn't a problem, as she had a standing invitation to dine at her brother-in-law Tayssen's house, and she could afford to eat at one of Tortala's three inns if she desired.

In her low moments, she wondered whether remaining so close to her late husband's family was stopping her from moving on, from leaving Olven in the past where, she knew in her heart of hearts, he belonged. Yet she was an aunt to Tay's two little girls and delighted in their company, and had become an older sister to Nell, Tay's wife. If she didn't have them, she'd have no one.

Senn was just getting ready to leave when there was a soft tapping at her door. Her *back* door, not the shop's main entrance. She frowned. It might be Nell or one of the girls coming to fetch her, or...

If it's Heft or one of the others, this won't end well. It was time to put a stop to all this nonsense.

"Who is it?"

"I need to talk to you," a voice she did not immediately recognise replied, speaking in little more than a whisper.

"You can do so from the other side of the door until you tell me who you are."

"I assure you, I mean you no harm. I need your help."

"First your name."

The voice dropped even lower, so she could barely hear it reply "Ryver."

Senn frowned. Ryver, squire to Halemon, Champion of Tortala, who was second only to Chieftain Marcham in the hierarchy of the village. *But Halemon isn't in the village—he went to patrol the northern borders.*

Ryver's voice became urgent. "Please, I can't be seen here. Will you let me in?"

Senn opened the door. He was no sooner inside her back room than he blurted out, "I need you to come with me at once."

"To your master?"

Ryver nodded, ducking his head as if he feared discovery. His evident anxiety contrasted strangely with his appearance: tall, muscular, and handsome, his blond hair braided into a warrior's knot that twisted and looped around the right side of his head, Ryver was every inch the fighter except for the discomfort in his blue eyes.

No, not discomfort. Fear. Something is terribly wrong.

"I'll come at once," she said.

Ryver kept them to the back streets and alleys of Tortala as he led Senn to the house—or rather, the hall—that was the official residence of the village champion. He'd covered his head and face with a dark cloak and insisted that she do the same, and avoided meeting anyone, staying in the shadows while other villagers passed them by. *So, no one is to know that he and his master have returned.*

Senn's guess was confirmed when they reached the champion's longhouse, a grand structure of timber and slate. It was surrounded by a sturdy fence that encompassed sparring grounds for the champion and his warriors, as well as several outbuildings. None of the lanterns on the fence or within the house itself were lit, giving the impression that no one was home. Ryver led them to a small postern on the opposite side of the main gateway to the compound and ushered Senn quickly inside.

"Are you going to tell me what this is all about?" she whispered.

"Inside."

They went to a side entrance to the longhouse, a locked door that Ryver opened with an iron key. Senn caught the characteristic whiff of a nearby midden. When they were inside, some of the tension left him. He straightened and removed his cloak, then lit a candle. Senn saw that they were in the longhouse kitchen. Smoked meat and baskets of vegetables hung from the ceiling.

"Now we can talk," Ryver said. Now that there was no danger of discovery, his voice had recovered some of the confidence Senn associated with the warriors of Tortala: an iron self-belief that occasionally bordered upon arrogance, the assumption that the world revolved around themselves and their doings. "But before we do, I need you to swear that you will not breathe a word of anything you see or hear tonight."

"How can I promise that when I don't know what to expect?"

Ryver frowned. "Isn't it enough that I tell you it's a matter of vital importance and urgency? Just swear."

Senn crossed her arms. "Clearly you need my help as much as you need me to hold my tongue. You can tell me what's going on and trust me to be discreet, or you can tell your master that I'm busy—and that he needs to improve your manners."

Ryver scowled. "Fine. Come with me."

He pushed his way through the curtain that covered the kitchen doorway and Senn followed him into the main hall of the longhouse. It was here the champion met with his warriors for feasts or councils of war. In the light of Ryver's candle, Senn saw a long table lined with benches. In the centre was a cloth-wrapped bundle. Ryver used his candle to light a second, then set one on each side of the bundle, creating a small globe of soft yellow light. Then he pulled the bundle open.

Senn gasped.

It was Skerrast, the Lifeblade, the sword of the Champion of Tortala. Forged with the aid of magic, imbued with the power to part iron armor like cloth.

And it was *shattered*.

Senn swallowed. "How did this happen?"

"I don't know!" Ryver's voice was a tangle of emotions; Senn heard frustration, fear, and anger warring for prominence. "My master went into the hills north of the Deglosii lands on some errand for their chieftain. He sent me away—he said it was too dangerous. When he returned..." His hands clenched into fists. "You are the Binder. You *must* repair Skerrast, before the Gretangs discover what has happened."

The Gretang clan dwelt in the lands to the south of Tortala. Smiths from both villages, assisted by a powerful mage, had come together to make Skerrast in an act intended to seal an alliance between the clans. Instead, it had been the cause of generations of bloodshed.

Men being what they were, both the Tortalans and the Gretangs had laid claim to Skerrast, based on their ownership of the iron mines that had yielded the ore from which the blade was forged. Dozens of maps were made and produced as evidence, each as spurious as the last. The truth was now lost in the past, and in reality, it no longer mattered.

The feud had been going on for hundreds of years. Whichever clan possessed Skerrast had the upper hand in battle, as its wielder, named champion by the clansmen, could cut down foes with ease, but there were always other means to get hold of it, and the sword had gone back and forth scores of times. It had been in Tortala's keeping for some fifty years now, since the time of Halemon's predecessor. Now, however...

Senn sat down on one of the benches. Her mind was reeling. "Slow down, Ryver. Where is Halemon?"

The young warrior jerked his head towards the back of the hall. "He is broken with grief, with guilt. He has barely spoken since it happened. He just stays in his chambers."

"Guilt?" Senn echoed.

Ryver came closer, lowering his voice again. "He knows that he has failed us—failed the whole clan. My master is old, almost sixty. He knows he has fought his last fight, yet that final defeat has brought ruin on us all. He can do nothing for himself now. We had spoken of the day when he would put Skerrast in my hands and name me Champion of Tortala, and that day was close. Was..." He tugged at his warrior's knot in despair.

"My master can do nothing for himself. I must now act in his stead, and you must help me. Use your magic to remake the Lifeblade, and I will take on the mantle of champion and keep our village safe."

Senn didn't know what to say. She fixed broken pots, damaged fences, and old furniture. Could she bind a sword forged with magic far more powerful than anything she could imagine, let alone summon to aid her?

In her heart, she knew the answer was *no*.

Yet she felt that she had to try. Not for Ryver, his desperate appeal notwithstanding. Not even for her clan. No, it was to Halemon that her heart went out. He had been a great champion, not merely because of his prowess as a fighter, but because he'd never used that prowess save in defence of the clan, never fought until it was clear that there was no way words could settle a dispute. Olven had been a smith, and the smith was an important man in an iron-rich village like Tortala. Her husband had told her of many councils he'd attended where Halemon had spoken for peace or calmed the hotheads amongst his warriors who would have answered insults with blood. Now none of that would be remembered. The old man deserved a better legacy than this—crushed by the knowledge that he'd lost the fabled sword charged to his care.

Trying wasn't the same as succeeding, though, and her desire to ease Halemon's pain wouldn't make her task any less impossible.

And my own failure will be another weight for him to carry. He will take it upon himself as part of his guilt, and the additional burden may be too much to bear.

Senn tried to mask her thoughts by examining the Lifeblade. Had the sword been snapped in two, she might have found cause for hope, but whatever force had broken it must have been immense, shattering it into dozens of small shards, some no more than slivers of metal. Senn couldn't even see how they fitted together.

What could have done this? Only a greater magic than that which had resided in the sword. Senn was no loremaster. She knew there were sorcerers and enchanted weapons in the world, powers of which she had no comprehension, but she'd never heard of such a power living in the Deglosii hills.

"Do you have all the fragments?" she asked. It was the same habitual question she put to all her customers, but it made Ryver start.

"If any are missing, can you still remake it?" he demanded.

Senn faced him. "I'm not going to lie to you, Ryver. Even if all the shards are here, I don't know if I can do as you ask. Skerrast was forged by a mage. I'm a Binder. There's a world of difference. You'd do better to find another mage. Even if I can reassemble the pieces and bind them together, I can't guarantee that Skerrast will be the same. The spell that gave it its power may have been broken along with the blade itself."

"But everyone says the things you bind hold together forever, and that they will never come apart!"

"There's some truth in that," Senn admitted, "though the magic weakens over time—"

"It doesn't matter!" Ryver strode up and down as if to relieve his angst by activity. "Skerrast is more than a sword; it is a symbol! It gives heart to our warriors and strikes fear into our enemies! In my hands, it will still be a terror to our foes, whether it possesses its old magic or not. Make the blade whole, and when I wield it, no man amongst the Gretangs will stand before me. If I must find a mage to enchant it, I will, but first, it must be repaired."

He won't take no for an answer. "Very well," Senn said. "I will attempt it." *Maybe that will be enough to assuage Halemon's guilt.*

Senn returned to the champion's longhouse the following evening, after dark. Ryver continued to insist on absolute secrecy and Senn obliged him, wanting to spare his master the pain of the truth coming to light. She'd repaired Kayla's mixing bowl that morning, then closed up shop and rested for the remainder of the day to regain her strength, sending a note over to Tay's to tell the family she'd come down with a mild illness that would prevent her from seeing them for several days. The news would get around and explain why her shop was closed, allowing her to sleep the days and work during the night.

It wasn't long, however, before an additional problem became apparent.

"I don't need you looking over my shoulder," she told Ryver, not bothering to keep the irritation out of her voice.

"Forgive me for holding your work in such importance," he responded sarcastically. "It's only the fate of the clan, after all."

He'd been waiting for her when she arrived, hustling her in through the postern and back into the hall, where he'd proceeded to pace up and down, stopping beside her at every pass to check on her progress, as if he expected her to start fitting the shards of Skerrast together like the pieces of a child's puzzle.

"I need peace and quiet. I need to concentrate and figure out how the sword fits together."

"I've not heard that you always take so long."

"I don't know who you've been talking to, but neither they nor you know what you're talking about. Can you at least sit down? No, behind me, or at least out of my eyeline," she added, when he moved around to the other side of the table.

Ryver clicked his tongue in frustration and walked around the table again, but it didn't help. Moving or motionless, she could still feel his eyes on her and almost hear his thoughts seethe with impatience.

"It's no good," she said after a few minutes.

"So, you have failed," he said, leaping to his feet and striding over to the table.

"You're not giving me the chance to succeed! Look, I know you won't let me take these away—"

"Impossible!"

"—but I have a suggestion. This is the first time I've ever been called on to bind a sword, or any kind of weapon for that matter. I don't know enough about how they're made."

"Wasn't your dead husband a blacksmith?"

Senn's breath came out in a hiss, but she controlled herself with an effort. "He made weapons for the clan, yes, but we didn't work together. Are you so ignorant not to know that smiths have their secrets?"

"What of it?"

"That's what I need. A smith. I need Tayssen—my brother-in-law."

Ryver shook his head. "This must remain a secret—"

"Do you want me to fail?" she demanded. "I'm doing my best, but I'm groping in the dark. Bring my brother-in-law here. You can trust him with your secret. Besides, your absence will give me some of the peace I need."

Ryver seemed to mull the matter over for a moment before giving a curt nod. He strode towards the kitchen door.

"Ryver."

He turned.

"If you ever disrespect the memory of my husband again, I will walk out of here, go straight to Chieftain Marcham, and tell him everything."

Ryver's blue eyes flashed, then he gave a slight nod. They continued to look at each other for a moment, their eyes locked, before he turned and left.

"Bastard," Senn snarled, then sat. Her whole body was shaking with anger, her eyes beginning to fill with tears now that he was gone. She blinked them away, refusing to let his words affect her. She heard the kitchen door close and then the retreating sound of Ryver's footsteps. Senn turned to stare at the shards of Skerrast as if the fury she felt could weld them back together.

Then she heard movement in the room beyond the hall. She whirled in her seat just as the curtain was drawn back and Halemon, Champion of Tortala, stepped into the light.

Senn had to look twice to be sure it was him. Halemon had carried his years with grace: still lean, fit, and iron-hard, his posture and movements were those of a man a decade younger. Now, his long grey hair was unbound from its warrior's knot, exposing the liver spots on his almost-bald scalp, while the man himself seemed to have shrunk, dwindling into a stooping elder with dark circles around grey eyes that had lost all of their sparkle. His movements were slow and stiff, as if the effects of a lifetime of battles and exertion had all come to him at once. Senn rose and went to help him to the chair at the head of the long table, and the fact that he allowed her to do so spoke to the blow that the breaking of Skerrast had dealt him.

"Champion, I'm so sorry," she began, but Halemon lifted a wrinkled hand to cut her off.

"I am no longer the Champion of Tortala," he said. Though his voice had lost much of its timbre, there was still strength in it, still a core as tough as Nassan iron.

He sat and clasped his hands before him as if by willpower alone he could hold back the ravages of age and grief. "Please sit, Binder. We do not have long."

Senn obeyed instinctively. Halemon's words still carried that much of the air of command.

"Before Ryver returns, there is something you must know. Something you must understand. I do not wish that *sword*," he said the word as if it disgusted him, "to be reforged."

He paused, but before Senn could ask the question, added, "It was I who shattered it."

There was a long silence. The old man's grey eyes were on her, conveying a deadly earnestness. Ryver had told her Halemon was broken by what had happened to the sword, but he didn't look broken. He looked resolute, as if he'd chosen his fate and was determined to meet it no matter the cost to himself.

"More accurately," he said after some moments had passed, "I had it shattered. Have you heard of the Aglarin folk?"

Senn nodded. The Aglarin were a scattered people, dwelling in small families and groups in the highlands and mountains of the Plains of Nassan. They were an introverted people, keeping apart from the Plainsmen of Nassan save for those few merchants who supplied their needs, which were scant. They were also rumored to be steeped in the old ways of magic, practitioners of arts the Plainsmen had either forgotten or never possessed.

"There is a small community in the Deglosii hills," Halemon was saying. "One of their number is a skilled weaponsmith, and more: he is a mage, a master of making weapons, armor, and all manner of other things enchanted with Aglarin magic. I heard of him from a Deglosii merchant of my acquaintance, and went to seek him out. Bhathe is his name, and after I spoke to him, he agreed to unmake the sword that our ancestors were pleased, in their naivety, to call the Lifeblade."

He met her eyes once more. "You wish to know why. Can you truly not see it for yourself? That accursed sword… Its name means "blade of life" in the old tongue of northern Nassan. It should have been named "blade of death." It has spilled the blood of hundreds, perhaps thousands, of Tortalans and Gretangs, for centuries." He held up his hands. "I myself have killed a dozen Gretang warriors, fine men with wives and families who only took up arms against me to possess that which took their lives. No more. I have seen enough death, enough grief, in my life, and *I will see it end.*"

Senn wanted to believe him, wanted it with all her heart. She had lamented the blood-soaked rivalry between the clans ever since she had grown old enough to comprehend the futility of it, the waste of young lives and the ruin of families. Olven had felt the same, and had wept whenever some new ferment of war required him to forge weapons and armor for the warriors. Yet he couldn't refuse the demands of his clan chieftain, and Senn knew the strain of having to meet those demands had contributed to the sudden seizure that had taken him from her.

"I know what you are thinking," Halemon said. "Given all that has gone before, neither Tortala nor Gretang need look too far to find a pretext for war. We have fought each other for long enough to add layers of other grievances, real and imagined, on top of the first cause, that of Skerrast itself. Yet I believe calmer heads can prevail, and that a better way can be found. I have used my influence to avert bloodshed many times in my life, though this does not outweigh the times I failed and was forced to take up that sword.

"It has taken me a long time to understand this—too long. But I have learned from those failures, and at last I came to believe—no, to *know*—that as long as we squabble over who truly owns that sword, it will always be a difference we can never overcome, a disease that cannot be cured and that will break out again and again like a plague, running its course until the landscape is covered in corpses.

"Maybe there will still be conflicts. Age has taught me that it is an undeniable, irrevocable flaw in the nature of mankind to fight and kill one another. But there is *no hope at all* for our clans while that sword exists.

"So." He unclasped his hands, spreading his fingers to present the shards of Skerrast like evidence in a case before a wandering judge of Tallich, the God of Justice. "My solution. It may prove to be ultimately flawed, but the attempt must be made, and," his gaze fell upon her and hardened until it had almost the force of a blow, "I ask—no, I beg—that you will not interfere."

"What about Ryver?" Senn asked. "You haven't told him. Why?"

Halemon sighed. "I intended to, as soon as I had made my own decision. But by then, I had come to know him better. Ryver…he is a good boy, at heart. He told me that when I chose him to be my squire, it was the greatest day of his life. He would revise that statement now, I think. Now he looks forward to taking my place as champion. He sees only the honor, none of the responsibility, the burden.

"This latest peace with the Gretangs has lasted almost ten years, but I fear what will happen after I am gone. Ryver is touchy in his pride, and were he champion, the first slight by the Gretangs would lead to as bloody a war as our two clans have ever fought, all so Ryver can add glory to his name. No, he would not understand. He might, in time, but time is one thing I do not have." He looked at Senn. "I must confess, I had forgotten about your gifts. I never dreamed he would come to you for help."

"Tell him when he returns," Senn urged Halemon. "You can make him understand."

"Do *you* understand?"

"I do." How could she not? "Though even if I didn't agree with you, I don't think I can remake the sword. With Tay's help, we might make *a* sword, but it won't have its former power."

Halemon started to rise and Senn stood to help him. "I think it would be better if you did not even do that," he said. "I heard what Ryver said, and he is right. Skerrast is still a symbol, still something for the clans to fight over. Better it remain broken forever."

"Then what would you have me do?"

"Tell Ryver that you cannot repair it, even with a smith's help. Tell him you believe some fragments are still lost in the Deglosii hills, or that only a mage can remake the weapon. Ryver will ride off to seek the missing shards or to find a mage, and in his absence I will take these pieces and scatter them, burying them where they will never be found. I would have done that myself, but Ryver sought me out and came upon me before I could do so."

"He might take them with him," said Senn. "If you can't convince Ryver, then go now, while he's gone."

Halemon stiffened, cocking his head. "It is already too late for that," he said, dropping his voice to a whisper. "I hear footsteps outside. Do not worry, Binder. Do as I suggest, and all will be well." He put his hand on her shoulder. "And *thank you*."

He disappeared behind the curtain to his chambers, and Senn hurried back to the table. She had only a moment to compose herself before Ryver came through the kitchen doorway, dragging Tay with him. Her brother-in-law looked confused and worried.

"Senn," he said when he saw her. "Ryver said you needed my help."

Senn moistened her lips. "Sorry, Tay. I think I've dragged you out of bed for nothing."

"What?!" Ryver hissed.

"I don't understand," Tay said. Then his eyes fell upon the broken sword. "Gods, is that..."

"You said you could fix it with the help of a smith," Ryver said, advancing on her.

"I said I didn't know where to begin. While you were gone, I had the chance to try. My Binding spell doesn't work. This sword must've been broken by a powerful magic—more powerful than mine. Whoever was wielding that magic clearly didn't want Skerrast to be remade."

Ryver's eyes blazed, but it was Tay who spoke. "You have to keep trying, Senn," he said, fear in his voice. "I mean, this...this is the Lifeblade. We have to do something!"

Ryver seized on this. "You are right, smith. We must leave no stone unturned! Can you reforge Skerrast? I promise you, your name will live forever in the songs and stories of Tortala."

Tay came closer to the table, his shock at finding the Lifeblade of Tortala sundered replaced by the practical concerns of his trade. "The blade itself...yes, though it'll take time. But I'm not a mage. It won't be nothing more than an ordinary sword." He looked at Senn. "But if you and I can work together, Senn, you might be able to do something, yes? Make it stronger?"

Oh, Tay. "What if some fragments are missing?" she asked, though without much hope. This was unravelling too quickly—no, she'd doomed it the moment she sent for Tay. Oh, she hadn't known, but in her ignorance, she'd dashed Halemon's hopes before he'd even expressed them.

"If you can accept that it'll not be the same sword as before, I can use the best steel I have to complete the work," Tay offered, turning to Ryver.

"It will suffice," the warrior said. "In my hands, Skerrast will be just as deadly as it was before."

And so it will remain a cause for war and death. Senn wanted to scream at them, to tell them what Halemon had tried to do for the good of them all. If Olven had been here, he would have understood, but Tay...Tay was not the man his brother was. He was a good smith, a maker and a fixer, and he took pride in his work, whether it was a set of horseshoes or a sword in the hands of a young man marching off to fight and die. That same simplicity of thought that made him good at his trade sheltered his mind from the bigger questions that had troubled Olven. Tay was also a good clansman, Tortalan to the bone, and as far as he was concerned, the Gretangs could be annihilated.

Senn believed she would be able to sway Tay if she could get him alone, but Ryver would not leave their side. Senn had no idea what to do. She had lost.

Then Halemon stepped into the room once more.

"Smith, do not remake that sword," he said. There was quiet authority in his voice, but something else as well, something like resignation.

"Champion—" Tay began, but Ryver spoke louder.

"Master! You... What do you mean?"

"I mean that I broke that sword. It shall not be reforged."

Ryver was speechless. "I don't understand..." he said, then his eyes widened as he was struck by a sudden suspicion. "You do not wish me to possess it!"

"I do not mean for anyone to possess it," Halemon said softly, but Ryver wasn't listening.

"Is that how it is?" he demanded. "You resent me because I'm better than you—faster, stronger, more skilled. You would cling to your reputation with one hand and hold me back with the other, all so that I won't surpass you, as you know I must! Don't you see that you've doomed our village for your old man's pride?"

"Binder," said Halemon, ignoring his squire. "Take the shards. You know what needs to be done."

Ryver's eyes burned as his gaze fell upon her. "So, you are part of this too? I might have guessed from your reluctance."

"Senn, what's going on?" Tay asked, looking from one to the other in mounting confusion.

"I'll tell you what's going on," Ryver said. "You, smith, will reforge Skerrast, without the help of this lying witch." He turned back to Halemon. "Master, it is not too late to redeem yourself. Go to Chieftain Marcham and tell him you are passing your title to me. We will see that you are cared for with honor for your remaining years."

"You have proven this night that you do not deserve to be champion, boy," Halemon said coldly. Ryver went white with shock and fury. "I will find another more worthy of the responsibility. Until that time, *I* am champion and you *will* obey me. Let these people go."

His words snapped something in Ryver. He cried in wordless anguish and advanced on Halemon as if he would strike him. The old man backed away. Senn darted forward and snatched up the cloth bundle on which the shards of Skerrast still lay. Ryver whirled on her. From beneath his cloak he drew a sword.

"Give them to me!" he thundered.

"Never!" she shot back.

Ryver advanced a pace, but was stopped short by the snap of Halemon's challenge.

"Turn, boy. Turn and face me. It seems I must give you one last lesson."

The Champion of Tortala had not retreated from his former squire's fury, but stepped back to arm himself. Halmeon now held a sword of his own, and as he settled into his stance, the years fell from him as though he were shedding a cloak.

"Run, Binder," he said calmly.

Senn needed no further urging. She grabbed Tay by one arm and pulled him after her as she made for the main exit from the hall. Ryver, defied on all sides, launched himself at

Halemon, screaming in frustration. Senn heard their blades clash once, twice, and again before she ran from the longhouse with Tay at her heels.

There were horses in the longhouse stables and Senn pulled Tay in that direction. He tried to ask questions but she told him to saddle two of them while she grabbed some horse blankets and a bag of feed. There was no telling what would happen inside the hall or how long they might have. Fortunately, Tay was good with horses and had them ready quickly. The gate at the main entrance of the champion's compound was open, and they were soon through it.

"Why do we need horses?" Tay called over the drumming hooves and the sound of their ragged breathing. "We should go straight to Chieftain Marcham and tell him everything."

"No!" Senn had thought of that and discarded the idea. Marcham would demand that Skerrast be remade, and his authority outweighed Halemon's. They needed a better plan, but there was no time to explain everything now. They had to get away from the village.

Senn knew the land around Tortala well, and led them as directly south as the terrain allowed. They passed through fields before plunging into the darkness of a nearby pine wood. There they had to slow their pace, but the track the Tortalans had cleared through the wood was wide and well-maintained, so there was no danger of being struck by a low-hanging branch.

Tay had fallen silent when he realised that Senn wasn't going to answer any questions until she was ready. However, when they cleared the wood and Senn kept them riding south rather than turning aside, he spoke up again.

"Senn, why are we going south? That's the way to the Gretang lands."

"It's the last direction he'll expect us to take," Senn replied, hoping that she was right.

"Look, when are you going to tell me what this is all about? What got into Ryver—and did Halemon really break the Lifeblade?"

Senn had to feel sorry for him, but they were still too close to Tortala. "I'll explain it all, Tay. Let's just put a little more distance between us and the village."

Tay had no choice but to go along with her. She led them by a trail she knew that ran southwest, skirting around the Tortalans' main ironworks. Beyond that was disputed land, claimed by both clans but left unoccupied by common consent. There they stopped for a while in a narrow gully that opened onto the main trail.

The walls of the gully provided shelter from the wind, but it was still cold, and the ground was even colder. Senn had only grabbed three blankets. They covered the horses and shared the third, huddling shoulder-to-shoulder for warmth. Now they'd stopped moving, Senn realised how thoroughly unequipped they were for anything more than a night's ride. Putting that aside for the moment, she told Tay everything. Somewhat to her surprise, he neither disbelieved her story nor argued with her concerning Halemon's decision.

"I've heard of that Aglarin, Bhathe," he said. "He's a legend amongst smiths, and if anyone could break the Lifeblade..." He lapsed into silence. "As for the rest...it sounds like something Olvi might've said, Senn. I could almost hear his voice when you were speaking. He cared about people—you know that better than anyone. Maybe he cared more than was good for him, I don't know. But what you're doing to help Halemon, it's what he'd have done as well, so I'm with you.

"But what are we going to do? Halemon said scatter and hide the pieces of the Lifeblade. Is that what we're going to do when the sun comes up?"

"I don't know," Senn admitted. "I need to think."

She also didn't want to say out loud that it didn't matter what they did. Halemon and Ryver had fought. She hoped that it wouldn't be to the death. If it was...

Senn steeled herself to face that thought head on. If Halemon won, that didn't mean all would be well. People in the village would have heard the clamor of swords and their own horseback flight. Halemon would have to tell everyone the truth, and Chieftain Marcham would send his men to find them and recover Skerrast. At most, Halemon would buy them time to complete his wish.

But would that suffice? Neither Senn nor Tay were woodsmen. They might try to hide their trail, but Marcham's own trackers would have little trouble finding them. Eventually, the pieces of the Lifeblade would be retrieved.

Senn closed her eyes as she felt hopelessness flood through her. That was also the likely result if the fight was stopped before one man killed the other. At best, all they could hope for was more time. If Ryver won—Senn shuddered at the thought—then they would not even have that.

Tay had felt her body shake. "Are you cold, Senn?" Then he snorted. "Stupid question. I can't make a fire, but maybe you can stand by one of the horses for a bit. They're well-trained, these two, and I don't think they'll mind so long as you don't do anything to spook them."

"It's not that, Tay. I just can't see a way out." She related her thoughts to him, hoping that stating their dilemma out loud would help them to find a solution. Instead, it left them feeling worse than ever.

Tay inhaled and let out a long breath that steamed in the night air. "Let's take it one thing at a time. That's what my dad would have said." Senn smiled faintly, remembering old Kellen. "We stay here till sun-up. Then what?"

Senn never had the chance to answer him. She never had the chance to make that decision. For at that moment, they heard the sound of a horse, ridden hard, approaching in the night. The gully walls had proved a barrier to sound, so before they knew it, the hoofbeats were close. Soon they could see light as well, the faint glow of a lantern. They held their breath, hoping that the rider, whoever it was, would pass them by.

It was their horses that betrayed them in the end. They had become restive at the sound of another horse, and as it came closer, they whinnied, calling out to establish contact. The horse on the road, recognising its stablemates, returned the call, then all three horses began to rejoice at their reunion.

Senn and Tay leapt to their feet, but there was nowhere to run. Their pursuer turned into the gully and raised his lantern. They couldn't make out the features of the figure behind it, but when it spoke, Senn knew their end had come.

"So," said Ryver, his voice filled with contempt. "There is yet another layer to this treachery. I suspected as much, divining the old fool's last command. To deny me my rightful position, he even went so far as to order you to deliver Skerrast into the hands of our enemies."

"That's not it, Ryver," Senn protested.

"Quiet! I want no more of your lies. Why else would you be fleeing to the lands of the Gretangs?"

"We would never—" Tay shouted.

"No more!" Ryver dismounted and set the lantern on the ground. In its light, they could see that his face was awash with blood. His clothes too were stained and torn, and his left leg dragged as he advanced on them, sword in hand.

"Give me the Lifeblade," he said, his tone promising death should they continue to defy him.

Senn clutched the bundle to her chest. "Halemon—"

"Dead. *I* am now Champion of Totala, *and I will have what is rightfully mine!"* Ryver started forward, his bloodstained sword raised.

Then three arrows struck him at almost the same time. One took him in the right shoulder, forcing him to drop the sword. The second stuck in his right leg, while the third scored a glancing blow on his left shoulder, close to his neck.

Ryver staggered forward, falling to one knee as his right leg buckled under him. Senn looked around for the attackers, but it was too dark to see anything. *They're above us!*

Tay grabbed her and pulled her back along the gully and against the rock wall, protecting her from Ryver and the hidden archers.

A second volley of arrows struck home. Ryver fell on his face, stretching out one arm, his fingers clawing for the bundle containing the shards of Skerrast. He was inches away from grasping the sword. Then he convulsed and was still.

Senn heard footsteps moving somewhere above, then the heavy sounds of men swinging themselves down into the gully.

"Neither of you move," a hard voice commanded. "You're covered from above."

A hooded figure moved into the light and checked Ryver. As he looked up, Senn caught a glimpse of a bearded face. "He's dead," the hooded man said. He stood up, lifting Ryver's lantern. In its light, Senn saw that the first speaker was a large man, muscled like a fighter, with the telltale bulge of a warrior's knot under his hood. The one with the lantern was taller and leaner, with a black beard cut short and a pair of dark eyes that were surprisingly gentle as he looked at them. He too had a warrior's knot, though none of his companion's pugnacity.

"I am Brynn," he said. "My companions are Rale and Parron."

Tay's eyes narrowed. "You're Gretangs."

The big man called Rale laughed nastily, but Brynn gave a slight shrug. "So we are. And, unless I'm mistaken, you are Sennelle, the Binder of Tortala, and he is Tayssen, a smith, brother to your late husband." He seemed to be the leader of this scouting party.

"You seem to think you know a lot about us," Tay said, blustering a bit, though Senn could tell he was almost as scared as when Ryver had them cornered.

Brynn ignored him. "We also know that your erstwhile attacker was Ryver." His eyes narrowed. "Did he speak the truth? Is Champion Halemon dead?"

"Why should we tell you anything, Gretang?" Tay demanded.

"What makes you think you have a choice, Tortalan?" Rale shot back. He took a pace forward, but stopped when Brynn laid a hand on his shoulder.

"Easy, Rale," he said, then turned to Tay. "For one thing, we just saved your lives. For another, you'd do well to tell us why Ryver was pursuing you. Are you outlaws? Fugitives from your village? If so, you're in a bad way, and you'll need our help." He studied them, his eyes still gentle as if he sought to understand their secrets rather than expose them.

"No, that's not it," he said after a long moment had passed. "There's something going on here that I don't fully understand. We heard him accuse you of plotting with us, which we both know isn't true. What else was he mistaken about?" His eyes strayed to the cloth bundle.

"You leave that alone," Tay said before Senn could stop him.

"An admission in itself." Brynn went to examine the bag while Rale stepped across to put himself in Tay's way.

"It's broken," Senn said. Brynn froze, and Rale's eyes went wide. She had their attention now. "Halemon broke it himself."

"Impossible," said Rale, but Brynn said nothing. He knelt and opened the bundle, gazing down at the metal shards. When he spoke, his voice was so soft that Senn barely heard him. "And it was for this that Ryver killed him?"

"In part, yes," she said.

Brynn rose. "A tragic end," he said. "You might not believe me, but I had great respect for Champion Halemon. He, more than anyone else, was responsible for the peace of the last ten years."

"He had you running scared, you mean," said Tay.

"Tay, please," Senn said, laying a hand on his arm. This was between her and Brynn, she felt. "I'll tell you what happened," she said to the tall man, "but first, I would ask you something. How is it that you know who we are?"

"Why should we tell you anything, Tortalan?" said Rale with a smirk, but Brynn once again studied her with his dark eyes before he gave his answer.

"Your clan has possessed the Lifeblade for many years," he said. "We wanted to keep an eye on your village. Sometimes we watch from afar, as we were doing tonight. At other times, we've sent agents into Tortala in the guise of merchants or travellers, to gather information."

"So you can plan to steal the Lifeblade," Tay accused him. Senn said nothing. She wanted to know how Brynn would answer this charge.

"Champion Halemon was a voice for peace, and your chieftain is shrewd enough to appreciate the benefits of allowing your clan to grow and build, free from the shadow of war," he said. "We would also see the truce continue, but we knew Halemon was old, and that his successor might not share his views. We need to know as soon as possible if circumstances are going to change—which brings us to tonight.

"Halemon is dead, as is Ryver. Skerrast is broken, and you were fleeing with the pieces. I don't understand why, or what your chieftain will do in response."

Senn couldn't help laughing bitterly. "Isn't it obvious?" She could see it all in her mind's eye, their hopes breaking under the hammer-blows of their clans' eternal rivalry. "Unless we return to Tortala tomorrow morning, Chieftain Marcham will claim it was a plot by your clan—that you killed Halemon and his squire in an attempt to steal the sword, which Halemon broke to keep it out of your hands."

There was a tense silence, which Rale broke after a moment by swearing angrily.

"Even if we let you return, your chieftain will claim the same thing," Brynn said, and though he masked it better than Rale, Senn could hear his anger too. His was a different kind of anger, though; a frustration born of his inability to prevent what was surely coming.

He doesn't want a war, but he doesn't know how to stop it, Senn thought. *None of us do.*

How many others have there been, like Halemon, or this man Brynn—people who strive to find an end, only to find that there is no end? We're like hillside trees in a landslide, resisting the inevitable for a while, only to be swept away by the momentum that has built up behind us or the shifting of the ground beneath our feet.

Perhaps all they could do was keep resisting. *"I believe that calmer heads can prevail, and that a better way can be found,"* Halemon had said, *"but there is no hope at all for our clans while that sword exists."*

Then she saw it: the answer in Halemon's words and in those of the Gretang warrior who stood before them. *The solution, like the problem, belongs to neither the Tortalans nor the Gretangs alone—it belongs to both clans, to all of us.*

"Take us to your village," she said urgently to Brynn. "I know what we can do, but we don't have long."

Brynn and Rale exchanged a look. "Is that wise?" the former asked.

"It's the only choice we've got," Senn told them. "If you don't want this to end in another useless war, let's not waste time with questions. I'll explain everything on the way."

The following afternoon, the warriors of the Tortalans and the Gretangs faced one another across an open field, their battle lines spilling out on either side of the seldom-used road that connected their lands. The Tortalans clashed their weapons against their shields and yelled at their rivals, shouting taunts or vowing revenge. The Gretangs were watchful but silent. Their chieftain, Allander, had made sure his fighters knew what to expect.

Nevertheless, Senn felt her heart pounding in her chest as she walked forward with Allander and his sons. Brynn was there as well, bearing a simple grey banner, a universally recognised token of parley in the Plains of Nassan. Tay was also at her side, carrying a bundle wrapped in cloth.

Chieftain Marcham emerged from the Tortalan line, also accompanied by his sons and several prominent Tortalan warriors. Both groups advanced to the centre of the prospective battlefield. Senn prayed to all the gods she knew to ensure that prospective was all that it would ever be.

She and Tay were behind the Gretangs, so Marcham and his retinue didn't see them until the groups were within a dozen feet of each other. Then the chieftain's eyes widened.

"You have...hostages," he said as they came close enough to parley. "I fear they may not be as valuable as you hope. Perhaps a better word for them would be 'traitors,' and returning them to us will not be enough to turn us aside this day."

"They are neither renegades nor hostages," Chieftain Allander replied. "The word I would use is guests, and like all guests, they came with a gift."

"A gift that you would do well to return, it being rightfully ours."

Allander turned to Senn. "I brought gifts that we can share," she said. She gestured to Tay, who unwrapped the bundle in his hands.

Revealing two identical swords.

"Halemon, Champion of Tortala, broke Skerrast," she said in a clear voice. "He thought it was the only way to stop our clans from fighting, but I believe I have found a better way—one that Halemon would have approved of.

"These swords are each named Lhuyn." The word meant "peace" in the old tongue of northern Nassan. "They are replicas of Skerrast, remade with my magic and that of Erith, Binder of Gretang. They were forged in the smithy of Bordin of Gretang, with the help of Tayssen of Tortala. With members of both our clans as witness, we swear that neither sword contains more of the original than the other.

"They possess none of the power of Skerrast, yet let us now let them be what the Lifeblade was always intended to be: a token of fellowship between our clans. Let us redress the mistakes of the past and leave behind enmity and conflict. Let these swords be true to their names."

She took one and gave it to Chieftain Allander, who immediately bestowed it upon Brynn.

"I name you Champion of Gretang," he said. "May you never draw it save in defense of our lands."

Senn took the other sword to Chieftain Marcham. He looked at both her and the weapon for a moment. Senn saw the doubt in his eyes. He had come here to avenge a betrayal, but now his world had changed, as it had for all of them. He was an intelligent man, but also a proud one. How would he react?

Senn had to hope that Halemon's wisdom had not died with him, that Marcham had not been deaf to his Champion's advice.

The warriors on both sides of the field were silent. Even the breeze had stopped rustling the leaves in the trees. It was as if the landscape was holding its breath.

Marcham's eyes met hers. At last, he spoke.

"I believe Halemon would have approved," he said, and took the sword. "Tortala's next champion will, I'm sure, follow the example he set."

"I deeply regret that Halemon isn't here to witness this," Senn said. The tension had flooded out of her as soon as Marcham accepted the sword, and at Halemon's name, sadness at his death began to fill its place. "This is what he wanted."

"Don't deny your own part in this, Sennelle," Marcham said. He turned to his opposite number. There was another pause as the two men, who had never met, though each had spent years attempting to guess the other's mind, looked at one another. When Marcham spoke, his words were stiff and formal.

"Chieftain Allander, tonight we mourn the death of Halemon, Champion of Tortala. In the spirit of the peace we now make together, I invite you to join us as we lay him to rest."

"We would gladly pay our respects," Allander said.

Senn left the two clan leaders to their business and walked slowly away from the group. Whatever relief she felt that there would be no battle today was tinged with sorrow, and not just for Halemon. She missed Olven more than ever right now, her old grief reawakened by this new loss.

"He would have been proud of you," Tay said from behind her.

She turned, tears forming in her eyes. "Halemon?"

"And Olvi. I guessed you might be thinking of him."

Senn nodded, unable to speak, and Tay took her in his arms. On either side of the field, Tortalans and Gretangs were sheathing their swords as their battle lines dissolved. There was no cheering, but Senn sensed a feeling of relief on both sides that no one would have to die today.

It might not last, she thought, but peace, however long it lasts, is better than the alternative. Halemon said it's part of our nature to fight and kill, but that isn't all that we are. We can come together in joy or sadness to honor those who tried to find a better way. We can choose to keep looking for that better way no matter how impossible it seems. We can all be Binders.

About the Author

Pat Woods is a writer from Nottingham, UK, who moved to Taiwan in 2008 for an adventure that turned into a lifetime commitment. He began writing in school and started to actively seek out publishing opportunities after becoming a part of the Taipei Writers' Group, which he now runs.

Pat writes fantasy and speculative fiction, and was nominated for the 2016 Pushcart Prize for his Sherlock Holmes pastiche "The Adventure of the Etheric Projection."

In addition to writing, Pat works as an editor for a number of his peers. He is also an actor and has performed in shows in England, Taiwan, and China. His books can be found at https://www.amazon.com/Pat-Woods/e/B011XVYIDY.

THE CONTENTS OF THE GRAIL

RICHARD ZWICKER

Rosskild led his horse out of the thick woods, dropped supine to the ground, and soaked in the midday sun. For two days, under a spotted shade of tree cover, he'd dodged swinging branches and climbed over fallen tree trunks. He'd reached his limit. On the ground he thought of Elaine, whom he'd not seen since he'd set out in quest of the Grail, two years before. In his mind he embraced her elusive, supple image, as if by force of will he could bridge the distance between them.

An equally exhausted Nascien emerged into the light with his horse. Before his eyes adjusted, he tripped and fell over his fellow knight's body.

"Oh, sorry," Rosskild said, remaining on the ground. His long, wiry frame, along with shoulder-length dark brown hair and a jutting red beard, made him seem conflicted. Nascien sat up and massaged his shoulder to little effect through his chain mail. In contrast to Rosskild, he was short, his tawny whiskers barely lining his face. He peered to the north, squinting.

"I do not see the castle."

Rosskild reluctantly sat up. "It should be just beyond the hill."

"That's where everything should be."

Their destination was Castle Mabuz. Mabuz was called a king but, in truth, no one knew who his people were. He reached out to no one, which created an array of rumors, the most persistent being that inside his castle lay incredible riches, and possibly the Grail itself. The second most persistent was whoever entered the castle never came out the same, if at all.

"He will not be happy to see us," said Nascien.

"Are you afraid?"

Nascien adjusted his chain mail. "I am *concerned.*"

"I suggest we rest a bit, then carry on until we are in view of either the castle or the setting sun," said Rosskild.

"Agreed, but I retain the option of changing my mind."

Rosskild closed his eyes and remembered a third rumor about King Mabuz, that he had died many years ago and that his unsettled spirit haunted his abandoned castle. The next thing Rosskild knew, Nascien was waking him up.

"I think I dreamed that I slept without dreaming," said the waking knight, as he grunted and rose to his feet. "It is not very satisfying."

"Neither as a dream nor an anecdote," said Nascien.

They rode forward, up a small grassy hill. The indistinct trail they followed could have been made by animals long dead. Nascien muttered he didn't like trails that forced him to concentrate. The top of the hill granted a panoramic view of the forest to the south and east, a plain to the west, and to the north, Castle Mabuz. Its central section looked like a darkened tooth, with its upright, rectangular form topped off by smaller, uneven squares. Two towers flanked the attached north and east sections like blank-faced sentinels. A lake wrapped around two-thirds of the castle, reflecting an ethereal upside-down image of the structure. Its tiny, irregularly placed windows reminded Rosskild of eyes that could see you but revealed nothing.

"What do you think?" asked Rosskild.

Nascien shook his head. "It looks as unwelcoming as I expected."

"We can camp under the shelter of that copse of trees." He pointed halfway down the hill.

It was farther than it appeared, and as the sky darkened, they noticed the drifting smoke of a small fire. As they got closer, they found the haunch of a hart hanging over the fire, not quite cooked, and a roan tied to a tree. Rosskild's right hand clasped his sword. A large drop of rain hit his head with a splat, then two more.

"Not the best conditions to cook a hart, I fear," said a third man, large and round, with a thick curly black beard, as he stepped from behind a tree.

"Denholm!" Rosskild said, recognizing a knight from the Round Table and lowering his sword. "We shall have food for sustenance and thought tonight."

"I have traveled mostly alone," said Denholm, as the three men feasted on the meat. "I want to find the Grail based on who I am, not who other people are. Have you two been together the entire time?"

"No," said Rosskild. "I started out with Agravain and Gareth, but after eight months a mob of hungry men ambushed us. I alone survived. Since then, though my path has crossed the lives of many, I have always ended up walking out alone, until I met up with Nascien a fortnight ago."

"What did you do before that?" Denholm asked Nascien.

Nascien took a gulp from the flask of wine that Denholm shared, then hesitated. "Talk is cheap," he said.

"Nonsense," said Denholm. "If the Grail is the nectar of purity, talk is the nectar of life! You would deprive us of its gifts?"

Nascien looked at Denholm as if he was a lunatic, then glanced at Rosskild, whose expectant eyes prodded him. "Very well, though you are the first to call my talk a gift. Like you, I have traveled mostly alone, but for a different reason. I see the chivalric codes as a means rather than an end. I am skeptical of them and the Grail, but both are an effective way of directing one's life."

Denholm shook his head. "I pity you."

"If it makes you feel better," said Nascien.

"Do not mind him," said Rosskild to Denholm. "His beliefs are unorthodox, but he doesn't force them on others. So, what will you do if you find the Grail?"

Denholm smiled. "If I am blessed with that great vision, it means I've done the utmost."

Rosskild chewed on his piece of hart. "Sounds like death."

"Oh, but what a death."

Rosskild nodded and turned toward Nascien. "What say you, brooding one?"

Nascien looked up, his mouth dripping. "Too much thinking weakens a man. If a wolf considers the pain of its prey, the prey escapes."

"You have a low opinion of man if you compare him to a wolf," said Denholm.

Nascien frowned. "There is a difference. If man meets his need of food and shelter, his life then requires a larger meaning. Mine is to spend my days searching for the Grail. It suffices as a direction. My greatest fear is that I will find it."

Denholm laughed. "Why on earth would you fear that?"

Nascien sighed. "We all have a picture of the Grail in our minds. Mine is a shining, golden goblet with ornate, incomprehensible carvings. What if I find the Grail exactly like this, and think, yes, I've seen this many times? Then I will have lost my quest, and I'll have to come up with another."

Denholm waved his hand dismissively. "You have nothing to worry about." He turned to Rosskild. "Is your vision as sacrilegious as your friend's?"

Rosskild wiped the grease from his face. During their quest there had been plenty of time to think. He'd wondered why Arthur gave it to them, breaking up the unity of the Round Table, yet did nothing himself. Even if one of his knights found the Grail, how would Arthur be able to see it if he'd not participated in the search, or, perish the thought, was not worthy?

"I seek the Grail because my king has ordered me to," he said softly. "Otherwise, I would have stayed closer to my lady, Elaine."

"Do not get him started on her," said Nascien. "I already know her better than I know myself, and I have never met her."

"What if you find the Grail?" asked Denholm, ignoring Nascien. "Will you strive to always be worthy of its sight?"

"As I would if I did not find it." Though Rosskild was trained to fight, he enjoyed comparing thoughts. "What do you see as the reason for pursuing the Grail?"

"It is part of God's plan to influence man to follow the correct path," Denholm said, with confidence.

"Though all is predestined?" asked Rosskild.

"Of course. God sees the past, present, and future."

"You may be right," Rosskild said. "But I see attainment of the Grail as a means to influence God."

"What do you mean?" asked Denholm.

"I believe if I find the Grail, my reward will be God's attention."

"And what would you do with that?"

"Ask Him to allow me to make my own life."

"You think you can do a better job than He?"

"The act of trying makes it better," said Rosskild.

The next morning, though all three of the men sought entrance to the Castle Mabuz, they thought it practical to stagger their approach. Nascien drew the short blade of grass, so he banged a gloved fist against the entrance. The lake threw its echo back at the other two knights, hidden behind some trees fifty paces away. Rosskild and Denholm heard the scrape of wood on stone as the door opened. A tall, hunched man stood in the entrance, looking as much a gnarled, climbing bush as a person. His voice was soft, the words fading out despite the propulsion of the lake. They seemed to talk a long time, the host maintaining calm while Nascien's voice became more heated. Finally, Nascien turned and walked to the waiting knights.

"He says he'll not let me in unless we're together. He's got better things to do than open his door three times."

"Rather haughty for a servant," said Denholm.

"That was Mabuz," said Nascien.

"What kind of a king opens his own castle door?" asked Denholm.

"A controlling one. You didn't have to tell him there were three of us," said Rosskild.

"You are right," said Nascien. "He already knew."

As they approached the door, it opened slowly, again revealing King Mabuz.

"Welcome," he said. His voice was deep, yet drained of energy, like a spirit's moan. His face was as lined as a scroll. Behind him stood a gaunt, longhaired woman of middle age and lost beauty. "The doors of my castle are open to all that dare enter. Maintaining such a place keeps us busy, however, and we are unable to show you around, but you are free to wander."

"Thank you for your hospitality," said Rosskild. "Rumor has it the Grail lies in this castle. Our only purpose is to seek it."

"That seems a narrow purpose for something as complex as a man," said Mabuz, "but so be it. I have labored to ensure most things can be found in my castle."

"What about our horses?" asked Nascien.

"I assume they are secured? No one will steal them on my lands," said Mabuz. With those words, he turned and walked away. Rosskild looked at the queen for answers. He'd heard her name was Lunete and depending on the legend, she hung over her husband like a restless ghost or a relentless force. The three knights entered, bumping into dank air. A blood-red carpet etched with runic designs stretched down a dim corridor. Spiny support beams lined the walls like stems of plants that had never seen the sun's light. Occasional mounted torches flickered. Dark red banners with the same symbols as the carpet hung stiffly over the walls. A larger than life suit of armor stood upright on an elevated base, its metal hands clasping a prickly mace.

Lunete closed the door behind them. "Seek," she whispered, then followed her husband as if floating.

Rosskild turned to Denholm. "Sometimes you visit someone's home and it surprises you. You see a side of a person you did not expect. This is not one of those times."

Denholm nodded. "Perhaps our expectations of the Grail will be met as well."

"Only the most pure-hearted can see the Grail," said Rosskild. "If only a fraction of the rumors associated with this castle are true, how could someone such as Mabuz see it?"

"How can anyone can see it?" asked Nascien.

They walked down the long corridor, their footfalls swallowed by silence. They passed another oversized suit of armor, posed in the same position.

"What's the first thing you notice about this place?" Rosskild asked.

"It is silent. No evidence of servants, of anyone." said Denholm.

"Walking down this corridor I feel I am going deeper into a bottomless lake. We do not get closer to anything. We just get farther away," said Rosskild.

"We know there are at least two people in here," said Denholm.

"All we know for sure is that the door closed behind us," said Nascien.

They walked, and walked, and walked. Behind and ahead of them, the corridor yawned like the night sky. Several times they passed intersecting corridors but shunned them for fear they'd lose their way.

"We should turn around," said Denholm.

"Our hosts could give us some direction," Denholm said, his tight face betraying fear.

"They made it clear that we are to find our own way," said Rosskild. "Perhaps we should split up. The Grail might not reveal itself if one or two of its admirers are flawed."

"If we spilt up, we will get more lost," said Denholm.

Rosskild had experienced many adventures and knew eventually he would encounter one from which he could not escape. He had always thought it would be tomorrow rather than today, but that was life. It went on, until it didn't.

"If we retrace our steps, we may find ourselves just as lost as we are now," said Rosskild.

"If we split up, at least I won't have to spend eternity looking at you two," Nascien said. "This is not the time to be timid."

Uneasily, the knights separated. Rosskild turned left into a side corridor, and for a time he passed more empty halls. He wondered if he would spend the rest of his life lost in the Castle Mabuz.

"Where are you going?" a melodic female voice asked. He whirled around but saw no one. Then a young woman stepped out from one of the perpendicular corridors. She wore a straight blue gown that hung to the floor. Light brown tresses flanked her head, reaching to her waist. She resembled a young Lunete.

Rosskild struggled to find his voice. "I am an Arthurian knight seeking the Holy Grail. Have you seen it?"

A frown stretched her sad features. "I have seen little. My name is Branwen, and my father has never allowed me outside of this castle. But I can lead you to the Grail if you promise to take me away from here."

Rosskild's heart raced. If the woman's words were true, he was close to completing his quest. On the other hand, how could he steal a daughter from a father, out of his own home?

"How would your father feel about that?" asked Rosskild.

"He would not stop you. He doesn't see life the way most people do. Time for him is a mix of past, present, and future. It sounds interesting, but it means he doesn't see the need to do anything because in his mind, he's already done it. I must break free... or I will become my mother."

The fatalism in her words chilled Rosskild. "I will speak to him."

She shook her head. "He appreciates only deeds, but you can try. Follow me."

They walked for what seemed a long time. Rosskild felt his legs tighten, yet Branwen strolled without effort. The corridors continued without change, dimly lit passages with showcases of armor and weapons.

"There," Branwen said, finally. They stepped into a wide, windowless room. Near the ceiling hung a golden goblet, ringed with jewels, emitting a dim halo. Rosskild stood, spellbound. Why was he seeing it? His life had been far from spotless. Had they misunderstood, or was the legend wrong? Was there a state higher than purity? Were some flaws desirable?

"That is not the Grail," he said sadly.

"Why do you say that?" she asked.

"It looks exactly as I pictured it, as if lifted from my mind. The true Grail would be beyond my imagination."

"It is the true Grail. Take it in your hands. Unless you're afraid."

If the quest had accomplished anything, it had diminished his fear. He reached up and grasped the goblet. It was cold. Inside was a murky liquid, which nearly reached the brim.

"What would happen if I pressed the Grail to my lips and drank from it?" asked Rosskild.

"The contents of the Grail are what is already inside you."

He did not understand her words. "What if I spill its contents?"

"What if you spill your blood?"

Tired of her riddles, he turned and walked back to the corridor but found he could not pass through the doorway.

"What is this?" he asked.

She stared at him. "I have taken you to the Grail. Now you must live up to your part of the agreement. My father will not give you permission, but he won't stop you. So what will you do for me?"

The question confused Rosskild. "I will free you from your father's dominion."

"Then what?"

"Then you will be able to follow a path of your choosing."

"What are my choices?" she asked.

"Someone with your beauty would have no trouble finding a man to marry."

"Not you?"

He smiled wistfully. "My heart belongs to another."

"What is she like?"

Rosskild's cheeks flushed. "She is the epitome of beauty and grace, whose honor I defend to the death."

"Very well. So I marry someone else. Then what?"

"You will have children and raise them."

"Can I not be a knight like you?"

Rosskild chuckled. "To become a knight, one must demonstrate strength, fighting ability, and loyalty to your kind. You also must have the means to buy your armor and weapons."

"How many women become knights?"

"I know of none."

"And you agree with that?" she asked.

"What I think is irrelevant. Women can become wives and mothers or nuns."

She folded her arms and turned away from him. "You seek the right to choose your life, yet accept such a limited choice for women? You profess to honor women, but only if they know their place."

How could she have known that was his quest? Was there anything the inhabitants of this castle didn't know?

"What is wrong with knowing one's place? Life is the search for such knowledge. I gave you my word. I will take you from this castle, but I cannot change the world."

She glared at him. "Cannot or choose not?"

He looked up and saw they were standing in front of the castle door. Between them and the door stood two over-sized knights in full armor, their swords raised. The first knight charged. Rosskild parried the thrust sword with his own. The Grail clattered to the floor, spilling its contents. The impact jerked Rosskild to the right, enabling him to avoid by inches the second knight's mace.

"I am a guest in King Mabuz's castle! Do you attack me at his behest?" Rosskild gasped but received no response, other than another sword thrust from the first knight. "This woman has asked me to liberate her. I will do so, or die trying. State your purpose, and perhaps we can come to an agreement without bloodshed."

But it was as if he was fighting empty suits of armor. Not only didn't his foes respond to his request; they did not grunt or gasp under his onslaught. With a mighty swing, Rosskild cut off the head of the first knight, its helmet clattering on the floor. Nonplussed, the second knight lunged at Rosskild, who sidestepped, causing the assailant to fall to the floor. Before he could rise, Rosskild impaled him through the belly. Both deathblows split no blood. Confused, Rosskild picked up the empty Grail and grabbed Branwen's hand.

"Let us leave this place."

He opened the door, and the outside air washed over them. As he dragged Branwen through, she screamed, and the Grail burst into flame. Rosskild dropped it to the ground, and the goblet smashed into fiery pieces. The knight dove to the ground, shielding his face. By the time the fire had burnt itself out, Branwen, the Grail, and the front entrance to the castle were gone. Rosskild pummeled the wall with his mail-clad fists, the sound sliding across the lake and bouncing off the hill. Twice he yelled, "Open the door!" though there was none to open. He was pulled back by Nascien and Denholm.

"She wanted the right to make her own decisions," said Rosskild to the other two men as they sat in a triangle back at their camp. "I said I would try to help her, but the moment she stepped outside of the castle, she disappeared."

"Was that her doing, or Mabuz's?" asked Denholm.

"I do not know, but somehow I feel she knew it would happen all along," said Rosskild.

"My experience was similar," said Denholm, scratching his belly. "Except I encountered an elderly priest who argued with me about faith. He was blasphemous, criticizing those who held faith without questioning. He said my kind of belief imprisoned religion in a stasis, that there was a gap between what should be and what was. He said actions defined the man. He challenged me to bridge the gap between belief and reality."

"Did you accept that challenge?" asked Rosskild.

"I said I had devoted my *life* toward bridging that gap. At that point, I saw the Grail, but just for a moment. Then the two knights appeared. It took all my skill to vanquish them. Once I did, the Grail was gone and I found myself outside the castle."

Rosskild turned to Nascien. "One always has to ask what you saw."

Nascien's eyes looked haunted. "I saw nothing. I wandered the halls of the castle for what seemed like years, though I did not need food or drink. The only proof that I walked was the echo of my steps. Had you two not insisted that only part of a day passed, I would have believed I spent ten years in that wretched castle. I never felt so pointless. I thought, if I ever get out of here, I would find a better reason for living than I'd had up to that point. Long after I'd given up, I found myself at the castle door, those same two knights guarding it. I thanked God, someone I have had limited conversations with, for finally giving me a means of escape, and I knew it would take more than two knights to stop me."

"So you never saw the Grail?" asked Denholm.

"I saw a flash of light when I thanked God, but I thought it was merely the steel of the two knights' swords."

"Have we been toyed with?" asked Denholm.

"Better toyed than killed," said Nascien. "Let Mabuz have his fun, as long as it is far away. His amusement is like a cat playing with a bird. Usually, when the game is over, only one walks away."

"But three have walked away," said Denholm. "And Mabuz did not see the result. Why did he not just tell us what he wants?"

Rosskild took off his helmet and scratched his head. "I think he did, and maybe he did see the result. Branwen said the past, present, and future were the same to him."

"Was this a test?" asked Denholm.

"For the Grail?" Nascien spat. "It's all a test. But what if the test is to avoid fool's errands?"

"We can live like the animal that obeys only its hunger and its instincts and never questions the meaning of things," said Rosskild. "But if we were meant to do that, why have we the power of reason? What kind of a God would give a gift that cannot be used, that reveals only what we cannot have?"

"God helps those who help themselves, but I am unsure of Mabuz's connection to all this," said Denholm. "And what about the Grail?"

"That is the question," said Rosskild. "I do not know if what I saw was truly the Grail, but when it broke, something about this quest broke in me."

Denholm pointed at the air. "I can bridge the gap between belief and reality only by helping others."

Nascien stood. "I too question our wandering. I need to find a home, though it may be too late for one such as I. Hence, though I thank you for your company, I must follow a different path. Farewell." He untied his horse from the tree, mounted, and rode off.

Denholm turned to Rosskild. "Would you like to help me?"

Rosskild thought. "Yours is a worthy quest, but I gave my word to Branwen. Though I do not know where or if she is, I need to see if I can right the wrongs in the code I live by. Good luck, Denholm."

Rosskild gathered his belongings and walked away, his mind ringing like a deep question. He felt the answer lay with his beloved Elaine. He would go to her, and this time, things would be different. He would actually speak to her.

ABOUT THE AUTHOR

Richard Zwicker is an English teacher living in Vermont, USA, with his wife and beagle. Some of his over fifty published short stories have appeared in such ezines as Penumbra, Perihelion Science Fiction, Phantaxis, *and other markets that don't all begin with the letter "P." Humor and seriousness often fight to a draw in his writing and life. In addition to reading and writing, he likes playing the piano, jogging (especially after he finishes), and fighting the good fight against middle age. Despite living in Brazil for eight years, he is still a lousy soccer player.*

Pooka Problems

M.C. Dwyer

Tessa dreamt of broken glass and woke to an icy draft slicing through her bedroom. Sitting up groggily, she shivered and wrapped her comforter closer around her shoulders.

Peering through the moonlit room, she blinked the sleep from her eyes and tried to make out what had happened. She reached for the bedside lamp, missing the switch on her first try but finally succeeding, and its warm glow showed nothing out of place apart from the draft.

With the comforter still wrapped around her, she crawled to the end of the bed and flopped down, reaching for the slippers she'd kicked underneath. After some flailing, she managed to brush her fingers against the furry fleece and pulled them out. She hopped off the bed, slid her stockinged feet into them and stood up. Abandoning the comforter, she snagged her hoodie from the back of the chair and pulled it over her head, shivering as she pulled up the hood and slid her hands into the front pocket.

Tessa walked into the hall and paused. The front door was ajar, swinging gently in the wintry breeze. A sound came from the other room, and she froze completely. Was someone in the house? She crept down the hallway, the rubber soles of her slippers making no noise on the carpet, then swept up the umbrella that was leaning against the hall tree. It was an old-fashioned one; black, with a generous hook for a handle and a wicked-looking metal spike at the top. Wielding it like a sword, she eased around the kitchen door and raised it to strike.

Only to stop, dumbfounded, at the sight before her. Her fridge was standing open, its various contents strewn across the floor. The fridge light combined with the moonlight to illuminate her intruder: he was small, only a child; he was dripping wet, and—perhaps most importantly—he was speaking to the empty air in front of the broken kitchen window.

"This one? You're sure?" He held up the bottle of chocolate syrup and gave it a vigorous squeeze, sending a stream of goo onto the floor where it mixed with the broken glass and food wrappers.

"What the heck?" Tessa said when she managed to find her voice.

The boy turned with a yelp, dropping the chocolate syrup and raising his hands as if to ward off a blow. They started to glow blue, and Tessa lowered the umbrella in surprise. The boy caught the tip in one glowing hand, and, with the sickening jolt of electric current, the world turned inside out, leaving Tessa with a pounding in her head and the lingering taste of fudge.

"Ugh," she groaned, dropping to her knees. Her ears were ringing, and her eyes stung. She blinked furiously to clear them and found herself in a field of flowers the likes of which she'd never seen before. They were vaguely daisy-shaped, if daisies could be striped in fluorescent orange and blue. The effect, when combined with her recent experience, was faintly nauseating.

"Look what you made me do!" a voice accused, bringing her head up. She saw the boy from before, illuminated now by the light of a newly risen sun—no, wait. She peered up into the sky and saw not one but two yellow orbs making their way across the greenish heavens. Tessa looked back at the boy, incredulous.

"Where are we?"

"That's what I'm saying! You threw off my transport!" In the daylight (if daylight it was; since the sun—suns?—were up, she guessed it was day), he looked to be maybe ten or eleven years old. His brown hair hung damp and messily on his brow and tumbled in a riot of curls to his shoulders. He pushed it back from his forehead impatiently and put his hands on his hips. His eyes were pale lavender, a color reflected in the long tunic he wore over a pair of pants and short boots. His damp clothes were steaming gently in the sunlight.

"What?" Tessa said, uncomprehending.

The boy stamped a foot. "You threw off my transport and made me lose the trace. Now I have to go back and find it again."

Tessa was confused, but of one thing she was certain. "Back? Yes, you should take me back."

He tossed his hair out of his eyes and scowled. "I'm not taking you anywhere. You messed up my transport, and you'd probably just do it again. Find your own way home." He sniffed. "Loser."

Tessa pointed the umbrella at him. "Listen, kid! You brought me here, so you can darn well take me home again."

At this, a spark of blue shot out from the tip of the umbrella, surprising them both. Tessa yelped and dropped the umbrella—or at least tried to. Her fingers didn't want to open, and when she tried to remove it with her other hand, it simply stuck to that one as well. She could transfer it back and forth, but it refused to be dropped.

She looked helplessly at the boy. "What's going on?"

He reached out a hand to the umbrella. It sparked at him, making him pull back with another scowl. He merely shrugged, however, and said, "Some of the transfer must have gotten caught in it. It should run out eventually." He turned and started walking away.

Tessa stared at him weakly for a moment, then climbed to her feet and started after him.

She strode through the flowers, her fuzzy slippers crushing the alien stems and releasing a pungent smell that was faintly reminiscent of anise. The boy had moved surprisingly quickly, and she was starting to work up a sweat by the time she caught up to him.

"Hey!" she said, brandishing the umbrella at his still retreating back. "I'm talking to you, brat!" The umbrella was inert in her hands, and she threw it down before grabbing the boy's shoulder and spinning him around.

"My name is not *brat,*" he said with a scowl as he shrugged off her hand. "My name is Owain."

"Tessa," she said automatically, but the boy merely shrugged again. "How am I supposed to get home?"

"Not my problem," Owain said coolly, narrowing his lavender eyes.

Tessa felt a rising urge to strangle him and forced herself to step back and breathe. *Pretend he's one of your students,* she cautioned herself, closing her eyes and inhaling deeply. *Think of the lawsuits. Breathe.*

After a moment, she opened her eyes to see his retreating back. Snatching up the umbrella, she ran after him again. As she neared, she saw his hands glow blue. Lunging forward, she brushed the sleeve of his tunic and felt the world flip-flop again.

"Hey!" The boy's indignant voice pulled her back to reality. It hadn't hurt as badly this time, though the stomach-dropping sensation reminded her of one of the nastier rides at the county fair.

"Huh?" she managed, looking up to see where they had landed this time.

Owain stood fuming, one hand on his hip and the other flung up and out as if to say, "Look at this mess!"

Accordingly, she looked around, but saw less to alarm her than last time. There was a full moon hanging low in the sky, but it looked like it usually did. They seemed to be in the midst of a forest, and there was a faint dusting of snow on the ground.

"Where are we?"

The boy took a deep breath and then looked around, startled. Tessa sniffed the air, too, wondering what he had smelled. It simply smelled like a cold, damp, winter night. And then she heard the roar.

"What was that?" she whispered.

Rather than answer, Owain spun in a circle, scenting the air. Choosing a direction seemingly at random, he started off at a jog. Tessa followed, hoping he was heading away from whatever had roared in the night. He sped up, and Tessa did too, wishing she were wearing her sneakers rather than fuzzy house slippers. She gripped tighter with her toes and prayed she wouldn't lose one in the dark of the forest. Worse than running through the woods in the dark would be running through the woods in the dark in stocking feet.

Somewhere off to her left she heard the sound of branches snapping as something large moved through the trees. A roar sounded again, seemingly right in her ear, and she squeaked in fear and put on another burst of speed. Owain was glancing from side to side, looking more frantic and flustered than she'd seen him yet, but just when she was about to say something, he slid to a halt. His hands glowed blue, and Tessa grabbed his shoulder, resigning herself to the imminent stomach-churning transport.

But nothing happened.

"What's wrong?" she whispered, opening eyes that had closed automatically at the thought of another trip.

"Shut up!" he hissed, then flexed his fingers. The blue glow intensified, then spread in a sort of bubble that engulfed him and came to a stop midway through Tessa's chest before vanishing. Looking down, she realized she couldn't see anything—nothing at all existed below where the bubble had vanished. She could feel Owain's shoulder under her hand, but she could not see either hand or her own legs—she was merely a floating head and shoulders.

A third roar sounded again, and her head whipped around in time to see something enormous and vaguely reptilian moving through the trees. The moon glinted on one eye, and with a sudden mix of horror and awe Tessa identified the shape. Her knees gave out, and as soon as she hit the dirt, she could suddenly see Owain and the rest of her own body once again. The blue glow hovered around them, shimmering and transparent, and in the glow of the—magic? Tessa had no better name for it—Owain's face glistened with sweat from the effort of holding it steady.

The creature—a *Tyrannosaurus rex,* her brain insisted—stalked past them, looked around for a moment, and then continued on. Owain started breathing easier, but he didn't release the blue glow. Tessa poked at the ground with her umbrella, trying to process what she'd seen. The umbrella's spike brushed the bubble, and it fizzled out with a spark and a quiet pop.

The boy dropped to his knees with a groan.

"You've got to stop throwing off my transport," he said, gasping slightly.

"I'm not doing anything," Tessa protested, keeping her voice low in case any other Jurassic creatures were nearby.

Flopping onto his back in the leaf litter, Owain draped a hand across his eyes. After a minute or two, his breathing returned to normal.

"Really," Tessa tried again. "I didn't believe in magic until about forty minutes ago. How could I be messing up your transport spell?"

He raised his arm and looked at her critically. "The mere fact that you consider it 'magic' is probably enough to throw it off."

Tessa raised her hands helplessly, and then jumped when the umbrella let off another spark. "What else could it be? As far as I'm concerned, I'm either having a really weird dream, or I just got kidnapped by the world's youngest wizard." She paused for a moment. "Did you run away from Hogwarts?"

Owain sat up quickly. "You believe that drivel?" he scoffed.

She rolled her eyes. "Not before tonight I didn't. How else do I explain you? Unless you're Legolas's kid brother?"

He scowled and muttered, "Tolkien didn't get it right, either." On a sudden impulse, Tessa reached over and flicked the curls away from one of his ears. He scrambled back, but not before she had seen the graceful, upswept curve of ear that culminated in a perfect point.

"You're an elf?" she said, and her voice came out in a squeak.

"Fae is the proper term," he said haughtily, "but I prefer 'elf' to the other one." He wrinkled his nose in scorn. "None of my people has *wings*."

He said this with such loathing that Tessa immediately guessed the word he meant. "Fairy?" she said, with just a hint of malicious glee. It had been a rough night, and the impulse to tease was irresistible.

"If you expect my help to return home," he said with his nose in the air, "then you will never use that word in my presence again."

"Ohhhh," Tessa said, "so I'm not on my own? Why would you help a *loser* like me?"

He shifted uncomfortably, suddenly looking younger than before, but said nothing.

"How old are you, anyway? 200? 300? Do you get an extra-long childhood?"

Crossing his arms over his chest, Owain straightened. "I'm fourteen."

Tessa rapidly revised the image she'd been forming in her brain. Older than he looked, then, but still basically a child. She sighed, then said, "How can I help? *Can* I help?"

Owain scowled at her for a moment, but then gave it up with a world-weary shrug. "You can scarcely make it worse. I need to find more transfer, and then I'll try another transport. I need you to contain your essence or you'll throw off the trace again."

Feeling her eyes glazing over, Tessa shook her head. "I'm sorry; what?"

With an expressive eye roll and a heartfelt sigh, he tried again with exaggerated patience. "I need to find more *magic* to move us away from the scary forest full of monsters, so I need you to not think about *anything* while I'm working the 'spell.'" He said this last with air quotes as sarcastic as any of Tessa's middle schoolers.

She closed her eyes and took a deep breath in through her nose, then let it out slowly. Fixing a smile on her face, she said, "Where can we find more transfer?"

"There's another pool nearby," he said, climbing to his feet and dusting off his back. "Practice turning off your brain while we walk."

With an eye roll of her own, Tessa climbed to her feet and followed after.

A few minutes' walk brought them to a small clearing but nothing that she recognized as a pool. Regardless, Owain came to a halt and started gathering the blue light in his hands again. Tessa put her hand on his shoulder and tried to turn off her thoughts, a difficult task under normal circumstances, but even more so after the events of the last hour. To make matters worse, her stomach was growling. That made her think of the *T. rex,* which in turn made her wonder about other animals who might want to eat them.

At that moment, the world flipped, and they found themselves standing on a barren, rocky plain edged in the distance with low, brown mountains.

Spinning in a quick circle, Tessa spotted something in the air—a large, long-necked *something* that was heading in their direction.

Owain was gazing at it with a look of resignation.

"I'm almost afraid to ask, but were you by any chance thinking of *dragons* while we transported here?"

Tessa bit her lip and looked at the approaching creature. "Maybe?"

Cradling his head in his hands, he groaned, then pushed his hair back. "Alright. Don't say anything, don't do anything, and for pity's sake, don't *promise* it anything."

The dragon was nearing as he spoke, and Tessa could make out the individual features. She was simultaneously terrified and thrilled, which must have shown on her face, because Owain added, "Just turn your brain off as much as possible. Dragons are low-level telepaths."

Tessa blinked and once more tried to calm her turbulent thoughts. It helped that most of those thoughts were along the lines of *Oh my goodness, a DRAGON! An actual dragon, actually in front of me!* She ignored those, and tried to silence the rest of them to a low murmur.

With a blast of hot air and dust kicked up from his wings, the dragon landed on the ground in front of them. He was enormous, and Tessa found herself craning her neck back trying to take him in all at once. His skin was smooth and scaly, a deep red around his head and trailing down his spine, then fading to a rich, pumpkin orange on his belly and clawed feet. He tucked his wings back and turned a large, slightly protuberant eye first on Owain and then on Tessa.

He's gorgeous, she thought, running her gaze the length of his body and back.

The dragon's mouth pulled back in what might have been a grin, and Tessa felt a wave of amusement wash over her. She shrank back, startled.

Greetings, younglings, a voice boomed in Tessa's head.

Owain swept a bow and flapped a hand at Tessa behind his back. Unsure what to do, she bobbed her head and smiled weakly.

"Our greetings to you, Elder," Owain said, scowling at Tessa from the corner of his eye. She chose to ignore this and returned her gaze to the heretofore mythical creature crouched in front of her.

What brings you to this fair realm?

Owain answered something about traces and an escape, but she wasn't really listening. She was too busy wondering if the dragon's skin would be rough to the touch, like the bearded dragon in her classroom, or if it would be smooth and silky, like a python.

The dragon's nearest eye glinted at her, and then he stretched his head around and rubbed it against the spiny ridge on his back, preening.

Tessa intercepted another fiery scowl from Owain and a mouthed, "Stop that!" She shrugged helplessly.

"We don't mean to bother you, Elder; as soon as I can gather more transfer we'll be on our way."

Unfortunately, the nearest source of transfer is about a day's hike in that direction. He swung his nose to his left, indicating the barren desert with the mountains beyond.

Owain sighed. "Thank you. We'll start walking."

He turned to go, and Tessa reluctantly moved to follow when the dragon held up a clawed finger.

I could take you there for a very small price.

Stiffening, Owain paused. Without turning back, he said, "No, thank you; we'll be fine."

Tessa, thinking ahead to the unpleasant walk, said, "What price?"

Owain interrupted swiftly. "We're not interested." He followed this up with a furious glare at Tessa, which she missed because she was caught in the dragon's gaze.

Just a small promise, he said, staring at her intently. ***And it's not even one you have to make.*** **I** ***will promise you.***

"Seems fair," Tessa said cautiously. Owain had given up trying to be discreet and merely clapped a hand to his forehead.

Then we have an accord, the dragon said, and without pausing to acknowledge Tessa's indignant squeak of protest, he swept up both of them in his clawed hands and leapt into the sky with a rush of wings.

Dragonflight was a novel experience for Tessa, and, she had to admit, one that was much more comfortable than Owain's transports. And that was even taking into account the umbrella that was currently digging into her ribcage, and the fact that she'd kissed her slippers goodbye about thirty seconds into the air. The view was spectacular, though it was nothing but rocky desert, and when she tired of that, she could always turn her gaze up to the dragon and marvel at the fact that she was flying through the air, being carried by a *dragon*. She studiously ignored Owain, who had apparently resigned himself and now seemed to be sulking.

About half an hour's flight brought them to a small oasis in the desert. The dragon landed gently and placed them on the ground with special care. Tessa still stumbled slightly, mostly from the lightheaded thrill of the flight. Owain brushed himself off, and stood haughtily.

As promised, the dragon said, ***transfer enough for a journey wherever you like, in exchange for one promise.***

"I didn't actually agree to your terms," Tessa said, a bit nervous now.

The dragon's mouth pulled back in what was definitely a smile. ***Hold out the weather guard you carry.***

Tessa looked down, confused, and remembered the umbrella. She held this up now, and the dragon carefully placed one heavy claw on it. It was so large it stretched the full length of the umbrella. His skin was warm and smooth to the touch, much more like snake skin than lizard.

A promise for you, he said with a solemnity that was at odds with his grin, ***I will see you again.*** At his words, a rush of blue gathered around the umbrella and pricked at Tessa's fingers. The glow faded, and Tessa was once more left with an inert umbrella.

"A boon, Elder," Owain said with equal solemnity. Tessa had the impression that the words were part of a formula she was unfamiliar with.

Ask.

"This human keeps throwing off my transport. If we cannot transport in safety, she will not survive long enough to fulfill your promise."

Tessa stood staring. Was Owain actually worried about her? She shook her head. It was much more likely that he was worried she'd get *him* killed instead.

At a gesture from the dragon, another faint swirl of blue coalesced above the umbrella before sinking into it and vanishing.

I have laid a geas of finding and returning on it. You will not be led astray, and* you*, human, will not misplace my promise.

That had a slightly ominous ring to it, but Tessa couldn't do much about it at this point.

With a final farewell, the dragon lifted into the air once more and quickly vanished from sight.

Owain sighed. "Fool," he said, but without much heat. "I told you not to promise him anything."

"What exactly did I promise?" Tessa asked, still gazing at the umbrella.

"That he'll see you again. Essentially, he can call you here whenever he wants, and keep you indefinitely." He said this matter-of-factly, as though it wasn't such bad thing.

Tessa felt her stomach drop to her feet, but at the same time couldn't deny the swirl of excitement that said, *I'll get to see the dragon again!*

"Too late now," Owain said, his hands glowing blue. Tessa placed a hand on his shoulder and the world turned inside out.

Tessa opened her eyes cautiously, unsure of what to expect, and was pleasantly surprised. No dragons, dinosaurs, or other obviously dangerous creatures were in sight. In fact, the only thing in sight was a vast meadow of pale blue flowers that were, if she were not mistaken, singing.

"Finally," Owain sighed, gazing around with faint satisfaction.

"I didn't throw off the transport this time?"

"No, we're right where I meant us to be."

"Why are the flowers singing?"

"Because they're singing flowers," he said, in a tone of voice that clearly said, "Duh."

Tessa nodded. Of course. Singing flowers sang, obviously.

"What exactly is this trace you're following?"

Owain sighed long-sufferingly. "Weren't you listening? One of our shifters escaped and managed to transport into the Realms. I'm trying to find it and get it home before"—here, he blushed, then continued—"before my father finds out that it's gone."

"Ahh," Tessa said. His pet had gotten out, and he'd get in trouble if he didn't find it. That was normal enough to understand. "Okay, what are the Realms?"

With another exaggerated sigh, Owain explained, "The Realms are what's left of the various worlds after the Cataclysm. They're no longer fully independent worlds like yours, but rather bits and pieces of worlds that exist apart from each other."

She furrowed her brow in concentration. "Sort of like shards of glass after you break a window?"

He shrugged. "More like shards of a mirror, because sometimes all that's left is a reflection of what used to be. The shards are all still fundamentally connected, however, and we can transport from the broken edges."

"Right, using transfer," Tessa said, mentally substituting the word 'magic.'

"Right."

"So, this shifter that escaped. Can it use ma—I mean, transfer?"

Owain scowled, though for once Tessa didn't think it was aimed at her. "Not exactly. Part of its nature allows it to move from one Realm to another as easily as you or I breathe. But it's been tagged, and that's the trace I've been trying to follow. But it's got quite a head start on us. It's already moved on." His hands glowed blue, and Tessa hurried to grab his shoulder before they transported again.

This time they were on a beach, but the sands were pink and the skies lavender. Owain stood, head tilted back and apparently listening intently.

Tessa listened for a moment, but heard nothing beyond the breakers on the shore. Gazing at the ground, she dug in the sand with one toe. The beach was littered with fragments of fantastical shells in a rainbow of colors. She picked one of these up and rubbed her thumb over the smooth, iridescent inner surface. It glistened in the sunlight, and she slipped it into the pocket of her hoodie. Her hand encountered the smooth plastic covering of a granola bar, and her stomach grumbled on cue. Owain hadn't moved, so she pulled the wrapper back and enjoyed the novelty of a late breakfast on the beach. She just wished she had some water to wash it down with.

"Do you want any?" she asked, holding out a portion of the bar.

He blinked, startled. "No, I'm fine. I'll eat when I return home."

Tessa tore off another chunk of chocolate and peanut butter and asked stickily, "Where is home? One of the Realms?"

Owain shrugged. "Based on your earlier metaphor, if the Realms are the broken windows, my home is the house that contains them. It is nearly whole—and is more complete than any of the Realms we travel to."

She mulled that over for a minute.

"So, what was the Cataclysm?"

He lifted one shoulder and returned to his listening pose. "It happened before I was born. You'd have to ask my father, but I wouldn't recommend it. He's a little touchy on that subject."

There was nothing more to be got out of him, so Tessa pulled her socks off and started walking down the beach, enjoying the feel of sand between her toes. She couldn't actually remember the last time she'd been to a beach. The water was perfectly clear and cool, and she dabbled her toes in it happily. Pausing just long enough to cuff up her pants, she waded out further and let the retreating tide pull the sand from under her feet as she wiggled her toes deeper. She stood in blissful silence for a while until a shout broke her from her reverie.

"Idiot!" she heard, and looked around. Tendrils of seaweed had wrapped themselves around her ankles and tugged insistently as the waves withdrew.

"Get out of the water!" Owain said, this time with a note of fear in his voice.

Tessa lifted one foot, but the seaweed trailed tenaciously and sucked her foot back down. With a suddenness that caught her off-guard, the seaweed tightened and yanked her feet out from under her. Arms flailing, she felt one hand caught in the transfer-tingling grip of Owain, who spoke through gritted teeth.

"Use the umbrella!"

With her free hand, she swung the umbrella at her feet. She knew it wasn't long enough to reach, but somehow she managed to brush one ankle with the tip. Blue sparked into the seaweed, and it released her with an inhuman shriek. Using that foot to help brace her, she managed to stab at the other. The seaweed withdrew, and Tessa could have sworn she saw a dark head peering at her with two large, luminous eyes from out in the surf.

"Help me," Owain said, tugging at her arm.

Tessa shook her head, and the creature in the sea was gone, if it'd ever been there. She rolled to her feet and managed to climb back above the water line on shaky knees. Owain still had her hand in his blue-glowing grip, and was staring out to sea with an intent look on his face.

Bending over to inspect her legs, Tessa discovered raw, red welts around both ankles. They stung like burns, and she hissed in pain.

Owain looked down at her. "I should have warned you about the undines. Sorry."

She felt her mouth drop open in shock. Had he really just apologized? He was destroying his surly-teenager image that she'd been building in her mind since they'd met.

"Did you find any sign of your shifter?" she asked, a conversational olive branch.

"It's here, I think, but not nearby." He hesitated. "Actually, I think it's out in the water."

"In the water?"

"Yeah."

"With the undines?"

A sigh. "Yeah."

Tessa was silent for a moment, contemplating that eerie face she'd seen. "Do you have any sort of plan?"

"Yeah. But you're not going to like it." With that, he tugged her to her feet, and pulled her back into the breaking surf.

"Wait," she said, stumbling after him, shocked at the strength of his arm. He was the size of a ten year old, but she was being dragged willy-nilly.

As soon as her feet struck the water, the seaweed was back with a vengeance. With a suddenness that took her breath away, they were both whisked off their feet and sucked under the waves.

Tessa expected to drown and, for the first couple of moments, was sure she was going to. A small hand clapped across her mouth, leaving a sticky film across her mouth and nose. She gasped in panic, but found herself breathing normally. Panic subsiding, she looked around and made out Owain next to her, still holding her hand tightly. He pointed to her face and gave her a thumbs-up, which she returned. She now turned her attention to where they were being dragged.

She was half-expecting an underwater palace like something out of Disney, but what met her gaze first was the literal tail end of the undine. She was vaguely mermaid shaped, but much less human on the front half. She was more or less human shaped, but covered from neck to tail in shimmering scales and strangely elongated in her proportions. The tendrils of seaweed extended from Tessa's ankles to the undine's hands. Owain's feet were likewise entangled.

Beyond the undine, Tessa could see that they were rapidly approaching what looked like a giant, opaque bubble. Her perspective shifted as they approached, and she realized it was even bigger than she'd thought. As they reached the edge of the bubble, it extended in all directions for as far as she could see. The undine vanished, moving through the surface of the bubble with a faint sucking sound, and then Tessa's feet hit the surface. She gripped Owain's hand even tighter and held her breath as they passed through the membrane.

Here on the other side of the bubble was the Disney landscape she'd imagined, though it was more like an ocean-themed Rivendell than a home for singing crustaceans. They were no longer swimming, but drifting gently toward the ground. The undine's tail split and left her with two human-looking legs and a long dress that rippled in the shifting light. She touched down first, barely seeming to notice the transition, and gave a sharp tug on the seaweed. Tessa's landing was not as gentle, and she tumbled to the ground, scraping her hands on the sandy surface. There was air here, though it felt thick and viscous. She noticed that Owain left his faintly glowing breath mask in place, and she did the same.

The undine opened her mouth, revealing pointed teeth in black gums, and screeched. The sound must have contained words, because Owain shrugged and gestured toward the largest building in sight. The undine screeched again and yanked on the seaweed, causing Tessa to stumble before she managed to match pace with the undine. Looking at Owain out of the corner of her eye, she held up her umbrella and raised her eyebrows in mute question.

He gave a slight shake of his head, and they followed the undine. Tessa resigned herself to whatever would happen next.

The undine led them through a shell-encrusted archway and into an open courtyard. Strange, feathery trees undulated in an unfelt breeze, and Tessa could see other creatures like the undine at work in the gardens and strolling down the pearly paths. Most stopped and stared in openmouthed shock as they passed. A few hurried away. One, a large male clad in skintight, leathery material that reminded Tessa of an eel, reached out a hand as they passed. Tessa shied away from his touch, but stumbled over the seaweed ropes and fell again on her bruised palms.

Owain opened his mouth for the first time since landing and shrieked at their captor in the same voice she'd used. She paused, glanced back, then advanced on the undine and delivered a stinging slap to his face. He flinched, bobbed an apologetic bow, and retreated. The undine met Owain's eyes briefly, then moved forward again. Tessa scrambled back to her feet, careful not to bump the seaweed with her umbrella, and followed after.

They reached the building proper and were ushered in by two armored guards carrying spears that looked like they might have been made from narwhal horns. Tessa wished for more time to examine them but was forced to stumble after the undine and Owain. They walked down several halls before emerging in a long, vaulted hall that screamed 'throne room' to Tessa. She looked for and found the raised dais at one end, and with some trepidation, she eyed the figure seated there. It was another male, this one clad in pale, spotted fur with a golden circlet on his black hair. He was leaning on the arm of the throne, his head resting on one hand, but straightened at their approach.

The female undine screeched again, and Tessa winced, wondering if everyone here spoke in this fashion.

The king, if that's what he was, waved her to silence and considered Tessa and Owain for a moment.

"Trespassers," he finally stated, and Tessa breathed a faint sigh of relief even as new worries sprang to mind.

"Visitors," Owain countered.

"Thieves," the king returned.

"Kidnappers."

The king's lip pulled up in a sneer. "Children."

"Protected," Owain shot back, and Tessa wondered if she'd imagined the sudden tension in the king's shoulders.

The undine shrieked, interrupting the conversation, and the king responded in the same tone.

"Liars," the king said finally.

Owain shrugged. "Test it."

Tessa felt like she was watching a tennis match and wasn't sure who was currently winning. The king was tense, but Owain, for all his nonchalance, was fiddling with his fingers in a way that suggested nerves. She wished, not for the first time, that she had some context for what was going on. That they were captives of the sea king was obvious; what that meant for their immediate future was less so. She was fairly certain the umbrella would be equally effective on the seaweed the second time around, but that would leave the two of them in the king's castle surrounded by his guards. And somewhere nearby, if Owain was correct, was the shifter. Tessa wondered what it looked like and if she'd know it when she saw it.

The king studied them a moment longer, then slumped back on his throne. "Trial."

Owain's shoulders tensed for a moment, then relaxed. He nodded once. "Begin."

Smiling faintly, the king shook his head. "Human."

Owain looked at Tessa in alarm, and she felt her stomach drop. "What?" She would have said more, but was caught up in the single word exchange and couldn't quite manage anything further.

With a flick of her wrist, the undine snapped back the seaweed that encircled Tessa's ankles. Tessa hissed in pain as the tender flesh was exposed to the air, but gripped the umbrella tighter in nervous anticipation. What kind of trial did the king have in mind?

"Weapon?" Owain demanded.

The king shook his head, and motioned for Tessa to drop her umbrella.

Reluctant to comply and unsure if she'd even be able to release it, she bent down and placed it on the ground. It was inert and laid there quietly. The king shrieked once, and a set of double doors on the side of the hall burst open to allow several guards to enter. Each one held two seaweed ropes attached to the creature in their midst. It was as long as a station wagon, and vaguely amphibian in shape. Its front half was loosely frog-like, but the back end was more nearly similar to a cricket or a grasshopper. It was too ugly to be terrifying, and Tessa noticed that Owain had stiffened at its appearance. The sudden thought occurred that this creature might be the shifter. If that were true, what should she do?

Glancing at Owain, she bobbed her head in the creature's direction and raised a questioning brow. He grabbed his wrist and mimed holding on no matter how hard he tugged. The undine noticed what he was doing and yanked on the seaweed, knocking him to the ground.

"Hey!" Tessa shouted, and started toward her. Before she'd gone two steps, a shout from one of the guards distracted her, and she realized with horror that the frog-creature was loose and heading right for her.

Grab on, Owain had said. And don't let go. That was easier said than done. Where to grab it? She dodged the creature's initial lumbering attack and sprinted past it. As it shuffled around to face her again, she scanned it, looking for a place to grab that would let her avoid legs and any possible teeth or tongue. The back would be safest, she decided, and launched herself between the two muscular rear legs. The creature shuddered under her, and she quickly buried her hands in the slimy folds of skin at his neck and held on.

Barely leaving her time to blink, the creature dissolved in her hands and left her holding a large, fluffy rabbit. She nearly dropped it in shock and it took advantage of her distraction to sink its teeth into the web of flesh by her thumb. She shouted in pain, but tightened her hold just in time for the rabbit to vanish and leave a snarling wolf behind. Tessa managed to hold the wolf at arm's length, then had to contend with a flapping of wings as a raven tried valiantly to free itself. She barely managed to keep a hand around the neck as it proceeded to turn in quick succession into a snake, a goat, a frog (a normal one, this time) and finally a sleek, black horse.

The horse nudged Tessa with its nose and rubbed his head against her shoulder even as Owain shouted, "YES!" from somewhere behind her. Tessa reached up to rub the horse's forehead and found that she was once more holding the umbrella. The horse tossed its mane, and seemed to invite Tessa to climb on its back. Though leery of the strange creatures she'd encountered so far in the most eventful day of her life, Tessa nevertheless couldn't resist the temptation to ride the beautiful horse. Gathering up a handful of mane, she pulled herself up, swinging a leg over and straightening up before finally looking around the otherwise silent throne room.

The king was glaring from his throne, but otherwise made no move to stop her. The guards had all withdrawn to the perimeter of the hall and stood watching silently. The undine still holding Owain's restraints opened her mouth, but closed it again without making a sound.

Tessa wasn't quite sure what she'd done, but it was obvious she'd won whatever it was. Nudging the horse with her heel, she walked it over to where Owain was standing with a smug grin on his face. She pointed the umbrella at the seaweed, and was gratified when a spark of blue jumped out, causing the bonds to withdraw. She pulled Owain up behind her with one easy move, then turned the horse out of the throne room.

Once in the halls, the horse picked up speed with no direction from Tessa, but since it seemed to know where it was going she let it run. By the time they reached the courtyard they were at nearly a full gallop.

"Does this horse know where it's going?" She yelled over her shoulder.

"Not a horse. But yes, he should be able to get us out of here easily," Owain called back. The heaviness of the air swallowed up their words, and Tessa was having difficulty catching her breath. She bent further over the horse's neck and simply hung on.

They approached the boundary of the bubble, and Tessa prepared for the transition back to the water. Instead, the stomach-churning feeling of a transport swept over her, and she felt herself falling.

She didn't black out, but things definitely went a little hazy for a few seconds. There was a confusing babble of voices—not just Owain's but other, deeper voices punctuated with a softer, feminine tone. There was a set of strong arms holding her; she was fairly certain they'd caught her in her tumble off the horse. The horse was nearby; she could hear its hooves striking the ground and the huff of its breath. Vision and coherence returned abruptly, and she found herself in another castle courtyard surrounded by tall, willowy, adult versions of Owain.

Elves, she thought with only slightly hysterical glee. A voice jerked her gaze upwards, and she immediately blushed under the close scrutiny of one of the fair folk.

"Are you all right?" he asked again, this time with a note of concern in his voice.

"I'm fine," she managed to say past her embarrassment. "You can put me down."

The elf's face split in a grin. "You lack shoes. It would be discourteous to put you down here in the stable yard."

Tessa bit her lip and gave herself up for lost. She was spared any further embarrassment by a sudden commotion.

The small crowd of elves split as another male approached, this one wearing a silver circlet of intertwining leaves.

She spotted Owain in the crowd and was surprised to see him wilt slightly under the stern gaze of the newcomer.

"Father," he said, and Tessa suddenly understood.

"Prince Owain," he returned. "Explain yourself, please."

Owain launched into a slightly expurgated version of his adventures. Tessa was a little surprised how much he'd been through before his arrival in her home. Apparently the chocolate syrup was to appease a pixie, the culprit of the broken kitchen window. Tessa wondered what pixies were, and how they compared in terms of nuisance with the various other creatures they'd encountered after she joined him. She rather thought the *T. rex* probably won.

Owain was describing her final challenge with the shifter, and for the first time Owain's father lifted his gaze to Tessa.

She blushed again under the scrutiny. When he approached her and kissed her hand, she nearly died of embarrassment. "It was nothing, really," she protested.

"You are too modest," he said. "You have quite probably saved my foolish son's life on at least two occasions today. That is not nothing. Furthermore, you have gotten trapped in a promise to a creature of the Realms as a result of your assistance. We owe you a great debt."

Tessa could find no words in response. She was fairly sure that everyone was making too big of a deal about the promise with a dragon, and she was very sure that Owain had exaggerated her help in the course of the day. She'd put him in danger at least as often as she'd helped him, but she couldn't quite find the words to explain this in the face of the king's gratitude. And there was another shocker—she'd been running around with a prince of the Fae all day and hadn't known it. She merely shrugged helplessly.

"Come," the king said. "You need food and healing, and then we will send you home."

Tessa was suddenly aware of her various aches and pains, and the fact that she was desperately thirsty. She managed "Thank you." The king inclined his head in reply.

With a great clamor, the group dispersed. Someone led the horse away, and the sole female grabbed Owain by the shoulders and directed him inside. The elf who had Tessa in his arms carried her inside and down a maze of hallways before depositing her in the care of a healer. He stayed and watched, lounging against the doorjamb with the umbrella tucked under his arm.

The healer introduced herself as Sol, then proceeded to bathe and bandage the welts on her ankles as well as the puncture on her hand. She tsked at the latter.

"Is it serious?" Tessa asked, wondering if you could get rabies from a shape-shifting rabbit.

Sol shook her head and dabbed an ointment on the bite marks. "Pooka's bites are rarely dangerous; I'm just concerned that it is so deep. I've cleaned it, and if Farin will lend me his aid, we'll add a bit of healing as well."

The elf in the doorway straightened up and walked over. "What do you need?"

"Just a slight touch to speed the healing," Sol said. She smiled at Tessa. "I'd take care of it myself, but I always seem to overdo it. Farin has a lighter touch."

Tessa glanced up at Farin, who smiled beautifully down at her and took her injured hand in his own. "You might want to put the umbrella down first," she cautioned, guessing that more transfer was going to be involved. "It sometimes reacts with transfer."

Farin looked briefly surprised, but he set the umbrella down before gathering blue in his free hand. He placed this over her injured hand and Tessa felt the cool tingling of the transfer settle over her aching hand, leaving a delightful coolness behind.

"Thank you," she said.

"Nicely done," Sol added. "I'm all finished with her."

Tessa stood up quickly as Farin moved toward her, afraid that he was going to pick her up again. He merely picked up the umbrella and offered her his arm in a courtly fashion. He then led her to a smaller courtyard that contained a covered gazebo and a table spread with a variety of dishes that Tessa had never seen before. She went first for the tall, silver cup that was glistening with condensation. It wasn't water, but it was something that was like a cross between apple juice and lemonade. It was heaven. Farin grinned at her and poured another glass.

A few minutes later, Owain appeared, freshly washed and in clean clothes. He also wore a silver circlet that was a simpler version of his father's. He joined her at the table and tore into the food with great gusto. Tessa chuckled at him and ate at a much slower pace.

Midway through the meal, a sleek, black cat crept into the garden and twined itself around Tessa's feet. Its purrs could be felt through the chair, and Tessa bent over and scooped him into her lap.

"He likes you," Farin said in surprise, backing up a step.

"Does he usually not like people?" Tessa asked, astonished. The cat had put his paws on her chest and was bumping her under her chin with his nose. She petted him absentmindedly, and he leaned into her hands and batted at her when she stopped. It was the friendliest cat she'd ever met.

"Pooka doesn't like much of anyone," Owain stated between bites, not even bothering to look her way.

She looked down in shock. This was the same creature she'd battled in the undine's home? The cat-shaped creature redoubled his purring.

"Although," Owain said, pausing thoughtfully with a loaded fork halfway to his mouth, "he might smell the dragon on you."

"Pooka likes dragons?"

Farin smiled crookedly. "As much as he likes anyone. Though I've never seen a reaction quite this strong before." He unhooked the umbrella from his elbow where it had been hanging. "Do you mind if I examine this?"

Tessa shrugged. "Go ahead."

After a moment of concentration, Farin's hands glowed blue, and he wrapped them around the umbrella. He stood with his eyes closed for several minutes before opening his eyes with a faint grunt.

"It's not as bad as we feared," he said.

Tessa was munching on what she'd mentally tagged *lembas*, though it wasn't nearly as filling as Tolkien's counterpart, and looked up with interest.

"The dragon's promise that he extracted from you," Farin clarified. "It's simply that you must return at some point in the next ten years and fulfill whatever task he sets for you. It has limits, however, about life endangerment and contract length. If it becomes life threatening, you're released; if the task takes longer than a month, you're released."

"Oh," Tessa said, processing and continuing to rub Pooka's ears. "So, sometime in the next ten years the dragon is going to ask me to fulfill a task, but if it threatens to kill me or takes longer than a month, I'm off the hook?"

"Essentially."

"He got all that in one umbrella?"

Owain snorted and Farin gave a slightly pained look. "It was in the shape of the transfer he laid on the object, yes."

Tessa eyed him and mentally translated, *those were the conditions built into the spell he put on the umbrella*. She nodded. "Got it. Now, not to be a bother, but I was supposed to be at a meeting about, well, a lifetime ago, and I have to teach school tomorrow, so would it be possible to get transport home?"

Farin bowed. "I would be happy to escort you."

Owain gave a half wave from where he was still shoveling food in his mouth. "Later," he said.

Tessa rolled her eyes and stood up, gently displacing the cat. He meowed in protest, standing on the arm of the chair as she walked away.

Farin handed her the umbrella, then offered his arm once more. His hands glowed blue, and with a plunge that upset Tessa's full stomach, they were suddenly back in her house. It was daylight, and a cold draft moved down the hall reminding her that she had a broken window to contend with.

She looked up at Farin. "How is transfer at fixing windows? A pixie apparently broke mine."

Farin laughed, a surprisingly hearty laugh for someone who was otherwise so elegant, and bowed. "Lead the way. I'll see what I can do."

Five minute's work left her with a window as good as new, after which Farin bade her adieu and vanished with a good-natured wave. She was left alone and had the strange impression that perhaps it had all been a dream. Except her ankles were still wrapped in bandages, as well as her hand. She looked at this for a moment, then shoved her hands into her pockets where she encountered the empty granola wrapper and something cool and smooth. She withdrew this in surprise and saw the shell she'd picked up on the pink beach.

Tessa clutched it tightly in her fingers and pressed it to her lips. It was good that she'd returned when she had; it would have been too tempting to ask to stay. She replaced the shell with a sigh then ventured into the hallway. The umbrella was back in the stand by the coat tree, but when she thought about it, it leapt with alacrity to her hand. She fingered it thoughtfully and returned it to its place, then returned to the kitchen. Here was evidence enough; the bottle of chocolate syrup lay on its side in a pool of sticky, congealed goo that had cemented the various food wrappers to the floor. Tessa sighed. At least the broken glass was gone. She pried the bottle off the floor and dropped it into the sink with a grimace of disgust before setting about to clean up the mess.

Scrubbing at the stain and wondering if she could go to work tomorrow as though nothing had changed, Tessa sighed.

Fairyland is not for you, she told herself fiercely. But tears that wanted to deny this pricked at her eyes.

And then from a fold in the air, a smooth, black form stepped into her kitchen and meowed piteously at her.

Barefoot and bandaged, in salt-stained pajamas with chocolate-saturated paper towels in both hands, Tessa sat on the floor and laughed. Maybe Fairyland wasn't for her, but apparently it wasn't done with her yet.

ABOUT THE AUTHOR

M.C. Dwyer grew up in a small town in Nebraska, has circumnavigated the globe at least once, and ended up back in Nebraska. She has been a student, a librarian, a store clerk, a teacher, a student again, and an occasional world traveler. Some day she might figure out what she wants to be when she grows up, but she isn't holding her breath. She enjoys binge-watching kdrama, learning new languages, and creating new fantasy worlds to escape into. M.C.'s debut novel Bleddynwood *was published in 2018. She is the author of the short stories "Of Grief and Griffins" in the anthology* Still Waters *and "Don't Wake the Dragon" in the anthology* Fell Beasts and Fair.

The Irrigation Ditch

B. Morris Allen

She'd shifted a cottage-weight of stone, lifted uncounted shovelfuls of soil, dug her way with mattock and sweat and bruised fingers. Before her, beneath her, all she had was a hole. The same as when she'd lifted that first shovel load, the same as she'd have after countless more.

She leaned over, let the sweat run slowly from her forehead to the tip of her nose, to gather there, in a swelling, glittering bulge just out of focus, until it fell at last into the hole and was lost in the dirt, became part of it. *Salting the fields*, she thought, though it was a hole, not a field, and not much of a hole. Forearm deep, about as broad, it wavered ambiguously across the hillside, dropping here to avoid a boulder, there to curve around a tree, turning on itself from time to time like a snake slowly undulating down the slope.

"Ditch," she said, when she had her breath back. "You're a ditch." A hole was just an empty space, a place where something wasn't. Bigger or smaller, it stayed the same, of no fixed dimension, but essentially negative. A ditch, now, had purpose, definition. A beginning and end.

She looked down the hill, to where the land flattened out, and trees clustered close to a cozy stone-weight of cottage, a round-cornered pile of shale and mud, with square-ish gaps for windows and a cheery little chimney at the far end. Inside, she knew, Rewk would be making jam or pickling carrots, or whatever it was the season for. Whatever it would be the season to eat, when winter fell heavy, and the windows wore wooden shutters laced snug with ice, and they sat by the fire under a warm blanket. The ditch began there, in Rewk's kitchen garden, with its ordered plots and raised beds and mysterious frilly greens, some sharp, some bitter, some crisp, like Rewk himself.

The ditch began down there, in Rewk's aching back and swollen joints and stolid silence. The channel would end there, once she had it dug, would peter out into little rills that stretched thin, wriggling fingers across the garden and laughed in the face of the well and its ever-deeper water, its ever-longer rope. But only if she got it dug.

She looked up the slope, stretching her back to straighten cramped muscles. She was about halfway, she thought. Halfway to the top, to the little cwm and its lake, to cool, clear water that filled the little hillside depression and trickled slowly out in just the wrong place.

Halfway, not partway. Halfway was a marker, a symbol, a turning point. At halfway, most of the work was done, the decision was made, the effort committed. At halfway, you had something. Not just a hole, but a ditch. You had a thing that came into being, once you called it by its name.

"Names are important," Rewk would say. "This is mustard, this is collard, this is kale. They're not just leafy green things." Though they were all leafy and green, and they all looked similar until he put them in his pans and turned them by magic into food.

She would smile and nod and let his magic melt down her throat while she talked about digging and channels and how important it was to irrigate the orchard that she hadn't planted, and how lake water was purer than well water, and how of course it wasn't just for his little garden, and wouldn't *that* be waste of time and effort.

Ends were the opposite of holes. A hole was a hole as soon as you started. An end was an end only when you stopped. Names were tricky that way; they had rules, and if you didn't play by the rules, you got something else entirely, no matter what you called it. The rules right now, she admitted, called for more digging.

He worked by the window, where the light was fair, though it would have been better by the southern doorway to his right, or outside, on the west side of the cottage where the sun angled down through pine trees with a warm, shady light. At the window, he could keep watch on the bubbling stew, and his eyesight was still strong enough to see the quick, sharp stitches he made in one of Derla's shirts.

He could see her past the hemlocks, as she dug her way slowly, tirelessly, up through the hill toward water. Like a mole, coming up from the earth into a sudden and unexpected rainstorm that would leave it drenched, refreshed, victorious.

He wondered, as he watched her, if he should make another token gesture to help, or another, firmer effort to convince her that fruit trees didn't need special irrigation, and that they would in any case be easier to grow on the flat. Then she would say something about grapes, and he would ask what they would do with grapes when neither of them liked wine, and she would mutter about taking wine to market in Hatherton, and it would go on until one of them stomped angry out of the house, or they gave it up and curled warm together like some complex braided bread that never went stale.

He pricked his finger as he watched her, and transferred the injured digit to his mouth until it should stop bleeding and putting Derla's shirt at risk of spots. He sucked on the fingertip, spreading warm saliva around and over it. It felt good on the perennially swollen knuckle. If only his mouth were bigger, he sometimes thought he would spend his whole day with his hands in his mouth like a baby. A pot of warm water might do the same, but how could he work with wet hands? And she would notice. She always noticed.

Already he suspected her of some buried motive for her ditch – a waterwheel, perhaps, or a duckpond. Something helpful and impractical that would tire her and knot her muscles and leave her limp and loving and righteous, until some day, in an argument about grapes, it would come out and he would feel cruel and hard and sorry all at once, and one of them would go off to Hatherton. One day, he suspected, one of them would not come back. Or they would come back, and no one would be home. And what was home without Derla? Just a word, just a place, not a thing, not a warm spot that your heart nestled into without even knowing it was there.

He took his finger out of its damp, warm resting place, and examined it critically. Slick with an old man's slobber, but not bloody. He gave it a tentative squeeze, and it smarted, but no blood flowed. Good enough. Pain was nothing but an ugly name for the scouts your body sent out to look for trouble. As you got older, they reported more and more frequently, until there was a constant stream of them in and out of the command tent. One more would make no difference.

"I'm over halfway," she announced that evening, over a thick stew of barley and lentils and chewy parsnip. Over halfway. It was definite when you said it out loud, irrevocable. You'd staked your claim, made your boast, like an empress asserting rights over land she'd seen through a window. You had to make good, or be forsworn, be shunned as a braggart, deposed in favor of some more modest ruler.

"That's good," he said, and she could see the cogs turning, the careful calculations. "Maybe I can come and help tomorrow."

She turned to her stew, sought quietude in its savor. It must be hard, she thought, to be strong and capable, and yet be overcome by such an insidious enemy as time. There was a pride in strength that she had never seen him display, never known until nature had taken the strength slowly away, leaving nothing but gnarled joints and empty confidence. She rolled her own shoulders, so broad now, so tight with work that he could no longer do, though he was younger by a year or two.

"Yes," she blurted, as the silence lengthened and she looked up to see brown eyes fixed on her. "Yes, come up with lunch." She could see the wince he tried to control, could see the tension in fingers that would never curl around a shovel again. That had never, it seemed to her, been entirely straight, entirely pain-free. "There's a gully there, where the lake overflows when the rain is hard. I was thinking of incorporating it, but I'm not sure how. You could help me decide, with your eye for detail. Maybe draw it for me," to indicate that of course twisted hands were no obstacle, that he could do everything she needed.

"Of course," he said, and reached out to squeeze her hard, rough hand with his smooth, knobbly one. It felt like a sprig of huckleberry – twigs covered with round berries full of juice and color, if only they could get free of their confinement. She lifted it to her lips and took a berry in her mouth to see the light spring up in his eyes. To her surprise, she felt a heat of her own, and they left the stew to itself as they sank onto warm blankets and a slow, easy exploration of this new sun – always bright, always hot, even for a woman who'd felt it many, many times before.

The bread was done, though it had used the last of their ready flour. With a waterwheel, they could do better than the coarse powder he coaxed from his small hand mill. It worked well enough to repay the winter he'd spent filing grooves in the lower stone, the quern, but even the simple rotary motion of the upper stone left his hands cramped and tight. It might have been better, he smiled, had they not been broken, or had they healed better. 'Crooked hands for a crooked man,' they'd said when they broke them, and who was to say they weren't right? One man's crooked was another man's curved, and one man's curved was another man's straight.

He took the loaves from the oven, breathed in their rich, yeasty fragrance. He set two on the counter to cool, wrapped the other in a coarse cloth, and laid it at the top of his little woven pannier. Cold bean salad, hot bread, and there would be fresh water from the lake. He tucked spoons under the light blanket. Derla would deride it as a foolish, townish extravagance, but she liked extravagance, for all her homespun simplicity.

The day was hot, and the pannier rode uncomfortably on his back, but he followed the route of the ditch up the hill, crossing back and forth, back and forth, waving to Derla at the near points, though she pretended not to see him, redoubling her efforts as if some hidden overseer were watching for sloth.

He cut across the last switchback, climbing straight up the hill toward the swing of her heavy mattock. It looked like a little less than halfway, but she had said half, and so it therefore was. He paused to wipe the sweat from his brow, and to admire the muscle across her broad back and still-slender hips.

"Ho there, young laborer. Have you time for a simple provider of provender, or must you toil until nightfall?"

"You got food, I got hunger," she said, setting her mattock on long grass and turning to face him. "And I'll eat *again* at night. That's how we are, out here in the foothills."

"And a fine breed you are," he agreed. "How about that tree over there?" A generous chestnut, it spread its branches wide and green over a flattish area at its base. He took assent for granted, and wandered over to set his pannier down and spread the little blanket wide.

"Oh my goodness," she exclaimed with a cultured voice he rarely heard and had never quite traced. "What a fine establishment you run."

"At your service, my lady." He laid down the spoons, the bowl of salad, and, with a flourish that wafted its scent her way, the fresh-baked bread. "We lack only water." He held up a generous gourd. "If you could..."

"Come with me," she said, herself again. "We can cool off in the lake, and I can show you that gully."

He bowed and tucked the gourd under one arm as she led off up the hill. She was a better engineer than he'd ever been, though less of an artist. Her sketches were all angles and calculations that left his head swimming. His were less accurate, but, she said, more true to life. Since they both knew the question of the gully to be one more of emotion than calculation, he supposed his skills might suffice.

They'd stopped near the crest of the hill to discuss the gully, to breathe, to admire the view. The cottage was a patch of grey stone amongst the green of wood and meadow, and she thought as always that it would have made a fine site for a manor, if only a wealthy merchant had cared to live out here near the mountains and far from culture. And if they had, she would be elsewhere, in another cottage that functioned as her manor, to protect everything she held dear, and keep herself and it from harm.

They climbed the last few steps hand in hand, waiting for the moment when a vista of grass and rock and sky turned suddenly, surprisingly, silver, and then blue, and then clear, and the lake water seemed to vanish entirely, leaving a bed of rocks and algae and ducks floating on little ripples of air until the wind blew, or a duck flew off, and the water was back in a shimmer of grey and green.

They looked out over the mirror-smooth surface of the lake, and the wind blew, and the ducks flew off, and a man rose out of the water.

Rewk spread his arms and stepped in front of her, fists knotted, as if either of them had ever fought, had ever held a weapon more dangerous than the gourd still gripped ludicrously in Rewk's left hand. As if a naked man were a threat, no matter how the water dripped from short hair onto wide shoulders and down over muscle to fall into the lake that even now he made his slow, sure way out of.

He smiled, a confident, knowing smile that sent shivers down her spine, and a chill through her heart. It was the smile of a man who knew what he wanted, and got it. The kind of smile she'd changed her life to avoid.

"What are you doing here?" asked Rewk, always blunt, always focused.

"Is it your lake?" the man asked as he wiped water from hair and chest and arms and reached for a fine grey blouse she saw, now draped over a nearby stone.

"No," Rewk admitted. "You just… surprised us."

"Surprise can be good. Revelatory." Muddy brown eyes caught hers and held them until he bent to pull on smallclothes and trousers.

"Sometimes good, sometimes bad. It doesn't matter what you call it." Rewk argued a point, that, she thought, no one had raised.

"Welcome," she said, stepping forward. "Though, as you point out, the lake isn't ours. Not formally."

"Formalities aren't everything," the man said as he sat on a dry rock to slip on socks and shoes. "If you call it yours, it's yours."

"No one said that," said Rewk sharply, still arguing his own track.

"So long as no one says different," the other added, with a wink at Derla that brought back forgotten nights of torches and stars, lively dinners, intimate dances. "I'm Merro."

She saw Rewk's look of suspicion and something more, and took Merro's outstretched hand in her own. It was hard, strong, dry, and it squeezed her heart with a gentle pressure. "Derla," she managed. *Now, anyway,* and she knew it was a quirking smile and dark eyes that made her think it.

He tipped his head toward Rewk, with a twitch of eyebrow toward Derla to share the joke.

"Rewk," said Rewk. He didn't offer his hand.

"A man of few words, but valuable ones."

Rewk said nothing.

"We were just coming for water," she said, taking the gourd still dangling from Rewk's hand.

"Let me," Merro said, taking the gourd and dipping it elegantly into the lake without getting so much as a finger wet, though his clothes were already damp from wet skin. "Shall we?" And then they were following him back down the hill to a picnic blanket and salad and still-warm bread and fresh fruit from a pack that somehow materialized on Merro's back.

In the morning, Rewk was up before dawn. "Just in case," he told her. She'd invited the stranger to sleep under the eaves, but he'd looked up at the clear blue sky and said the meadow was fine with him. And there he was, a still, dark shape against the lightening sky, with his back against a tree and his legs up on his pack.

"Morning," Rewk said.

"Morning," Merro replied, and said no more.

Rewk grimaced. In the old days, he'd have known how to winkle the stranger's secrets out from under his tongue with just a smile. In the older, darker days, when he'd known how to speak. When had he become so taciturn, so quiet that even a greeting was an effort?

The stranger seemed content to watch the sun lighten the sky beyond the hill, to let the rose-tinged clouds give false light to dark hair. Muscles moved beneath rich skin as he shifted to make space beside the tree without a word.

Rewk sat, slowly, a stride away. "You're far from home," he said at last.

"Am I?"

"Anyone who's here is far from home," Rewk said, knowing that he gave away more of himself than he learned.

"Home is what you make it," the stranger said. "Or what you make of it, perhaps."

"You're a fine one for words." And dangerous for it.

"You've spied that out, have you?"

And there it was – the knife behind the back, and the chill down his spine. Rewk's twisted fingers hurt as he failed to keep them from clutching at the grass.

"What do you want?" He'd already paid the price, paid with pain in past and present and future, paid with memory and absence.

"Little enough," the stranger said, and white teeth gleamed against brown skin. "Just to know you and pass through your lands."

"You know me well enough," and more. "How about you skip straight to passing through?"

Merro chuckled. "We've barely met; I'm sure there's more we can learn about each other." He smiled a smile so full of hunger that Rewk twitched back, remembering the hot feel of hands and breath and muscle against his back.

He swallowed and rose. "You know me enough to know I don't want that."

"Perhaps. Perhaps Derla does." The smile was menacing now.

"Try to find out." If there was one thing Derla had in plenty, it was constancy. "Try, and then leave."

Merro winked and settled back against his tree. "Fair enough. We'll see whether Derla knows herself as well as you do." And though there was a message there as well, Rewk turned his back on it and looked to gardens and stews and things that could be predicted, that were safe, that had no secrets to divulge.

Merro's back was broad and bare, with muscles that stood out against the sun and sweat. He used the mattock like a water wheel, dipping into the ground and out, with a blade full of soil on every steady stroke. He stopped only when she stopped, dripping wet but never tired, never out of breath.

"You're like a machine," she said at last, when she couldn't lift another shovelful, when arms like soft wax refused to rise again. Already in one morning, they'd done more work than she had in two days.

"It's the steam," he said, and turned to wave toward where a mist rose off her wet blouse and faded into nothing. "It drives the pistons that do the work."

"Well, your linkages are certainly well made," she said, and only then wondered whether she had already given herself away.

He winked as if she'd said nothing more than flattery, and made a joke of flexing muscles. "They'd have to be, to keep up with your pace." He dropped the mattock and wiped a hand across his brow and the short, tight ringlets that held beads of sweat to his scalp like pearls. "If this was a test, I concede." As if a fit, youngish man could be bested by an old woman whose only virtue was practice.

"No test. Already you've put me days ahead of schedule, and we've nothing to offer in exchange."

"A chance to rest from wandering, to eat real food, talk with real people. That's not nothing."

"Little enough, if you call this a rest." She nodded toward the slope, and the lake that lay behind it. "Real water, in any case."

He followed her up the hill. "That lake water," he agreed, "finer than the finest Bourgnon vintage..."

"...and just as sweet," she laughed, completing the joke. A joke she'd not heard in years, a joke that relied on an urban view of water as a flat, lifeless commodity rather than a sweet, heavy gift from the mountains.

He climbed past her, walking straight into the cold clear chill of the lake, letting it soak into his thin trousers and plaster them to his skin.

"Your boots will be wet," she said unnecessarily.

He sank slowly into the water up to his neck before turning back toward her to climb out. "I'll stay until they're dry, then. They needed a good cleaning anyway." He stood dripping in front of her, and she noticed for the first time that his brown eyes were level with hers. "Sometimes it's good to wash away the remnants of the past." He set on a rock to pull the boots off, as if his words hadn't struck her to the core and taken away her power of speech. He swished the boots this way and that, canvas and rope and cork floating slowly back and forth while her thoughts raced. "Even a past that's bright and plush."

"Who are you?" she asked, her tongue freed from its chains by a gaze that weighed her up and knew her worth exactly.

"Just a visitor. Just passing through." His dark eyes belied the easy tone, held her pinned to the rocky shoreline that hid a ditch and a slope and a home.

"And will you go back, when you're done passing?" Back to a city, and soft cloth, and groaning tables of every kind of food, and whispers in dark hallways.

"That depends," he said, and set the boots to dry on a warm stone. Water seeped out to leave a dark stain across the stone. "Let's see about that digging, why don't we?"

The ditch was done. The channel, as Derla called it, with the gully incorporated, and water flowing clear and quick from the lake and into his garden. It fed his plants and slipped past them, to collect in a little pond at the edge of the forest. Already, it drew deer and foxes and little glitterbirds that hovered just above the surface, their wings causing ripples that never quite seemed to fade, but never reached the shore.

They'd looked at his drawings, she and Merro, and talked knowledgeably about the rate of flow, and the thrust of water, and how the walls would get slippery and might start to fall. And every now and then they'd turn to him and smile or wink, and say how they couldn't have done it without him. And what exactly had they done?

They were outside now, in the rain. Merro had come in and seen him grinding his slow, painful way through a handful of wheat. He'd taken over without a word, just taking Rewk's old, twisted hands in his warm, strong, straight ones and setting them aside with a look that could have meant anything. He'd had a full bag ground within the hour, and it took that long for Rewk's heart to stop its nervous flutter.

Merro had said nothing at lunch, and yet somehow Derla had seen the bag of flour in their little larder. She'd looked at the stranger's hands, on which no speck of white remained, and looked at Rewk like her heart was breaking.

He'd been sharp with them both throughout the meal, until his acid tongue had driven them out to work in a foggy drizzle, shoulder to shoulder in the gully installing board and batten to guard against slippage. And he was here, warm and dry and alone, with only a bowl of beans to drain and soak and drain again.

It had been easier, in the old days. Then, he'd had clear goals, and a purpose, and a role. The role had been important. He'd clung to it, in the dark times, let *it* define him, rather than the things he did and that were done to him. It had all been the role, not him at all. He'd saved lives. He knew he had. They'd given him a medal, or rather shown it to him and then taken it away – for safety, for secrecy. They'd given him money instead. A lot of money. Gold and silver and pitying looks and kind words. They'd avoided him, in the barracks, in the streets, in the offices of the ministry, let their guilt eat at them until it hurt to see them watch him, to force their eyes to look even as it hurt their souls to do it.

And why not? They'd been the ones to send him. He'd volunteered, yes, along with some of the other boys, when it had been clear they needed boys. Slight ones, smart ones. And they'd picked him, the slightest, the smartest.

"I'm to be a spy," he'd said at last, putting a name to it. And they'd grasped at the straw.

"Yes," they said, "a spy. To gather their secrets and communicate them to us. We'll put you with the enemy's high command. We have a way."

It had been exciting, heroic.

"You understand what you'd be doing?" they asked, though he could see the words turn bitter in their mouths.

"Of course." There was nothing new about that, though he'd never done it before, never wanted to.

"We… it's… there's no other way," the general had gasped, as though the weight of guilt were crushing her flat.

"It's nothing to me," he'd said. Brave, heroic. Smiling in the face of danger. And this wasn't even that.

"It's revolting," said the minister, standing. "I'll have nothing more to do with it." The door clicked quietly behind him.

"It's not revolting," he'd said, confused. "The sergeant and Peter the cooper do it all the time. So do Lieutenant Ekar and Captain Laro. So do..."

The general had laughed until she looked like she might cry. "No need to list *all* the fraternization that's not supposed to happen between ranks."

"I watched. I know how to do it. I asked Laro if I could try, but he said no." It hadn't looked hard.

"It's not that. It's your age." She'd taken his hand and squeezed it tight. "If there were any other way..."

"But catamites have to be young, don't they?" And then she really had cried, and he'd been taken off by a hard-eyed sergeant.

"You forget all that," the man had said. "You're doing your duty, son. Don't ever question that. We have a job needs doing, and you're the man for it, young as you are. Like it or not, you do that job, and don't ever forget why. You're doing it for your mother, your father, your uncle. For that general in there. You're even doing it for me. When the war's over, you come find me, and I'll buy you a beer, and you'll tell me it wasn't so bad, eh?"

He'd remembered that beer all through the war, through the good times, and the bad, through the parts he liked, and the parts he didn't. And mostly it wasn't bad.

He'd never found the sergeant, of course. Their forces had been decimated, and decimated again, and again, until by the time they'd won, almost half the population was in the army, and over half the army had died. But they'd won, and he'd played his role, and the only hard part had been the end.

"You set him on edge," she said as they climbed up to the lake to wash off the mud. "He's not usually quite so brusque." Harsh, sometimes, and direct. But kind. Always kind.

"Well," Merro said, helping her peel off a sodden, mud-slimed blouse. "I can see why he'd be jealous." Did his hands slide a little too closely along her arms? Did they want to?

"Jealous! Don't be ridiculous." And yet here she was, waist deep in a lake in just her undershirt and small clothes with another man. They were both muddy and tired, of course, but she hadn't thought twice about it. Hadn't thought for a moment about how it might look to Rewk. But she'd thought about how Merro might look to her. Almost against her will, her eyes slid back to him, to his strong shoulders and tight-curled hair. He smiled.

"I'm going to swim," she blurted, and threw herself almost sideways into the cold water. She stroked hard, straight and sure with the form she'd learned in the mill-pond back home, when she'd been young enough that being friends with the miller's daughter felt natural.

"You're a natural," came Merro's voice when she stopped halfway across to tread water. He swam so smoothly she hadn't even heard him. "You know, they do this competitively in some places."

"Do what?" Not drown?

"Swim. They race. Only the upper classes, of course. And canal pilots. No one else has the time to learn non-essential skills." And she wasn't a canal pilot.

"Do they." She imbued the words with as much disinterest as she could manage, though the clear water showed that he'd taken the time to drop his own clothes, all of them. He kicked his feet, swept his arms, and she felt the water wash across her.

"What's at the bottom?" he asked, and before she could answer, he'd turned to jackknife cleanly into the water, buttocks and long legs rising up above the water before slowly, sleekly sliding in.

"You," she whispered. Hadn't he come out of the lake to begin with? But he hadn't vanished. She could see him down there, his wavering, flickering form straightening out to scull along the bottom and through the boulders that lay there.

She turned away and continued her swim, stopping to rest at the other side, and watching his dark head pop up through the rain that had turned to mist. He swam back toward their clothes, and once she'd rested, so did she.

"Gold," he said as she stroked close. "Jewels. Magic swords. Caves and creatures."

"Rocks, in other words." She came up out of the water and turned away to wring as much of the water as she could out of her undershirt. It clung to her anyway, cold and wet.

"Not as hard as you," he said. "Or me, come to that. We're tough, both of us. Not like Rewk."

"He's harder than the two of us put together," she said startled. She blushed, as if she'd forgotten all about him, as if she'd been caught at something. "He's granite. You're just marble. Pretty, but soft." And what was she? Sandstone, so easily worn away? She pulled her blouse over her head, fighting with the wet cloth. This time, he didn't help.

"You'd be surprised," he said. "Rewk may be more fragile than you think."

"What would you know about him?" And how had they gotten here? How had hard work together turned into an analysis of personalities?

He smiled. "What do *you* know?" He walked out of the water, gathering up his neatly folded clothes from the side of the lake and disappearing over the edge of the slope, leaving her with just an echo, and a doubt.

What did she know about him? That he'd been a soldier. That he'd built this cabin when he was younger and stronger, that he'd shopped in Hatherton when she'd been passing through, looking for a place to hide from obligation and society. That he'd done something that ate at him, something that had brought him enough money to live on, something that made him cry sometimes at night when he pretended to go out to pee.

"That he's a good man," she told the lake, and herself. "That he's never asked for anything. That he's never done me wrong." Even when they argued, when they were angry, he'd always played fair. Never undercut her, never tried to bind her to him with word or deed. That was why she had stayed, all those times they'd fought over stupid little things, imagined slights. Why she'd always come back, always fearing that he might have gone on. "That he loves me."

And that she was here, half-naked, half-disappointed that Merro had taken his muscle and his youth and his beauty and left her to feel wretched and cold, and to know that she was wrong.

He came in the door naked, his clothes a dripping pile before him. "Mind if I hang these to dry?" he asked, turning to the hearth.

Rewk closed his eyes, but he still saw taut muscles, a chest dripping water down a hard belly. "You and Derla are done, are you?" He tried to keep his voice flat, disinterested, but it came out harsh and bitter. "With your work."

Merro stayed silent, making a lean-to out of twigs and his shirt. Done, he rose and turned, still naked, still perfect. "Derla and I haven't even started, Kell. You know that."

Rewk froze, feeling the blood drain out of his face and shoulders to hear the name he'd tried so hard to kill, to bury. He didn't react when the other man stepped close, took him by the hand.

"Your fingers are cold," Merro said. "Let me help." He slid Rewk's hand along his chest, held it tight under his arm, surprisingly warm despite the rain that still clung in drops.

"How…?" There were too many questions to ask. "Who…?"

"Does it matter? One name's as good as another." Without letting loose Rewk's hand, he pulled a stool close, settled on it. He took Rewk's other hand, slipped it between warm thighs. "What matters is what we do, don't you think?"

And he knew. Clearly he knew, as he took Rewk's gnarled hand from beneath his arm and kneaded it, finding the knots and lumps of poorly healed bone and pressing heat into them until they felt almost straight. He knew exactly what Rewk was, and what he had done.

The relief surprised him. He'd thought the memories locked up tight – safe and secret in locked chests in locked rooms in deep vaults in his mind. Yet here they were, exposed and open, and he felt no fear, only respite.

"It's all right," said Merro, and kissed him. It was warm and soft and comforting, and he sank into it. There had been other days, other kisses, other arms around him. Others who had cared for him.

Abruptly, he pushed Merro away. "No." Though his heart trembled, his voice was firm and hard.

"Are you sure?" Merro asked, twining his young fingers into Rewk's damaged ones.

"I'm sure." He pulled his hands free.

"You can't hurt me, Kell."

"Don't be so sure. I'm a professional."

"I'm sure," Merro echoed. "I know you."

"Do you?" And if so, whom did he know? The bold, foolish boy who'd learned the enemy's plans from inside their commander's bed? The dutiful adolescent who'd passed the plans along to other, older spies with the same hands that evoked pleasure? The young man who'd sat silent as soldiers held him down and his lover broke his fingers one by one while an army made its last stand around him? The broken soul who'd watched with his hands in bandages and tears in his eyes as they strung a man up and taunted the death erection on his dangling, naked corpse?

"I know all I need to," Merro said softly.

"So do I," said Rewk, and turned away.

Derla stood at the door, little rills running down her face. He took her in his arms, felt her flinch, then shudder, then relax. "Rewk," she said into his shoulder. "I'm so sorry."

"We're a sorry lot," was all he said. Over his shoulder, he said to Merro, "You'll be gone in the morning." There was no answer as they moved awkwardly into the little bedroom, arms still tight around each other.

He told her the whole story that night.

"I've heard of you," she said. "You're the one who won the war for us."

"Yes," he said. "I'm sorry."

She held him tight. "I didn't realize you were so young," she said after a while. "I mean, not you..."

"The spy."

"Yes."

"No. That was the secret. Even after the war. They felt guilty."

"They should have. Of course they did. Sending a child. A *child!*"

He nodded, his head warm against her breasts. "It was wrong. I know that now. But what choice did they have? That's what he liked."

"It was wrong. That's what we fought against!"

"Pedophiles?"

"No! Yes! That's what they said about him, to whip us up. What *we* said."

He shrugged. "He was kind to me."

"Except..."

"I knew what I was getting into. I wasn't that young."

"Too young!"

"Yes. It happens, though."

"Not like this. Not..."

"Procured?"

"It was wrong. And they sent you off..." She began to cry.

"With nothing but a sackful of money," he said, raising his head to kiss her.

"We can change that," she said. "I know people."

"Don't think about it."

"No, really. My father is… was a minister."

He stilled. "A minister." He remembered a stern face, the click of a door as a man washed his conscience clean.

"During the war. After, he quit politics. He started a school. And an orphanage." He felt her breathing stop. "Oh!" she gasped. "Oh. Oh." He held her as the gasps turned to sobs.

"It doesn't matter," he said.

"It does," she mumbled. "It does. He made you a ..."

"A catamite," he said calmly. "A spy. And a traitor." He smiled. "I did too. It doesn't matter. Whatever name you put to it, I did what I did. I am what I am."

"It does matter," she insisted, rising above him. "You're not just some leafy green thing. You're Rewk. And I love you." And though she didn't put a name to it, she suited action to words, until she collapsed shuddering on top of him and held him as tight as she could.

In the morning, Merro was gone, as though he'd never been. The cottage felt larger without him, less oppressive without his presence, though the day was hot, and the air was still and close.

"Was he someone you knew?" she asked as he opened a sluice to let water into the garden.

"No. Maybe someone from intelligence, checking that I hadn't spilled the secret." Though he had spilled it to her thoroughly now, and doubtless would continue to spill for years to come.

"Or maybe a lake spirit, come to bring our secrets out in the open," she said. Or her father, topping off payments on an endless debt.

He smiled. "We'll have a good crop this year," he said. "I may have to expand the garden." He turned to admire the lake water as it ran down the hill and into his greens. Whatever she'd built it for, it would work wonders on their salads.

"It's an irrigation ditch," she said, calling it what it was, what she had always meant it to be.

"Is it?" He nodded approvingly. "It's a good one. I was thinking, though. How would you feel about a little waterwheel? My hands aren't what they used to be."

"That's okay," she said, taking his swollen hand in hers. "Right now it's a ditch. But we can always rename it."

About the Author

B. Morris Allen is a biochemist turned activist turned lawyer turned foreign aid consultant, and frequently wonders whether it's time for a new career. He's been traveling since birth, and has lived on five of seven continents. When he can, he makes his home on the Oregon coast. In between journeys, he edits Metaphorosis *magazine, and works on his own speculative stories of love and disaster. His dark fantasy novel* Susurrus *came out in 2017. You can find him at www.bmorrisallen.com and @BMorrisAllen.*

Going Home

Kelly A. Harmon

The small, silver disk materialized at nose height, tumbling in the air like a tossed coin, and clattered to the scarred wooden table before Volara could catch it. She closed her eyes and counted to ten, willing the disc to return from whence it came. While she counted, the disc thrummed on the table, buzzing against the wood, dancing itself to the edge.

Summoned.

She pushed the bowl of flax cereal away, no longer excited by the prospect of breaking fast, though she'd looked forward to the meal for quite some time. She'd sweetened the cereal with honeysuckle dew, the first of the season and hard won this late spring. Simple pleasures were all she had left.

There was a time she would have been thrilled to answer the call. But not now. Not when her magic no longer worked and she had nothing left to give. How could she possibly help?

Volara palmed the disc and clamped it hard, feeling the heavy weight of it pull her hand down to the tabletop, the solid edges cutting into her curled fingers. She stood and dropped it into a clay jar on the top of a high shelf, shoving a rag in after it to keep the disc inside. It didn't belong with the other tokens in the jar, symbols of completed quests. But it was magic, and that's where she kept all things magic these days. Precious little.

Well, she could still make the finest dandelion wine in the valley. And she didn't need magic to do so. Volara grabbed a shawl and wrapped it around her withered wings, tucking the ends of it underneath the shriveled tertiary feathers, then dragged another over her head to hide the russet fur that started at her temples and covered the rest of her body like a silky pollen robe. She fled the confines of the hut, grabbing up her reed basket as she left.

The wooden door drooped to a close on leather hinges behind her as Volara wandered out into the grassy fields. It was a cold spring, the blossoms late. The sky was overcast today, as it had been for many days.

Her basket was only half-full of yellow blossoms when Amia fluttered into the field with an ungraceful kilter to her flight.

"'Lara! 'Lara!" She somersaulted in mid-air and lost her balance, wings folding with a snap, and tumbled to the ground, oversetting Volara's basket.

Volara looked nervously around the clearing.

"You know better than to come here like that," she said, "someone could be watching."

"Too excited to care," said Amia, smiling wide. "Did you get your token?" Amia snapped her fingers and a bronze disc, shiny and bright, appeared in her palm.

Volara looked up from the dandelions. "So excited you didn't think *I* would care? I've found a life here. You'll ruin it, if someone sees you like that."

Amia frowned. She snapped her fingers twice and the fine pink fur on her jowls and arms smoothed into peach-colored flesh, her wings into a colorful collar on a lemon-yellow cloak. "Better?"

At Volara's nod, she said, "You should move back to the Grove, be with your own kind."

"I *am* with my own kind," Volara said. "The *un-magicked*."

She scooped the spilled dandelions back into her basket and walked two steps to another large patch of blooms. Amia followed.

"They don't find your... *hump*... distasteful?"

Volara looked back over her shoulder at her covered wings, frowned, but shook her head.

"No more than any other old woman's." She plucked a sunny floret from its stem and tossed it into her basket.

"But you're not an old woman!" Amia said. "You're a sprite. And you're younger than I am."

Volara gave Amia a sharp glance and placed a finger to her lips. "Shhh."

Amia quieted and looked around the valley. She lowered her voice and hissed, "If you quit shaving your face and hands, you wouldn't look like an old human woman."

Volara shook her head. "Here I might be an old woman, but at least my age and wisdom are respected. No one pities me." She ripped another blossom from its stem. "I'll take respect over pity any day."

"What about the loneliness?"

Volara unbent and thrust the basket into Amia's hands. "If you're going to stick around, you might as well carry the basket." She put her hands on her hips. "I'm not lonely. The villagers visit me sometimes; the young girls come for advice."

"You're younger than they are!" Amia said.

It was true, the way sprites count maturity. But losing her magic had aged Volara.

"I don't feel young anymore."

Over dinner, Amia broached the subject again. "Did you get a token?"

"No," Volara replied, pushing aside a plate still filled with turnips braised in sweet butter and a wedge of her favorite blue-veined cheese. Her appetite vanished.

Amia looked puzzled.

"Why should I have been summoned?" Volara said. "It's been years since the Elder called me. My magic is dead."

"But—"

"But nothing. I'm unneeded."

"The Elder said—" Amia stopped, covered her mouth with a downy pink hand.

"Said what?" Volara asked, her brow furrowed. "Summons are secret calls. No one knows who's been mustered until all are assembled to commence." She stood and walked her plate to the compost bucket, flinging the food into it with vicious force. Had her nerves not been so jangled, she'd have wrapped the dinner for later. But at that moment, she didn't care.

Across the tiny room, the jar on the high shelf teetered and fell to the floor, breaking into a thousand shards. The lone silver disc vibrated against dulled bronze ones, tinkling like a tambourine. It flew from the pile towards Volara, turning end over end in front of her nose, then dropped to the dirt floor at her feet, naming her a liar.

"Silver," said Amia. "You're the hinge-pin of the quest. You *must* go."

"I must do nothing," said Volara. She looked down at the coin, frozen. After long moments, she said to Amia, "You know the quest already."

Amia nodded.

"As I thought. The Elder seeks to pull me back into the fold. This quest is supposed to make me feel one of you again." She stared into the fire. "It's not the first time she's tried."

"You *are* one of us," Amia said. She knelt and scooped up the broken pottery, separating the clay fragments into one pile and bronze discs into another. "You have to do it. You're the only one who can."

Volara shook her head.

Amia nodded back. "Before you left the Grove, you gave a gift to the Elder."

"Motherless eggs, laid in a nest of thorns." She remembered them well, smooth and cool. Blood red with veins of black. They'd looked like marble effigies in their nettle bower, already dead when she found them. It was the last time she'd used her magic.

"They're beginning to hatch," Amia said. "You have to return them."

"Nothing could have hatched from those stones."

"They are witch babes," Amia said. "And the witch wants her brood back."

Volara shook her head. "Then she can get them from the Elder."

"They need to go back to the nettles," Amia said, laying the shards and the bronze tokens on the table in separate piles. "They're be-spelled, and they must live or die on their own—from within the nettles. They must be replanted."

"Someone else can go in my stead."

"But you're the only one who knows where the nettle bush is," Amia said. "They need to be returned to the exact spot from where they were plucked."

"Well, then, the witch will just have to suffer the loss if she was so careless to leave them unattended."

"She threatened to ice the world over," Amia said. "No more spring, no more summer, no fall. Only ice. No crops, no fish." She raised a wooden mug to her lips. "No dandelion wine."

"Impossible," said Volara.

"Not," said Amia, turning bleak eyes towards Volara's. "She's already begun. Have you noticed the late spring? The cool nights? This is only the beginning." Amia snapped her fingers.

The sharp-edged nest appeared on the table, four blood-red eggs coddled within.

Grief consumed Volara, the eggs' presence flaring the constant leaden weight she carried in her belly into a sharp stab. Volara took a deep breath and made the decision: she would go, but she wouldn't return to the Grove afterward. There was still no place there for an un-magicked sprite, no matter the good intentions.

They exited the forest and walked north across rocky plains toward the Erto Babbia Mountains. Without the break of the trees, the wind blew cold and blustery, battering them with long gusts.

"Just the two of us," Volara said, twin spots of color rosying her cheeks. "I should have known."

"It's not what you think," Amia replied. She'd abandoned her human clothing, but walked beside Volara. It was easier, Volara knew, than flying against the wind. Volara wore her shawls, carrying naught but a small sack of brown bread and a rind of her favorite blue-veined cheese. The eggs lay deep in the pockets of her apron: two on the left, two on the right. The nest of thorns she wore on her head, like a crown.

"It is what I think," Volara said. "This quest is for me. You're my keeper." She turned glaring eyes on Amia. "There is no witch, no curse upon this land. This is all the Elder's doing."

"If that's true," said Amia, "Then what about the frost this morning?"

Volara pulled her shawl tighter around her shoulders. "An aberration."

Three days into the climb, snow whirled down from clouds above the mountain. Where the sun breached the high trees, the rocky paths ran with mud. Volara's skirts and shoes were coated with it. Amia was clean as a sprite could be, floating above the mud like a dandelion wisp.

"How much longer?" she asked.

"Don't know," Volara replied. "I flew up here the last time." She slipped, but cognizant of the eggs in her pockets, twisted, hitting her right shoulder and hip hard on protruding rocks. They traveled more slowly then, Volara favoring her hip, scuttling across the outcroppings, using her hands for support.

They walked in shade, the mountain curling over them now, like an awning. Volara couldn't wait to be done with it. Prove that any un-magicked soul could have done the job, then return to her hut in the dale. Maybe the Elder would quit bothering her if she finished the job. Ignoring her certainly wasn't working.

At midday, Volara said, "We're almost there. This will be the hardest part."

The mountain rose up, steep and rocky, arching over the plains they'd abandoned. The nettle bushes grew in the lee of the curve, in the darkness, where the wind swirled up and was captured by the curl. When she had found the eggs, Volara used her magic to protect her from the wind; her wings to get her safely away. Now, she had nothing. A tiny ledge traversed the mountainside, the only path to the nettles. A false step along the slim ridge, and she would fall to her death in the stone-filled plains below.

Volara stopped, scanned the mountainside. Snow swirled *up* the path behind them, riding whistling winds. It smelled of steel and frost. Amia, buffeted by the eddy, fluttered down next to her. "What do you see?" she asked.

"Can you make out that white strip of rock?" Volara asked, pointing into the curve of the mountain.

Amia nodded. "On the far side, almost outside the overhang."

"The eggs were protected there, away from the roiling wind." She looked at Amia, stared at her wings. "You could get these eggs there far easier than I."

Amia looked as though she might agree. The wind billowed up again before she said, "No. You received the silver coin, it's your task."

Volara drew a deep breath and pulled her shoulders back. She snapped, "You could wing over and set them in the bushes in a trice. No one would know."

Amia stared back unblinking. "*You* would know."

Volara turned her back on Amia and scrambled up the steep path. Here and there, she slipped on loose rocks, listened to the wind sing up the mountainside. Her hip pained her, slowing her progress. Finally, she reached the area where the bushes grew. She need only scuttle across the ledge to be done with the task. An hour's work, maybe less. She would be glad to have it done.

Here, the sound of the wind was different. When she and Amia had walked up the path it whistled, sliced thin by rocks, producing a singing whine; but from this vantage, the gusts roared up out of the plains. Awesome bursts, expansive in breadth, swept up the mountainside hitting the curve of the slope, then rolled back down upon themselves, like great crashing waves on the ocean.

Volara thought perhaps she could crawl between the gusts, and hold on for dear life when they blew.

"Be careful," Amia said, then lit on a high boulder nearby to wait.

The wind lulled. It began to snow.

Volara stepped out on the ledge and wrapped her fingers around a rocky outcrop. More rock than dirt created this mountain, Volara realized. It amazed her the nettles found any purchase to thrive in. She took a few tentative steps, feeling the strength of the ledge, then, more confident, moved ten steps onto the ledge out over the plains.

Holding onto a rock with one hand, and a clump of wind-burned vegetation with the other, she felt the wind tickle the downy fur at her ears. A precursor. She tightened her grip. And the wind hurled upward with a plaintive howl, ripping at her skirts, tugging the shawl covering her wings, loosening it from its tucks. White-knuckled, she pushed her face against sharp, cold stone, closing her eyes.

I could just let go, she thought. Why fight the wind? The witch? The spell is already in motion. Will she reverse it when her brood are replaced? Likely not. And I could end all this grief by simply letting go.

The wind stopped and she relaxed, loosening her grip on the scrub. She could move now, but stayed put. *I could do it,* she thought. *I could jump.*

Amia fluttered over. "What's wrong?"

"Just debating the wisdom of the trek," Volara said. She squinted at Amia, floating far enough away to be bathed in the white brightness of snowfall. "How can we be sure the witch will keep her promise?"

"How can you be sure she won't?" Amia asked. "It's a chance you'll have to take."

"I can leave the eggs with you," Volara said. "I can still refuse to do this."

"It's your quest," Amia said.

"The witch doesn't care who returns her eggs. She just wants them back." Volara looked down over the edge and calculated how long it would take her to fall to the stony plain below. It would be terrifying for the brief span before she hit the ground, but then it would be all over.

"You take the eggs," she said, sticking a shaking hand into a pocket and pulling out one smooth, red oval. In the mountain's shade, it appeared almost black in her palm.

"No," Amia fluttered backward over the ravine. "You have to do it. If you don't, you'll never be able to return."

Volara nodded. She knew that already; the price for failing a quest. But banishment was the least of her worries right now. The wind rose up. Amia retreated to the path, and her boulder. Volara clung to the rock wall, her right shoulder burning with exertion.

When the second gust passed, Amia was back.

"If you don't do this, I won't forgive you," she said.

Volara shook her head. She almost smiled. "Empty threats, Amia. If I had a dandelion for every time you said that to someone in the last seventy-five years..." She shrugged.

"There'd not be enough casks in the Grove to bottle all the wine."

Volara started moving again. Two steps, five steps. She was more than halfway there. Amia floated above the gorge. She talked encouragement, but Volara wasn't listening.

Then the wind roared up from below, surprising both of them.

It captured Amia, pushing her higher. She rose up with a squeal, somersaulting until her wings caught purchase.

Volara fell.

She tumbled end over end, like the silver token that had called her to this quest, falling down the side of the mountain. The eggs flew from her pockets as she hurtled down the cliff-side. The surging air ripped the shawl from her shoulders, tossing it out into the wind. The nettles scratched her forehead as her descent tore the nest away from her head.

Volara's wings, unused for so long, fluttered in the wind like two broken kites flown into each other, knotted by strings and tales. Scratching together, rattling, the joints near her neck and bottom of her spine twisted as the wind clawed at the paper-thin appendages, pulling them as she turned.

Down she fell.

It's better this way, she thought. Rather than living a hundred human lifetimes without magic, she could be done with it, in one short fall.

"Volaraaaaaaaaaa!" yelled Amia, swooping down with her. "Fly, beat your wings."

"You know I can't," said Volara. She was smiling now. There was no way Amia could help her; she was falling much too fast. If Amia grabbed her, they would both plummet to their deaths. She knew it. And she knew Amia knew it.

"You can," Amia said. Her eyes were full of sorrow.

Volara shook her head, continuing to smile. "This is for the best. I know you forgive me."

The eggs hit the stony floor of the valley, thumping like hail.

A hundred feet from the ground, Volara's wings snapped open in a gust of wind— unfurled to full span—revealing dull and brittle feathers, dry from neglect and missing in patches. She'd not preened them, these many, many years. But her wings fluttered outward, the wind tugging them apart, catching the updraft, spreading, despite atrophied muscles. She glided.

She glided!

She possessed magic yet. And flight.

A shallow smile flitted across her face. And hope, she thought. Where there's flight, there's hope. *I have to find the witch's brood.*

Volara soared over the muddy valley, searched feverishly for the eggs, landing when she found them, exploded in puddles of grey dust. The dried remains of witch-beasts lay scattered in stones, grey and husky like wasps' nests. Volara sank to her knees and cried, pulling her wings over her head to shield herself from the falling snow.

"It's okay," said Amia, hovering to her left. "Don't worry about the eggs. Everything is all right now."

"It's not," moaned Volara. *Why did I think everything would be alright?* She said, "The witch, the snow. We've got to get them to the nettle bush." She clawed the mud, trying to scrape the battered shells together. Her touch crumpled them to bits.

Amia hovered lower, smiled at Volara. "No witch. No curse."

Anger streaked across Volara's face. "The snow?"

"An aberration."

"Then I was right all along," Volara said, rising from the mud, stripping the human skirts from her lithe figure. The wind was barely evident here, a mere breeze, tickling the delicate membranes of her wings where feathers were absent.

Amia rocketed above her and triple-flipped in the air, her giggle tinkling above the wind rattling higher in the valley. She soared away, but not before Volara heard her yell, "Not about everything..."

The silver summoning token tumbled down in front of Volara's eyes, somersaulted once, twice, three times, then dropped into the mud at Volara's feet. She bent and fished it out, feeling the muscles pull in her back. They ached, but in a good way. She hadn't felt this alive in some time.

The token was dull now, no longer thrumming with energy. It lay still in her hand.

Quest complete.

She beat her wings experimentally. They hurt, but she could be home in a day or two if she rested every so often. Soon, she'd be doing somersaults with Amia. Oh, but her wings looked terrible. It would take *months* of preening to make them beautiful again. She would start on that right away, as soon as she got home. Home to the Grove.

ABOUT THE AUTHOR

Kelly A. Harmon's short fiction has been published in Flame Tree Press's Swords and Steam*; Parsec Ink's* Triangulation: Dark Glass, *Spring Song Press's* Fell Beasts and Fair, *and elsewhere. She is the author of the Charm City Darkness series, an urban fantasy that takes place in Baltimore, Maryland. Her website is kellyaharmon.com.*

THE FINAL PIECE

JASON J. MCCUISTON

"Apep, you old serpent! Wake up! Come out!" he called into the reeking cave. "I am Pharaoh, King of the Upper and Lower Kingdoms, and I have come to treat with you!"

There was no reply.

The scorching sun climbed higher into the pale blue sky and a hot breeze wandered over the vast sandy dunes below the craggy hilltop. He was exhausted and every part of him ached from the perilous climb; his body was not what it once was, and old wounds hurt as if they were fresh. But after three decades of pain and death, of privation and slaughter, he had reached the final challenge and he would face it with all the strength he yet possessed.

As it was just a few hours after dawn, he knew that Apep was just as tired and probably hurting even worse. The serpent god had suffered yet another defeat at the hands of Ra.

Sweat beaded on Pharaoh's bald head and ran from beneath the crest of his polished blue helmet, down his neck and under the weathered bronze scales of his battered cuirass. He wore all the finery of his war glory; one did not face a god in rags, even a god of chaos and darkness. In one scarred hand he gripped the long-bladed spear which had been the death of countless lions and nameless beasts, and in the other he held the broad, curved khopesh that had taken the heads of hundreds of his enemies. For all their lethal splendor, they would count for nothing in the presence of the immortal serpent god. Pharaoh knew that he risked nothing less than all eternity. And he was willing, even happy, to do so.

"Come out and speak to me!" he shouted again. "I am Pharaoh, descendant of your eternal enemy, Ra, God of the Sun!"

A rumbling hiss emanated from the inky blackness, and the stench of a thousand corpses washed over Pharaoh. He coughed and covered his face. When he looked again, two golden eyes like evil moons stared back from the pit.

"Why should I speak with you, old man?" the god whispered in distant thunder. "Why should I not simply devour you, body and soul, and return to my rest?"

Pharaoh opened the pouch on his girdle and produced a glowing gem as long as his hand. In the morning light it shone in a blazing golden flame. "Because of this! And three others like it which I possess."

The unseen serpent god inhaled, drawing the scent of the mystic gem into the cave on a breath of avarice; smelling its power. "If I kill you, they will all be mine."

"True," Pharaoh said, returning the precious jewel to his belt and cinching the bag. "But then you will not know how to use them."

"Use them?"

"To defeat Ra," the king said.

The sound of granite scales sliding over one another rumbled in the cave. "Speak."

"First," said Pharaoh, "let us make a deal."

Apep's giant head shot from the cavern like a loosed arrow. Razored fangs longer than spears extended inches from Pharoah's face, flecking his armor with sizzling venom that burned the metal. "I am Apep, god of chaos and darkness!" the titanic snake roared. "I do not make deals with mortals who foolishly come to my mountain and offer themselves as sacrifice!"

Pharaoh did not flinch. "Nevertheless, serpent, you will make a deal with me. Or you will suffer another defeat at the hands of Ra come the dawn, just as you will again every day hereafter for all eternity."

Apep hissed and lashed, causing the mountain to shudder at his wrath. But in the end, he asked, "What is this deal?" just as the king had known he must. Apep's one true desire, and thus his only weakness, was to defeat Ra and plunge the world into his darkness forever.

Pharaoh leaned his spear and sword against a rock and sat down. "I have a story to tell you, and when it is done, I will show you the key to defeating Ra."

Apep coiled around Pharaoh's stone seat. "What do you get out of this? Why forfeit your eternal life to tell me a story and bring me treasure? You are a son of Ra! Why would you betray him?"

Pharaoh removed his shining blue helmet, stared at the golden vulture and cobra on the brow and said with a sad smile, "For love."

Apep made a sound which the king took for laughter, and though it was not a pleasant sound it made him smile. After all the many strange and horrible things he had encountered these many years, the sound of a serpent's laugh was truly the most bizarre.

The dark god reared above Pharaoh and studied him, his head swaying slightly. "Very well, old man. Tell me your story. But you have until dusk when I must go and do battle with Ra. If you have not told me how to defeat him by then, I will devour you, body and soul, and take your jewels and add them to my hoard."

Pharaoh nodded agreement and said, "It began just over thirty years ago. I ruled in peace and prosperity all the lands of the blessed Nile with my Queen at my side. She had just given birth to our son, and all was perfect in the world.

"And then the sorcerer came," he said, his brow darkening with the memory. "He was a Berber from the west, and he demanded half my kingdom lest he curse me and my household. He claimed that our western lands belonged to his people by right, but I knew that my grandfather's grandfather had taken those lands with his sword, and had even paid the Berbers in silver and gold to compensate their widows and orphans for the loss of their men."

"So you had this sorcerer killed," Apep said.

"I should have," Pharaoh conceded. "Instead, I ordered him to leave and never to return to my kingdom. I said that the next time he saw my face he would surely die. And that much, at least was true.

"However," the king said. "Before departing, the vile old man raised his staff and uttered his curse. At my side, my Queen gasped in pain and tumbled from her throne. I pulled her into my arms to discover that she was as cold as the grave. I looked to the wizard and saw that in his hand he held a large glowing gem filled with every color of the rainbow and more besides.

"He grinned cruelly when he said, 'Pharaoh, you and your people have taken what is rightfully ours. Therefore, I have taken that which is most precious to you!' He held up the gem and declared, 'In this jewel I have the Queen's soul in all its varied parts. And here those parts will remain until you give us back our land!' And then, in a burst of light and smoke, he was gone."

Apep snorted. "That's why I don't like to treat with people. It's usually best simply to kill anyone who annoys you."

Pharaoh ignored the observation and continued. "The priests and magicians examined my Queen and said that her body was indeed without life – and yet she had not truly died, and therefore could not be prepared for the sacred journey into the afterlife. Until her soul can be freed from the gem, she will forever be trapped between life and death.

"I ordered that she be placed in a crystal sarcophagus, and demanded that rituals and spells be performed to keep her body safe from corruption until the day that I should retrieve her soul.

"Then I marshalled my armies and we invaded the Berber deserts to the west. For five years I put their hordes to flight and their people to sword and fire. My wrath was unquenched and my cruelty without limit until I finally discovered the location of the sorcerer's hidden fortress.

"And in his secret fastness, after overcoming a legion of his monstrous servants, I slew him. But not before he told me that he had broken the soul gem into five pieces and scattered them all over the world. Dying, choking on his own blood, this evil man had his last revenge; he laughed as his soul winged its way to hell.

"From his lifeless fingers, I claimed this," Pharaoh produced the golden shard and lay it on the sand before Apep. "This holds my wife's *Ba*; her personality. When I close my eyes and listen, I can hear her laughter and her soothing voice."

Apep's tongue flicked appreciatively. "I can feel its power."

Pharaoh continued his tale. "After the war with the Berbers, I returned to my capital to confer with the priests and wise men. Using mighty spells of divination, they learned where the wizard had hidden the other pieces. Assembling a fleet of the fastest ships, I set out at once with the best of my elite warriors to reclaim the rest of my Queen's soul."

The king pulled a shard of glimmering black beauty from his bag. It absorbed all light and twinkled as if filled with an infinity of stars. "It took three years of searching, but in the seas to the far north, I found an island inhabited by a race of mighty and savage giants. I lost two hundred men in the battle with those man-eaters, but after killing their chief in single combat, I took this from his treasury. It is her *Sheut*, the shadow which gives her form and essence."

"Lovely," Apep hissed.

Pharaoh sighed and continued his tale. "In the land of the Canaanites to the east, for eight long years I hunted down a demon called a *shedim* or a *jinni*. Though it slew scores of valiant men and laid extra years on my body with but a touch of its hand, I again prevailed and secured this." Pharaoh withdrew another exquisite fragment of the soul gem; this one clear and pure as summer sunlight and air.

Apep's head bobbed knowingly. "This is her *Ren*; her true name and the key to her immortality."

The king nodded, touched each of the three gems lying in the sand with love and reverence. "And then, in the harsh wilds of Arabia to the south of Canaan, for five years I wandered among the haunts of their walking corpses, the *ghuls*, until I came to the court of the Queen of the Dead. It was in battle with her army of those accursed things that I lost the remainder of my band of heroes, but in spite of the cost I was victorious.

"I took this from the crown atop the undead monarch's severed head." Pharaoh produced the last gem from his bag. "Her *Ka*, the vital spark of her life and spirit," he said as the jewel burst forth in blinding white light at his touch.

Apep's forked tongue flicked the charged air around the largest of the gems, tasting its power and purity. "Which brings us to the last piece, I presume."

Pharaoh placed the jewels side by side in the sand and looked up into the glowing yellow eyes of the serpent god. "Yes. I have searched the wastes of this desert for ten years because I believe the wizard gave you the *Ib* jewel to guard. You have the last piece of my Queen's soul, Apep, and I would have it."

The dark god made that awful laughing sound again. His huge head darted to the west before hovering above Pharaoh. "Ra's sun barge draws near the edge of the world, old man, and yet you have not told me how your pathetic little story or your broken jewel will help me defeat him."

"Bring me the Heart stone, Apep, and I will show you."

The giant serpent hesitated, sensing treachery. "If you are attempting to trick me, know that I will devour you, and your soul will never have the chance to face judgment. You will writhe in my bowels for all eternity."

Pharaoh smiled. "Bring me the gem."

Apep disappeared into his foul den and quickly returned, a blood-red ruby the size of a large man's fist coiled in his tail. He dropped the treasure at Pharaoh's feet and hissed.

"Thank you," the king said, kneeling in the dust. Carefully, he took the five shards and put them together so that they joined in bursts of multihued light. He chanted the prayer the priests had taught him as he did so: the ritual of *se-akh*, the joining of the soul for passage into the afterlife.

With the last word of the prayer spoken, there was a blinding flash. For a moment, Pharaoh saw his Queen's *akh*, her unified soul in the form of a great white falcon with her smiling face atop its mighty wings. And then she was gone.

Apep roared and the mountain shook.

In Pharaoh's hands was a cracked husk of burnt black glass. He smiled, knowing that his wife's soul would find her way to the afterlife. He also knew that their son had grown into a good man who would be a just and strong king, and that he would sit on the throne for many years to come.

"You tricked me, old man!" Apep howled, lashing the air and mountainside, spraying gouts of burning venom in his rage. "I told you what would happen!"

Pharaoh smiled up at the dark god. It was his turn to laugh.

"You don't understand. My Queen was my life and her soul was *my* soul. Wherever she goes, there also is the greater part of me. I may not face judgment before Anubis and Ammit, but I know that my heart is lighter than the feather of truth, for I have saved my one true love.

"So do your worst, you old snake, for I am free at last."

ABOUT THE AUTHOR

Jason J. McCuiston's story "The Last Red Lantern" was a semi-finalist in 2016's L. Ron Hubbard's Writers of the Future contest and is now included in Parsec Ink's Triangulation: Appetites *anthology, and his story "The Wyvern" can be found in Pole to Pole Publishing's* Dark Luminous Wings *anthology. His story "Solomon's Key" is included in Left Hand Publishers'* A World Unimagined *anthology.*

Grimoire

Jennifer R. Povey

The shards of glass reflected the light as the apprentice swept them up. Leola was furious.

Of course, she was not the type to show her fury by yelling or screaming, although the unfortunate apprentice was being very quiet indeed.

She did feel sorry for the child, and would have taken on the task herself, but she felt it more important to turn her skills toward identifying the miscreant. Who would throw a rock through a library window? Into, for that matter, a study carrel. Only luck had not put her head or, perhaps worse, that of a visiting scholar, into the path of the missile.

She picked it up. It was only a rock, it held no obvious clues, but she handled it only with gloves. A mage might be able to determine who threw it, but not if she confused the matter with her own touch.

Only a rock. It could have killed somebody.

Worse, it could have damaged the books. Shaking her head, she slipped the rock into her pouch and headed out of the library.

The library formed one side of the quadrant, the university resting at ninety degrees to it. On the other side of the plaza were restaurants and stores that catered to scholars.

The restaurants were cheap, of course, and sold simple, filling fare. The scholars who came here were seldom wealthy. If they were, then they ate elsewhere, generally with their patrons.

Patrons. She made a face at that. Patronage had gone sour for her many years ago, when she had discovered that Count Rocfor had wanted more from her than a book.

Well, no. It had gone particularly sour when Count Rocfor's wife had discovered the same thing. It had not mattered to the woman that Leola had pushed him away and was in the process of telling him to go take a long walk off a short dock.

She would never be able to set foot in that county again. Somehow she had come to rest here, where she worked at the most basic yet most important level of scholarship.

Without somebody to keep the books in order and make sure everyone could find them, scholarship itself could not happen.

Leola often wished more people understood that.

Patrons. She saw a rich man in a velvet gown cross the square who likely fell into that demographic. A wealthy merchant, either showing off or, perhaps, hoping somebody would invent something to help him in his business.

She narrowed her eyes as she recognized him, and she elected to take a slightly circuitous route to the Proctor's office rather than risk interception.

The man thought she could do better than being a librarian, and he defined "better" as being his second wife. Having no interest in his overweight form (or, for that matter, in men in general), she elected to avoid him rather than being obligated to produce yet another refusal. He was so un-used to hearing the word *no* from a woman that she felt sorry for his daughters.

Stepping into the Proctor's office, she waited while that worthy looked up. Proctor Davox was a southerner, his skin almost the color of the darkly bound books on his desk. He had risen to his position in spite of the general assumption that his people were, in general, less literate than those of the north.

It was true to a point. But Leola suspected much of it was that if one was fortunate enough to live in a land with no winter, one did not have long stretches of the year in which the only thing you could really do was exchange stories (and, in the case of the far north, hope you got snowed in with a good bard). Certainly Davox was smarter than she was, and smarter than many of the scholars who came here.

Smarter than the wealthy ones, for sure. "Ah, Librarian. I have a task for you."

"I have a task for *you*." She set the rock down on his desk. "Some careless person threw this through the library window into a carrel. Fortunately, it was an empty one."

Davox scowled. "Probably a childish prank."

"One that could have killed somebody. Could you please get security to identify the problem?"

If it was a child, they would probably get two beatings–one from Davox and a second one from their parents. Hopefully, anyway.

If it was something more serious, Leola wanted to know. "So, a task for me?"

"A task for you. There is a merchant who is offering to sell us a book. He claims it is of considerable age and comes from the library of the White Tower."

If Leola had the ears of a cat, they would have pricked upwards. As it was... "If..."

"If it is, then it would be worth whatever he charges for it. But identifying books..."

"...is my specialty. I will look at it."

"And I will find the rock thrower and send him or her home to their mother with a sore bottom," Davox promised.

The idea lightened her mood. It made her forget about the rock throwing – well, until Davox brought it up again and restored her scowl momentarily.

A book from the White Tower.

Only four were even known to exist. This would make five.

More likely it was a fraud. Leola considered. "Where should I meet him?"

"At the Carradine Cafe."

She nodded. "I am going to take an escort."

"Wise."

"When I tell him it is a fraud, he may hit me." It had happened before and while Leola could defend herself, taking a burly student with her seemed smart. She knew exactly who to call.

The merchant turned out to be from the western steppe, a short, slender man with the peculiar narrow and slanted eyes of his people. They were nomads still, but their cities, even if they were not always occupied–or always occupied by the same people–were one of the things Leola wished she could see. She was not, though, made for the hardship of traveling such long distances.

Perhaps it was a weakness, but she liked things... comfortable. Sleeping on the ground, the times she had tried it, had simply meant not sleeping at all. There was nothing romantic about it.

Still, she did wish she could see Karil-Lor, especially during the summer fair when tribes met to exchange livestock and brides.

This man was clearly from a more settled background. She wanted to know how a western merchant had obtained a book from the White Tower.

"You are the expert?" he said, a little skeptically.

She glanced at Ballen, the student she had brought with her, then nodded.

"I thought your women were less likely to seek scholarly pursuits."

Great. He had just all but called her a bluestocking. "I am the university librarian. Let me see the book."

He pulled out a box. He had the book wrapped in silk, which was reverence but also a basic precaution. Books from the White Tower had a reputation, so she could not blame him for taking steps to ward against stray magic.

When he unwrapped it, she felt a hint of static. White Tower or no, this book…

"You're careful, I see."

"Supposedly it is cursed. I have seen enough to warrant… caution."

She nodded, then lifted it out of the box with great care. The binding was in good condition, but that tingle she felt could be a preservation spell as easily as a curse. "White Tower books generally had wards placed on them to reduce decay and repel bookworms," she explained. "It could be that."

Or, of course, it could be a book from one of the lesser wizards' academies. It was old enough, though, to have come from the golden age of magic.

Before the Prophet had drained most of the magic from the world and left them only with cantrips and the like.

Science had risen to fill the gap, but Leola did wonder what it had been like to live in a time when men could cast fireballs or women heal with a touch.

"Indeed. I suppose something more potent…"

"Something more potent would have no energy to fuel it." She opened the book. "The script is correct. The binding is appropriate to the time period, but that does not prove it is from the White Tower itself."

Still, even if it was from a lesser school, it was still...

...something that should have been destroyed. She could read only parts of the text, but her scalp prickled again.

When the Proctor had said a book from the White Tower she had assumed a history, a book of lore...

This was a grimoire.

This was a surviving book of true magic and it was in her hands. There were spells in here that could, if cast by a mage of sufficient potency, level this city.

Or end a plague.

"How much are you asking for it?" She could show no sign of her true opinion.

Shards of glass, she thought. *Shards of magic.*

It was not dangerous now. Not since the Prophet had shattered the crystals to drain the magic.

It was only a book.

"A dangerous find," Davox said. He refused to touch the book. "I have half a mind to burn it."

Leola frowned. She was averse to destroying any book. "The knowledge in it is useless without the power, and the power is gone."

He stood up, paced behind his chair. "The five crystals of power that held magic stable in the world were smashed."

"Right. And the knowledge of how to make more is lost."

"Unless it's in that book." He looked at her. "If it is, we burn it."

He was right. She knew he was right. But she could not bring herself to burn a book. She resolved instead to find a way to hide it.

Even though she knew that if it was a true grimoire, it might still have the power to cloud her mind.

"And even if it is not, some of those spells, if somebody had both the book and a shard... and do not forget..."

...that there was a crystal shard below the school. Leola nodded. "Still."

"You did right to acquire it. And right not to tell the merchant what he had."

"As it was, he knew enough to be greedy," she quipped.

"Merchants always are."

East, west, or south–Leola knew Davox was right. All merchants were greedy because only greedy people became merchants. A law of nature, that. Or perhaps a law of humanity.

And perhaps only those greedy for knowledge became librarians? She was certainly not greedy for money.

But she did not want to burn the book.

The crystals of power. The book.

Her fingers itched for that book, she realized, and perhaps she was unsafe. But there had been magic before, great magic, beyond anything that could be achieved or dreamed of now.

Part of her wanted that magic back.

Most of her knew Davox was right.

The price Leola paid for the book made her wince even if it was not, after all, her money. The school could afford it.

Barely.

But the school could *not* afford to have this book fall into the wrong hands. She carried it into her office and held it in her gloved hands, not wanting the chemicals of her skin to mar it.

That could happen with a book this old. A single touch could be, in fact, enough to destroy it. To cause the paper to crumble.

She took it into her office and, hesitantly, opened it. It contained knowledge she could not really grasp or understand.

A grimoire, full of magic. Spells, real spells that went beyond the small magicks some scholars could manage, the weak things left over when the magic had drained out of the world.

This might contain the knowledge necessary to call it back.

She flipped through the pages, feeling the book call to her, feeling it draw her in.

Burn it, Davox would say. She could hear those words in his voice, could hear those words in her mind. Almost a command.

Burn it.

The command was urgent, as urgent as words came. A command woven into the wards around the book: somebody had tried to destroy this book and, failing, had laid a compulsion on anyone who held it – or perhaps on anyone who read it.

It was a weak spell, surely? But she felt the force of it on her.

Burn it.

Compulsion magic was difficult, and even when it worked it was only supposed to compel something close to what the person would do anyway. Had it compelled her to read the book, she would likely have given in. But librarians save books; they do not destroy them.

Abruptly, she closed the book. Davox would agree with the compulsion. He would argue its very presence was enough. But she knew better.

No, she was no mage, but she *was* a librarian. Furthermore, she was a librarian who read. She knew the laws of magic as they had been, and as they now were.

The fact that she was starting to reach for a match, the fact that it was taking everything in her being not to do the one thing she would never, without coercion, do?

That was old magic. Somebody, somewhere, had brought enough magic back to do this. Enough magic to do *this*.

She stood. She put down the match. She slipped the book into her bag.

Davox was outside. "What about the book?"

"I'm still studying it. Excuse me." Her heartrate went up. If he found out what she intended to do, he would stop her.

He might be right to do so.

Could it be that the compulsion was intended to be fought? Reverse psychology. Command her to burn the book so she would use it. Davox might be right.

She walked past him nonetheless, around the wall, entering the old tower from its far side, where he would not see her. From there she descended into the catacombs.

Skulls lined the walls, the skulls of scholars past and before that of mages, from when this place was a mage school.

Not as prestigious as the White Tower, no, but it had been a mage school.

If magic had returned, would it be one again? To her, it did not matter. They would still need a librarian.

The crystal shard was what remained of this school's crystal—all that remained of it. It stood on its plinth.

Nobody dared move it. Superstition combined with sharp edges to hold it in place, to keep it where it was as a memorial and a monument to things which had been.

It was white, with the faintest hue of rainbow. White light shattered into a rainbow, she knew that.

Nobody knew, in truth, where the White Tower had been. Supposedly it had been destroyed when the crystals shattered.

She did not touch the crystal.

Sharp edges.

But she opened the book. The command to destroy it bubbled up in her mind as she tried to find the right page, stronger with every moment.

Burn it, burn it, burn it.

Burn it all.

The compulsion was reaching past the destruction of the book and toward the destruction of the school, and suddenly she knew her error, knew it keenly.

This was the book they had used to shatter the crystals, to destroy the White Tower, to destroy magic.

It wasn't the book she was supposed to burn.

"No," she said out loud. And she threw the book away from her, at the crystal. It was, perhaps, some instinct.

The book hit the crystal and the crystal tore through its pages. Something shrieked, something ancient and terrible, shrieking in agony.

Librarians did not destroy books, but this was not a book. It was a monster. The shriek died down...

...and it was just a damaged book.

Davox was right. She should have destroyed it. But she stood there looking at the crystal, what was left of it.

The book. She picked it up, bits of paper falling from it. She would burn it, after all. But she looked at the crystal, with its sharp edges, and she put a hand on it anyway. She felt her skin part, saw her blood start to flow down it. "I'm sorry about that."

As if it was a person to whom she needed to apologize. It wasn't, but it had been once. When it had been one of the crystals of magic. She picked up the book and left to find a fire.

Behind her, unnoticed, the crystal glowed faintly.

ABOUT THE AUTHOR

Jennifer R. Povey lives in Northern Virginia with her husband. She writes a variety of speculative fiction, whilst following current affairs and occasionally indulging in horse riding and role-playing games. She has sold fiction to a number of markets including Analog, and written RPG supplements for several companies. She is currently working on an urban fantasy series, Lost Guardians.

HEART OF STONE

ALEX MCGILVERY

Baz stomped into the village. At least the trolls called it a village. Baz had never seen any human village, but he imagined it would be more impressive than this ragged collection of stone huts. What did a being made of stone need with walls and a roof?

"Baz." Mic walked out of his hut followed by Gran and Slat. They towered over Mic; as far as Baz knew, they were the biggest trolls of the Thousand. Mic wanted to be the most important.

"Mic." Baz nodded slightly, the black rock of his neck grinding. The gods hadn't meant for trolls to bend and scrape. "What do you want from me?" He planted his feet and met Mic's eyes. Gran grunted and Mic flapped a hand at him irritably.

"You've been watching the humans again." Mic picked at the sheets of rock on his arm. "We don't need them to be thinking about trolls. Your memories should include what happened last time."

"What difference does it make?" Baz threw his arms up. "We are the Thousand. No matter what the humans do, we will return from the rock."

"Stay away from the humans, Baz. If you want to spend your time thinking, climb a mountain and sit on it."

Baz shifted his feet and made a fist. If trolls had emotions he'd say it was anger, but rocks don't feel.

"I could have you thrown from the Cliff and find out if you return from the rock more amenable to good sense." Mic put up his hand to stop Gran's step forward.

"You could." Baz relaxed his hand. Fighting with Mic would achieve nothing. "But each time we come out of the rock we come out more extreme. A day will come when even trolls won't talk to trolls."

"What's there to say?" Mic pointed at Baz. "We are what the gods made us."

"Did it ever occur to you to ask *why* the gods made us?"

"We're trolls." Mic shook his head. "So act like a troll. Stay away from humans."

Baz turned to go, but words snaked out of his mouth. "I may spend time watching the humans, but at least I don't want to be one." Gran and Slat stomped forward, so Baz turned and walked as fast as he could from the village.

"If I ever see you again, you'll go over the cliff." Mic yelled at his back. Baz lifted his hand in a gesture he'd seen the humans use when they were angry. It was appropriate for the situation.

Gran and Slat didn't even walk to the edge of the village. They might be big, but their size made them slow. They'd been Mic's bodyguard for thousands of years. None of the memories in Baz's head showed Mic without them.

He headed down the mountain, the memories arguing with him, calling him a traitor.

"Enough." Baz slapped his head. "Do you want to go grovel at Mic's feet?" The memories went quiet. His own thoughts weren't as easily silenced.

The gods had made trolls from the rock. The oldest legends said the other races were fearful, so the gods decreed there would be a thousand trolls; never more, never less. Only Baz of all the Thousand asked why.

The landscape shifted to meadow and scrubby trees. Baz walked carefully to do as little damage as possible; another one of his oddities. Not that there was anything like a normal troll, they were as different as the rock they came from.

The trees grew taller and farther apart. Baz no longer had to pick his way through the vegetation. Now he placed his feet in slow motion, so as not to make the ground shake and warn whoever camped on the trail leading to the pass. The memories woke and muttered at him, but now they were about the landscape. At one time the trolls used to come down the mountain. *Why?* An ancient memory floated up, a wisp-thin image of long-ago Baz talking with a human. The other memories swirled, of human mages taking trolls to torture; attempting to find the secret to immortality.

Now when trolls climbed out of the rock, they stayed in the mountains.

The memories showed Mic was right about the humans. They had come with armies and magic, and the trolls fought back with rocks and the mountains themselves. The humans left, and the trolls stopped talking with humans.

Am I wrong? Baz froze in the forest. *Will I only start a new war?* The stone in his chest gave him no answer. Rocks didn't feel, didn't change. The only difference between the basalt in the mountains and that in his chest was whatever the gods had done to make him live. He supposed if he were human, he'd be afraid.

Something moved in the dark. The sun had set while he'd been lost in the memories. Baz stayed still. A person in a red hat collected sticks, muttering too quietly for Baz to hear. When the wood gatherer headed away with a bundle as big as himself, Baz followed as slowly as he could. Up ahead, light flickered in a clearing. He crept as close as he dared.

A circle of dwarves huddled around a fire. The one in the red hat sat beside his bundle of wood, feeding the fire. Their breath made fog as they talked.

"I ever tell you 'bout the time I saw a troll come out of the rock?"

If Baz had had a heart, it would have been beating loud enough to alert the gathering. The other dwarves made a mix of groans and expressions of interest. The old dwarf grinned and rubbed his hands together.

"'Twas back when I was a Red Hat."

"Why do all these stories happen when dwarves are Red Hats?" The younger dwarf in the red hat shoved more wood into the fire then adjusted his hat.

"Because when we're Red Hats we do foolish things, and foolery makes for good stories." The old dwarf thumped his foot on the ground, and stared into the fire as if the story he wanted to tell was hidden in the flames. "We were climbing Zareth's Pass, late in the season, but Tompin Wellsdeep had spotted a deposit he wanted to explore, and we'd spent extra days chipping off samples for him. So there we were, sitting around a fire like tonight, and Tompin sent me off to fetch firewood. 'Red Hat fetches the firewood.'"

"Red Hat fetches everything," the dwarf in the red hat said, but he grinned and ducked his head as he spoke. The dwarves on either side elbowed him. The storyteller glared them into silence. Baz silently urged him to continue.

"The path down toward the trees was lit well enough by the moon, but the shadows it cast were stark black. I about jumped out of my skin when a loud crack echoed across the valley. Flakes of rock littered the path where I'd just been. Above them, coming out of the rock was a hand as big as my head." The dwarf shook his head. Baz looked at his hand, clenched it making a slight grinding sound. The crowd around the fire stiffened and looked around, Baz held still until they relaxed and the old dwarf took up the story again.

"I ran back to the fire and told the others, who of course laughed at me, but without anything better to do they followed me back to the rock face where the hand had become an arm waving madly in the night. It knocked my hat off and I scrambled back to grab it. The others shouted at each other, and I thought they were mad at me. I shoved the hat on my head and turned to glare at them, only to see I was alone on the path with the arm reaching from the rock."

"So what did you do then?" The Red Hat threw more wood on the fire.

"I might have been a Red Hat, but I wasn't a complete fool. I chased after the others. Took me all night to catch them too."

"But you could have caught the thing as it came out and taken the immortality stone from its heart."

"There is no immortality stone." Baz's voice surprized him as much as the dwarves. With a crunch of rock, he shrugged and stepped out into the light. "It is just the way we were made. You could kill me here, and try as you might, you'd find nothing but shards of rock. Another me would claw its way out of the rock of my birthplace."

The dwarves huddled on the other side of the fire, the light making their eyes into flame and impossible to read.

"I'd heard trolls hate all other living things and destroy them when they get a chance." The Red Hat stepped forward and looked up at Baz.

"Some of us do." Baz held up his hand and peered at it. "It is wisest when meeting a troll to run first and live to ask your questions of another being."

"What's it like to live forever?" The storyteller stepped forward and put his hand on the Red Hat's shoulder.

"We don't live forever. We die and are reborn as ourselves, but not with all our memories. Each time, something is lost."

"What can a troll die from?" The Red Hat tilted his head.

"What do dwarves die from?" Baz pushed the fire together a little with his hands. "Mostly, we erode, get weary of life, and become lifeless rock to let a new troll come forth." He nodded his head at the group, then pulled a chip of rock from his torso and tossed it across the fire. The Red Hat caught it and stared wide-eyed at Baz. "I thank you for your time and the light of your fire." He stepped back into the shadows, then walked away through the trees, making no effort to hide his footsteps.

There were times Baz envied the soft ones the emotions he saw on their faces. Other times, like now, he was satisfied to be free of the fears and griefs of the flesh. Baz stumbled through the forest until he stepped off the edge of a cliff.

He had no time to curse himself for his stupidity before he hit the water. It slowed him enough that the rocks on the bottom of the lake only knocked chips from his torso and broke off his left foot. Baz pushed himself upright and picked his way through the rocks until he found a place he could climb out.

The memories called him all kinds of a fool, and Baz didn't argue with them. This was what Mic had warned him about.

He looked around to see if anyone was there to watch. The strangest urge to hide came over him and Baz almost returned to the water. The threat of deep mud made him walk away from the lake. Quar had told him about spending a thousand years on the bottom of a lake buried deep in the mud. Of course, for Quar that would have been a perfect place.

The ground sucked at Baz's feet, and at times he sank in as far as his knees.

"Bah," he grunted aloud. He ripped a nearby tree from its roots and stripped it of branches with his hands. Using the makeshift staff to test the ground, he meandered his way onto solid footing.

He'd been walking for days using the tree to compensate for the missing foot, when he heard sounds of fighting coming from the distance. The smart thing would be to head away from the fight. Whoever was trying to kill whom, it made no difference to him. But his feet carried him toward the clash.

A tall human had her back to an immense boulder that towered above the trees. A smaller human lay unmoving beside her. Four other humans faced her, mounted on beasts that might have been either bears or dogs. They roared and batted at an invisible barrier. Two of the humans hammered at the barrier with swords, while the other two held staves in front of them, red light hitting the barrier and sending cracks through it.

"Foolish," one of the sorcerers spoke casually. "Your refusal to take a life weakens you."

"Not as much as being murdering scum would." The woman's voice didn't betray any strain, though her hands shook and sweat ran in rivers from her face.

The sorcerers growled and pushed more effort into their staves.

"Troll." One of the sword-swingers yelled and pointed at Baz. The sorcerers spun and aimed their staves at Baz. One of them spoke a syllable; the other's mouth had just opened when the tree Baz still carried struck them and sent the pair soaring into the trees. One swordsman rode at Baz screaming, blue flames licking the edge of his weapon. Baz hammered him into the ground; the flames vanished. The other turned his steed and vanished into the forest.

Silence fell. Baz dropped the tree. Whatever he wanted, he was still a troll, and every human knew that trolls killed without reason. The remains of the swordsman and beast accused him. The other beasts must have fled. Their masters' mangled bodies hung from branches high up in the trees.

"He said you don't kill." Baz turned to the woman, who gazed back at him out of eyes which might have been cut from sapphires. "I apologize for the shedding of blood." He lowered his head and turned to leave.

"Wait." The woman crouched beside her companion and checked him. "You took no oath, and there is no blame for aiding strangers. If Willard hadn't been injured, he would have championed me."

"Your champion, Willard. He is badly injured?"

"I'm afraid so." The woman sighed and wiped at her eyes. "Beyond my ability to heal at any rate. I must go for help."

Baz looked around at the wilderness.

"I have ways of traveling swiftly, though the price is high." She adjusted the man's cloak minutely. "I'm loathe to leave him alone, but traveling the ways would kill him."

"I will stay with him." Baz stomped over to where he could get a look at the man's pale face. His cheek twitched as if pain were torturing him even in unconsciousness.

"The Council is *not* going to believe this." The woman spun in place and vanished. Baz caught a glimpse of a tunnel formed of light, then he stood alone in the forest.

He didn't like the corpses lying around, proof of his murderous ways. Baz dug a hole in the soft soil of the forest floor. His hand tingled oddly when it got too close to the sword, so he used the tree to push sword, swordsman, and beast into the hole. Since the bodies of the sorcerers repulsed him even in death, he left them in their trees and filled the grave, tamping the soil down.

"My lady Qwyneth?" The man's voice rasped. Baz stomped over to look at him. Brown eyes pleaded with him.

"She has traveled the ways to bring you help."

"It is just like her." The man let his head fall back. "Wins an impossible battle, then kills herself to rescue me."

"The lady said you were injured beyond her ability to heal."

"Did she now?" The man's eyes closed. "I suppose even she has limits. The Rahadlian death curse is incurable. I am glad not to die alone."

"I promised to wait with you until her return."

"You are a most unusual troll." Willard's voice weakened.

"You've met others?" Baz couldn't stop the question. Quar was the only troll outside the village he'd ever met.

"A few." Willard winced and gasped. Baz guessed he would die soon.

The troll looked at his hand. Though his litany of questions made him an outcast, he wondered: what was it that kept him alive? He could almost perceive energy running through the black rock forming him. Death was so easy. Why did life have to be hard? Baz put his hand over the man's chest, now barely moving.

The light flashing through his hand wasn't much different than the light fading from Willard. Baz experimentally tried to push light from his hand into the human and suddenly lightning flashed from one to the other. The man arched his back and screamed, black fog lifting from his skin and vanishing in the lightning.

Then the light vanished with a snap.

Baz's hand crumbled into gravel. The disintegration traveled up his arm. Willard sat up and reached toward Baz, his pitch-black eyes open wide in shock and grief.

It was the last thing Baz saw before the rest of him fell into a heap of rock.

Qwyneth jumped from the roc then helped the Healer down. The great bird walked to the edge of the clearing and sat. Qwyneth ran to where she'd left Willard and the troll then stopped in shock, the healer bumping into her. The Arch-mage had ranted at her for risking her life for a dead man, but curiosity made the Healer willing to fly on her roc to meet a troll who apologized for killing.

Qwyneth had prepared herself for anything but this.

Willard looked up from the rock in his hand.

"I see you made it through the ways." He dropped the rock on the pile and knelt at her feet. "I'm not deserving of that level of risk. I'd rather die than live knowing I'd caused your death."

Qwyneth pulled him to his feet.

"How many times must I tell –" Her words broke off in a gasp as Willard looked at her. His warm, brown eyes had become hard, black stones. Yet he clearly saw as well as he ever had.

The Healer stepped around Qwyneth and laid her hands on Willard's arm, then snatched them back like they'd been burnt.

"What happened?"

"Don't rightly know." Willard sighed and sat on a rock. "I woke enough to talk with Baz. I could feel the curse working its way toward my heart, and thanked the troll for being there with me at the end."

"But where did he go?" Qwyneth looked around as if he'd step out of the trees at any moment.

Willard pointed to the pile of black rubble.

"The darkness was coming for me when a bolt of light struck through me, blowing the curse into tatters. I sat up and watched as he fell apart in front of me." He put his head in his hands. "What do people see in me to be so willing to die for my sake?" Willard jumped up and stalked away into the trees.

"Willard isn't human anymore, at least not completely." The Healer slumped down on the rock Willard had vacated. "His heart is stone, yet the life energy in him is beyond anything I've experienced, and I've healed dragons."

"Artisan preserve us." Qwyneth picked up a piece of rock from the pile which was all that remained of the troll.

"I must ask you to release me from my oath." Willard stumbled into the clearing and threw himself at Qwyneth's feet. "I swore an oath on my life to serve you until my last breath, but Baz has been reborn missing most of what makes him Baz. I must make what is broken whole." His shoulders shook.

Qwyneth reached down and lifted Willard to his feet.

"You know I cannot release you from that oath." The buzz of energy in Willard's hand stung her, but she set her teeth and kept her grip. "So I will journey with you and give you what aid I can."

Willard opened his mouth to argue, but Qwyneth gave him what he called The Look. He sighed.

"Then let us set out."

The Healer mounted the roc and flew away as Willard led them vaguely north.

The troll crawled from the rock and roared at the heavens. He smashed stones with his fists then threw the pieces far out into the canyon. He knew he was a troll, but he had no name, only whispers of memories taunted him, just out of reach. A tug from far away pulled at the cavity in his chest, aching to be filled. The troll turned his head as if he sought a scent in the air. Crushing one last rock between his hands, he thudded away down the path, always aware of the distant need.

Baz. His name fit loosely, leaving unexplained gaps in his mind, not touching the emptiness inside him.

The path moved from bare rock to trees to open meadows. Valleys filled with green slowed him as he had to find a safe way down abrupt precipices. Massive trees grew on valley floors, big enough even a troll must go around. He walked when he had to, ran when he could. Always downhill, always toward the ever-stronger pull of what had been stolen from him.

Baz only paid enough attention to keep from running off a cliff. He didn't question his rage, or how a rock could burn with hate. The open spaces grew larger, the slopes more gentle. Baz increased his speed, leaving the ground shaking behind him.

Momentum carried him half way through the army before he crashed to a halt. Men with uncertain eyes surrounded him, others on strange beasts gathered behind them. Confusion kept him in place. He'd seen these things before; the memory almost came to him.

"Surrender and serve me." A man carrying a tall staff and blue fire burning in his eyes strolled over to contemplate Baz. "You creatures are easy enough to kill, but how you live in the first place intrigues me. Imagine an army of stone warriors at my command. You could be my General."

The pull became painful. Baz shook his head. Then a memory struck him with the force of a boulder. A man like this stole his heart. He screamed his defiance. Rage and pain mixed. A man tried to stick him with a spear glowing with blue flames, and Baz spun and snatched him up. Completing the spin, he threw the spearman at the one with the staff. The sorcerer's bolt of red light was deflected enough to strike the troll's arm instead of where his heart should be.

The arm exploded sending red-hot rock toward the humans. Baz thumped the ground with his remaining fist, making everyone close to him stagger and fall to their knees, even the one with the staff. Baz threw a handful of dirt and rocks as another bolt shot from the staff. The blast left a wide circle of moaning humans.

The irresistible pull drew him into a run. The humans scrambled to get out of his way, and none followed him into the forest. He left a path of destruction through that day and the next. Pain ruled what mind he had.

In the night, he didn't see the cliff of black rock towering over him. Baz ran into it at full speed, splashing into the basalt cliff as easy as water.

It enfolded him, eased his pain, comforted the distress in his mind. When Baz moved to claw his way out of the rock, a voice whispered, *Wait*. So Baz let the rock cradle him, the first troll in the millennia since the gods had made them to return to the rock.

Willard opened his eyes to Qwyneth leaning over him, tears dropping on his face.

"It wasn't your fault."

"I swear you're a mind-reader." Qwyneth sat back and rubbed her face.

"The only time I've seen you cry is when you're blaming yourself for my fate. I made my choice; I'd make the same one again."

"If I'd just..."

"Just what? Been faster, stronger, able to see the future? Don't blame yourself for being human."

"But being human is such a nuisance at times." Qwyneth stood up as Willard laughed.

"It has its good points too, my Lady." He rubbed his arm, surprised to find it still attached.

"What happened?"

"Pain, like my arm had been torn off, a spear stuck in my back. Anger, grief, fear–whatever happened to Baz hurt him badly. It's stopped now, but he's still out there."

"I can only think of one thing which could hurt a troll like that." Qwyneth stared north as if her vision could cut through forest and rock to show her the Rahadlians.

"I will take care not to walk into them." Willard stood, picked up his pack and let the way through the forest. He didn't dare ask how long he'd left Qwyneth vulnerable with his weakness. They didn't talk as they journeyed; Qwyneth was used to silence as a safety measure.

A deep valley beckoned, already in shade, an immense black cliff on the far side. Willard guided them on a roundabout route, avoiding open spaces. They arrived at the cliff without incident.

"Something about this..." Willard stretched his hand out to touch the smooth black rock.

"No!" Qwyneth reached toward him, but too late; his hand vanished into the stone, pulling the rest of him inexorably. Willard snatched at his sword to cut himself free and twisted to see Qwyneth's horrified face.

"Sorry, my Lady." The last thing he felt was her fingers sliding off his.

Memories floated in the rock. He couldn't tell if he was Baz or Willard. He wasn't sure there was any difference anymore. The panic of climbing from the rock with only half a soul washed through him. The guilt at standing between an arrogant young girl and those who would harm her, blood dripping from his dagger. He wanted to know. He needed to atone. *Why?*

Amusement touched him gently.

He lived the memories of Baz refining his curious nature, desperate to find a purpose beyond existing. The worry as the trolls grew apart, uncaring even for each other. Then a memory of training floated to the surface.

"Dying is easy." The instructor had paced in front of him. "Life is hard. I'm training you to live. *They* told you to be prepared to give your life for your mage. I'm telling you that if you die, you've failed."

The knowledge that he could always be reborn – he saw how it weakened him, made him careless of his life. What had he done in the thousands of years as living rock? Only died and been made new. How had the world been changed?

His first meeting with Qwyneth as a mage. Against all advice, she'd bonded him as her companion.

"Guilt is not a good reason to do things." The Arch-mage had looked into her eyes. She stared back, unafraid.

"It isn't guilt. It's the desire to make the world a better place."

"You almost believe that." The Arch-mage had dropped his head, then took her hand and Willard's and incanted the words linking their fate. He would not survive her death. She could not kill even to protect herself; he was her shield against danger.

"I must find her."

His heart raced, his hands shook, and he gasped for air. Willard fought to ease his fear then opened his eyes.

Baz stood and put his hand on his chest, then turned his gaze to Willard.

"This is what it is to be human?" He tapped his finger against the rock. "So frail, but so determined."

Willard stood and swayed on his feet. "Trolls do not lack courage."

"What is courage?"

"The choice to live a hard life instead of taking an easy death." Willard pointed to the ground. "There was a squad of warriors riding fell-beasts. They've taken Qwyneth."

"How do you know she lives?"

"If she were dead, you'd be standing alone here." Willard looked around, but they must have taken his pack along with Qwyneth. "We follow this trail." Baz thumped along behind as Willard loped toward his Lady.

Mic looked at the village; discontent filling him. The trolls could be so much more if they would just listen to him. A scant hundred out of the Thousand lived in the village, most of them going through their life as if they were alone. Baz's words before he left irritated him. The only thing needed was a little discipline.

Gran and Slate loomed behind him. They'd followed him for millennia. Mic didn't know what they found by serving him, unless the occasional chance to toss someone from the cliff was motivation enough.

Mic didn't really want to be a human, but he wanted what human leaders had: respect, obedience.

"Mic." Felds thumped up behind him. "A human army has been spotted at the bottom of the pass."

"Gather everyone you can find and bring them to the canyon. We'll discourage them." Felds departed, bellowing to the others in the village. Trolls left the village looking for others who lived close by. "This is Baz's fault. I warned him."

"Should've pitched him," Gran rumbled behind Mic.

"He was right about one thing." Mic clenched his fist, sending flakes of mica falling to the ground. "He'd have just come back. We need a better way of dealing with him."

"Deep hole," Slate said.

Mic turned around and stared up at Slate for a moment. The troll hadn't spoken in a hundred years. Then he shrugged.

"We'll deal with that when we've sent the humans running." He headed off toward the canyon.

The edges of the canyon on both sides were lined with loose rocks of all sizes. Trolls on the other side waved. There had to be almost a hundred there, watching the pass intently. Almost as many stood on Mic's side. If he'd known an invasion would bring them out, Mic would have sent Baz out himself. He rubbed his hands together in anticipation. This would alleviate his boredom, at least for today.

The sun dropped below the horizon, but the trolls didn't move. What did rock need with rest? It rose again, showing a small group of humans riding beasts up the path to the canyon.

Mic held his hand up, waiting until the invaders were too close to escape. The humans didn't look to be in any rush. None of them looked up. They wouldn't live to regret their foolishness.

The sun had risen halfway to noon before Mic dropped his hand. A hail of boulders plunged toward the interlopers. Trolls threw one, then picked up another to throw before the first one hit. They went through half of the boulders placed for this purpose before Mic saw that not one rock had hit its target.

They slid to the side or off to the rear of the group. The humans were pointing up and laughing. One stopped and made a face up at them. The human in front, carrying a staff, turned and made a cutting motion with his hand. The impudent human returned to following, but as the train reached the end of the canyon, he turned and made a gesture at the trolls.

A boulder lifted from the edge and plunged down in a blur and wiped the warrior from the trail. The leader didn't even look around.

"Wait here." Mic told the trolls. "I'll go find out what the humans want." He eagerly walked back toward the village. Gran and Slate followed, in step as always.

The humans waited in the village. The one with the staff stood a little in front of the others.

"I suppose I should apologize for the manner of our entry." The human nodded to Mic. "I didn't want damage any of your people, but did need to demonstrate my power to do so. The fact you are here shows you received my message."

"What do you want?" Mic glared at the man. He could squash the human with one fist. But a glint of challenge showed in the man's eyes.

"To the point." The man planted his staff on the stone. "I am the High Sorcerer of Rahadlia. If I am going to rule the world as I should, I need an army unstoppable by any normal means." Blue flame danced in the sorcerer's eyes. "That army would need a general."

Mic smiled. His face wasn't used to the expression, but it felt good. "Let's talk about what the trolls would gain from being your army."

Baz and Willard slipped through the forest. Baz watched Willard move and emulated him. The longer they went the more separate the two became. Baz knew without a doubt he was Baz, the troll, and Willard, the man. Willard glanced back and nodded in approval.

Baz watched for the human to stop and rest, but he moved as relentlessly as any troll. Maybe there was stone in him now. Was there flesh in Baz? He nudged at the memories trying to find something to show how he'd changed, but they were as confused as he was. Something tightened in his gut. Baz stopped to put his hand on his torso.

"It's fear." Willard didn't turn around. "While we are our own selves, it seems we still share some things."

"Fear?" Baz explored the sensation. It made him think of landing in the water, unsure if he'd survive in one piece.

"I think you trolls have as many emotions as any other race, but how long have you told yourselves stone can't feel?"

"Forever." Baz put his hand on his head. "Yet we live, and rock should not live either."

Baz explored his memories with his new insight. How could he have missed it? But looking back his life, it took on shades of emotion, many he couldn't name. Was this true for the others too?

Willard held up his fist and Baz froze in place.

"Let me go forward alone. Your skills are amazing for someone of our size–your size–but this is beyond you."

"I will think on what I've learned."

He stood still and sifted through his memories, comparing them to what he'd gained from Willard.

Willard ghosted through the forest, avoiding sentries. They were good, he'd give them that, but none had the training of a companion. Close to the clearing, Willard climbed a tree high enough to get a view of the camp. Warriors bustled setting up tents and corrals for their beasts.

In the center of the camp, a wagon sat surrounded by two layers of guards holding swords or spears, some burning with blue flame. On the wagon, Qwyneth had been chained in a kneeling position, arms bent awkwardly. Willard's shoulder twinged in sympathy.

Qwyneth's head lifted, and the guards in the circle rustled. She knew he was watching. He had no idea how she did it, but she always knew he was watching. Her head dropped again and the warriors relaxed.

Her hand stretched as if she were trying to relieve pressure on her shoulders.

Danger, trolls, sorcerer. At least Willard expected she meant "troll" when she signed "golem."

He wasn't sure if she meant danger to the trolls or from them. Maybe both. He couldn't see the High Sorcerer anywhere in the camp. The man had made Willard's skin crawl when he'd visited the Council to leave his ultimatum. Willard had thought he was used to magic, but the sorcerer felt like a viper among rat snakes. The man intended to rule the world, no matter the cost to the people who lived in it.

A fragment of memory drifted into his mind–Baz confronting the Sorcerer; the High Sorcerer inviting Baz to join him and lead the trolls. Willard's stomach sank as he imagined even a few trolls marching against the Council forces. Only magic could stop them, and the Mages were forbidden to kill.

Willard slipped down the tree and crawled his way out of the forest to meet Baz.

"The sorcerer wants the trolls to fight for him," Willard said without preamble.

Baz nodded. "Mic would like that. Not the fighting, but the importance of leading."

"Mic?"

"A troll who wants to organize us into–something. I'm not sure even he knows. A chance to be a General would be irresistible."

"How would the sorcerer know about Mic?"

"He wouldn't need to. He would just have to keep asking until someone says yes." Baz clenched his fist. "I need to go talk to Mic."

"The High Sorcerer may be there."

"It won't be the first time we've met."

"I remember. Go safely." Willard turned away as Baz vanished into the trees. Willard sighed, then turned to sneak back to the camp. This time he needed to infiltrate the Rahadlian army. It would be easier with the High Sorcerer missing, but there were others he'd need to watch for: he wouldn't have Baz to heal him of any death curse this time.

Getting to the camp was child's play compared to taking a sentry silently. They were warriors, strong and alert. He'd only have a short time before the gap in the line was discovered. Then he spotted a warrior headed to the woods, unlacing his trousers. In any army Willard had seen, he'd be disciplined for his actions, but his laziness served Willard well.

The man leaned against a tree making noises of relief. Willard waited until both hands were occupied with putting his clothes together. The warrior never knew he died. Willard hauled him farther from the camp, but not far enough for the first ring of sentries to trip over him. He changed clothes as quickly as he could, hiding his own knives out of sight.

A man in a brass helmet stormed over as Willard entered the camp. It wouldn't be good if he ended up in the stockade.

"What the blazes do you think you were doing?" Brass Helmet didn't give Willard time to respond. Just as well, since his Rahadlian was rusty. "March double time! You can stand in the inner circle for a day. Maybe the witch will strike you first. The sorcerers say she's bound not to kill, but that still leaves a lot of nasty." He pushed Willard, who marched over to the circle. The men thumped him as he pushed through to the inner circle. He'd chosen his entry point to end up in front of Qwyneth. The others held weapons at the ready and stared steadily at the wagon. Willard drew his sword and waited.

Qwyneth's hand moved in the circle she used to tell him he was being especially crazy.

You're one to talk.

Baz climbed up the back ways to get to the village. The first thing he noticed was the number of trolls present. They'd at least doubled in number since his last visit. Mic must be happy – and there he was, with Gran and Slate behind him, talking with the man who'd used magic to take off Baz's arm.

The sorcerer stiffened and pointed to Baz. He looked ready to fire a bolt, but Mic stopped him. They argued briefly before the sorcerer waved in disgust and stomped off.

"I told you the next time I saw you, you'd go over the cliff." Mic looked to be holding himself straighter, more confident.

"Need to talk to you." Baz ignored Gran and Slate, who'd taken his arms. "Maybe you can walk with me, and make sure they do it right."

Gran growled, but Mic shook his head. "You've always been a strange one, Baz, but I should thank you for sending the High Sorcerer to me."

"I'm guessing he's told you he's out to conquer the world. Wants you as his General commanding the troll army."

"That's right. The others are bored, and a little destruction will provide some new and interesting memories."

"I can see that. Any troll would love to be torn to pieces by magic–then the dragons. They'd be a lot of fun."

"The humans won't expect us, Baz. They won't have time to respond."

"They have short lives, but their race has a long memory. They adapt fast."

"You would know." Mic sneered. He looked to be about to turn away.

"If you're their leader, you need to have a plan for every possibility," Baz told him. "Including a plan for what to do if that sorcerer decides that conquering the world includes ruling the trolls."

Mic fell back into step. "He's just one more human."

"He fired a bolt of magic that blew my arm off. His men have swords and spears that will cut rock."

"It will only take one blow to kill him."

"Then plan that blow well, Mic, because you won't get a second one."

They arrived at the cliff. It wasn't the first time Baz had seen this view. Through the ages, he and Mic had never seen quite eye to eye.

"You're their leader, Mic. It's your job to have plans. He won't expect trolls to think ahead."

Gran and Slate picked Baz up and threw him over the cliff as easily as he'd toss a pebble. They'd given him more distance than last time.

Curl into a ball. Willard's memory prompted him.

Baz obeyed the thought. As high as the cliff stood, it didn't take more than handful of seconds to hit bottom. He crashed in the pile of shattered trolls sending shards in all directions. Baz rolled to a stop almost buried by rock. He stood up and inspected himself. He'd taken a few chips here and there, but that was all. Mic would not be pleased.

Let's not do that again soon.

Baz laughed, stunning his memories. They could not recall any troll laughing before. The day was filled with new things. Baz pushed his way out of the rock pile and headed down the valley. He'd be able to cross over the ridge and get back to Willard.

Willard stopped himself from falling by sheer willpower. Something had happened to Baz, and it had sent echoes through him. Not as bad as the first time, but he'd come close to fainting and giving himself away. Now all he got from Baz was a vague feeling of happiness.

Qwyneth looked at him, her eyes concerned. Willard lowered his brows briefly. Not much could be communicated with such miniscule expressions, but Qwyneth relaxed slightly.

Time for patience and endurance; even with his training, Willard couldn't imagine being forced into such a position for hours – never mind days. Qwyneth once commented that mage training made companion's schooling seem mild in comparison.

Willard knew two things for sure. First, that Qwyneth had a plan, and probably several plans; second, that he wouldn't like any of them. The High Sorcerer had grossly underestimated the Lady, and Willard didn't intend to let the man learn from his mistake.

Later in the day, the High Sorcerer returned, followed by a collection of trolls. More than a hundred of them accompanied the Rahadlian, if Willard's count out of the corner of his eye was accurate.

The Sorcerer strolled over to the wagon and waved the guards away. A single troll followed him. Where Baz had been formed of chunks and columns of black rock, this one was made of sheets which reflected glints of light from the sun. He picked at the stone of his arm. That must be Mic, the leader Baz had mentioned. If the troll had been human, Willard would have guessed he had a case of the nerves.

"For now, you are a useful hostage against the Council." The High Sorcerer's voice carried to Willard's ears. He held a cup of water and made a point of ignoring the soldiers. It didn't matter, as most of the guards broke into groups to sit or lie on the ground and rest. Willard sat and put his head on his knees. He missed Qwyneth's reply, but he could imagine her response to being thought of as a hostage.

"The Council *will* surrender, or my trolls will tear down their city around the Council's ears."

A grunt came, sounding like rocks grinding together, and Willard forced himself to stay still. Was Mic having second thoughts? Did he know how dangerous that was?

As the sorcerer left, the Rahadlian warriors reformed the circle around Qwyneth. This time Willard had a place off to the side, without any view other than the wagon, the camp, and the forest.

The sun dropped toward the horizon, and even Willard grew tired. He was seriously considering stealing a break when shouting at the other end of the camp roused him. Qwyneth's fingers twitched.

Golem, trouble, treason.

Willard forced his breathing to stay even as the younger warriors around him peered toward the source of the noise. More senior men thumped them and yelled for everyone to keep their eyes on the witch.

Be ready.

The chains holding Qwyneth's arms flared white and vanished in a shower of sparks that burned wherever they landed.

Willard jumped up on the cart and put his sword to Qwyneth's neck.

"Look scared," he whispered. Qwyneth snorted and began trembling realistically.

Willard looked around the camp to take in the chaos. The trolls were huge and fearsome, but no match for the trained warriors. He saw a huge troll shatter, and Baz racing toward an even bigger troll.

"Put a shield on me." Willard prayed his crazy idea would work.

Baz threaded his way through the forest toward the huge meadow where the army camped. Willard already had joined the army. He'd be near his lady. Baz put her out of his mind.

He bumped into a sentry and took advantage of the warrior's shock to hammer him into the ground. The blood on his fist accused him, but there would be worse to come if Willard's memories were anything to go by.

Baz watched for the second sentry and sent him after the first. A few more steps and he stood in the shadow of the trees with the sun behind him.

Mic stood in front of the High Sorcerer, looking in Baz's direction.

"We are not *your* trolls. We are not your beasts of burden."

"You are my General, and Generals obey their leaders." The High Sorcerer's voice made that uncomfortable twist in Baz's stomach worsen. Fear, Willard had called it. He'd also said trolls have courage. Baz readied himself to intervene.

"We obey your orders to fight, not to be servants!" Mic pointed at the High Sorcerer, who simply touched his staff to Mic's torso. As it reddened, Mic looked toward Baz and nodded, then suddenly exploded. None of the shards hit the sorcerer.

Baz waited for the rest of Mic's trolls either to attack the High Sorcerer or to run from the field. They did neither. A troll bellowed *rockslide,* and they split up to move in all directions. Most ran into the camp smashing wagons and tents, swiping warriors out of the way with their fists.

The High Sorcerer raised his staff and sent up a bolt of light which boomed like thunder. In response, the warriors in the camp formed up out of the way of the rampaging trolls, some carrying spears and swords glinting with blue flame. Their beasts roared and growled, asking to join the fight.

That signal almost cost the Sorcerer his life. Slate leaped forward, both fists lifted to crush him. Baz ran across the field at top speed as the sorcerer swung his staff, red light flaring as Slate was cut in half. His legs fell into rubble, but his arms and head held their form.

The human turned toward Gran just as the giant brought his fists down on the ground. The ground shook, and the Rahadlian stumbled and almost fell into Slate's grip. He managed to twist out of the way, dodging both Slate and Gran. Rolling to his feet, he pointed the staff at Gran, and a bolt struck the huge troll and tore through to hit Baz dead on.

I tried.

To Baz's shock, however, the bolt splashed against him, causing no pain or damage. He didn't slow to wonder about it. Astonishingly, Gran took another swing at the Sorcerer, whose hair moved in the breeze of Gran's fist passing. This time, the blast took Gran's head off and sent it flying toward Baz.

Gran's head had a broad grin plastered across it. Baz laughed as he caught all that remained of Mic's bodyguard. He hefted the stone before sending the head screaming back at the sorcerer. The human blew it to pieces with a jerk of his staff. His grin was identical to Gran's as he put both hands on his staff and aimed it at Baz.

Then Slate's hand swept the High Sorcerer's feet from beneath him. The bolt shot up into the sky as Slate's other hand crashed down on the human, driving him into the ground. The troll fell to pieces, and Baz slowed to see what remained of the sorcerer.

The human shot out of the ground with a shriek of fury. As he swung his staff in an arc, Baz rolled forward out of the way, coming to his feet with a chunk of stone in each hand. He fired them at the sorcerer's head. The man dropped as he cut the rocks from the air, but for an instant his staff was pointed up. Baz leapt forward and wrapped his hands around the High Sorcerer's waist, trapping the staff against his body.

A shield pushed against Baz's hands, stopping him from crushing the Rahadlian. Bolts of magic flew harmlessly away into the sky. The human fought, throwing every bit of his power against the troll.

"You may be a sorcerer," Baz ground out. "You may be the strongest man in the world. But I am made of the stuff of mountains."

The chaos in the camp stopped, and the warriors and trolls backed away from each other. Willard escorted Qwyneth through the center until she stood only a little distance from the raging sorcerer.

"You are going to burn out, the way you're behaving. Didn't they teach you any discipline?" Qwyneth spoke casually, almost in a friendly tone. "It doesn't have to be this way. Vow peace to the Council and you can go home."

"And be the weakling puppet of the Council?" The High Sorcerer put his head back and screamed.

Baz clenched his fists and the sound cut off. He dropped the crumpled remains of the human on the ground.

"I had a shield around him," Qwyneth said, "but that works too." She held her hand out over the remains of the sorcerer, and they sank into the ground. "Give me a minute, Baz." Qwyneth sauntered over to the stunned Rahadlians. "Go home. The Council has no interest in ruling you. They are lazy, and governing is a lot of work. Any who are sorcerers are welcome to visit, but only if you swear peace. Otherwise stay away."

"Tell your generals, your kings or sorcerers or whatever," Baz stepped up beside Qwyneth. "If they want to invade, they will face the trolls." He turned to look at Qwyneth. "That goes for your Council if they get too energetic. We trolls have been looking for something to do, and I think keeping the peace will work well enough."

Qwyneth grinned at Baz. "I will pass on your message. They may want to visit to discuss details. The Council is big on details."

"They can wait at the foot of the pass and fly a flag. We'll come and guide them to the village."

Willard's lips twitched, and his amusement tickled at the back of Baz's head. The rest of the trolls gathered around Baz.

"I've been thinking about you and Willard," Qwyneth said. "I had a little peace and quiet to do so." Willard rolled his eyes. "If you put the palms of your hands on the palms of another troll, you may be able to share your memories. Not as completely as with Willard, but enough maybe to give you a common ground."

Felds stepped forward and raised his hands. Baz put his over top. His hands tingled and memories buzzed in his head. When he dropped his hand, memories from Felds were being welcomed and given a place.

"Thank you, Lady Qwyneth." Baz bowed to her. The other trolls copied him. "Let's go home." Baz turned and walked away, the others following in his footsteps.

Baz looked up from where he talked in a circle of trolls. Mic was walking into the village, flanked by Gran and Slate.

"You were right." Mic said.

"But you had a plan." Baz held out his hands palm up. "Put your palms on mine."

Mic reached out slowly and connected with Baz. The other troll's memories flooded in, his centuries of frustration trying to do something—he didn't know what—with the trolls.

Mic dropped his hands and stood still. Baz waited.

"What do you want me to do?" Mic looked at the circle of trolls behind Baz.

"We've been waiting for you. We want you to lead." Baz put his hand on Mic's shoulder. "It is, after all your gift." He led Mic to the circle; they shifted to make space for him.

"Let them tell you what we've been doing, then you can give us your ideas from there."

Baz backed out of the circle and headed out of the village. He'd be able to make the pass by sunset. Maybe he'd find a campfire and hear some stories.

ABOUT THE AUTHOR

Alex McGilvery has been reading as long as he can remember and started writing novels in grade school. He lives with his wife and muse, Alexandra, along with their two dogs and occasionally his son. His website is http://alexmcgilvery.com/.

Antonio's Beast

Bokerah Brumley

Hatred Caves
The Barren

Stiff scales squeezed the dragon's middle, and he rolled over in his stone bed, adjusting to loosen the corset of plates that squeezed his heart. The fracture in his firebox had been growing a little more each year. It wouldn't be long until loneliness would steal his fire breath, force his heart apart, and release poison shards in his veins. A dragon could live without fire, but the shards would kill him.

His inevitable end loomed over every moment he spent awake, but he had been asleep for almost a year, ignoring the problem with no solution. On this day, his hunger had grown too great to ignore.

Water dripped from the ceiling to the underground lake in a rhythm that never changed. The sound echoed backwards and forwards like a clock ticking.

Dragons weren't created to live alone. As time passed, his loneliness had grown large enough that he wondered if he might not fit through the mouth of his lair this year. A breeze tripped in, and the cool of winter tickled his nose. The cold season came early in the mountains, and it meant late summer in the valley. The time had almost come.

He shifted until the rocky points scratched the itchy places between his armored plates. A pleased groan vibrated in his throat. He had been hungry since the air turned hot, but the village needed time to gather livestock enough to feed him his annual meal. It was the agreement that kept them safe, an agreement he'd made impulsively in his youth. He didn't mind waiting for the men of Rivenbourne to amass his offering. They treated him like a diseased king, but he hadn't counted on the short life of man or the misery of solitude.

The dragon was the only one left who remembered the circumstances behind Dragon Day, and he was the only one sworn to uphold it. The Rivenbourne men had almost forgotten the words their grandparents passed on from their grandparents. Even he could barely recall the face of his last hero.

Centuries ago, the Master of the Keep had called him forth from his home. The man had braved the Hatred Caves to strike a bargain. His bravery had touched the fire in his dragon's breast and stoked something more than hatred.

The dragon agreed to eat only what the town offered. For three hundred years he had reveled in the freedom of not having to hunt, and for the first eighty of those, the hero visited every full moon. To his last breath, the man begged the dragon to keep the covenant.

Smacking his lips, he tried to remember what fresh meat tasted like. It had been a long sleep since he had tasted red mutton and flossed his teeth with wool. His stomach groaned. The vibration knocked boulders from the ceiling. They landed in a pile near his clawed feet.

The bonds of his oath were whip's teeth in the hands of forever. Ravenous hunger swelled his stomach. He lumbered to his feet, roaring into the empty places, sending gouts of fire through his lair. At the next full moon, he would consume his due. The dragon had awakened.

RIVENBOURNE TOWNSHIP
THE MASTER'S ESTATE

Antonio rolled over on his sleeping mat. Nightmares had kept him awake, and the thin straw did not make up for the discomfort of the hard, stone floor in the Master's storage room.

Fire and ruin were coming on leathery wings. If Antonio did nothing, Mary and the rest of Rivenbourne would burn on Dragon's Day.

Antonio laid his arm across his eyes, willing his mind to quiet. The sun would be up soon. He should get more sleep before the stars disappeared. He still had to earn his keep in the Master's house. Chores needed to be done. He would not leave them undone. Even in hard times, laziness would not be his legacy.

The famine in the country impacted all of them. The maidens no longer giggled and gossiped about the stable boys while they folded linens. Cook spent portions of her day fretting over the larder. Most livestock had already been made into meals. Guilt salted the meats, and dread flavored the watery soups and stews. They all knew what was coming.

Mary's cousin, the mayor of Rivenbourne, had fled to the mountain caves to wait out the day, only the poor and foolhardy remained. It took donkeys, horses, and money to flee.

Oh mio.

A breath of wind crept along Antonio's spine. He didn't want to be eaten, but he didn't have a choice. Destiny does not wait on convenience, his father had always warned. He turned over again.

Dragon Day.

It comes every year, but this one is different. This one seems…

Antonio smelled the air. *Angry somehow.*

The village had nothing left to feed the hungry beast. The dragon wouldn't care that a drought had killed the town gardens. Their harvest withered in the field. Winter would starve them all.

If the dragon did not dine on their bodies and pick his teeth with their bones first.

No hero would stand against the winged horror to defend Mary or the people of Rivenbourne. That was the truth the daylight would bring. Yesterday, he had spoken to the old woman at the corner of the city gate. She could read the future by recalling the past. She had reached for his hand and warned him to hide.

"Fear does not guide me, grandmother." Antonio squeezed her hand.

"Soft years make weak men, but a boy shall lead them all." She uttered the words as though they were a benediction, and then she reached into her basket. When she pushed beneath her stock of tattered rags, three short swords glinted in the sunlight.

"Don't stare, Antonio," she whispered as her hand hovered over them. "Hard times make criminals of the weak-minded." From beside the weapons, she swiped an ivory tusk. "This is the horn of the Breidbore bear. It will keep you safe from the dragon's magic, Antonio, and keep your mind clear. Use it when you meet your moment." She pressed it into his hands and then lifted her basket to her hip. A frayed tassel tickled his wrist. The white shape was the length of his hand and nearly as heavy as the milk bucket. When he looked for the woman, she had disappeared in the throng.

Antonio rolled over once more and placed his hand over the tasseled relic of the Breidbore bear. It gave him courage, but maybe she had known that. He would stand on the crest of the Hill to wait for the appearance of the fell beast.

In all the times before, the mayor secured the gates that led into the walled city. With the coward gone, who would see to it? Rivenbourne would be wide open to the hungry beast. Perhaps not even the Master would remember to close the gate to hide the village. Out of sight. Out of the mind of the beast. Dragons never craved what they couldn't see.

Antonio shivered. He didn't want to be eaten, but he didn't know if anyone else would protect Rivenbourne. *The dragon will come to feed, and I will beg his mercy for Rivenbourne.*

If the Dragon was too hungry to give them mercy, then he would offer himself in place of Rivenbourne. Antonio hoped he would be enough of a meal.

The day passed quickly.

RIVENBOURNE TOWNSHIP
THE MASTER'S ESTATE

Something tickled Antonio's nose, and he snorted at it, unwilling to stir. "Feathers?" The hen would be the death of him. He was always chasing her out of the kitchen, back into the barnyard, and finding her eggs in strange places.

"Get up, sleepy bones." Somebody giggled.

That's not right. Antonio cracked an eye and peered around the storeroom. "Who's—"

Cold rained down on Antonio's face, and he bolted to his feet, sputtering.

Mary, the water girl, stood nearby. Her brown hair was bound in twin braids and twisted together on top of her head. Her hands rested on her hips, but her eyes sparkled with mirth. The dousing pleased her so much the smattering of freckles nearly danced across the bridge of her nose. At her feet, an empty bucket rested on its side. She made a perfect replica of Cook when the older woman studied the storeroom. "Serves you right, Antonio," Mary said. "Sleeping away the mornings. You're almost as bad as my cousin." She nodded her head, but only once.

"We don't all have someone else to wake us up at a decent hour." Antonio scowled at her and crossed his arms. He would never be as bad as that coward of a mayor.

She laughed again as though she hadn't a care in the world. "But I wokes you, so you do, too." She glowed with self-satisfaction. "The creatures wants their breakfasts." Mary always spoke with too many s's. When she was a girl, her father was an angry drunk, and he'd been angry every night. Cook said Mary's speech came from being mishandled when she was a babe. She had come to live with her auntie Cook on her sixth birthday. She'd been Antonio's friend ever since.

"I haven't slept late later than the rooster in a long time." Antonio couldn't remember ever having slept late.

"Maybe so, but Cook said once was too many." Mary tapped the bucket with her bare toe. "She sent me to wake you so she could inventory the spence."

Antonio waved toward his night shirt. "Go on then, let me get dressed enough to be decent." Her jovial mood disrupted his focus. She didn't understand what would happen later that afternoon.

At that, Mary laughed. "I've never seens you decent, Antonio Ricci."

"That's not true." He was decent every day. She didn't know what she was looking at.

"Mary," Cook called. "Where are you, girl?"

"Coming." Mary scooped up the bucket and dashed out of the room. "See you at the dinners bells." She tossed the words over her shoulder as she disappeared around the corner.

Once she had gone, Antonio dressed quickly. He could hear their cow, Daisy, lowing in her stall. The stable hands would have already led her into the barn so he could milk her. He needed to hurry. Cook would want the milk for Mistress' morning meal.

He must hurry through his scheduled tasks and head to Hillcrest. Destiny waited for him outside the city's walls.

RIVENBOURNE TOWNSHIP
THE MASTER'S ESTATE

Antonio tapped Daisy's rump as she chewed on a bit of hay left over from last harvest. They rationed it carefully—she received five handfuls each morning. Then she would be prayerfully turned out on withered pastures. Antonio hoped she would grow as fat as she could despite the drought.

"Good girl." He spoke quietly to her as he milked her, comforted by her warmth in the first light chill. The tusk bumped against his hip as he worked. He'd used a frayed bit of string to tie it to his belt, and its presence made him less frightened than he'd been before.

Daisy didn't like many people, but she cooperated with him. She provided cream and butter for the house. As long as she produced well, she would avoid the butcher's knife. Daisy seemed to like Mary, and Antonio hoped the cow would let Mary take on the task.

Mary appeared at the end of the stall, her smile bright and her cheeks rosy. "Is it ready? Cook's in a moods today."

"Just finished," Antonio said, drawing down once more with each hand. Daisy stomped her back foot. She was tired of waiting to see her calf. He stood and then lifted the wooden pail and handed it to the waiting Mary. She took the bucket and started down the aisle between the stalls and back toward the kitchens. .

Antonio took a deep breath and let it out slowly. *Now or never.* "If anything ever happens to me," he said, "promise me that you'll take care of my Daisy. She won't let just anybody else milk her. I want you to take care of her." Antonio spoke to Mary's back as he smoothed his hand over Daisy's flank.

Mary turned back slowly, pivoting on her heel, careful not to spill the precious liquid she carried. Her smile disappeared. "What would happen to you, Antonio?" The inner portion of her eyebrows turned up, meeting in a wrinkle.

Antonio peered at her, unsure what to say. The moment stretched. "I don't know. Things happen," he offered finally. The reason sounded flimsy as soon as he said it. He tried to smile, but it felt more like a grimace on his face. "Promise me?"

"I promise." She drew out the words, and stared at him for a moment before returning to her task.

Antonio turned to Daisy's lead rope and pushed against her withers. She ambled out of the stall and turned the opposite direction from that which Mary had gone. Daisy had gone this way so often that she led Antonio. She wanted to see her little one.

As the pair rounded the edge of the barn, Daisy lowed to her pied calf, waiting behind the gate. The baby was smaller than any other bull calf Antonio had seen. If Daisy couldn't produce enough milk to feed him and give enough milk for the house, the Master might choose to butcher the calf.

Antonio rubbed the velvet nose of the moon-marked face, and the calf leaned into it. His other hand drifted over the tusk. "I hope you survive, boy. I hope we all do." To survive, the rains would need to come soon to refresh the pasture grasses and turn them green. Even if rain came in the next few days, it might still be too late to save anyone. Antonio undid the latch, and Daisy lumbered inside.

The orange hen darted by, and Antonio chased after her. He would catch her, drop her back in the coop yard, gather her eggs, muck Daisy's stall, and finally be on his way to Hillcrest.

A rumble shook the ground. Antonio lifted a hand to shield his eyes from the sun and stared toward the mountains. Thunder did not come from a cloudless sky. He sighed. That meant only one thing.

The dragon is awake.

RIVENBOURNE TOWNSHIP HILLCREST

Antonio crept along the inside of the city's outermost stone wall. Every few steps, he stopped beneath the darkened skies. Clouds billowed on the horizon like warriors preparing for battle. The quakes had increased in frequency, but the dragon had not yet shown its scales.

A foul wind spiced with sulfur blew through the town. The ground shook, and a rumble rolled through the stones and up through Antonio's legs until his heart quivered in his chest. His mouth dried. His hand drifted over the ivory tusk of the Breidbore bear and a short segment of cord, both tied to his waist.

The empty streets chilled his blood and dried his mouth, souring the morning's meager meal. The nightmares played again in his mind, and he stumbled in front of the grocer's. As he climbed to his feet, he saw the grocer's daughter peering out beneath the corner of a curtain, her eyes wide and as frightened as he felt. A hand grabbed her shoulder and pulled her back into the hidden parts of her home.

Almost to the city gate, doors of homes stood open, as though the inhabitants had vanished in the middle of their normal days. All he had to do was trip the gate and slip through before it closed. It didn't matter if he could get back in. He wouldn't need to.

The gargantuan wooden gate stood wide open. If it had been closed, iron cross pieces held the thick slats together with the force of a giant, but what good was an open barrier?

Antonio's mouth twisted. It was no doubt an instruction left behind by the town mayor—a provisional measure for a selfish man at the cost of the town. The mayor imagined himself safe if only the dragon would consume the town.

Soft years make weak men, but a boy shall lead them all.

He tugged the ivory tusk from his belt. The frayed tassel fell across the back of his hand, a soft sensation in the middle of the tumult inside him. The old woman's promise took the place of the nightmares.

It will keep you safe from dragon magic, Antonio. Use it when you meet your moment.

The ground shook beneath him again and again. The steps of fate were heavy on the hills.

Antonio frowned. The footfalls had stopped, but women wailed and babies cried out.

A hush descended.

A screech filled the air, the depth and breadth of it drowned out the world, and a shadow blocked out the sun. He wanted to drop to his knees and press his hands over his eardrums. The sound nearly sent him back to the straw mat in the larder. A winged silhouette crossed over him, and the stench of brimstone filled the air. The fell beast had come.

His moment was upon him.

He looped the short cable around the gate lever and walked through the opening, keeping the end tight in his hand. He took a deep breath and pulled on the rope.

The city gate slammed behind him, sealing his fate.

Antonio's knees shook. His throat worked. Bile hit the back of his throat and he clamped his mouth closed. Spots danced at the edges of his vision.

He could run back to the gate and scream until they let him in. The Master would hear him. He would tell them to open the gate. Antonio shook his head and straightened his shoulders.

The creature circled once and then landed on the crest of the grassy hill in front of Rivenbourne. Sunlight shimmered across its scales in myriad iridescent greens and blues and blacks. Great and terrible. It sniffed the barren ground in the corrals. For hundreds of years, livestock had been offered there, but both were empty.

The dragon screeched at the sky and then sent plumes of fire far overhead, so tall it reminded Antonio of an exploding mountain. After a moment, the beast directed the destruction at one wooden pen. Within moments, the enclosure dissolved in ash.

Even as far away as Antonio was, the flames warmed his cheeks. Overhead, he heard a scuffle. Men yelled to one another. And then someone he didn't recognize cried his name. He pressed his palms together.

The dragon turned to face him, eyes as bright as the forger's fire. Antonio's mouth dried, and he froze, his confidence withering in the heat of the beast's gaze. A shake of the giant, horned head, and the creature turned toward the second empty pen. It took a deep breath and blew flames over the planks, but it shuddered and the fire stuttered, winking out before the blaze devoured the second pen.

"Antonio," Mary screamed from the top of the wall. "What are you doing? Come home. The soldiers will let you in."

Antonio glanced up, but he couldn't see her. He bolted forward and then spun toward her, cupping his hands around his mouth. "Mary. Go home. Take care of Daisy. Keep the calf alive until it rains."

"Come home, Antonio." Her voice broke at the end.

"I cannot. This is my moment." Antonio waved to her and offered a smile. He hoped she couldn't see how it shook. Mary pressed her hands over her face and then crumpled down behind the parapet. Two soldiers dragged her into the tower at the corner. "Don't let her watch!" Antonio bellowed, but the men-at-arms didn't answer, and Mary disappeared from view.

Behind him, the dragon hissed.

Rivenbourne Township
Hillcrest

The man-child straightened his shoulders and came nearer as though he didn't feel the fear-stench that filled the serpent's nostrils. The dragon stomped the ground to watch the boy flinch. The child shrank away as all the others did on this day, but there was something about him that reminded the dragon of…

The boy stopped where his front claws scratched a groove in the ground. "Happy Dragon Day," he said, holding up his hands. "I have come to offer myself in place of the village."

The loneliness in the dragon's belly urged him toward the boy, but he held back. The bargainer was only a child, unable to bear the weight of friendship with a beast of Dragonkind. And yet... the boy strode toward the dragon as though the nobility of the Master of the Keep coursed through his veins.

The dragon licked his teeth until the points dripped with saliva. Hunger yawned in his belly. Horse, mutton, and beef—he had been promised his fill of food. Loneliness grew fat on the emptiness, the absence of connection.

"What is your name, boy?" The rumble of the dragon's voice made the boy's eyes go wide. The creature's breath ruffled his hair, but he did not shy away.

"I am Antonio." His chin lifted slightly.

The dragon leaned close. The boy was shorter than one of his irises. "What makes you think you're enough to take the place of what has been promised?"

"I am not enough to fill your belly." Antonio drew himself to his full height. "But I would ask that you do not kill the villagers to feed yourself. I offer myself as payment of Rivenbourne's Dragon Day debt. Rain will come, and they will feed you more next year. For today, I ask you to spare them." He held out his hands once more, entreating. His face held no malice, no hint of regret or bitterness.

Antonio's soul shone in the dragon's mind like a diamond worth hoarding. His loneliness reached for the child once more, but the boy drew back, studying the reptile from the tip of his nose to the end of his tail. Antonio had courage in him, of a kind the dragon hadn't expected to meet again. Perhaps Antonio could heal the crack in the fiery beast's heart.

Antonio frowned and laid a hand on the plates beneath the dragon's eye. "Are you so starved that you are shrinking, dragon?" He waved to the hills that surrounded them. "I'm sure there are creatures enough for eating. I can even show you where there are pack horses and mules."

"Why would you do this?"

"To spare my village."

"I could devour you and then eat your people."

He tilted his head. "I don't think you will."

"How can you know?"

"Something in you reminds me of Daisy. She dislikes cruel men, but she is gentle toward Mary, even though Mary tugs too hard when she milks. She's a stubborn cow, but she's good-hearted." Antonio's eyes widened. He jerked his hand away and clamped it over his mouth as though too many words had spilled from his lips.

"It's the dragon magic, boy. It pulls truth from the hearts of all men so I can know the ambitions in their souls." The dragon tapped a toe on the ground; the long claw gouged the earth. The boy had shown a loyalty that had already seeped between his scales.

"The old woman said this—" Antonio held up a white crescent shape "—would protect me." He dropped the tusk on the dirt beside him, sending a little burst of ash upward. "I think she knows less about dragons as she thinks she does."

The child amused the dragon, and his hunger had abated in the boy's presence. The searing pain in his firebox had also lessened. That was something worth exploring.

Rearing back onto his hind legs, he stretched his wings above them, and someone screamed on the castle wall. The dragon scooped the boy into his claws and leapt into the sky.

To his surprise, Antonio did not beg. He did not cry. He made no sound at all.

HATRED CAVES
THE BARREN

Instead of eating him, the dragon deposited him at the mouth of a cave, and Antonio struggled to find his footing on the loose shale incline. A large rock slipped out from beneath his heel and tumbled down the slope. He pitched forward to land on his knees instead of his back. Sharp points gouged his kneecaps and his shins.

More cautious the second time, Antonio climbed to his feet, steadied himself against the mouth of the cavern, and studied his surroundings. He had to be sure Mary was safe.

"Where are we? Is this the Barren?" He limped across the small clearing and stopped at the beast's side. A rumble vibrated beneath Antonio's palm. "Will you let Rivenbourne live?"

The dragon leaned closer. Its slit eyes glowed, and the pain disappeared from Antonio's legs. He gaped at the behemoth. The villagers said the great serpent lived in the Hatred Caves, hidden away from men, but that cave system was in the Barren. Antonio studied the green trees, laden with nuts. Rainberry bushes surrounded them, covered in bright blue flowers. It would soon be time to harvest the delicious yield. Cook made Mary's favorite jelly from them.

"This is my home, but your people call it the Barren. Like most things they do not understand, they are wrong about it. Food is not scarce here." The dragon pointed his long nose downhill. "If you're thirsty, the creek is that way." The creature rolled over and scrubbed its back against the rocks. The ground trembled with his weight.

"Rivenbourne looks more like the Barren than the Barren does." The villagers could forage in the Barren for weeks. Antonio wondered if it was the same where the mayor hid. "Has it rained a great deal?"

The dragon flipped back to his feet and drew a claw between each of his teeth. "Rain goes where it is sent."

"It's been sent here, dragon, but not to my people." The people of Rivenbourne would eat for weeks, maybe even months, on the bounty within the valley that surrounded the Hatred Caves. Antonio reached for the dragon's shoulder, and it did not move away. "Do you eat rainberries?" The berry bushes covered the hillside. Leaf robins darted from plant to plant. It had been a long time since Antonio had eaten poultry. If the dragon didn't eat the berries or the birds, perhaps he wouldn't mind if the people of Rivenbourne did.

"Red flesh is all that interests me." The giant head swiveled toward Antonio, and its nostrils flared.

A breeze blew over him, almost too hot to stand in. He feared for Mary.

"What should I call you?" Antonio studied the colors that moved across the reptile's pupil. The length of the iris seemed shorter.

"Call me what you've been calling me."

"Just dragon?" Antonio moved his hand over the scales. One direction, it was as smooth as the Master's metal armor, but the other way it was as rough as tree bark. He might have imagined it, but the dragon seemed to lean into Antonio's touch.

"You cannot pronounce my name." The dragon sighed.

"You could teach me."

"Why would I bother?"

"Why haven't you eaten me? Are you not hungry?" Antonio didn't want to be eaten, but there must have been a cause for the creature's mercy. Maybe that reason would help him understand what would come next, even to prepare for it.

The dragon met Antonio's gaze; the reptilian eyes drooped. "I have not had a conversation in four hundred years." Then he turned toward the cave and slipped inside. The scales on his side brushed against the mouth of the cave. "No one cares enough to speak to a lonely dragon."

Antonio stared after the creature in shock, his jaw slack. He remembered what it was like after his father died, before the Master found him, before Mary, before he had a place in a warm larder behind a fireplace and a warm mat to sleep on.

His heart broke and tears clouded his vision.

He would do whatever he had to, to keep them safe.

HATRED CAVES
THE BARREN

The dragon had disappeared. At least he had not reappeared from the depths of his home. Antonio didn't want to wake him, but he'd been sitting outside the mouth of the cave for hours, waiting with a brace of coneys.

Perhaps Antonio could bargain for Mary's life by befriending the lonely creature.

The pair of hares wouldn't make much of a dent in the dragon's hunger, but they were the best Antonio could do in the limited time he had been there. If Antonio could convince the dragon to take him flying, he could lead him to the animals the mayor had spirited into the countryside.

Mary had shown Antonio where they'd gone. He and Mary knew the hills better than most, exploring trails when Cook gave them free time. Rivenbourne needed the meat and pack animals more than the selfish mayor did. It would be an easy meal for the dragon.

Sharp shale points dug into the fleshy part of Antonio's backside, and he shifted to alleviate the discomfort. The movement sent an avalanche of shale bits down the hill. The shards knocked against each other, and the sound reminded Antonio of the broken glass wind chimes that hung in Mistress' garden.

An unexpected snort vibrated the ground and nearly sent Antonio tumbling down the slope. Antonio grabbed the hind feet of the rabbits and scrambled to his feet. He held the duo up as two large nostrils appeared at the mouth of the cave.

"What do I smell?" The voice rumbled through Antonio's middle.

Antonio grinned. "Red meat for you. I found them eating rainberry bushes. It does not take long to create a trap. After I had them, the rest went smoothly. Should I skin them for you?"

"Mmm?" The dragon poked his head out of the hole. "Oh, no, I eat them whole. At least I think I do. I've never been fond of rabbit." He disappeared again.

"You are hungry, dragon. Your hunger starves you, and I believe you are shrinking." Antonio held the coneys higher. "They aren't much, but they are a beginning, and I know where we can find more livestock to fill your belly."

The dragon sniffed. "It would take hundreds to fill me."

"Not rabbits." Antonio tossed the food into the lair. "Beef cattle, dragon. I know where you can find a small herd to consume." The sound of smacking filled the air followed by the sound of crunching bones.

After a moment, the dragon appeared. "You would give away someone else's hard-earned livestock?" He slipped from the cave. That time, his sides did not even brush the entrance at all. The dragon was definitely becoming smaller.

"I would give you our own." Antonio studied his hands a moment before continuing. "The drought has made livestock scarce, but the mayor of Rivenbourne took the meat animals we set aside for you and fled our town before you arrived. He did not even close the gate behind him. I know where he is staying until you're gone. You can eat what we meant for you." Telling such things, even though they were truth, still made him feel like a traitor.

"Indeed." The dragon blew a long breath through his mouth. Flames danced in his eyes. "Perhaps beef should be on the menu."

"I will show you where." Antonio crept across the shale and positioned himself directly in front of the giant beast. "But you must promise not to hurt the men."

The dragon froze, staring into the distance over Antonio's shoulder. Then he dipped his head toward Antonio, moving low enough to meet Antonio's gaze. The beast sniffed at Antonio as though searching for something. Finally, he asked, "Why would you care about the cowards who left the town defenseless?"

Antonio did not flinch as the dragon's warm breath swirled around him, moving his hair and his clothes. He laid his hand on the creature's chin. "They are still men. I would not see them hurt for their cowardice. Perhaps they had no father to teach them a better way."

"Do you have a father, Antonio? Will he miss you?" Dragon moved away, each footstep sending shale tumbling down the steep incline into the draw. Some pieces even made it as far as the stream, splashing into the cold water.

Antonio followed, picking his way across the uneven ground. "My father died when I was six. When I was seven, Master caught me trying to steal apples from his tree. I was so hungry and no one would let me work." Antonio couldn't help the grin that spread across his face. "He dragged me back to his kitchen and his Cook and told her to scrub me down to see if there was a boy beneath all the dirt."

"Cook was kind to you?" The dragon started toward the water.

"Oh, mio," Antonio laughed, still following. "She burned my clothes. Then she scoured me with boiled water and horsehair brushes until I howled and my skin turned bright red. When I told her what I thought, she boxed my ears."

The dragon stopped short and snorted. "Why would you stay after that?"

"Because even though she told me she didn't know what the Master saw in me, at the end of it all, she hugged me. I couldn't get my arms around her fast enough. I cried and cried on her apron. I missed my father. I had been so alone; then I wasn't. If Cook wanted to box my ears every day, I would have let her, if she would hug me. It meant more to me than all the apples in the world." Antonio sighed, remembering. "When I finished, I looked up to tell her thank you, and she had tears on her cheeks."

The dragon started walking again. "Did they let you stay?"

"I think Cook wouldn't have let me go after that. She piled a plate full of biscuits and smothered them in butter." Antonio rubbed his belly. "It was the first time I'd tasted butter. I ate until I couldn't eat another bite, then I asked to see the cow that made the butter. Cook laughed and laughed, but then I met Daisy. I've been taking care of her ever since."

"Who will care for Daisy now?"

"I taught Mary how to do it before I came."

Dragon glanced over his back. "You planned to meet me?"

Antonio shrugged. He eyed a rainberry on a bush and plucked one. "When the mayor left, someone had to try to reason with you." His mouth puckered when he tasted the fruit. Not yet ripe, it was still filled with tannins, but those farther down the mountain, growing closer to the warmth of the valley, would be ready soon. He must find a way to get them to the town.

At the edge of the stream, the dragon dipped his face into the crystal liquid. He drank long and deep. When he finished, he turned to face Antonio, water glistening on his scaled snout. He sat back onto his rear legs. "You are a foolish boy, Antonio. You should have let the men protect Rivenbourne."

"Perhaps." Antonio nodded. "But I wasn't sure they would, so I did." He took a seat on a shaded boulder situated beneath a giant evergreen. "I have been given much, dragon, and if I had not come, I would not be conversing with you." Antonio paused. "'*For unto whomsoever much is given, of him shall be much required,*'" he quoted. "One of the things my father taught me before he died. I do not know where he learned it, but it pleases me to keep it."

"I think that must be why I did not eat you." The dragon leaned forward and started shaking, his size growing smaller with each shiver that rolled through his body.

Antonio leapt down from the rock. "You are too hungry. We must feed you." He waved to the scaled beast. "If you let me onto your back, I can show you where our cattle have gone."

The convulsions faded as quickly as they had come, and the dragon shook his head. "It is not my hunger that makes me smaller, Antonio." He sighed a deep, rumbling sigh. The skin around his eyes pinched as though his next words pained him. "Dragons are not made to live alone, and I have been alone long enough that my firebox has cracks."

"Your firebox has cracks..." Antonio repeated the words, testing them. They did not make sense to him. "Why does your firebox have cracks?"

"When loneliness grows too large for a dragon's heart, it breaks the firebox and swells inside the dragon, forcing the beast to grow larger and larger. A dragon can live a long time with those cracks. As I have." The dragon started back up the hill, moving slowly.

Antonio scurried after. "But it cannot live forever?"

"Dragons can live without fire, but, eventually, our fireboxes shatter from disuse. The shards spread throughout our bodies and slowly poison us."

Antonio stopped. His heartbeat thundered in his ear. Finally, he asked, "Are you going to die?"

"My loneliness is shrinking, Antonio, so I am returning to my original size." The dragon sighed once more, long and slow, still plodding up the hill as though marching to a great doom. "In the morning," he said, "I will return you to Rivenbourne."

The boy watched the beast make his way back to the cave, the large tail swaying one way and then the other. *That would mean...* He frowned and ran up the hill. "Why would I go back?"

"I am not your people." The dragon disappeared inside the darkness of his lair once more, twice as much space between his sides and the circumference of the mouth of the cave.

Antonio tilted his head, studying the void where the beast once stood.

To save Mary, I will gladly make this dragon my purpose.

HATRED CAVES
THE BARREN

The next morning, Antonio woke, shivering, just inside the door to the dragon's lair. It was the dawn of his new life as the dragon's friend, and the dragon needed to learn to trust him.

He clambered to his feet, jumping up and down and rubbing his upper arms. His clothes weren't right for so high on the mountains. If he stayed into the winter, he would have to find a way to keep from freezing to death. Behind him, the lumbering steps of the dragon filled the cave. There was a deep breath and then a stream of flames landed on a pile of sticks beside him.

"Your fire breath returned?" Antonio winced at the high pitch of his voice. At least he didn't yet have the uneven tones of the older stable hands. After the revelations of the day before, and thinking of the unburned corral outside the city, Antonio had been certain that the dragon had lost his fire. He whirled toward the beast and found himself nose to nose with a diminished version of yesterday's creature.

"You can scream." The dragon ducked and brought his eyes nearer, his ears twitching, but did not back away. "My firebox contracted in the night," the dragon continued. "It makes it easier."

Antonio tilted his head. "That's not all that's changed."

"Becoming smaller solves all sorts of things for a dragon."

"Today is the day we feed you." Antonio threw his arms around the dragon's neck, tugging the creature closer. The sharp ridge scales scratched Antonio's forearms, but he didn't let go. A shudder traveled through the scales beneath his palms.

The dragon eased out from beneath Antonio's arms and moved to the mouth of the cave. "How will you take me there?"

"You are still bigger than the Master's horse, and he was able to carry me." Antonio studied the reptile. "May I climb onto your back?"

The dragon turned back. His irises had changed from reds and oranges to blues and purples. He leaned to the side. "Which way do we fly?"

"Toward the rising sun." Antonio grasped the upright ridge scales, searching for a place to settle. Over the dragon's withers, the scales were less pronounced. They'd either broken off or worn away. Antonio threw his leg over and marveled at how much like it was like riding his broad-backed cow, Daisy.

Before the sun could reach its zenith, they dropped down through the bottom of the cloud cover and circled a camp situated in the curve of an oxbow. Men moved from tent to table to fire, probably preparing their midday meal, yet none had yet noticed the serpentine shadow crisscrossing the camp.

"There," Antonio said, pointing to a corral filled with the largest beef cattle left in Rivenbourne. "You can eat from there. I'm certain the town would have offered them to you if the Mayor had not run away."

The dragon glanced over his shoulder and smacked his lips. "I think one will suffice."

"Take two, then, and save one for later." Antonio squirmed in place. He wasn't happy about witnessing the Dragon's hunt, but he'd always known that the beast had to eat. It was the natural order. He hoped the cow the dragon picked wouldn't remind him too much of Daisy.

A shout sounded below. The cry of "dragon!" echoed in a hundred voices.

"Hold on, Antonio. I do not want to drop you." The dragon pitched his head downward and his body followed. Antonio squinted to shield his eyes from the sting of the rushing wind. As they flew, the men grew from ant-sized to man-sized.

Dragon dove toward the adjacent forest, dipped down into the trees, and touched down. "They'll rush wildly for a moment," he said. "Hurry, Antonio, wait here, between the trees, and I will return for you after I've frightened the men away."

The dragon wouldn't hurt him, and he wouldn't leave him. He'd proved it time and again.

Antonio jumped off and ducked behind the largest trunk. He raised his hand once. The dragon leapt upward once more, his wings beating against the air.

In the clearing, men lifted swords and spears toward the sky, shaking them as though daring the creature to eat them. The dragon circled once and then landed beside the corral, hissing and growling like the barn cat that had kittens in Daisy's stall. He belched fire at the first group that came near.

"Where is the mayor? Where is your leader?" His roar shook the trees and echoed off the mountains. Each man considered the other, and the movement repeated into the camp. Finally, the line of men split and a trio pushed a sniveling man through.

The mayor fell to his knees. "Please don't eat me. Have mercy."

"Did you abandon your city in its hour of need?" the dragon bellowed.

The mayor pointed to the cattle. "I meant only to protect our interests."

"You are a coward. You are no leader. You aren't even a man."

From his hiding place, Antonio cheered, dancing on his toes as the corrupt mayor earned his reward. Justice could be sweet.

The dragon darted forward and wrapped himself around the mayor. He licked his cheek and took a deep breath. "You will make a delicious meal."

Antonio gasped. He couldn't mean it. Surely, he wouldn't... Antonio dashed out, his legs pumping as hard and as fast as he could make them go. He skidded to a stop before the man and beast.

"Don't!" Antonio put up his hands.

"I could take my share from him, Antonio."

"I didn't bring you here for you to consume a man." Antonio dropped to his knees. He hadn't wanted death. Justice did not mean death. "Give him mercy. You are not fearful for your life, and you are not his judge. Let him live."

The dragon drew back. "Do you mean this?"

"I do. No men must die." Antonio stood. "And I cannot lie... I have been around your dragon magic."

The dragon dipped his head and sauntered away, appraising the cattle that cowered in the corner. He spun back to the mayor. "You must return the animals to your people."

The mayor nodded. Tears glistened on his cheeks. "I will. I will."

Later, back in the cave, the dragon made happy, purring noises and cleaned his teeth. His forked-tongue darted in and out of the space between his sharp incisors.

"Would you have eaten the mayor?" Antonio licked his fingers. The scent from the steak piece Dragon cooked for him still lingered in the air. He hadn't been stuffed so well since… he couldn't remember when.

"My mouth would not have opened far enough for that." Dragon moved on to cleaning his scales.

"Your mouth is large enough."

"I made a promise to eat none of the men. When I give my word, it binds me. Breaking it is impossible." The dragon's ears swiveled forward. "It's the dragon magic. It keeps us both honest."

Without warning, Antonio's laughter bubbled up from his middle and poured out, the sound echoing on the cave walls. "You only meant to scare him?

"Someone had to return the livestock to Rivenbourne." The dragon winked. "And maybe the mayor will think twice about committing cowardly deeds or cheating his people."

"You are the smartest dragon I know."

"I am the only dragon you know." The beast chuckled and the unfamiliar sound wrapped Antonio like a hug.

When the dragon leaned back, Antonio could see the bulge in his middle, and, in a strange way, it made him content. He chewed on the tips of his fingernails, not wanting to break the goodwill between them.

But if Antonio was going to earn the dragon's agreement, it would be best to ask while he had a full belly and sleepy eyes. He must seize the moment, or he would not ask at all.

"Dragon?" Antonio climbed to his feet.

"Yes, Antonio." The dragon made a sound that was half-way between a snore and a growl.

"Will you promise to not eat the people of Rivenbourne?"

After long moments, the dragon sighed. "I promise always to spare Rivenbourne."

Antonio leaned into the dragon's side, his heart filled to busting. He had made the dragon see reason *and* he had avoided being eaten. There was just one more thing …

"Dragon?"

"Yes, Antonio?" The dragon's voice sounded more like a snore that time.

"The people of Rivenbourne are starving." Antonio pressed his hands together, the way he'd seen Cook do when she prayed. "They are my people."

Dragon's eye popped open. "There's a drought in the valley." He said it as though it made perfect sense and nothing to do with him.

"You have rainberries here, and there is other food closer to the valley."

"Your kind tries to kill my kind."

"Yes, but you could stay in the cave, and I would protect you."

"From grown men?"

"I protected grown men from you." He lifted his eyes, stepping forward. He laid his hands on the dragon's chin. "I think they will listen."

"Men are not reliable…"

"Then only the women will come. If you stay in the cave, they can forage farther down the hill. We can test them. We can warn them that they will be eaten if they approach your lair. Rainberries are Mary's favorite. If I do nothing, she will starve, and I don't want Mary to starve. Who would take care of Cook… or… Daisy?" The words tumbled out of Antonio in a torrent.

Silence stretched between then. In the trees beyond, crickets and frogs sang the last mating songs of the season. "For you, Antonio, I will allow it."

Rivenbourne Township

The dragon touched down beside the two corrals, in view of the lookouts. He leaned to the side, and Antonio slid off his back. The boy lifted his hands and approached the walled city. Men ran one side and then the other, stopping at equidistant spots along the perimeter.

Archers.

They nocked their arrows and raised them, the tips trained on the beast. The dragon was a threat. It was the only way they saw him. He didn't want to leave Antonio to their mercy, so he held still, scarcely moving at all. He was diminished to about the size of two horses. A bevy of arrows would cause more damage than his magic could heal.

On the wall, someone screamed, "Antonio."

"Hello, Mary," Antonio called back. He waved at a girl barely tall enough to see over the rampart. "How's Daisy?"

"Open the gate. Open the gate." Mary didn't even stop moving. "He said they would come. He said they would come." She disappeared down into the city.

"Did the mayor come back?" Antonio yelled at the wall. The dragon couldn't tell who he was asking, or even if he asked a specific anyone.

The gates opened and a crowd poured out. Mary ran ahead of them all, her arms outstretched. "The mayor came and told us everything. He even brought back the cows."

The archers still did not lower their weapons, and the dragon considered the distance between the offering pens and the tree line. If he could disappear into the forest, even with the foliage mostly gone, he could hide and fly back toward his lair.

Antonio raised his hands and the throng quieted. "Dragon has rainberry bushes near his home. Coneys abound, and he has given us permission to fish his stream."

The horde did not respond.

Not even the bugs or birds called.

"The dragon has been kind to me," Antonio called. "He has promised to be kind to Rivenbourne in exchange for peace between us."

The silence went on.

Until another child took a step forward.

Mary.

Despite the chill, the dragon could see the sweat on her upper lip. She pressed trembling hands together. When she opened them, she hesitated, and the dragon took a step backward, expecting the movement to break the archers' restraint.

Instead, her face broke in a smile, and she clapped.

And everyone joined her.

The dragon flinched when Antonio waved his hand toward him, but the spear-tips did not lodge in his side. Dragon tilted his head. It was an oddity — a town led by a child, a boy not old enough to have whiskers. It seemed as if Antonio had his own magic, of a kind Dragon did not understand.

Once the applause died down, a man approached, his chest puffed out. "Antonio," he said. "Tell us how to find this bounty you've brought us."

The two made plans and re-worked them until, finally, they were shaking hands.

"You should stay," the dragon said. Antonio belonged there... with his kind.

"I think I would like that." Antonio faced Rivenbourne and didn't move for long moments.

The dragon turned away, his head drooping. Loneliness hurt most when preceded by companionship. The brave boy had bound him by oaths and now abandoned him, much as the man had long ago. He passed the corrals, and the noisy crowd filtered back into Rivenbourne.

Soft footsteps followed him, and a small hand stroked his scaled side. "Someday, dragon," Antonio added. "But today I would rather keep my purpose and come with you."

ABOUT THE AUTHOR

Bokerah Brumley is a speculative fiction writer making stuff up on a trampoline in West Texas. When she's not playing with the quirky characters in her head, she's addicted to Twitter pitch events, writing contests, and social media in general. She lives on ten permaculture acres with five home-educated children and one husband. In her spare time, she also serves as the blue-haired President of the Cisco Writers Club.

In 2016, she was awarded first place in the FenCon Short Story Contest, third place in the Southern Writers Magazine Short Story Contest, fifth place in the Children's/Young Adult category for the 85th Annual Writer's Digest Writing Competition, and selected as a 2016 Pitch Slam! finalist. More recently, she accepted a contract with Clean Reads Press and moonlights as an acquisitions editor for The Crossover Alliance. Her website is https://superbokerah.com/.

On Falcon's Wings

R. K. Duncan

Alssia saw Idris for the first time in three years against the whitewashed wall of the temple. The first gleam of dawn made his skin shine like polished rosewood. In his hands, the new idol, a tangle of flutes and chimes, bells and reeds and rattles. Every breath of wind woke soft sounds from it, music for an enchanted meeting. Old Qadim ruined it. He scuttled from the temple before either of them could speak, his eyes like shattered glass, glistening even as he kept in shadows, where the sunlight would not weigh him down. The old man was breathing ragged and clutching the absence of a wound in his belly.

Inside the temple, his god was dying. The black bull of Belhadid had broken him. Three days ago, when warriors from the iron city came with battle, Siad-Amak had met them, and when the foemen loosed their god, he had raced to meet it, cast his net about it, pierced its side with his bright spear. The bull had been too strong. It tore the starry net, and scorched the sky with its burning breath, and ripped his belly with its horns. He had fallen, but the bleeding bull ran wild from the field, and half the raiders ran after it. Alssia had been in the front rank as they routed the rest, and brought their broken spears and cloven shields into the temple, but the fisher of the skies was still dying. He lay in the temple, too broken even to return to his idol-cage of mirrors and prisms.

Idris was red-eyed and limp from working through the nights to finish his new idol, and now Qadim told her that she must take him deep into the desert, into the demon waste to trap a thing of wind to be Belmaladh's new god. The old man pressed amulets of polished shell and sea-glass on them, to guard them from the demons and bid them go quickly. Siad-Amak would not live past the sunset.

Alssia wanted to speak, to tell Idris, to ask if he still thought, but the moment was more broken than the priest. Instead, she led the way south in silence, past the fields inside the rampart, and past the olives on the first ridge, out into the wastes. Her spear rested easy on her shoulder and a sling hung at her belt. Idris followed her, cradling the new idol like a child, stroking it with his long, clever fingers. He blinked long lashes at the glare when they stepped into full sun beyond the ridge.

The air turned hot, without the breeze off the water that kept the city cool. Idris was sweating before they left the empty lands, close enough to the city that Siad-Amak had emptied them of demons. She kept an eye on Idris as often as she could. He was not used to walking in the waste, and every misplaced step and grunt of effort made her hunting senses twitch. Her eyes lingered on him each time. She had seen too little of Idris since he went to be old Qadim's apprentice and craft his idol in the temple, and she liked looking.

She shook her head to clear it. She needed to focus on keeping them safe, not on Idris' bright eyes and his smooth skin. The first demons had started buzzing around them, pleading on the edge of perception for worship and tribute and strength to grow. A little patch of dust shaped itself into a man and raised its fist to rail at them, then fled a salamander of smoke with a burning ember at its heart that dug its way out of the soil. Jeweled birds and winged women, all small as pinheads, danced in the air. These were only midges, fragments of hunger and power sifted from the wind. The strong ones that might be worth trapping lived farther into the waste, where there was no risk of angry gods. She felt the ragged pulse of Siad-Amak's heartbeat in the trinket at her throat. His power was still on them, to blind and warn away the greater demons. There should have been a score of hunters and warriors to guard Idris, and the other five apprentices, in case he could not hold the god alone, but only a trickle of power still flowed with that ragged heartbeat, only enough for two. Without a ward, demons would tear apart a hundred warriors, just like they would strip Belmaladh without a god to guard it.

She had to break the silence, drown out the ragged echo. "We should try and keep out of sight. It's dangerous farther in."

Idris was staring ahead blankly, plodding, sweat drenching his skin. He flinched at her voice and struggled to focus on her face. She almost laughed. He looked like an owl startled from its burrow into unaccustomed sunlight.

"The amulets should still protect us. This will only draw the right sort of demon. The kind we want."

She tried to turn her snort into a polite throat-clearing. He had not learned much of the land beyond the walls while he made his idol.

"There's more in the wastes than demons, and most of it can see us. We'll keep to the valleys and work our way south. You need a high place, right?"

He nodded, smiling a little. Because she had listened and remembered Qadim's instruction? Because she made him smile?

"Yes, a high place where we can catch the wind from all four quarters."

His eyes unfocused again, thinking of gods and demons and the binding instead of the ground under them. She pulled him along, keeping to valleys and ravines where she could. The hills ran across their path south, though, so they crossed saddles and ridges quickly, bending low to keep from sight, half sliding back to the low ground in their haste. It was hotter in the valleys, even in the shade. The hills on either side stilled the wind so that they walked through parched, dead air, like an oven. Idris sweated and puffed. Alssia was comforted. The valleys were safe from prying eyes, and safe from hunting beasts too, if they kept to dry ones. The rains that had wept at Siad-Amak's fall were over and sunk into the dust; no floods would sweep down the narrow valleys, and no hunters would come without a stream to draw prey. The baking air was a blanket, wrapping her in comfort like a mother's arms.

Alssia felt the raiders as Idris struggled up the slope behind her, a harsh screeching note like metal against metal, sounding in her spirit from the demon they carried. Idris felt it a moment later, more sharply. He nearly reeled back down the hill, clutching his head. A quick glance showed her the flash of eyes and a raised hand. They had been seen.

"Run. Now."

She sprang forward along the ridge, and Idris stumbled after her, idol jangling. They needed speed now. It might only be two or three raiders on whatever errand had brought them here, and running would make them follow instead of gathering the rest for a sure kill. Small hope; the raiders would have felt Siad-Amak's fall and seen the sky weep for him. They knew Belmaladh needed a new god. Very likely a whole raid was waiting, ready to take blood and spirit for their demon.

Idris slowed her. Alone, she might have outpaced the raiders and left them to search for easier prey, but he was no hunter, no fighter. Her instincts screamed at her to run faster, as fast as she could. She felt the demon's breath like a hot wind on her back.

There were five raiders, weathered men decked in mismatched finery, stained silks, chains of coins, hacked and broken chunks of silver. They wore all that would have gone into a temple if they had a god instead of kneeling to a demon.

It rode them, fed on their treasures, sipping lightly at their spirits. It was not real, yet, but the shadow of a stone lion, with sullen flame glowing from its mouth and cracked skin, paced alongside the men.

Alssia stopped, but waved Idris to run on. He skidded into her, nearly threw her to the ground.

"What are you doing? Come on, we have to run." Fear made his voice harsh, not the soft, rich bell it should have been.

She didn't push him away. "Go on. I'm faster than you. I'll catch up, but I want to try and slow them."

There was a moment's hesitation, where he still half-held her, but then he let her go and ran. The absence of his arms was cold, despite the sun.

She readied her sling and spun it until it whistled around her head. She let fly straight at the leader's face. The stone lion leapt into the world and caught the shot in its mouth. It coughed out slag and contempt. Now that it was manifest, she heard its growl like the grinding of stones. Its feet tore the ground as it ran, as though they fell with the force of great hammers. The voice at the back of her mind screamed louder, telling her to flee. Her sling was useless against that. Her spear was no better. She looked around. Was there anywhere they could lose the raiders?

There, the slope of the next hill south was steep, and it looked loose. Maybe they could scramble up it where the heavier raiders couldn't. She ran after Idris. It didn't take long to catch him. He was flagging, breathing raggedly and starting to stumble. She pulled at his shoulder to turn him.

"Come on. Up that slope. Maybe they can't follow us."

He had no breath to speak, but he lowered his head and followed doggedly. They slid and stumbled down from the ridge. Idris landed awkwardly on his backside. She pulled him up, and they ran for the slope. The raiders came down behind them. This was nearly a cliff; they climbed more than they ran, and Idris still had one arm taken up with the idol. She had to drag him up by his shirt more than once, and she nearly fell half-way up when she missed a handhold looking down to help him. Idris lost his hold completely and grabbed her ankle just as her hands reached the top. It felt as though her foot would rip off where he held her. She tore her nails scrabbling at the rocks, but she managed to keep hold and pull them both up. She lay on the ground for a moment, panting, and the world beyond the slope in front of her returned. She felt the sweat trickling down her skin, heard the raiders shouting from below, half taunting, half baying like wild dogs. It didn't sound like they were climbing up.

Idris gasped. The ground shook loose a skitter of stones. She rolled up to look over the edge. The demon was tearing at the hillside. It finished carving one ledge and stood on it to reach higher. The raiders would have a stair soon, and Idris was in no shape to run and leave them. She barely was herself. She struggled to her feet and readied her sling again, but before she could load and loose, Idris was standing beside her, fouling her swing. He whispered, but not to her, and there was a strange, grinding undertone to his voice. A web of fine cuts opened all over his skin. Smoke trickled from his mouth.

"No. Why wait? ...take them now...blood there, spirit and treasure. Feast now... don't need them... Feast now!"

He roared, and the stone lion leapt up the cliff. It covered a quarter of the distance in one bound and sprang again, but the hammer-blows of its paws cracked the stone, and it landed askew on a patch of loose earth and little pebbles, and went tumbling down along with half the hillside. The raiders' laughs and taunts turned to screams as the rocks broke and bloodied them, and the demon roared its joy as it fed on their dying.

Idris put his hand on her shoulder. The cuts had closed ugly and black, like char. "Come on. We should go. It will come after us if we're still here when it's done with them. Demons are never full." His voice was still too deep, grinding, hungry.

Alssia took the lead again. It was easier to think about finding a path farther up than about what Idris had done, how much he had sounded like the stone lion, speaking the demon's thoughts to make it jump. Were his footfalls heavier than they should be?

She was bleeding. When the fear of the chase was still pounding in her, she'd thought it was only sweat, but now that fear was faded to bitterness in her throat and a throbbing in her jaw, she felt the sluggish, sticky flow down her leg. She'd cut herself climbing and not felt it. It was barely bleeding anymore. She tied it off. Idris made a wincing noise and held out his hands to help, but she waved him away. She would love to feel his fingers on her, but not while those black scars were still fading.

She could still keep up a better pace than Idris, even with the pain stabbing at her ankle. Blood was dangerous in the wastes, though. Demons and their servants weren't the only things hunting here, and Siad-Amak's tokens wouldn't cover their scent. She pushed it to the back of her mind and walked on. She needed to get Idris far enough into the heights to catch his god.

The jackals were better hunters than the raiders had been, but Alssia was more alert now. She had grown accustomed to Idris beside her, was no longer so distracted thinking of how his smooth skin and clever fingers would feel if she reached out and touched him. She heard their eerie, coughing whine when it was still soft with distance. Idris didn't. No point saying anything yet. Her limp would mark her as prey when the jackals saw it. Maybe they would lose interest when they saw she wasn't alone.

It was noon now, no shadows anywhere. She felt the sun like a giant's eye, pinning her down and showing her up. She needed somewhere to hide. The jackals were louder now. Idris heard them.

"They're following us, aren't they."

"They can smell the blood. It means something's weak. That's what they like."

She paused a moment to scan the hills ahead.

"There, do you see that flat-topped hill, just away to the left?"

He followed her pointing finger. "I see it. That will do, yes."

"I'll stop at the next good spot and deal with the jackals. You get on with the binding. I can catch up, or you can come back and find me once it's done."

He stopped walking and looked at her. Really looked at her. She felt his bright, eager eyes studying her like they never had. She clamped down on a shiver, on the urge to pull her hair back over her ear. She saw him thinking, and still not understanding why she wanted him to go on.

"There's half a dozen of them at least. I can help. I'm not leaving."

"You don't know what you're doing. You'll just get in the way, and you'll be in danger. We need a new god. You have to get there and catch one."

She had to get him away, out of danger.

"Then you can protect me. If it's that dangerous, you'll die alone, and if it's not, there's no trouble and we can go up together when it's done. Either way, I'll stay with you."

He had always been able to talk circles round her. She'd forgotten that, forgotten how stubborn he could be.

He broke a branch from one of the lonely cypresses that dotted the hills as they walked, and, a little later, there was a patch of steep slope that would give them a wall to put their backs against. As good a place as any. She set her spear ready, and drew her sling again. Idris put the idol down and stood in front of it, holding the cypress branch awkwardly. He still didn't understand the danger.

"If I go down, take that thing and run. They won't follow."

He didn't answer, just looked at her with those big, bright eyes and shook his head. She should make him go. The city needed him. She could die alone. If he died here, could any of the other acolytes trap a god in time? Belmaladh might die with Idris. Still, there was a warm feeling that he wanted to stay. She hadn't known how he felt, since he went into the temple.

They had a clear view of the jackals, in the bright sun. It sent a cold finger trailing down her spine. They were too tall, four feet at the shoulder at least, and their tongues were dark and long and never swallowed. There were seven.

"They're demon-touched."

Idris realized it too. They had to be, made by one of the stronger demons, or fed on blood from a dead one.

They loped closer, casual, playful. She wanted to think they were intelligent, toying with their prey. They didn't recognize any threat as she whirled her sling around and sent a stone into one. It took the jackal in the lower jaw, left it hanging by a rope of gristle at one side. The jackal fell, gushing blood, and the rest scattered, yipping and coughing. They did not flee, and now they wove behind rocks and trees and kept her from another easy cast. She loosed a few more stones, but hit nothing, and the jackals laughed at her failure. She threw down the sling and set her spear. Idris was shaking, only a little, but she could hear his foot grinding on the loose dirt. She hoped he could see her eyes pleading with him to go when she looked, but she couldn't speak. Her mouth was dry. Sun and fear beat on her like a hammer, tightening her muscles until they were wrung-out and weak. She tried to relax, tried to be the serpent, cool, loose, coiled ready for her prey to come in reach.

They sprang across the last yards all at once. Alssia snapped her spear out, quick as a viper, and pricked once, twice. They skidded to a wary halt and she drew back for a stronger thrust. Idris' scream drove a knife into her gut. One of the jackals had gotten under his club and closed its jaws around his leg. He'd stumbled left, away from her, too far for a quick thrust. She spun on her back heel and threw the spear. It took the jackal through the neck, perfect as a dream, and then the others buried her. They smelled of blood and dust and the scorched heat of the waste. She fell backward, flailing her legs to keep them from biting and tearing. One landed on her chest and she fought to hold it away from her throat with one arm while she fumbled for her knife with the other. Her arm buckled for a moment. It lunged. She got her arm between its jaws and shoved it back. Then her knife was out and across its throat with a spray of blood that covered her face and chest in crimson stickiness.

She kicked again and rolled to get a little space, trying to come up into a crouch, but something gave in her injured leg, and she fell awkwardly to one knee. One jackal was quicker than the other, diving for her weak side. She lurched into it and pulled it close, rolling with it, holding it round the belly and plunging her knife into the back of its neck again and again, until the paws tearing at her belly spasmed and stilled.

She finished the roll on top, and a third jackal landed on her back, biting for the junction of shoulder and neck. She was no gazelle. She caught it by the scruff and swung it over her shoulder onto its back, then opened it from neck to tail with one long pull.

She leapt up. Idris was fending off the last two jackals with wide, wild swings of his cypress branch, but they were baiting him, darting in to nip him and dancing away before he could hit them. His legs were bathed in blood from knee to foot, and she could hear his gasping breath from here. She ran toward him. One long pace, two. On the third, her leg gave out again and she pitched forward, trying to turn it into a dive. She landed tangled in the nearer jackal's hind legs. It twisted round to snap at her. Idris bellowed and charged at it, swinging the branch down heavily, but he left himself open, and the last jackal sprang onto his back. He went down under it, and there was blood. She pulled the one Idris had stunned closer and put her knife through its eye, snapped it out, and threw. The last jackal must have heard it whistle through the air. It snapped its bloody muzzle up and caught the knife point first in its open mouth, then fell, and did not move.

She dragged herself to Idris and shoved the jackal off him, wadding his already torn shirt to press against the wound. She wished she could pray, but god was dying already. She felt herself weeping, tears pulling themselves out despite how much the wastes had dried her. There was so much blood; she couldn't tell how much came from his wound as she packed more and more of his shirt against it. She tried to quiet her ragged gasping. She couldn't hear if he was breathing.

And there were his hands, his strong, warm, clever hands, wrapping around hers where they were pressed at the hollow of his shoulder. He reached a bloody finger to her face to wipe a tear, and they both collapsed and buried their faces in their arms and laughed. They were alive, and in a moment they could go on, and that was enough for joy overflowing.

They were both shirtless and wearing trousers torn to loincloths by the time their wounds were bound. His leg was the worst, and his shoulder next, but her ankle would not take her weight. They broke her spear in half for walking sticks and struggled on. Idris was pale from bleeding, and she felt no better, but there was no way home but on. Alone, she might have made it back by nightfall. With Idris, only a god could bring them safe through the waste.

They didn't speak, not more than to point to the next task. She had seen his eyes when the jackal went for her, and that made it easy to imagine what he had seen in hers. He was as sorry they were parted as she. It didn't change a bit of what they had to do for Belmaladh, of what it would take from them.

They were safe from men and beasts this far south. Only demons lived so deep, and Siad-Amak's amulets still hid them, as long as they stayed far enough from the great demons and the way the world twisted round them. The slopes were steadier as well, and Alssia kept them on the easiest course for the hilltop she had chosen. They wound around the hill three times instead of taking the straight way up. Halfway along the first turn, Idris broke the silence.

"I know what you think. That this means we have to be apart." She looked over to him. He was staring studiously forward, face and voice stiff. "I've known you thought so since I went to the temple, and you never visited."

He was right. She tried to see behind his face, to see what he was thinking, but it was a beautiful mask, and he was breathing in the calm rhythm of temple meditations. It made his words sound like prayers, broken into verses by the rhythm of his breath.

"You're wrong, though. It doesn't need to be that way. You'll always be welcome in the temple, when I'm priest, and just because Qadim never took a wife, it doesn't mean..."

"I'll be welcome, but you'll be gone." That was enough to make him turn and look at her. "I've seen Qadim, how he shies from the light, sees things that aren't there. Being a priest makes you something else. You won't be you after you do it, after today."

He looked angry now. She could hear him struggling to keep his voice measured, not to shout. "It's not like that. Binding a god changes you. It will change me, but I'll still be me. I'll be better, stronger, with the god to help me."

"I never needed you to be stronger."

He stood there, staring at her, so full of pride, so eager, so much like the young warriors, beautiful and fierce. Broken, now. They were silent again, climbing.

The sun was starting to sink noticeably when they reached the hilltop. People in the city would be worrying, glancing to the south and shaking their heads. Alssia and Idris should have returned by now, if all was well. The council would be meeting, except for Qadim, to think what they would do if Idris failed. How they could find another god for Belmaladh before Siad-Amak died and left them open to whatever came from waste and wave to break them. Alssia had no answers to whisper to the desert wind. The ground shook under them. An obsidian giant, taller than a tower, strode across the plain, shaping it new with every footfall. A few hills east, a great pine with silver needles and a trunk skinned with silent, screaming child faces sprouted to the sky. She felt it watching her, spreading out her mind like a parchment to read, felt scratching fingers across the inside of her skull.

Idris' hands shook her back into her skin. She was safe. The tree was rooted. It could not come, even with its branches stretched toward them. But the amulets were failing.

"Do it. We need to get out of this place."

Idris took up the idol, and readied to play. It wrapped him from shoulder to hip in a cage of bone and silver. He blew into one reed, and then another, and he swayed in the breeze that sprang up with the music. Chimes rang and jangled, and reeds whistled and moaned. The sound seemed small, lost in the emptiness of the rising hills and the coastlands spread below them, and smaller still when a demon came near to listen.

A wind from the blazing desert beyond the hills blew up in an instant and nearly slammed Alssia to the ground. It screamed past her and whirled around Idris, spinning up dust-devils as tall as she was and making the idol clatter and scream. Idris spoke.

No, something used his voice, but made it harsh and rasping, nails scraping gravel in his throat. The dust around him spread into great wings and the air rippled with a wall of heat between them.

"Kneel! Offer me blood or burn beneath the winds. I will strip your meat and make your bones sing for me."

The voice broke off in a snarl, and Alssia saw Idris' eyes narrow. His fingers shifted, and the tunes the idol played shifted with them. He spoke again, in his own soft voice. Small and frightened after the wind's scream.

"Name yourself."

That was the first test. Qadim had forced a little wisdom into his mutterings when he sent them out. Only the strongest demons made names. That was the first test to be a god.

The desert wind growled with Idris' throat again. A little softer now. It was learning to use his mouth.

"I am Harmattan. Kneel and weep."

Idris was calmer the second time, but his voice was raw, harsher, more like Harmattan. The dust danced to it. Heat haze clustered on him like a cloak.

"Name your virtues."

That was the second test. Demons were born in hate and hunger. Ones that lived long and grew strong enough had virtues they claimed, as well as vices they despised.

The burning wind wrested Idris' voice from him again, but it seemed softer this time. Perhaps Alssia was only becoming used to its harshness, but it seemed to her that already Idris and Harmattan were growing together, becoming something else, killing her sweet, soft boy with clever fingers and inquisitive eyes. Her skin crawled, trying to pull her eyes away from looking.

"Who dares command me? Kneel, and offer blood and weeping and I will spare you. You are bold, at least."

She could barely hear the change when Idris spoke again, only see it in the way his eyes re-focused, as though he had been out of his body altogether while he let the wind speak through it.

"I will kneel if you are worthy. Speak your virtues. What is best in you and in mortal men?"

Why was he still dealing with it? It was only rage and hate and death. It knew nothing of fair winds to speed a ship or rain for fields and orchards. What could it give Belmaladh but blood and fire? Was he so lost already that he couldn't see?

The rasping scream cut the air again. It hurt her ears. It stabbed hot fingers down her throat into her lungs.

"Fury is best, fire is best, rage and blood and burning. Kneel before me or feel them all, but wait; I like this toy that you have made to give me voice. I will keep it, and you will carry it. We will eat the woman. She is only a worthless worm."

The wind redoubled, and it hammered into Alssia's chest like a doubled fist. She stumbled back. Idris opened his mouth, but all that came out was a strangled croak. The burning wind Idris had raised wrapped around her and lashed her with oven-hot sand. Idris looked at her, eyes pleading. He saw something in hers that made him harden. His hands danced on the idol, and he clenched his jaw. The music changed, a rolling counterpoint to the howling of the hot wind. For a moment, bands of wind and sound played over her, hot and screaming, cool and musical. Then, Idris seemed to become somehow more solid, more real, to step from somewhere else and stand heavily there on the hilltop. He bent himself to one of the idol's many mouthpieces and blew a deep, loud horn blast. The cool wind shredded the hot, and Harmattan faded to a whistle on the breeze and dwindled down to silence.

Idris set the idol down, gently as an infant, and came to stand over where she had fallen while the winds whipped her.

"Are you all right? Did he hurt you?"

"Not worse than I already was. Did you mean to call that... thing?"

"It doesn't work that way." He stepped back half a pace. "The idol calls spirits that fit. I made a prison for the wind, but any wind can feel the pull."

At least he had the grace to look sheepish, after what he had almost become. He understood how clear his lie about not changing showed now. His face squeezed the way it did just before he said something sweet and clever to charm her, but she never heard it.

The air screeched loud as thunder and sharp as needles. Great waves of wind swamped the hilltop. Idris ran to take up the idol and play again. Alssia looked up and saw the demon like a shadow of mist across the sky. A great falcon with wings that reached the horizon, the sun its blazing eye. The greats wings beat with a wind to send ships speeding across the wave, or to shatter them with its strength.

Idris began his music again, but it sounded tiny, lost in the falcon's whirlwind. Still he challenged it.

"Name yourself."

The wind's reply cut her ears like a knife of ice. This demon did not use Idris throat. It spoke from the idol like a choir of glass tongues and metal teeth. "Bash-Irem." A woman's name.

She heard Idris' voice shaking now in answer, as humble as she felt beneath the demon's gaze.

"Great lady, speak your virtues. What is best in you, and in men and women below?"

"To see the truth of what must be and swiftly make it so: just rewards and swiftest retribution for injustice; never to delay when they must act."

The falcon's voice was fierce and huge, but it felt clean, not hateful like the desert wind had been. Alssia could hear its wisdom. Belmaladh needed the virtues it named. Siad-Amak had been careful and he had made them over-cautious. Never had they sailed back to Belhadid or Belrustam to recompense a raid and make them fear to come again.

Idris spoke again, his little voice against the wind. "Come then, and take the gift I have brought for you."

Now was the contest. Gods and demons could feed on crafts and treasures as they did on blood and life, but they must encompass each thing to grow from it. The idol had to shift and change enough to trap the demon and tame it for a god. Idris' fingers danced, and his lips went from pipe to pipe as he played a riddle of music for the falcon. Bash-Irem screamed louder than before, and Alssia felt her passing as a river of wind. The falcon made a faster, sharper music of trilling flutes and ringing chimes, and it cut through the overlapping horns. They buzzed and sighed against each other for a breathless moment, but then the idol screamed. There was a crack, and Idris was thrown away and tumbled to the ground. The idol hung on the wind and played a fierce exultant music for Bash-Irem.

Idris had fallen, and the demon about to break the idol and depart unbound. She should have been terrified, but Alssia found that she knew the tune. It was the pounding blood of the strike that ended the hunt, the moment when all of mind and will and body were united in a single perfect release; the thrust of the spear, the flight of the stone. Without thought, Alssia ran to make the kill. She seized the idol and felt out the holes that would channel the falcon's song and confuse it, and she found a harmony with the demon of the hunting wind. Idris came up, and his clever fingers guided hers to play the notes that caught Bash-Irem in the chimes and reeds, still restive, like a hunting bird testing its jesses, but bound in earnest. She felt her limbs lighten, like a bird. It was a strain to focus on his face, but she could see every leaf on the olive trees outside the city. They made music together, the ones who had been huntress and acolyte, and she knew that they must do so again. The two of them had caught this god, and both of them would be what it made them.

She thought of the long road back, the road she had been dreading as they climbed. She laughed, and felt for the stops she needed, and they rode back to Belmaladh on falcon's wings.

ABOUT THE AUTHOR

R. K. Duncan is a new, hopefully up-and-coming, author mostly of fantasy, with a dash of sci-fi and horror thrown in. He writes about fairies and gods and ghosts from a ramshackle apartment in Philadelphia. In the shocking absence of any cats, he lavishes spare attention on cast iron cookware and his long-suffering and supportive partner. Before settling on writing, he studied linguistics and philosophy at Haverford College. His occasional musings and links to other work can be found at rkduncan-author.com.

The Palace of the Mind

J.E. Bates

The following myth of the Chiorli people presents an example of somagnosticism, a belief in the body as a conscious entity distinct from the ego mind.

Many years ago lived a man named Ral Tam who did not care for his body in the manner prescribed by the oracles. He did not chew the *hetez* nut to clean his teeth as ordained or bathe in the sea as often as custom demanded, for he hated the taste of the hygienic nuts and grew winded walking the long trail to the shore.

Ral worked as a weaver and all day he sat at his loom, crafting tapestries, capes, and carpets from reeds dyed cobalt and marigold. Though merchants came from afar to buy his wares and enrich his purse, his sedentary ways and fondness for honeyed mash earned him the nickname Ral the Stout. No maiden left *chiorli* blooms by his door, not even Kalur the

Dyer's Widow whose slender hands mixed his pots of dye with such deftness. Ral lived alone and would not mend his ways.

Then came the Night of the Solar Moon, that festival where children take the part of village elders, and wives gamble and bellow at their husbands in good humor. All night long, the people would sing around the bonfire, drinking cane wine and performing sand dances.

Ral remained within his hut. He told his neighbors that his knees ached but in truth, he feared gibes about his girth. Instead, he ate an extra-large meal of honeyed mash and went to bed early.

Sometime near midnight he woke up, unable to move. From the shore came distant singing, but another presence filled his hut, unseen in the darkness.

"Who is there?" Ral called out, trying to move. An unseen force like ropes held his muscles fast. "Is it the oracles?"

"It is I, your loyal body," said the presence. The voice came from his throat, identical to his own.

This frightened Ral. "My body? What do you want?"

"Ral Tam, for years I have been your faithful servant, carrying you from bed to loom and back each day. Yet my legs grow flabby from disuse while my fingers grow crooked from overwork upon the loom."

"What… what of it? Is this not the duty of a body?"

"It is," said his body. "Yet my belly grows immense from honey mash and my heart sick from a surplus of cane wine. We shall die within the next few moons. The oracles tell me so."

"I heed your warning," Ral said, for he did not want to die. "I will change my ways, eating less honey mash and more of the green *karu* shoots with the unpleasant taste."

"Ral, I am your body. I have heard such empty promises before. I propose a bargain instead."

Ral grew fearful again because the body spoke true about his promises, and he did not want to die. "What bargain?"

"Let us switch places. You shall labor in the temple of the heart while I reign in the palace of the mind."

As much as he feared dying, Ral did not like the sound of this bargain. What might his body do in his place? How could his body weave patterns at the loom? His livelihood and reputation could be destroyed. "What if I refuse?"

"Then surely we shall die," his body said. "If not tomorrow, then a week hence, or a month. Who can say? The oracles are fickle, but it shall come sooner than the monsoon season."

"How can you be sure?"

"I am your body. I know."

"I see," said Ral. He could not deny the arguments of his body; if the oracles said it, then it must be true. He did not want to die for he enjoyed life's offerings: sunlight dappling upon the quays, the smiles of those who admired his wares, the slender hands of Kalur the Dyer's Widow. "Then I accept."

"Good. Let us sleep."

In the stillness before dawn, Ral's body leaped from the reed cot and threw on a tunic.

"Why are we rising at so unholy an hour?" Ral asked.

His body only laughed, running out the door on their flabby, shared legs, jogging down the path at the best pace it could make. Ral began to wheeze and gasp, but his body pushed them on, relentless.

On the way they passed a group of fishermen walking to their boats, long nets slung over brown shoulders. They saw Ral and made gibes.

"Ral the Stout, where do you go so early in the morning?" one called.

"Look, brothers!" called another. "He seeks more honeyed mash."

Ral cringed. He wanted to slink back to his hut. Such humiliation he could not bear.

His body only laughed. It waved a greeting at the men and ran on.

Every shared step became an agony, every footfall a fire raging through his lungs and pounding like a smith's hammer upon the anvil of his heart, but his body never slowed its pace. At last, they reached the long pier where fishermen put out to sea.

Ral bent over double, gasping for breath. "Enough of this folly," Ral said. "Return home at once, and begin to work on the loom."

His body only laughed, resting only long enough to regain its wind. Then it stripped off the tunic and waded into the sea, swimming toward the end of the pier.

Ral shouted in protest, only to swallow a mouthful of seawater.

Weeks passed in agony. Each morning, his body rose before dawn to run and swim and labor without end. Each noon, it drank clean water and ate the green *karu* shoots with no taste. Some afternoons it spent clearing heavy stones from footpaths. Other days it hiked in the hills above the sea. It neglected the loom altogether.

Each night, Ral collapsed onto his reed cot, half-starved, bone-tired, helpless prisoner to another's will. One night, he could take no more.

"Body, in the name of the oracles, I beg you to end my suffering. I'd rather die than endure another day of this torture."

His body only laughed. "Be glad I do not drown you in honeyed mash and cane wine."

Finally, there came a day when his body no longer swam after each run or labored to clear stones beneath the hot sun. Instead, it returned to the loom. Tapestries, capes, and rugs came from their shared fingers in patterns bold and colorful, of marigold and cobalt and green. The new work resembled nothing Ral had made before.

"Body, how do you make such patterns? How can you work so well on the loom?"

His body only laughed. "Have I not sat here every day with you, working until my fingers grew bent?"

Within the week, Kalur the Dyer's Widow came by his hut, bearing pots of fresh dye.

"Ral," she said. "You look hearty and your new work astounds the marketplace. I have brought more tinctures for you."

From his new place, Ral noticed what he had not before: how Kalur's smile followed him about the room, how she lingered in his hut, how her hands touched his tapestries.

His body poured *karu* tea and spoke with passion about dyes and patterns. After a while, his body did not speak with words anymore. His body secured the blinds across the hut's windows and then took Kalur's hands and drew her down onto the woven cot.

They painted their naked bodies cobalt and marigold, and Kalur's hands proved deft indeed.

In the next moon, Ral found a *chiorli* bloom outside his door. It was tied with a twist of red and gold cord, Kalur's sign.

Ral picked it up. "Body, she has brought a proposal of marriage."

"Isn't it wonderful?"

"For you," said Ral. "This is your work."

"Ral, I let go so gradually you never noticed. It is you that have sat in the palace of the mind this last moon. I, who never aspired to be more than a loyal servant, have already returned to the temple of the heart."

Ral blinked, and moved his arms and legs, and found that his body told the truth.

"Thank you," he said.

"Did you not mark the passing of the seasons?" his body asked. "Tonight, the Night of the Solar Moon comes again. Tonight, the oracles shall take away my gift of speech."

"You're leaving?"

"In part, though I shall remain with you always as your most loyal servant."

"Farewell, my friend," Ral said, but he knew his body spoke true. They would be together until the oracles parted them at the last.

He took his token of acceptance to Kalur and then, with their hands clasped, they walked to the sand dance beneath the light of the Solar Moon.

ABOUT THE AUTHOR

J.E. Bates is a lifelong communicant of art, literature, and other mind sugar and screen candy. He has lived in California, Finland and many worlds between and now resides in Singapore. His website is https://jebates.com/.

Glass

Jade Black

Meredith rolled her capri legs higher as she waded into the frothing surf. It murmured around her ankles, drawing back and revealing more waterlogged sand beneath her feet. She leaned down, eyes intent on hunting through this small patch before the water covered it again. Shells and broken coral littered the sand, but no glass. She took a second to look around at the rest of the beach. It was empty in the early morning light except for her. No footprints marred the sand, and only kelp decorated the high tide line. Even her footprints were rapidly eroded by the surf as it hissed up and down the sand.

The water drew back again, and with her eyes glued to the newly revealed beach, Meredith kept walking.

Something in the sand almost glowed in the sunlight, and she reached down and scooped it up just before the wave crashed back over her fist. Water sifted through her fingers, taking sand with it and leaving only the small piece of glass in her hand. She pulled it out and slowly opened her fingers in the sunlight. Blue shone through her fingers like the water of the Caribbean, and she gasped.

This wasn't an ordinary piece of glass! A perfect convex arc, it was rounded and well-worn at the edges with an uneven frost on all surfaces. It was luminous in the sun, and Meredith knew she was holding something special.

She swished it again through the water to get more of the sand off before holding it up to examine it. No stamped markings marred it, and it obviously wasn't the rim or base of any bottle. She thought it might be a bit of an old glass fishing float, but it wasn't nearly thin enough. It was about the size of two of her fingers put together; quite large for a bit of sea glass, but she ignored that fact. It even felt warm in her hands instead of being inundated with the chill of the waves.

Without even having to think about it, she stuffed it in the zip pocket of her pants instead of the mesh bag she usually put sea glass in and kept looking. She didn't find any other pieces of that caliber that Saturday, but she knew she'd be back looking for more.

The piece went in a little stand on her mantle, and visitors commented on it whenever they noticed it among her bottles of sea glass.

She found others over the next few weeks, and they joined the first in a special wide-mouth bottle that she found at a thrift shop. They were assorted colors ranging from the deep blue of the open ocean to the green of the shallow water, the white of the peaks of the waves, and the brown of the shallows over the seagrass fields in the Keys.

Meredith was out for the third weekend in the row on her special glass beach, soaking in the early morning sun, when she realized she wasn't alone. The stooped form of an older woman peering down at the glass was easy to spot, draped as she was in mourning black. It was unusual clothing for beach combing, and all Meredith could think about was the fact that the woman was probably going to fry.

She picked her way across the sand to where the woman was bending over, obviously in pain, peering hopefully at a patch of sand.

"I heard tell there was special glass to be found at this beach," the old woman said without looking at her. "I have been searching a very long time for such… special glass."

Meredith thought of the glass she kept at home, the ones that glowed almost on their own and picked up the colors of the ocean whether they were in the sunlight or not.

"I've seen glass like that," she said.

The old woman turned a face forlorn with wanting to Meredith. "Was it here?" she asked. "I saw glass like that in my youth, and I would give quite a lot to see it again."

Something in Meredith's heart twitched. It wasn't something that would have normally happened. She was notoriously jealous with her glass hunting beaches, and rarely gave any of her found glass away. But there was something about this pitiful old lady who walked as though she was barefoot on burning hot sand that summoned sympathy, and Meredith opened her mouth to answer.

She was interrupted by a squeal that couldn't have come from anyone but the old woman, and Meredith inched back just a little.

"There!" The woman nearly swooped down and picked up a piece of black glass that seemed to glow.

Meredith's heart lurched. Black was one of the rarest colors of beach glass, and for the woman to find one of the luminous pieces made her hands ball with jealousy.

The look of newfound purpose on the woman's face, however, wasn't one of greed. It was one of hope, of newfound faith, and Meredith almost envied her as she pulled a black bag out from under her shirt and with shaking fingers, placed the piece of black glass in with a clink. The bag went back under her shirt, and the old woman turned back to Meredith, a few wrinkles smoothed from her face.

The elderly woman's voice was strong and smooth. "In my youth, I made some rather unintelligent decisions. I thought I knew better than my family, and I sought to be with a man my father warned me I would not have. I told them—all of them—that I would be with him or die, and I bargained away part of myself for that chance."

She paused for a moment, looking out at the ocean as it frothed and rolled towards the shore. "When he finally noticed me, I was unimportant to him. And by the terms of the bargain, I would die.

"But family is very important to my loved ones, and they entered into a second bargain to bring me home. The man died in my place, and as punishment, I have to find pieces of... something that was broken a long time ago... before I can see my family again. I have been looking for a very long time, and I only need a few more pieces."

Meredith frowned. The story sounded familiar, but she just couldn't place it. Against her better judgment, sympathy stirred inside her. "I may have more pieces of that glass," she said.

The woman's face lit up. "You do?" she breathed.

"I'll be right back," Meredith said.

It didn't take her long to rush home, pick up the bottle, and get back to the beach. She lived a scant few minutes from the ocean, her first love, and parked in the same spot she'd just left.

The woman was waiting patiently on the sand, and Meredith let an ugly thought surface. What if she just took the pieces and never came back? The old woman would never be able to find her. Something inside her whispered, and Meredith remembered how happy she'd been to find that one glowing piece of glass. She was far happier than Meredith herself had been. How could she deny the woman that joy?

She walked back to the black-clad figure waiting on the beach. She wasn't even sweating in the growing heat, and Meredith envied her. Meredith's own skin was tanned a dark nut brown from wearing only a bikini top and capris to go glass hunting, and she knew the skin on her neck and shoulders was starting to look like leather.

Meredith pushed the thought aside and held up the bottle as she approached. "Is this what you're looking for?" she called.

The old woman's eyes grew wide before they filled up, and she fell to her knees in the sand. "Thank you," she whispered. "Thank you, thank you, thank you."

With shaking hands, she reached out to take the bottle, and Meredith was proud to say she only had a little trouble letting go.

"My name is Ariana," the woman whispered. "I can finally go home."

Curiosity got the better of Meredith. "What do you mean?"

"I used to live out there," Ariana choked. "And now I can again."

Ariana held up one hand, and water coalesced from the air to form an orb that spun lazily above her palm. Bubbles surged in the clear liquid, and Meredith stared at it, then through it at Ariana's face. "You're not lying," she breathed. Astonishment filled her from head to toe, and she felt a surge of triumph. Even though she was letting the glass go, she was going to help someone no one else could.

"Please," Ariana said. "Help me go home."

There was nothing else Meredith could say. "Okay."

Ariana tipped the bag of glass that had been in her shirt onto the dry sand above the high tide line, and followed it with the glass from the jar. Her face smoothed further as her goal lay so close.

Holding two pieces together that looked like they didn't fit, Ariana pursed her lips together and blew on them. Brown and yellow, the colors of a surf dark with sand and the yellow of the sea under the setting sun, they looked like they'd never once been part of the same structure, let alone the same piece of glass.

Together, with her breath upon them, however, the shards grew tendrils towards each other that weren't of either hue. Purple and red pieces of fan coral sutured the glass together in a mesh of color, and between the pieces of glass, gold shone bright in the sun.

"Add another," Ariana directed, and Meredith held another up. "The black," Ariana said, and Meredith searched through the pile until she found it.

"Here," she gestured with her thumb, and Meredith held while Ariana blew. More coral, more gold glints, and the piece that Ariana cupped grew bigger.

Piece after piece with Meredith's help and Ariana's breath, they grew into a frosted orb held in Ariana's hands, until the whole thing sat cradled there, stitched together with coral and gold. It looked like a shattered glass float that had been pieced together by sea life using molten gold as a seal, and Meredith looked at it longingly. It was one of the loveliest things she had ever seen.

"My soul," Ariana breathed happily. "It's been so long…"

The last of the years fell away from her face, leaving a fresh-faced young woman dressed in old lady clothes.

A glow lit her face as the setting sun turned the ocean into fire.

"It's time," Ariana said. "I cannot wait any longer."

She kicked off her shoes and shrugged her jacket off, dropping it into the sand.

She handed Meredith the work of art that was her soul. Meredith held it as gingerly as she could have held anything, terrified to break it.

Ariana leaned over, peeling the support stockings from her feet, then the hose that lay beneath.

Meredith caught her breath as bruises beneath were revealed. They were deep, ugly things, and must have made every step torturous.

Ariana shucked her shirt, then her pants until she stood before Meredith as naked as anyone could be. She took the orb back gently but firmly, holding it pressed to her chest above her breasts, and turned back to the water.

Meredith watched as Ariana walked back into the sea.

ABOUT THE AUTHOR

Jade Black is an American author whose career in law enforcement is used to fund a profound penchant for all things macabre. She has a dual bachelors degree in criminal justice and anthropology. Prior to beginning her law enforcement career she worked as an archaeologist.

Reunions

Ben Howels

Janessa flicked a glance back down the tunnel, fearing the sight of unnatural shadows dancing on the edges of the torchlight—but there was nothing except the six flame-cast echoes she trusted, all running from an evil darkness into an unknown one.

She held up her hand, the polished steel of her butterfly axe glinting orange, and halted the group. "Vardan, how are we doing? Are they still behind us?"

The Tracer knelt, placing his fingertips on the cold stone, a whisper of blue light pulsing into the ground, then speeding away along the path behind them. Moments passed, then more, before the light returned, absorbed back into Vardan's hands. He stood, milky white eyes turning to Janessa.

"The entrance. They have found it, and they are coming."

"Darkness take them, we'll have to keep going."

"Lady," said Taj, "the darkness will take *us* soon as well. The torches are almost out. I estimate that we have no more than—"

Janessa held a hand up to stem the philosopher's analysis; clinical it may have been, but the children were already scared enough. And, unlike what pursued them, they needed the light to see by. "We keep going. Come on." She turned and carried on into the black, periodically craning her neck to check that everyone was staying close.

Vardan was a stoic rearguard, always alert. She knew he'd buy the rest of them as much time as he could, if the Skinwarped closed in. Taj's movements were strangely stuttered—not by fear, but by curiosity. He wanted to know who had made this tunnel. And the children…

The children should never have had to go through something like this.

The little twins, Lindra and Salomon, were struggling with the pace, but Brock was helping them along, always smiling, always offering encouragement. Janessa couldn't have been prouder of her nephew—twelve cycles, and already showing his promise as a man. She just hoped he'd get the chance to be one.

Time passed in a blur of shadow and flame, booted feet thudding on dirt and stone, a small parcel of light traveling beneath the mountains, full of uncertainty and fear. But the parcel of light kept shrinking, pulling the group tighter together, until they were hunched and staggering beneath only one torch.

A final burst of incandescence, and then there was only darkness. Janessa opened her eyes to after-images of the torchlight. The twins started sobbing.

"Vardan, how much time do we have?"

"Not long. They will close on us now."

"Can you use your trace to show us the way?"

"It will help a little, but I cannot maintain—"

"No," said Taj. "Don't pulseglow. I can see light ahead. It's faint, but it's there."

"Where?" Janessa squinted in the direction she thought she had been traveling, willing her eyes to adjust to the blanketing darkness. "I can't see anything. I can't—"

And then she could. Almost nothing, but still something—a whisper of light. A beacon to follow.

"Hold hands, everyone. Me, then Taj, then the twins, then Brock, then Vardan."

Two quick bursts of pulseglow gave the group just enough visibility to get themselves in order, then—once Janessa had got her bearings again—they stumbled towards the light in the darkness.

They closed with it far faster than Janessa had expected—a wan glow, gently pulsing in the guts of the mountain. She'd only taken a hundred paces or so, and she could already see the axe in front of her again—but the metal was tinged green, not white. Whatever was ahead, it wasn't daylight.

"Taj, can you see what it is yet?"

"No."

"Vardan?"

"No, but we should be wary. The light's not—"

"I know. Be ready."

The green glow blossomed, until finally the tunnel opened out, the path terminating in a steep slope that led down into a rubble-strewn, circular chamber. The green light pulsed from three small shards of rock that extruded from the center of the roof. They looked like jagged sword-blades.

"It'll be tough to climb back up this slope," said Taj. "And I don't see a way out down there."

"No," Janessa replied, "but we don't have much of a choice. We can't go back, and—if it comes to it—at least we will have light to fight by. And cover." She pointed at a large pile of boulders that lay on the far side of the chamber.

"Lots of rocks." Vardan chuckled, patting the sling which hung on his belt. "I will thin the warped ones, if they do follow us in."

"I know you will." Janessa forced a smile onto her face, hoping it didn't look as hollow as she felt. "Come on, let's head down. I'll help Brock. Taj, Vardan, take the twins."

As she clambered down the short slope, she noticed how the green light gave the chamber a mellow, comforting glow. That didn't stop it feeling like a tomb—for her, and for all of them.

No. Not for the children. They'd be taken. The Skinwarped would…

No. She'd find a way to save the children. Whatever it took, she would save them.

When they were all gathered at the bottom of the slope, Janessa gave her orders.

"Taj, take the kids and see if you can find them hiding places. If we can dig into the floor a bit, cover them up, then we do it." She turned to Vardan. "See how easy it is to get back up the slope, and then run a pulseglow again. Let me know how much time we have."

"And what about you, Auntie?"

She smiled down at Brock. He'd never called her by her full name. Not once, not ever. "I'm going to have a look at the pile of boulders. See if maybe I can shift some of them. They may be hiding a way out of here."

"Okay. And then we can find my parents."

As her nephew scurried off with Taj and the twins, Janessa's eyes met with Vardan's. They'd both seen what had happened when the Skinwarped had hit the refugee caravan. It had been absolute chaos, with people fleeing in every direction—but not everyone had made it. Maybe S'ainn and Kurgan had made it into the foothills. Maybe.

"Go. Tell me how much time I have."

Vardan nodded, clapped her on the shoulder, then headed towards the slope. Janessa turned, and started to clamber up the pile of boulders. She was cautious at first, but soon found the stones to be solid and unyielding. Safe to climb, perhaps, but unlikely to be easily moved.

"Lady?"

"Yes, Taj?" Janessa looked down and to her right, where the philosopher was stroking the floor with his palms.

"The surface here is smooth. Very smooth. Almost flawless. Not like the walls of the tunnel we came down."

"That's lovely to know, Taj. Just keep looking for—"

"Who carved it?"

Janessa tugged at a thigh-sized stone beneath her feet, halfway up the rock pile. "Don't worry about that. Just focus on how you can—"

"It wasn't us."

"Had to have been. These mountains have been empty since the Mythtime. The Tome tells us that we're the only things that ever came across the mountains, and—"

"I'm telling you, this wasn't us. I've read the Tome, read all our books, all our scrolls, and I'm telling you, we were never able to carve Wyrdstone this smoothly. Even when we still had the old magics… even when the Patriarchs wielded the Lighthammers… we could never do this."

"Fine. Trust to your learnings, Taj, but it doesn't—"

Hammmmerrrr?

It was a word without a clear voice—something Janessa felt, rather than heard. A faint tremor tingled through her leather boots. "What was that, Taj? Did you—?"

Hammmmerrrr?

The thigh-sized stone shivered in Janessa's grip, dust trickling from where it sat amongst its kindred. It shook; shifted.

Janessa's first thought was that she had moved it. Her second thought was that it wasn't the only stone that was moving.

"Get everyone back. Back! This is coming down." She leapt to the floor of the chamber, then paced away from the pile of boulders. She needed to get clear. She needed to…

Why was Taj just standing there? What was he looking at? Janessa turned back to the pile of rocks, and she froze.

The thigh-sized stone she had been pulling on earlier folded neatly into two, then slid sideways, revealing similar, segmented stones beneath. They fanned out, just like fingers in a hand. Exactly like fingers in a hand. Another was forming on the other side of the rockfall. Two large boulders at the base of the pile were cracking and sliding apart, revealing stone toes. Eight of them. Then there was a rumble of dry thunder, dust cascading down as the pile of boulders unfurled—the top half stretching, straightening, leaning up and back against the wall of the cavern.

Brock was suddenly beside her; hiding behind her. The twins were cowering by Taj's knees. And in front of her…

In front of her was a giant, humanoid rock creature, sitting against the chamber wall.

Hammmmmmmmmerrrrrr?

There was a dry, crackling sound, then eyes the size of Janessa's head opened wide, a green light blazing out from within.

Softskins.

No mouth had opened; the words felt like a drumming in the bones. The emerald gaze flickered quickly over everyone in the chamber.

No hammers.

A thin gash opened in the stone face, curling up at the edges. One of the rock hands closed into a fist.

Mouth tasting sour, Janessa held her axe in front of her, and pushed at Brock to head back towards the slope. "Get back with Vardan. All of you, get back up the slope."

The creature's stony smile remained, its eyes turning to the back of the chamber.

A gritty thrumming droned out, making the floor shiver. Janessa heard Vardan yell, then a slithering, heaving crackle—turning, she saw the scree slope dissolve into the room, Vardan sliding with it. Dust and debris washed across the floor.

The back wall was now smooth, the lip to the path four times her height. Seeing the Tracer stagger to his feet, she pushed Brock towards him.

"Go. Vardan, try and get him up the wall."

Their eyes met for what she thought would be the final time—they both knew there was no way out. At least if the rock-thing killed them all, it meant the Skinwarped wouldn't get the children.

Turning, she saw Taj was still immobile, just staring at the creature sitting in front of him. "Taj, the twins. Taj! You've got to get the twins—"

A huge, cratered hand started to reach forwards, and Janessa knew she had no more time. Sweeping past Taj, she screamed a war-prayer, and brought her axe around in a wide arc, slamming it into a stony palm. There was an awful grating sound, and a flash of sparks—then a chuckle like a mudslide, and the impact of rock against her chest-plate.

The creature had done no more than flick her with its finger, but she hurtled backwards, wind slammed from her lungs, axe skittering across the floor.

Vision pulsing, eyes feeling squeezed in her skull, she sensed Brock move towards her; Vardan, too. But Taj remained stricken, and the twins with him.

Small first. Scared. Easy prey softflesh. Vengeance.

The words came to Janessa through the earth again, as though they had vibrated through her back, and into her head. There was raw emotion in them, so powerful it rattled her teeth. She could taste it. Rage, and something else. Something behind it. Sorrow.

The creature's fingers spread wide, reaching for Salomon's head. Taj was doing nothing; Salomon could do nothing but cry and shake.

Janessa found the breath she needed.

"Not the children!"

Her scream echoed through the chamber, halting the stone fingers just as they came close to Salomon's head.

Children? Know word, from the Long-ago. Softflesh young? Softflesh shards?

The green eyes briefly glanced towards the ceiling, then turned to Janessa.

Small things softflesh shards?

This time the thrumming in Janessa's back made her think less of rage and more of disappointment. She took a few ragged breaths, then managed to force more words out.

"Shards? I don't understand. What are shards?"

Mine. Ours. Killed by the softflesh, in the Long-ago. Rolling hammers. Great hammers.

"I don't understand what you—"

"You're a trullock!" said Taj, finally breaking free from his stupor. "Divinity take me, you're *real*!" He turned to Janessa, looking as giddy as a child riding their first unihog. "The oldest scrolls—the ones from the Mythtime—they talk of trullocks. Rock-people, with lava for blood. When they died, they explod—"

"The Mythtime scrolls? They're just stories to entertain the children. The Tome denies their—"

"Really?" Taj just pointed to the rock creature. "How is that not proof? That *is* a trullock."

Myth... mythtime? The Long-ago?

"What?" Taj turned back to the trullock, seemingly oblivious to the threat it posed.

Janessa could see uncertainty in the stone face now. Whatever the creature was, its face was as expressive as her own—apart from the mouth, which still hadn't opened.

Waken when you come. How long since war? Since kill shards?

"What shards? What war? What...? Oh. Oh, yes."

Janessa sensed Taj was suddenly uncomfortable—as though he'd just remembered something unpleasant.

"What war, Taj? What—?"

"In the forbidden texts, there was mention of a war. The Sundering, I think it was called. When the Patriarchs found... when they found the trullocks, they fought them. They wanted the wealth in the mountains. Our old magic was strong. The Patriarchs—"

Killed my shards. All our shards.

The hand that had been close to Salomon's head shifted at blinding speed, wrapping itself around Taj's body, pinning his arms to his side. The twins ran to stand with Brock, who hugged them close. Janessa tried to stand, but Vardan held her in place, shaking his head.

He was right. If the trullock had meant to kill Taj, he'd already be paste—and besides, their weapons could do nothing to harm the creature.

Why kill us?

"I... I didn't. *We* didn't." Taj's voice was far calmer than Janessa would have given him credit for. "The war was hundreds of land-cycles ago, in the Mythtime."

Hundreds?

"Yes. I know very little about it. To be honest, even I thought it was all just legends and—"

Hundreds of land-cycles?

"Y... yes."

Show.

The trullock's free hand suddenly swept forwards, and a finger extended, pressing against Taj's forehead. The philosopher went rigid, mouth open in agony, but only for the briefest of moments. His head sagged as the finger was withdrawn, and the creature stared at him until he had regained his composure.

Scrawled lies. False heroes. Killed my shards. But long ago. Too long. It released Taj. *Not you. Not even sires. Not even sires' sires. I sleep too long.*

"How did you... what did you do to me?"

Memories just echoes. Tremors. Rock good with tremors. Feel all.

"And the talking... the language... how can I understand you? You aren't speaking, but—"

Of earth. Tremorvoice language of it. First language. All life talk through land. Softskins forgot how to speak it, in the Long-ago.

The trullock looked thoughtful for a few moments, then seemed to come to a decision. It brought its arms back to its sides, and started to settle into the shape it had been in when they first found it.

"Wait," said Janessa. "Please. Is there a way out of here? Is there some way we can get through to the other side of the mountain?"

The head reappeared, eyes opening and looking at Janessa with disdain. A finger extended, and pointed towards the lights above. *Shards long dead. But when die, leave piece of selves. Final rock. No child, but echo of core. Of beat. We collect. Place together. Revere. In Long-ago, had great echohalls. Hundreds. Thousands. Now…*—the trullock's head shook slowly—*…all I have left*. The head and finger folded back into itself again. *No kill. No vengeance. But no help.*

"But we can't go back. The Skinwarped are already in the tunnel behind us. They're coming, and they'll kill us."

Skinwarped?

"They were once like us, but they chose the wrong gods. Re-learned the old magics. The dark ones. We cannot fight them. We have all had to flee."

All? All softskins run from death? Pity. There was a faint rumble like laughter in the ground.

"They have no hammers, but they have powerful weapons. They may even be able to harm you."

Then I join shards in the longdark. In the endless cave. My time.

Janessa was getting desperate. She looked across at Vardan.

"Not long, Priestess. Two sand units at most. We will be able to hear them soon. Their bloodmutts will already be able to hear us."

Janessa turned back to the trullock. There was only one plea she had left, she just wished she didn't have to voice it. "If not for us, then for the children. Please. For the shards. The Skinwarped will kill us, but the young ones… they don't kill them. They have rituals, and…"

She couldn't bring herself to describe it, not in front of the children. She was about to ask them to cover their ears, when the ground rippled with a fresh urgency.

Tell.

"I can't. I don't want them to hear what—"

Show.

Before she was even aware of it, the trullock had unfurled, wrapped her in one hand, and pressed a cold, stone finger against her forehead. Green eyes bored into Janessa, expanding and then enveloping her, drowning her in an emerald lake. An agony she'd never known tore into her skull, clubs pounding at it from the outside, knives gouging it from within. Then the *tremorvoice* sounded—but only through the finger touching her forehead, not through the floor. Somehow she knew that this time, only she could hear what the trullock was saying.

Let in, no fight. No pain.

And suddenly she realized, for the first time, how warm the voice was. It wasn't cold. It wasn't lifeless. It was compassionate.

She relaxed, and the pain sloughed away. She felt nothing more than the gentle touch of fingers, turning the pages of her memories, finding the darkest one—from her scouting trip only one moon ago, when she had looked down on a Skinwarped encampment, and heard the screams. Seen the horrors of what they did to the little ones. She also got the faintest of glimpses at the trullock's own memories—a faint backwash of emotion, but enough to make her pity the creature. Death, loss, and a deep loneliness.

Surfacing from the green lake, Janessa found herself back in the present, resting against a stone palm, the fingers no longer encasing her. There was a strange rustling sound. She looked around, saw nothing, then turned back to stare at the trullock, and understood.

Small pillars of dust fell from its eyes, drifting towards the rock-floor of the cavern, tiny motes glittering green in the dim light.

The shards.

Those words came through the floor, felt by all, and the vibrations conveyed nothing but the horror and disgust that Janessa had felt since she'd first seen the Skinwarped's encampment. She raised a hand to one of the stone fingers beside her, and gripped it tightly.

"I'm sorry. For you, and for your shards. I'm sorry for what my people did, in your Long-ago. But I must get the children out of here. Is there a way?"

The pillars of dust slowly diminished, then stopped falling. The trullock glanced up at the light-giving shards in the ceiling.

Yes, my time now.

There were the myriad sounds of a landslide as the trullock stood, its head brushing against the ceiling of the cave. Where it had sat, a circular opening was now exposed. A gust of fresh air swept into the chamber.

Janessa saw Vardan breathe deep, then smile at her.

"Grass and evergreens, my Lady. Spring Heartslips and Yellowstems." He pointed. "That leads through to the other side, or I'm no Tracer."

Mine, dug in the Long-ago. Met other tunnel. Made chamber. Good for last echohall.

"Thank you." Janessa didn't know what else to say. She didn't even know the trullock's name. She grabbed her axe from where it had fallen, then motioned to the others. "Come, we have to leave." She moved towards the freshly opened passage, only to be blocked by a huge foot sliding in front of her.

"What? I thought you were letting us go?"

Am. But tunnel dark. Need light.

"You have torches?"

The trullock shook its head. As it moved towards the middle of the chamber, realization dawned on Janessa.

"No! They are the memories of your children. You should keep them with you. We cannot—"

Can and must. For the children. The trullock gently stroked each of the three ceiling shards. *Would understand. Approve.*

"But you can just sit back down and block the tunnel. The Skinwarped won't get through. They'll—"

Strong magics. Powerful, like the Long-ago. You said.

"Yes, but maybe not this group. It's a scouting party, ahead of the main force. Probably no shaman. And besides, they might think we went another way."

No other way. Will realize.

"Then come with us."

No. Grown with age. Tunnel back, take too long. They catch.

"I will stay."

No. Shards need you.

"Then I will stay," said Vardan.

No. She needs you. The trullock pointed at Janessa. *You two are one. Easy see. Land tells me. Now go.*

"We can come back for you," said Janessa.

Won't be here.

"What?"

Go to longdark. Journey to endless cave.

"No," said Taj. "I want to come and talk to you again. There's so much I can learn from—"

The stone hands shot out again, encasing the philosopher, and placing a finger against his forehead.

Hear my echoes. Hear all.

Taj shook briefly, then was released, falling to his knees and groaning. Tears funneled down his cheeks.

"How could… how *could* we? I'm so sorry. So sorry. So many shards… so many killed…" He staggered to his feet. "We were *monsters*! We were—"

No. They were. Not you. Teach your shards truth. Be better.

Then the trullock reached to the ceiling, and delicately withdrew the three light-stones from the rock, handing one to each of Janessa, Vardan, and Taj.

Always part of me. Always know where are. When you out of mountain, I go endless cave.

Janessa found tears welling on her cheeks. Brock was crying, too. Twelve, and already learning the pain of sacrifice.

Huge hands descended, sweeping the group firmly, but gently, into the tunnel beyond.

One ask. When safe, longways from here, bury stones deep. Meant to be lights in darkness. Like me, soon.

"I promise," said Janessa.

Then the trullock turned, and sat back into its original resting place, sealing itself in the darkness.

For brief moments, there was nothing but the sounds of sobbing, and deep breaths. Then Janessa placed her fingertips on the spine of the trullock, and whispered thanks. The others followed her lead, before she took them down the tunnel.

It was a long scurry through the darkness, cocooned in a green wash. Janessa didn't know how long they had been running before she heard the faint strikes of metal on stone; or how much longer it was before she heard the first shrieks. The thump of firmer impacts.

She did know when she saw the light—white, not green—ahead of her. Her axe hacked at a mass of wayward vines, and they were through. Out into verdant foothills, some foliage familiar to her, some not.

The sun felt wonderful on her face; the air begging to be sucked in as deeply as possible. Brock and the twins rolled in the grass. Vardan gently brushed her shoulder, then knelt, sending out pulseglows. Taj kept looking back up the tunnel, clutching his still glowing shard like a lost child.

Moments passed, and blue light returned to Vardan's hands.

"My Lady, more have entered from the far side. Many more. We must leave."

"Then why are you smiling?"

"Because I didn't just check behind. Others have made it. In the valley." He pointed over her shoulder. "Our tribe. Your family."

She let out a cry of joy, then wrapped Vardan in a hug. "Then let's go." She was about to call everyone together when she heard a rumble in the mountain, a rumble that turned into a roar.

Everyone fell silent and looked towards the tunnel.

As the roar faded away, Janessa felt the gentlest of vibrations in the ground. No words as such, but a feeling of peace. Then other vibrations joined it, coming from all directions; the faintest of ripples in her toes.

She smiled.

ABOUT THE AUTHOR

Ben Howels' fiction has previously been published by Writers' Forum, Writers Online, Shotgun Honey, Devolution Z Magazine, Phantaxis Magazine, Red Sun Magazine, The Arcanist, Earlyworks Press, Sirens' Call Publishing, B Cubed Press, *and* Lit Select. *If he's not writing, he's either in the gym, or on Twitter at @BenHowels.*

Stained Glass

Chloe Garner

Carter leaned in the doorway, arms folded, legs crossed at the ankle.

She hated when he did that.

She ignored him for another good five minutes before closing her book and looking up at him.

"Why are you wasting your time like that?" he asked.

"Because sometimes I like to just read a book," Samantha answered. "What do you want?"

"We have work."

There was a very long, very moody pause.

"So?" she finally asked.

He shrugged, just shifting against the doorframe and resettling his crossed arms.

"Mind reader is not on my list of special skills," she said. "What do you want me to do?"

His nostrils flared, subtle humor, and he pushed off of the doorway, walking for the front door. Samantha sighed, cursing this most recent demon who had sold her a lock that he'd *sworn* would keep Carter out of her closet bedroom.

She put the book under her bed and pulled her backpack open, peering into it as the front door opened. She had until the elevator got up to their floor, maybe forty-five seconds. She knew everything was where she wanted it, but she checked every time, anyway. She downed a testing concoction, smiling at the feeling of warm, spreading power from her stomach. She was still as light as she could possibly be in a human body.

She stripped her shirt and put on the harness she'd had custom-made for Lahn, her angel-forged shortsword, sheathing the blade in a familiar motion and pulling her shirt back on. She grabbed her backpack at a flat run to make it out just as the elevator doors dinged. She slipped between them, bending time to keep from touching the one in front of her, but her backpack brushed the one behind her and they opened again.

Carter sighed loudly.

It was going to be one of those days.

He had her park in one of the invisible parking spots of New York. They were magic, and you had to be one of the people who knew they were there in order to see them, so while it didn't make parallel parking in traffic any easier, at least she had a place to leave the car. Carter got out and looked up at the historic cathedral across the street, tugging at the cuffs of his suit jacket.

Samantha came to stand next to him.

"We going in there?"

"Yup."

"Thought you weren't allowed."

He grunted without saying anything, starting across the street despite traffic.

It wasn't that the world bent around him. That wasn't the kind of power he had. It was that the world, in general, wasn't willing to see what happened if it bumped into him.

"I'm serious, Carter," Samantha said, catching up as he pushed open a door. "I didn't think we were allowed to go places like this."

"Just don't talk to anyone," he said. "It's a public space."

Carter took a hard right, going through a door Samantha suspected was locked and up a spiraling set of stairs. They passed small, iron-barred windows at intervals, and ultimately they reached a landing where a man stood, leaning on a dustmop, looking out at the city through a glassless window.

"Get out," Carter said passionlessly, stopping next to the man to look out the window. The janitor stirred himself as if he were surprised that Carter was there, then shook his head and nodded at Samantha on the way down the stairs. Samantha frowned after him, then looked at the floor.

There were footprints there in the dust.

"Weak minds, strong magic," Carter murmured, then drew a sharp breath, stirring himself. He started setting out small vials from his pockets onto the floor, putting a sharp, curved knife in the middle like a totem, though it wasn't a magic Samantha recognized.

"I assume you brought simple oil," he said.

"I'm insulted," Samantha answered. "Are we going to have a conversation about why the window's missing?"

"Because someone took it," Carter answered. "I need it now."

"The window?"

"The oil," he growled. Samantha smiled to herself, setting her backpack down against a wall, unzipping it, and pulling out the full rack of vials from inside.

"How much?" she asked.

He looked back.

"How much do you carry?"

"Well, there's this," she said, pulling the vial and holding it up, "or there's the bottle I use to refill it."

"You're going to be four feet tall when you die," he answered. "That's plenty."

"Something's going to kill me long before my backpack has a chance to shrink me," Samantha answered, tossing it to him and going to look at the window. There was a smell of rosemary and… she breathed… wimple stain.

"Why would they take it?" Samantha asked.

"They wanted it," Carter said, his mind focused elsewhere. She glanced, watching him draw a pattern on the floor with the oil and then smear it with a red, gummy solution that he had covered his palm with. He was forming a symbol she knew.

"Who?"

"Don't know," he grunted. "Are you planning on being useful?"

"I'll take my oil back if I'm bothering you," she said.

"They say," he said, "that when they first built the cathedral, the archbishop blocked and locked the entrance to that stairwell. The demons say that an angel, a real, white one, sat up here for two dozen years weaving magic." He stood up, looking down at the pattern, then turned, holding out a hand. "Need your blood."

"Don't do blood magic."

He narrowed his eyes.

"Then your spit."

"Why me?"

"Virgin."

She considered this, then wrinkled her nose.

"You know the concept of virgin spit seems antithetical to me."

"Take it up with the idiot who wrote the rules," Carter said.

"Don't talk like that," Samantha answered coldly. His head ticked to the side slightly and she sighed.

"Fine. Where?"

He held out his red palm and she grimaced.

"Ew."

"I'd prefer blood, too," he answered, and she drew a long breath, spitting in his hand. He turned and continued to work.

"It's like a demon sword," he said. "That many layers of magic, no one knows how it all works, but the window was right in the middle of it."

She looked back at the metal spokes that had held pieces of glass in place.

"How did they get it out?" she asked.

"Hell if I know."

There was a slight pop, like something had quietly imploded behind her, and she turned to watch as Carter finished his cast.

He spoke a set of words, mostly a combination of human languages to form a natural magic cast. His real power was with dark magic. Samantha could feel it just as clearly as he could, though—this space wasn't going to tolerate dark magic.

There was a small ripple of blue flame across the red goo, and then pale green smoke came up off of a thick drop of oil, curling in the mostly-still air. It caught a draft from the window and coiled away, almost disappearing as it reached the ceiling and began to pool. Carter looked up at it.

"Well?" Samantha asked.

"Not good."

"It's never *good,*" she said. "What *is* it?"

"I have no idea."

"Should have been red, blue, or black," Carter muttered as they jogged back down the stairs. Samantha thought he was going faster simply to make her backpack's weight harder on her, but she couldn't tell what was simple lack of awareness and what was intentional malice, these days.

Fifty-fifty, probably.

"What would those mean?" she asked. He stopped, and she almost ran into him as he looked up at her.

"Sect," he said. "Always sect."

"You think a demon took that glass?" she asked.

"I think we need to get it back," he said. "Whoever took it wasn't an angel."

"Why not?"

He stopped again, this time not looking back.

"White angels don't need to do scavenger hunts for ingredients," he said. "They cheat."

"It isn't cheating," she said, and he chuckled darkly, continuing on.

"A demon couldn't get into that room for anything," Carter said. "I was having a hard time breathing. Nothing else weaves that kind of magic."

"So not an angel and not a demon," Samantha said. "That only leaves humans."

"One of these days you're going to impress me, and I'm not going to know what to do with myself," Carter answered. He hit the door to outside at speed and she saw the way his shoulders eased.

"You're human," she said. "It shouldn't impact you like that."

"I'm complicated and you know it," he answered, continuing into traffic like it wasn't there. Samantha stopped again and waited, darting across at the biggest gaps she could find.

He got into the car on the passenger side and she waited for a car to go past before opening her door and sliding in.

"So if the only ones who could have gotten into that room were human, why would they have a demonic sect?"

"Because who would know about that glass and want to take it but a demon?" he asked.

"I don't know," she said, "maybe a mage?"

He opened and closed his mouth.

She blinked.

"Did you get demon tunnel vision?"

"Human," he said. "I don't deal with humans."

"Then maybe this isn't our problem," she answered.

He shook his head.

"That glass has more ceremonial magic in it than any other piece of flotsam wandering around this hemisphere," he said.

"How much is it worth?" she asked. "If you knew the market well enough?"

His face darkened.

"Take me to Celeste."

She smiled out the windshield, starting the car. He was a jerk and he wasn't willing to admit it, but she was useful.

She really was.

Celeste was a tricky person to find at the market. She didn't have a stall, not one that Samantha had ever seen, and she tended to just show up when she wanted something, but Carter spoke to several merchants and they pointed directions. Ten minutes later, Carter opened a door—just a piece of corrugated metal that looked like debris lying against a wall—and Celeste turned to face them.

She was in dark, dark gold today. Samantha had never seen Celeste's face; the woman wore a long, draping satin cloak that covered every inch of her. She only took her hands out of the opposite sleeve to complete a transaction.

"Carter," she said. "To what..."

"Glass," Carter said.

She shifted.

"I don't have anything remarkable to offer you," she said. "What kind are you looking for?"

Carter pushed her back into the cubby and pulled the metal closed as Samantha scurried in behind him.

"Angelic cathedral glass," he hissed.

There was a long silence.

"I don't know anything," Celeste finally said. "But that's too dangerous."

"I agree," Carter said. "You hear anyone looking to offload it, you leave a sign for Abby."

"Yes," Celeste said, and the light came back to the small space as Carter pushed the door open, leaving it askew against the wall behind them. His posture was even bigger than normal. Every vendor here knew he carried Diana, one of the greatest epic blades in use anywhere in the world, and every one of them knew about his temper.

They weren't going to do anything worth risking his attention unless it was very, very lucrative, but he was putting on a show, in his subtle, egotistical way. They saw him—today—and they knew who he was. It would make them think twice. Celeste's reaction had been enough to affirm Carter's estimation of the glass in Samantha's mind. Carter could outsize the importance of things when he took them personally, but Celeste was a businesswoman. About anything else, she would have been indirect and noncommittal. And in the way of things, if she'd come across the glass, she'd have moved it, at the right price.

"Why can't Abby just find it?" Samantha asked as they got back to the car again.

"It's warded," he said.

"Why ward glass?" Samantha asked. "It's just supposed to sit there."

"That room is private," Carter said. "Anything that ever happened in it, it stayed there."

"Could that be why they want it?" Samantha asked. "For privacy?"

He sighed at her.

"I can name a dozen much less interesting ways to guarantee that no one could possibly overhear or record anything that happens in a space. Mute juice, if it came to that."

That meant something to her.

Actually, it meant a lot.

Mute juice was an expensive potion, full of things that were difficult to get and expensive to produce, and a single cast of it could cost nearly a million dollars.

The cathedral stained glass was more important—more interesting—than mute juice.

She was still trying to get her head around the economy Carter lived in, but a million dollars was still a big number. Big enough that some of the men behind them would be willing to risk their lives to sell it to the right customer.

"Oh," she said.

"Yeah."

They got back to the car and he put his foot up on the dashboard, resting his wrist on his knee and stared at nothing as Samantha drove. She was headed for Nuri's club. It was where Carter normally went to consult about important things that happened in the city, and Samantha wouldn't mind getting to sit with Nuri for a while, either. The demonic woman was one of the oldest in the world, as far as Samantha could figure, and she was both terrifyingly foreign and hauntingly familiar, as far as demons went. She engaged Samantha's curiosity with an open sense of bribery.

"Nuri's," Carter said some time later.

She nodded. His fingers, lax, tapped a rhythm on the air that kept drawing her attention, but his gaze remained distant as she turned into the parking lot under Nuri's club and turned off the engine.

He was in motion again without looking at her, in and through the club, to the hallway outside Nuri's office.

The pipsqueak demon sitting at the door was supposed to demand that they state their identity and their business, but Carter had never, in Samantha's experience, stopped to talk to one of them. He went into the office and sat down on one of the chairs, resuming his tapping motion with his fingers on the air as they waited.

Samantha roamed the office, looking at things. She knew that the desk was off-limits, and she knew better than to touch anything, but the things that were on the walls and on shelves were there to display, and she liked to see what was new and what she hadn't noticed before.

Nuri took perhaps twenty minutes to glitch into the room, appearing on her black velvet chaise lounge with a bored expression.

"Do you know?" Carter asked. Samantha went to sit next to him so she could see both of them as they talked.

"Come sit next to me, child," Nuri said, and Samantha slid out of her chair, going to sit on the floor next to Nuri. The woman was beautiful, tall and lean with skin that really wasn't brown but truly black. She had an elegant, well-featured face and a lack of expression that bespoke intense concentration and control more than lack of expressiveness. The tiniest motion at the corner of her eye or twitch to her mouth spoke volumes.

"Do. You. Know," Carter said again. Nuri split her lips with the tip of her tongue and let her mouth open slowly as she spoke.

"I know more than you can conceive of," she said.

"Someone took the glass out of the stained glass window in the angel room at the cathedral," Carter said.

Her mouth tightened. Anger, perhaps. Maybe surprise, though Samantha found that difficult to believe.

"No," Nuri said. "It's been a… parlor game among demons for many years, how we would take that glass, but it *is* the nuclear option. No one would do it, even if they could."

"What would you do with it?" Samantha asked. Nuri put her hand on Samantha's shoulder like a drifting cloth and shook her head.

"I would not speak of that with you."

"I know what you'd do with it," Carter muttered. "And what anyone else would do, too."

"Who has it?" Samantha asked Nuri.

"I do not know," Nuri said. "But I would."

The tall demon looked at Carter.

"What will you do?"

"Green smoke off of a mix of oil and wimple stain," Carter said.

She frowned.

An honest-to-goodness frown, with eyebrows and everything.

"Green."

"What does that mean?" Carter asked.

"Unaligned," Nuri said. "Whoever took the glass hadn't had dealings with a demon."

"Why would they take it?" Samantha asked.

Neither Nuri nor Carter answered.

"Could someone *pay* someone to take it?" Samantha asked.

"The power of the demon would come through the money," Nuri said quietly. "You have much to learn about currency."

"And what about mages?" Samantha asked.

Both heads turned to look at her.

"Green does suggest magic," Nuri said. "Just magic that I do not control."

"Like a mage," Carter said flatly.

"Yes."

"I don't *do* mages," Carter said.

Nuri looked at him, then down at Samantha, motioning at Carter with her head.

"Child, we need to speak privately."

Samantha twisted her mouth to the side, but she stood and went out to the bar, anyway, sitting on a stool at the bar and taking a glass of ice water from the demonic bartender.

She liked drinking ice water at a demon bar.

It bothered them.

It wasn't but a few minutes before Kjarr came to join her. Nuri's husband was a huge Norse king with a ready laugh and a huge smile, but today he just sat next to her.

"There will be a war over that glass," he finally said. "You should be sure to stay out of the crossfire. If it goes badly, I will avenge you, but it would be better if you stayed in one piece."

"I'm harder to kill than I used to be," Samantha said, pleased nonetheless, and he chuckled mirthlessly.

"I won't avenge Carter," he said, nudging her with his elbow as he stood. "You matter more than he does."

"Don't tell him that," Samantha said, taking a drink. Kjarr did laugh at this, clapping her on the back twice as he left.

She watched after him, curious.

Carter was another thirty or forty minutes, and Samantha was chilly and sloshy when he finally did walk past her, not pausing to make sure she would follow. She pushed the glass at the bartender and hopped after Carter, following him to the car.

In the parking lot, Carter stopped and faced her.

"There's going to be a war," he said.

"Kjarr just told me that," Samantha answered, which startled him.

Huh.

Maybe she hadn't played that card right. Fun to be able to disrupt him like that, though.

Finally he shook his head.

"A human has glass that every sect and family of demons who has ever heard of it is going to go after. If he isn't already splashed, it's because he's... well, he's one of the three most powerful mages in the city. They're the only ones who could hold it. But I need to get it and I need to take it out of play."

"How?" Samantha asked.

"You're going home," Carter said.

"Nope."

"It wasn't a question."

"I think I was clear."

"This isn't part of our normal game," Carter said, grabbing her wrist. "There's no power balance here. The threat that I pose to the demons isn't going to keep them from killing you if you're in the way. And, knowing you, that's exactly where you're going to end up."

"What are they going to use the glass for, if they get it?" Samantha asked.

"Demons can't handle light magic," he said. Samantha gave him a dour look and he mirrored it. "That glass contains all of the light magic they could possibly need to do anything they wanted. It's like a mage with dark magic power as strong as Nuri's, and light magic power as strong as any angel's. They don't need much natural magic in the middle to keep those two separated, and they can *do anything*."

"But both you and Nuri knew what she'd do first," Samantha said. He nodded.

"Every dark demon wants human sacrifice. They'd send the city into chaos and sit back and watch," he said.

"And the gray?" Samantha asked. Like Nuri. And Kjarr.

"They want power," Carter said. "There is magic they could cast that would siphon all of the magic out of the city into themselves. They'd be untoppleable."

Samantha paused.

"And if it were Nuri?"

Carter shook his head.

"You don't want to see what she would be, if she could do it."

"But why would she *not* want that?"

"She does," Carter said. "She just doesn't want to risk someone else getting the glass first. We're in a race with every demon in the city, including her, but she's willing to back us as the next best option."

"You just said *us*," Samantha said. He frowned and turned to face the car.

"You're going home."

"What are you going to do?" Samantha asked, unlocking his door and going around to get in. A warded car would keep itself safe on a public street, but demons were never above messing with an unlocked car below Nuri's club.

"I'm going to find the idiot who took that glass and I'm going to beat him until he gives it to me."

"Where first?" Samantha asked.

"Home."

"Where first?"

A very long, stony silence. He didn't look at her. This no longer bothered her.

"You stay in the car."

"Where first?"

"You stay in the car or I will handcuff you to it myself."

"You taught me how to get out of handcuffs."

"Not if I put them on you," he said darkly, just his jaw working to tell her how angry he was.

"Where first?"

He gave her an address she recognized and she nodded, starting the car.

"If it's that important, I'm not letting you go on your own."

"You're just going to get yourself killed," he muttered.

"Look at the bright side," she answered. "If I die, at least you'll have Kjarr on your side, instead."

He looked at her, eyes wide, and she smiled.

"He likes me."

He sighed.

"That you're proud of that isn't even the strangest part," he answered.

The apartment complex was an embodiment of luxury. A pair of uniformed doormen stood at attention outside, and one of them opened a brass-and-mahogany door for Carter and Samantha. A concierge greeted them and asked if he could call a resident for them.

"I need to see Russell," Carter said. "Tell him Carter is here."

"Yes, sir," the man at the desk said, picking up an antique phone with a wooden handle and brass mouthpiece, dialing. Samantha peeked over the desk at the rotary dial, just to watch him use it.

"Mr. Andrews?" the concierge said. "There's a man, Mr. Carter, here to see you."

He listened for a moment, then gave Carter and the phone a civil smile and hung up.

"If you'll step onto the elevator, I'll send you up," he said.

Samantha gave him a long look, tempted to test him to see if he was a demon, but Carter didn't show any sign of concern. She followed him onto the elevator and watched his reflection as the doors closed.

She was here to save him. She'd come back from the dead to do it; she just had no idea how. It didn't seem to have anything to do with keeping him safe or alive. Nothing she'd done since she'd come back had *felt* like the thing that had brought her back, that singular *thing* that was so important.

What she did know was that she didn't expect to save him from the car.

Having a mission gave her a certain measure of fearlessness that was refreshing, even if she'd learned the hard way that being fearless about everything could cost her dearly.

The elevator doors opened into a large sitting room. Carter put an arm out to stop Samantha from walking into it, though she hadn't yet taken a step.

"I'm not here for a fight," Carter said. "You know why I'm here."

"That door is going to close again in about fifteen seconds," a voice said. "You push the button or hold the door, the entire car is going to explode. You step off, it goes boom, too."

"You think I didn't find that?" Carter asked. Samantha looked at him, not sure if he was bluffing.

Sometimes she could tell. This was not one of those times. He peeked at her out of the corner of his eye, then let his face rest calm again, his arm dropping.

"You have them," Carter said.

"Just sitting in the open like that?" the mage answered. "How could anyone expect them to stay?"

Russell Andrews was a tall, lean man in Samantha's memory, always wearing ill-fitting brown clothes and shoes that couldn't decide if they were *shoes* or *slippers*.

He had a wicked way with magic, though, and a poor temperament that made him impulsive and reactive, which was a dangerous thing in magic. Most of the mages she'd met had huge egos, certainly, but they were measured. Thoughtful.

Russell flew off the handle at bugs. She'd once seen him turn a cockroach into a purple giraffe plushy.

"They're going to kill you for it," Carter said.

"Like to see them try," Russell said.

"I'm more powerful than you," Carter said. "And I'd have left it where it was. I wouldn't want to try to protect it."

"Who says I'm protecting it?" Russell asked. "Maybe I'm going to use it."

"For what?" Samantha asked.

"You brought her?" Russell asked.

"Who do you think is going to handle it?" Carter answered. "I'm surprised you could even touch it."

"I brought tongs," Russell said.

"Can we come in?" Carter asked.

The doors started to close and Russell dashed across in front of the elevator, lifting a red string as he ran, and Carter grabbed Samantha's elbow, dragging her across the threshold as the doors closed behind them.

"What are you going to use it for?" Samantha asked, starting to follow Russell in the direction he'd disappeared. Carter grabbed her elbow again to stop her.

He took a stone out of his pocket and handed it to her. She felt it in her palm, then put it into her pocket. It wasn't a cure-all, but it would keep a lot of the more tricky magic off of her. A disruptor cast, by the touch of it.

"You getting tea?" Carter asked. "Sam doesn't drink it."

"Everyone's trying to get in," Russell called, his voice coming from the wrong direction. "If you wanted to help, you could pick up a bucket."

Carter looked at Samantha.

"You're the one who wanted to be here," he said. "You got this?"

"Yeah, I got it," she answered, walking across the extravagant sitting room to a long wall of windows that looked down at the city.

Windows were an excellent way to get into a place, if you knew how to work boundary magic. The elevator was the one that would be obvious to people constrained by getting to a place by having been in the place next to it, first, but angels and demons didn't think that way. Windows were a thinness so fragile that even light could get through.

Upside for her: they had a strong symbolic tie to *light*, which made them an excellent anchor for the magic that she had in mind.

She took out her bag and started mixing things, laying out a set of light components on the window sill. That, alone, would strengthen it, and it gave her a moment to tease out what Russell already had on the apartment to keep himself safe.

"You know that there's a very good chance you die at the end of this," Carter called, taking off in a third direction as Samantha started working. Not the way Russell had gone, nor where his voice had been coming from. He knew something Samantha didn't. Curious as she was, she kept working. If he was going to trust her with a task, she was going to kill it. Not because it would keep him from criticizing her later—he would, regardless—but because they'd both know that he was having to make stuff up to do it.

The dove feather drifted around in an invisible draft, coasting up and down the windowsill for several moments before finally falling to the floor.

That was the weak point. Any seep from dark magic coming through the window was strongest there.

So that's where Samantha started.

She pulled out a mesh bag full of gullseed, sprinkling it along the metal sill, then got out a vial of suspended angel hair. Normally she used the fiber dry, but if you let it distill in an oil mix, it could transfer a lot of its properties to the fluid, making it so that she could mix it with other dry things directly - like the gullseed powder. It formed a cement of sorts, and she continued working, using shapes, colors, specific powers, symbols, everything she could think of, working her way along the window in both directions. She ducked her head through a doorway, finding more windows in the next room, and she just kept going, crystalizing the light in the glass until the glass glowed with it. Russell's magic was intricate, but dark. A mage was a master of light, natural, and dark magics, but most of them tended to drift dark over light, because light was the least compatible with the others. Natural and dark got along quite well if you knew what you were doing.

Carter came back through, Russell darting through the doorway behind him and stopping to stare at the windows and then Samantha, and then chasing after Carter again.

Samantha kept working.

Russell was powerful.

She respected that, for as odd as he was. She didn't want to go toe-to-toe with him in a fight over anything. Maybe not even with Carter on her side. He'd assumed that his power was keeping him safe, though, and his home wasn't anywhere near as impenetrable as Carter's apartment. Ten thousand years hellside makes you paranoid. There's just no getting around that.

Once more, Carter stormed past. Samantha straightened from the symbols she was painting on the windows in a mix of lamb's blood and purging chalk.

He glanced.

"Like the pink," he said, continuing through into the next room. Samantha saw Russell as he looked around a doorframe and she narrowed her eyes.

"You stole angel magic," she said.

"I've heard you might take that personally," he answered, looking at his windows again. "You're trapping me in here, aren't you?"

Samantha shrugged.

"He didn't say I couldn't."

"You know I could break you," he said, still peering.

"You're welcome to come out from behind that wall and try," Carter called, coming back into the room. Samantha didn't turn. "She's trained with the angels. Longer than you've been alive. Don't mistake her lack of a killer instinct for lack of skill."

Russell looked at the windows once more, fully frosted now and gleaming bright, pure light. That wasn't sunlight, though she was using the sun to power it. She watched him.

"What are you planning on doing with the glass?" she asked.

There was a thud, like a giant bird hitting the apartment window, and then a faint shower of ash.

"That was a big one," Carter commented without any real sign of concern. "They're coming for you, Russ."

"What were you planning?" Samantha asked louder. Russell took something out of his pocket and tossed it at the windows. There was a huge cracking noise and the light in the room dimmed.

"Shouldn't do that incautiously," Carter murmured. "She's the only thing between you and them, right now."

"That and that sword of yours," Russell said bitterly. Carter scoffed, leaning against the wall and crossing his legs at the ankle as he shifted to put his hands into his suit jacket pockets.

"They show up, man, I'm gone. We know what *they're* going to do with it, but I'm a *survivor*. I'll figure it out after."

"They can't touch it," Russell said as the room dimmed another fraction. Samantha put her fingers on the glass, feeling the force of magic against it.

"You think they haven't thought of that?" Carter asked, his voice rising.

"What were you planning?" Samantha asked. She found that she was yelling now. There wasn't *noise*, but there was the impression of noise, the way the glass was buzzing against her head.

Russell shook his head, trying to focus, trying to keep his mind in the game. He looked at the glass like he might charge it and Samantha braced to stop him, but he turned, waving her to follow. Carter pushed off of the wall, waiting for her to go before he followed her up the stairs and into a small, dark room.

The glass sitting on the floor glowed. Red and yellow and blue and green, it glowed, the pattern a dramatic burst of color. She'd seen the framing for it at the cathedral, but she was still unprepared for the beauty of it.

Lahn, the sword on Samantha's back, surged with a strange sort of awareness and power.

"They're nothing," Russell said drunkenly, looking down at them. "They're conduits. They mean nothing."

"I think you're mistaken," Samantha said. "You… you don't *see* the symbolic magic in that? Something that lets light through, but that gives it *color*?"

He looked up at her and she widened her eyes at him.

"Seriously? You thought they were just melty-glass magic flasks?"

Carter chuckled. He hadn't even come into the room.

"You should let her take them off your hands," he said. Something hit the side of the building, making the floor shake, and ash rained down on them again. It hissed and sizzled and sparked where it landed on the glass.

"No," Russell said. "No. They can't take me. Not with this much light magic in my hands."

He stooped, his hands shaking as he held them over the glass.

"They can't take me," he muttered.

He grabbed a piece of the glass and lifted it over his head.

Samantha was in the middle of thinking that this was the worst possible time for dramatic displays of lunacy when he melted.

Well.

Melted was the wrong term. It implied that he turned into a fluid. What he did was ash, only he didn't turn into… anything. He fell apart into nothing, and the thick shard of glass clattered back down to the floor, glowing orangely among its peer glass shapes.

The building shook harder and Carter looked over his shoulder.

"Decision time, Sam," he said. "Anything Russ had holding this place up is gonna disappear *fast*. We can't fight our way out when it happens." He looked back at her. "You woman enough to carry those or are we leaving them?"

She put out her hand.

"Let me use your jacket."

He snorted.

"You really think a layer of fabric is going to protect you? Either you're pure enough to handle them or you aren't."

She put her hands over them like feeling a campfire. They radiated so much *power*.

"What will you do with them?" she asked. He laughed again, that dark noise he made when he was giving up on something, but trying to do it without letting it hurt him.

"I can't touch them. Ever. Can't use them for anything. All I want to do is get them somewhere that they aren't going to make a lot of people *die*."

She stooped, feeling Lahn twang on her back in a sort of harmonic vibration to the glass.

Paused.

Faith.

Either she was or she wasn't. She tested herself almost daily, afraid that she wasn't.

So afraid.

She'd chosen to come back from death. For a reason. But it was so hard to stay clean, in this life.

She scooped up the glass, clasping it to her chest as she picked up the stray pieces, purple and green and blue and yellow. They cut her fingers where she was careless, but she knew Carter was right.

They had to move, or they were dead.

The demons of New York knew the glass was here, that it was unprotected. She'd put up a signal flare for all of them, and then Russell had lowered the gates.

It might already be too late. Her magic downstairs was holding, but she wouldn't know when it failed, other than that the ceiling would stop raining ash on them.

They ran back downstairs, Carter pushing the button for the elevator and Samantha standing with an armload of glass slipping and slicing at her skin. Her fingers were bloody. Not in the way that they would have been if the glass had done any real damage, but the way a good paper cut wouldn't give up bleeding until you finally squeezed it hard shut.

And then she saw it.

Lahn buzzed and throbbed and there was another thump against the glass behind them.

Samantha knelt, laying the glass out on the floor in its original pattern.

"Can't go back," she murmured.

"Can't put it back," Carter agreed. "Won't work."

She nodded.

"Very sad," she said. He turned to look at her, frowning, perhaps hearing something in her voice and then seeing the pattern on the floor. She didn't know how she'd known where each piece had gone, but it was like fitting a jigsaw puzzle. There was only one right answer for each. The building shook, and there was a hellscream as ash fell and sizzled and sparked. She looked up at Carter.

"Really," she said. "You'd do nothing?"

"Nothing," he said, watching her with intense eyes. She drew Lahn.

Brought the shortsword down pommel-first on the smallest central glass piece, a tiny, round, blue shard that shattered like a hard candy under Lahn's platinum-and-gold handle. For a moment, Lahn was too hot to hold and too powerful to let go, then the feeling faded, though Samantha could feel that Lahn was changed.

The glass lay flat at her feet, just so much colored silica.

She looked at Carter.

He shook his head.

"There are going to be demons out there who are going to try to kill you for that," he said.

"They'll get over it," she answered. "You know how to summon one of Nuri's bound servants?"

"Always," he said, taking a vial out of his jacket, uncapping it and tipping it against his finger and back, then putting it away.

He snapped.

A kid with shaggy hair and a surly expression appeared, looking around with a lack of surprise to see where he'd ended up.

"Look," Carter said. It was an order, not a request. The teenage-looking boy came to stand next to Samantha, giving her a hostile, standoffish side-eye as he nudged the glass with a sneaker.

"What happened to it?" he asked.

"You recognize it?" Carter asked. "That it's the cathedral glass and not a decoy?"

The kid looked at him, wild and resentful, but he squatted, picking up a piece and smelling it with a grimace.

"That's it," he said.

"Go," Carter said. "Tell Nuri. I will ash any demon who glitches in here and they'll be coming for something that no longer has any power."

The kid stood and sniffed.

"Can I pick a few to keep out of the loop?" he asked, then ducked his head and glitched away before Carter's glare reached full-force. Samantha looked at Carter, taking a deep breath and blowing it through tight lips.

"You sure she won't hold back telling some of the demons she'd rather see gone?" she asked.

"Not and risk me dying," he answered, drawing Diana anyway. The elevator doors dinged behind him, and Samantha went to get her backpack, loading the glass carefully into it as Carter stood with an evident lack of patience.

"Should have left you in the car," he said. "What are you going to do with it? Put it on the wall in your room?"

"No windows," she said, looking up. "It's still got symbolic power in it. People who look at it know what it is."

He shrugged, yawning and leaning against the door to keep it open. Diana rested point-down on the elevator floor.

"Obnoxious, how much that blade does to take care of you," he said. She spread her hands for him to see them. Even the blood was gone.

"She heals," Samantha said. "How can you be surprised?"

He snorted.

"Get moving," he said. "I've got better things to do today."

ABOUT THE AUTHOR

Chloe Garner acts as the conduit between her dreaming self and the paper (or keyboard, since we live in the future). She writes paranormal, sci-fi, fantasy, and whatever else goes bump in the night. When she's not writing she steeplechases miniature horses and participates in ice cream eating contests. Not really, but she does tend to make things up for a living. Her website is blenderfiction.wordpress.com.

THE BROKEN GARGOYLE

TOM JOLLY

Pika Kahne was literally a basket case.

Dr. Matthew Hamilton looked down at the basket of stone fingers, toes, forearm, and foot, then back up at the patient, and tapped his pen on his lower lip thoughtfully. The stone gargoyle stared back at him hopefully, unblinking. The two of them were sitting across from each other in one of the exam rooms in Backside Clinic, the only clinic in town that accepted—or even knew about—the supernatural community.

Hamilton glanced down at his clipboard. The nurse had conscientiously written down "no pulse" on it, along with a weight of 370 pounds and a temperature of 72 degrees. Well, no surprise there. That's where the clinic's thermostat was set.

"When did you first start losing parts of your body?" Hamilton asked.

"As far back as I can remember, every time I bump into something hard, a crack forms. After that, it's usually just a matter of time before the part comes off. A little water gets in there, a freeze comes, the ice expands, and there goes a finger.

Or foot." Pika touched his prominent, arched nose. "I've been lucky with the nose."

"How far back can you remember? Someone had to have created you, right? I mean, gargoyles don't reproduce, right?"

Pika frowned. "You don't actually know very much about gargoyles, do you? Maybe this visit was a waste of time." He bent over to pick up the basket of loose bits as though to leave.

"Mr. Kahne, I can't help you if I don't know the details of your case. Answer a few questions for me, and if you don't like what you hear, feel free to get a second opinion."

A second opinion! Pika sighed and stared at the basket. The list of supernatural clinics in California was very short. "Fine. Ask away."

"What's your first memory?" Hamilton asked.

"I was lying on a wooden table, and my master, Logarian the Ept, was hovering over me, chanting some arcane language. When I moved, he stopped chanting. Leaning over me, he asked me who I was and I replied that I did not know. So he gave me the name I have now."

"Logarian the what?" Hamilton was writing notes on his clipboard.

"The Ept. Like inept, but opposite. Like 'the Capable'."

"I see. Not a native English speaker, is he?"

Pika shrugged. The gargoyle also had an accent that Hamilton couldn't quite place.

"So when you were first created, your body must have been carved standing up? Or lying down?"

The gargoyle tipped his head slightly. "Why is that relevant?"

Hamilton walked around the gargoyle, looking at the details of his structure. Pika looked back at him with stone eyes; disturbingly featureless solid orbs of gray. "If I were to carve a gargoyle, I would carve it crouching, ready to loom over the streets below. Gnarly and grotesque, probably with wings of some sort. You nearly look human but for your somewhat skeletal appearance and your nose. Why would someone create your original stone form standing up or lying down?"

The gargoyle gaped. "I...I had never considered the question. It is curious. When Logarian brought me to life to guard his estate, he never told me of my origins, nor, as his servant, guardian, and roof ornament, did I ever question them. It was not my place to ask." Pika looked up at the ceiling, thinking. "Once, while he was standing on the balcony with an associate sorcerer, I overheard him mentioning the rare stone of Moloka'i as he pointed up at me, apparently bragging in some way. That is the closest I can come to a clue."

"Are there other gargoyles at the estate you guard?"

Pika nodded. "In fact, that is how I arrived here without being seen. Rather than create some disguise and sneak out of the house, one of the flying gargoyles carried me here this evening. He is still on the roof of your clinic, waiting for me."

"Which explains why you were banging on our skylight entrance. I was wondering how you got up there. So, these other gargoyles, are they falling apart as you seem to be?"

"No. They can feel things. I, on the other hand, seem to be numb all over. I feel nothing, as one might expect from someone made from stone. But the other gargoyles are sensitive to bumping into things, while I can never tell when I've damaged an appendage by smacking into an object too hard. It's curious," he said, frowning, "and makes me wonder if I'm a true gargoyle at all. I cannot serve my master well if I'm shattered into dozens of pieces."

"Uh huh." Hamilton looked down at his notes, thrilled that he had something new to add to his notebooks on the supernatural world. He tapped his pen on the clipboard and sat down. "What we try to do here at Backside Clinic is find a logical and scientific reason for supernatural afflictions. It's my belief that everyone that walks into this clinic has some scientific explanation for their existence and their problems. We try to find out what that explanation is. We've had pretty good success so far."

Pika looked doubtful. "Have you?"

Hamilton shrugged modestly. "My patients have included a werewolf, a glass person, a ghost, a sphinx, a dryad, a troll..."

"Okay, I get the idea. So do you have any speculations on my condition?"

"First off, I question your origins. You might not have started out as a gargoyle."

"Well, I am now," the gargoyle grumbled. "What else?"

"The closest human analog I can think of for your condition is brittle bone disease, osteogenesis imperfecta, or perhaps osteoporosis, where bones become brittle. Bone tissue is constantly replaced in the body in that case, but new bone creation doesn't happen as fast as old bone removal."

"Bones, huh?" Pika held up his broken-off foot. "Does it look like there's a bone in there?" The stump appeared to be solid stone across its diameter. "And what's the cure for that?"

"Symptoms can be treated but it can't be cured. Same with brittle bone disease." He shook his head and chewed on the end of his pen. "Have you tried construction glue or cement?"

"Really? Is that what you ask an amputee? Have you tried glue?"

"Have you?" Hamilton persisted.

Pika cleared his throat and looked as sheepish as a stone face can look. "Actually, yes." He held up a little finger. "I reattached this one, but I can't move it. It's lost the flexibility the rest of my body has. It's dead to me."

A ghost blinked into existence in the middle of the exam room, making the gargoyle jump. "Ah, sorry, sir," the ghost said, then turned quickly to Dr. Hamilton. "Doctor, there's a man in the lobby insisting that we stole his property. He appears to be holding some artifact that's pointing to this exam room."

"Thank you, Corwin." The ghost disappeared. Hamilton turned back to the gargoyle. "That would likely be your master, Pika."

The door to the exam room flew open and a short, rotund balding man stepped in. He locked eyes on Hamilton and said, "So you're the fellow who absconded with my gargoyle!" Pika picked up his basket of appendages and hugged them close to his chest, looking fearful.

"Hey, aren't you Logarian the Ept?" Hamilton said, his eyes wide.

The man paused, surprised, then self-consciously straightened a short purple cape hanging from his shoulders. "Why, yes. You've heard of me?" He had a thick accent, but Hamilton couldn't place it. Eastern European, perhaps.

"Your fame precedes you. Everyone in Torrance knows of your amazing prowess."

Logarian raised an eyebrow. "Using my incredible powers of observation, I detect sarcasm." He looked accusingly at Pika. "You told him, didn't you?" Then his eye caught sight of the basket of stone body parts and the abbreviated limbs marring Pika's body. "What's this?" He turned angrily back to Hamilton. "What's wrong with my gargoyle?"

"I keep breaking off parts of myself," Pika explained. "I have no feeling in my appendages, and I keep hitting things by accident. I thought the doctor could help me."

"You could have asked me first," Logarian muttered. "I am the Ept, after all."

"I thought you would be angry with me," Pika said. "Can you reattach my limbs?"

Logarian thought for a minute, then said, "No, I don't think so. Nothing in my vast repertoire of amazing spells will allow me to fuse living stone to living stone." He turned to Hamilton. "Did you have some ideas, Doctor?"

"Besides glue?" Pika mumbled.

Hamilton stared into the distance. "I want to research this a little further. There's more to this than it seems. Did you pay to have the gargoyle carved?"

"Oh, no. I buy old stone figurines and statues here and there and animate them myself. It's much cheaper than paying a sculptor, and they seem to be more obedient that way." He eyed Pika askance. "But I must admit, Pika seems to be a bit more independent in thought than the others."

"Why did you name it Pika Kahne?"

Logarian laughed. "When I bought the statue in Kaunakakai, the sorcerer that sold it to me said that it was that name of a Hawaiian god, and this was the sculptor's interpretation of his likeness. He seemed to be amused at the time. 'The god of broken marriages,' he said." Logarian shook his head. "They have a god for everything."

"A sorcerer? Do you remember his name?"

"Akoni Kekoa. He's been on Moloka'i as long as I can remember."

Hamilton nodded his head. "I'm due for a vacation. Hawaii is as good a place as any to take it."

"I'm not paying for your vacation to Hawaii to find a cure for my gargoyle," Logarian grumbled.

"No need. I'll take care of that," Hamilton said.

Later that evening, Hamilton put together a backpack for an overnight stay in Hawaii. A prior encounter had introduced him to a closet imp who had access to a network of shortcuts through closets. He could travel anywhere in the world in a matter of minutes. With one strap of his backpack slung over a shoulder, he went to the clinic's walk-in closet. "Mbuzi!" he called out. A minute later, a short ugly imp appeared at the rear of the closet, eyes glowing a soft red in the dark shadows.

"Hi, Doctor Hamilton. How's business?" Mbuzi said.

"Strange, as always. Hey, I need to ask you if any of your closets lead to the Hawaiian Islands."

"Do they use coat hangers there?"

"I suppose so," Hamilton said. "All those Hawaiian shirts have to go somewhere."

"Then I probably do. That's a good twenty-minute walk, though. Any particular island?"

"Moloka'i."

"I can take you there. I'll have to fetch an oxygen tank for you. You know… no oxygen in my domain."

"Yeah," Hamilton said, "I remember. How are the wax beetles doing, by the way? All gone?"

The imp squoodged out an ear with a thick fingernail, then examined the glob of wax. "My ears haven't itched in months, so I guess they're gone. Thanks again for that. Let me get that oxygen tank, and we'll be on our way."

Hamilton checked the straps on his oxygen mask every few seconds. Some of the metallic smell of Mbuzi's pocket dimension seeped in at the edge of the mask. The air wasn't toxic, but it was very acrid. Around Hamilton were millions of wooden boxes, three feet on a side, marked with illegible and arcane symbols; labels in some demonic language telling Mbuzi where each small portal led, to which closet in the world it was connected. And even though the millions of boxes were crowded tightly together, there was still room for mountains of twisted coat hanger wire piled around the boxes. It looked surreal. A reddish-gray haze hung over everything, and a dim light illuminated the bizarre landscape without any discernable source.

"So this is home?" Hamilton said. His voice sounded muffled through the oxygen mask. The only other sound in the place came from random pings and groans from the shifting mountains of steel wire. It was eerie.

"Home until I've paid for my mistake. You get used to it, like anything. Ah, here we are." He pointed at an isolated pile of thousands of boxes. "Moloka'i."

"Can you give me a closet exit where no one is living? Maybe a hotel?"

Mbuzi rubbed his chin, then climbed over a half-dozen boxes to one that looked just like all the others. He read the symbols inscribed on the door out loud, and the frame around the door glowed with a light blue. He turned to look down at Hamilton. "Gimme a second to check the room." The imp disappeared through the door and returned a few seconds later. "All clear!" he said, and held the small door open for Hamilton.

Hamilton climbed over the other boxes and knelt down to crawl through the small passage into the closet, then stepped out of the closet into the empty hotel room. The imp called out behind him, "Give me a shout when you need to go back."

"Thanks, Mbuzi." Hamilton handed the oxygen mask and bottle back to the imp, and the panel closed behind him. The seam where it had been faded away.

Hamilton took a breath and stepped out into the empty hotel room. The bed was made and no bags were present. A window was open, letting in a damp breeze. He adjusted his backpack and went to the door just as someone rattled the knob, accompanied by the click of a card-key. The door opened and a startled couple gaped at him.

"Sorry to bother you!" Hamilton improvised. "The room's clean now, just finished making the bed. Enjoy your stay, and call the front desk if you need anything else." He shouldered past them and hurried down the corridor, exiting out a side-door of the hotel. Circling around, he came back to the front desk of the hotel and got a room for the night.

Even though Hawaii was two hours behind California, it was already dark outside. Hamilton visited the bar on the patio, bought a beer, and sat down in the muggy evening air, listening to the ocean waves a hundred yards from the hotel. He pulled out his phone and searched for more information about Akoni Kekoa. He had his own web page, advertising himself as a sculptor, and apparently a fairly successful one, occupying a mansion on a hillside overlooking the beach east of Kaunakakai. He wasn't that far from the hotel, just a few miles down the road.

Hamilton put his phone away and enjoyed the rest of the evening. The mystery of Kekoa's sculptures would wait until morning.

The next morning, after a light breakfast, he took a short taxi ride to a car rental agency in Kaunakakai. He spent the brief taxi ride staring out the window at the vibrant emerald greenery of the mountainsides and wondered why he'd never taken a vacation to Hawaii. Too busy, perhaps. That, and other excuses.

Hamilton rented a Honda Civic and drove out to Kekoa's, arriving early-afternoon. He pulled into a small parking lot, just large enough for four cars, got out, and found himself in a garden surrounded by dozens of small, realistic stone figures of animals and plants, interspersed with a few abstract sculptures. Dozens of tall palms shaded the garden, along with a small jungle of flowering plants. The overall effect was entrancing. Hamilton had wandered through half the garden before realizing someone was following him. He turned to face the man.

"Akoni Kekoa?" Hamilton asked. He recognized him from a photo on his web page.

"The very same. Are you interested in a sculpture?"

Hamilton ran a hand over the cold stone surface of a cat caught in mid-leap, hovering at the top of a steel rod, ready to land on some unseen prey. "The detail is amazing."

Kekoa smiled. "It is my trademark. I strive for accuracy and realism in my work."

Hamilton nodded. The attention to detail was incredible. Impossible, even, and Hamilton couldn't help but think of magic. Was it possible that he started with real animals, and somehow converted them to stone? "Let me look around awhile," he said.

Kekoa nodded. "Take your time. Most of the sculptures weigh quite a lot, but we can ship them anywhere in the world. Are you vacationing? Or here on business?"

"Vacation. Any recommendation for local sights to see?"

"Have you visited the colony at Kalaupapa yet?"

"Colony?"

"Where the lepers lived. Those with leprosy used to be sent here, to keep them isolated from the rest of the population.

Thanks to the surrounding mountains and cliffs, Kalaupapa is almost a natural prison. There are still a few scattered cases, but for the most part they've all been cured. The history is fascinating."

"Leprosy?" Hamilton looked like he'd been hit in the head by a stick. Leprosy, or Hansen's disease, deadened the nerves; in the past, victims often lost limbs and digits because they weren't aware of damage they'd done to themselves, and infection often killed off the limb. Could Pika's problem be due to some strange version of leprosy, converted to stone?

Kekoa waved a hand and chuckled. "No reason to be scared of it these days. Thousands of people tour the colony every week with no ill effects. You should take a tour if you have any interest in local history."

Hamilton nodded. "I think I will. Medical history is a bit of a hobby for me."

He finished touring the lifelike sculptures while Kekoa approached another potential customer, coming back to the sculpture of the leaping cat. He looked closely at the details, the way the hair flowed, the sharp claws extended forward. But was that a flaw? He narrowed his eyes, peering at a stray filament sticking out of one of the cat's rear claws, and touched it. It looked like a strand of grass, turned to stone. Hamilton glanced suspiciously over at Kekoa, who was still busy with another customer, then returned his attention to the unexpected stone blade of grass. Who would add that detail to a sculpture?

He walked back to the parking lot, lost in thought. Sitting in his car, chewing on his lip, he looked up Pika Kahne on his phone, and found a 'missing persons' notice from two years before. Pika's wife, Iolana Kahne, was listed as a contact and lived in Kaunakakai. The coincidence was too strong. The tour of the leper colony would have to wait. He needed to talk to Iolana Kahne.

Iolana's residence wasn't much more than a cottage. Dozens of potted plants decorated the perimeter. Hamilton pulled into the gravel driveway, unsure how he was going to approach the matter with Iolana. He got out of the Honda just as a woman came to the front door. She appeared to be in her thirties, tired looking, but still striking. Hamilton nodded to her and asked, "Mrs. Kahne?"

"Yes? Can I help you?" Her voice was soft and level.

"I may have some information about your missing husband, Pika." He saw the sudden look of hope in her eyes, mixed in with suspicion and anger. Others had approached her, he thought, con artists or worse.

"Who are you?"

"My name is Matt Hamilton. I'm a doctor from California. Do you happen to know a sculptor by the name of Akoni Kekoa?"

Iolana's fists clenched suddenly and she bared her teeth, then shook her head and looked away, back at her house, then back at Hamilton. "You should come inside," she decided. "I will make tea."

While she put the water on, she called out from the small kitchen, "What do you know of my husband, Pika?"

"I first have to ask you if you believe in magic," Hamilton said.

"You're speaking of that evil monster Akoni, the sorcerer on the hill, aren't you?"

"I suspect I am," he replied.

"Then yes. What of my husband? What do you know?"

Hamilton struggled with how he should explain it, but there was no easy way. "I believe I saw a statue of your husband in California, where I work."

"A statue? What made you think it was a statue of my husband?"

"The statue was named after your husband. And the statue was purchased from Akoni Kekoa."

Iolana sat down on her threadbare couch, put her face in her hands and cried. After a minute, she said, "Before, he was only missing! There was always hope he might return. Now I'm sure he is gone forever."

Hamilton bit his lip, wondering when he should tell her the rest. He opened his mouth to talk, and she interrupted.

"The rat Akoni, he had always wanted me for himself. Even in school, Akoni and Pika fought for my attention, but Pika had always been the one I knew I would spend my life with. After we married, Pika found out that he had a rare form of leprosy, resistant to most antibiotics. Our marriage became chaste, but our love was still strong. But we could not afford the drugs required to cure him. Akoni came and said he could cure Pika of his illness with magic, and in our desperation we accepted his offer of help. He took Pika up to his mansion and that was the last I saw of him. Akoni said he cured him of the illness with his magic and Pika left. He assured me he did not know where he went. He suggested that Pika might have only married me because he knew I would take him, sick or not, and now that he was cured, he could go anywhere and be with anyone. I knew he was lying." She clasped her hands together, squeezing until her knuckles were white and stared angrily at the floor, remembering. "He still drops off little gifts, calls with little hints that he is there for me, and I ignore him. He still wants me."

The teakettle began to whistle and Iolana glared at the kitchen. She stood up and went into the kitchen.

Hamilton thought about Akoni's garden of statues, waiting until she returned with the two cups of tea. "He turned Pika into stone and sold him, didn't he?"

Iolana nodded quietly, new tears trickling down her cheeks. "I suspected it. I could never prove it. How can you tell the police that a sorcerer has turned your husband to stone? And I never saw the statue, anyway. I was never certain. What if what he said was true? But Pika wouldn't leave me like that. I filed a missing person's report and hoped."

Hamilton leaned back on the couch, thinking.

"Where is this statue now? I want to see it," Iolana said.

"The statue is being used as a gargoyle on top of a building in Torrance, California," Hamilton said.

She stared at the floor and said, "I cannot afford to fly to California."

Hamilton glanced at her bedroom, looking for a closet. "How badly do you want to see this statue?"

She followed his eyes, misinterpreting his intentions. "I would walk through Hell to see my husband again. But if you are suggesting…"

"Hell? That's fortunate." He stood up. "Do you have a closet handy?"

Mbuzi guided the two of them through the twisting corridors of wire and boxes while Iolana gawked at the bizarre landscape. Hamilton considered exiting from Logarian the Ept's closet, but thought that appearing uninvited inside a sorcerer's estate might be a bad idea. He reappeared in Backside Clinic's closet, returning the oxygen masks to Mbuzi as before.

"We are in California? You are a sorcerer, too?"

"Not me. Just a doctor with the right connections." He looked over his shoulder at Mbuzi. "Thanks again, Mbuzi."

Mbuzi lifted a hand in farewell, and disappeared into the shadows in the back of the closet.

It was dark outside, just after 8PM. A brief call to Logarian assured that Pika would be carried via flying gargoyle to the clinic yet again.

"There are a few other important things you should know," he told Iolana. "First off, this other sorcerer animated the statue. He wanted a living gargoyle, and didn't know that the statue had ever been a human."

"Pika is alive?"

Hamilton waggled his hand. "Sort of. He's still made out of stone, and he's lost most of his memories. He may not remember you. You should be ready for that."

She put a hand to her mouth and choked.

Hamilton continued. "Also, he still appears to have leprosy, but a stone version of it. His body is brittle. He's lost a forearm and a foot." He saw tears forming in her eyes again, and she sat down in one of the clinic's folding chairs.

"I have lost him all over again," she sobbed.

A few minutes later, Pika was pounding on the skylight door, and a nurse let him in. He came down the stairs awkwardly and carefully, using the stump of his broken leg like a peg-leg. He finally looked up and saw Iolana and stopped dead at the bottom of the stairs, staring at her. She stood up slowly, then stood still, hands at her side, and said softly, hopefully, "My Pika?"

He struggled with flashes of memory and looked at her closely, then his stone eyes widened. "Iolana?" he whispered.

She fell into his arms, crying, and he gently wrapped his stone limbs around her.

"I have an idea or two," Hamilton said when Logarian showed up an hour later. He pulled a bottle of Scotch out of his desk and poured tumblers for the two of them. Pika and Iolana were talking together in another room. Hamilton heard Iolana laugh, and he smiled. "First off, I want to reimburse you for the cost of your gargoyle. I have plenty of Coin to pay for him." Coin was the currency of the supernatural community, unique gold coins that let you know what sort of person you were dealing with.

"That's not necessary, Doctor Hamilton. I'm already embarrassed that I was tricked into buying a human turned to stone. The sorcerer's guild has rules about that, and Kekoa has certainly broken them."

"Don't do anything to Kekoa yet. I might still need him," Hamilton said.

"For what?"

"Stone antibiotics. I've come to understand that Kekoa does custom sculptures. I intend to take in a plant, say, a fruiting pepper or tomato, and ask him to create a sculpture of it. I'll stuff the fruits with packets of strong antibiotics to treat Pika's leprosy, and when Kekoa turns the plant to stone and sells it to me, I'll have stone antibiotics. Just break the fruit open."

"Ah, that might very well work. The Law of Similarity will nearly guarantee it. We might even be able to reattach some of his lost members. Duct tape and antibiotics!"

Hamilton raised his eyebrows. "There are laws in sorcery?"

Logarian snorted. "Well, of course. There's the Law of Contact, Law of Contagion, Law of Association, and so on. How do you think we sorcerers sorcer?"

"Hmm." Hamilton thought about all the notes he needed to take. He'd be up all night. "And as far as Kekoa is concerned, he still needs to be dealt with. We do have access to the closet in his bedroom. Perhaps a midnight visitation from Pika..."

Logarian laughed out loud. "The Council frowns on skull-bashing, but I can provide Pika with a powder that he can sprinkle on the sleeping form of Kekoa to temporarily paralyze him. The Council would be happy with that; they're big on retribution, and what better justice if Kekoa is paralyzed like a statue himself when he's brought before the Council, by the man whom he turned into a statue!"

Hamilton looked to the room where Iolana and Pika were catching up. "Will he be stone forever?"

"A good question. Though I personally don't know how to change him back, I suspect it isn't possible. You will notice that his internal parts seem to be all of a sort, a puree of moving stone. I doubt that there is a way to turn them back to their original purpose. But I'm not certain. I will ask around. There are many sorcerers with a variety of skills. I do wonder how a marriage of stone and flesh will work."

"Love will find a way," Hamilton said, and tossed down the last of his Scotch.

ABOUT THE AUTHOR

Tom Jolly's stories have previously appeared in Analog, Daily Science Fiction, Perihelion, Something Wicked, *previous Spring Song Press anthology* Fell Beasts and Fair, *and elsewhere. Find him on the web at silcom.com/~tomjolly/tomjolly2.htm.*

TAROT OF THE ANIMAL LORDS

HOLLY LYN WALRATH

There are many ways to play this game. In the forest of secrets, the past is always the first card drawn. To interpret the cards, one must keep in mind the divinatory and symbolic meaning of every single card. This works best in partners—an oracle and a querent. If a card appears upside down, its meaning changes, suggesting the opposite. These other meanings may be seen as yin and yang, black and white, dark and light, but the best oracles learn how to read between the lines.

Zero. The Fool (Badger)

Spirit of initiative, desire to travel, *thoughtlessness, selfishness, ignorance.*

Adele's skin was stretched hard over her bones as she stood in the ditch, rubbing mud on her arms, hoping the pat might soften her cracked skin. Smelling death, she followed her nose down the ditch and there she found two foxes, their small hands curled around each other as if in embrace. She felt bad for the foxes, with their tails so pretty and fluffy. Her own shorn hair was strange to her as she ran a hand through it—safer to keep it short rather than give a solodat something to hold onto in a fight. Heaving herself back onto the road, she slung the foxes over her shoulder. It was rare for foxes to become roadkill. They were usually fast and smart, but the road was so littered with glass and metal debris even Adele found it hard to navigate in her heavy-soled boots.

Up ahead, some human bodies lay on the ground near the edge of the road, face down. She was grateful for that; face down was better. Around them sprayed jutting shards of caccia, glittering like cavern jewels brought out into the light. The bodies were clean on the outside, skin naked of any indication of the chemical weapon within. She'd never had the courage to break open the bodies like others, to see the caccia. Piercing skin, it sank into the veins and made its victims heavy, filling them with a thousand luminescent formations of hard crystal.

Still, Adele walked toward them. Because this was the last safe road. Because the trees were too overgrown for travel, too snarled and wild. Because she was alone and even dead men made for better company than the sound of her beating heart.

She heard the camion's rumble long before it arrived, its giant treads crushing debris beneath its wake. Two metal belts wrapped around a craggy hull with a large caccia-filled gun at its head, turning, ever seeking a victim. There was no place to hide but the trees and night was a dark flush in the shadows. She'd have to build a fire or die. Better to let the camion pass first.

As it crested the road behind her, she fell flat on her stomach beside the heap of bodies. She tucked her elbows in, turned her face away from the road, prayed the camion wouldn't stop to investigate the bodies, and if it did, the solodats would assume her dead. She wiggled, allowing the dead man beside her to spoon against her. He smelled bitter and his body felt cold and hard. Refusing to look at the man's face, she willed her skin to still, her limbs to rest, her face to slacken.

Adele heard the camion trundle to a stop. Its engine fell silent and she held her breath. She heard the steps of the solodats, two of them.

"More villagers," one said. The solodats walked toward the bodies, their boots crunching glass and broken concrete. Adele squeezed her eyes shut. Pressing down fear, she thought of dark caverns, of hidden jewels sparkling away in the night. If she kept her thoughts dead, perhaps the men wouldn't see her.

One of the men kicked a nearby body. "Hard as stone," he said. "We'll radio ahead the road needs clearing here. If these bodies break open they'll germinate."

They walked to the other side of the road. Adele felt relief fill her, but she did not move. "Droppings," the man remarked. She heard him kneel, shift the debris to inspect the ground. "Others are close, perhaps in these very woods."

"Should we hunt them down?" the other man asked.

Green as a fresh mown field, Adele thought. The second man's voice quavered with a tinge of fear.

"No, the trees are theirs, for now. Until we discover why the wild grows so fast, the brass doesn't want us meddling."

The second man, younger, coughed, his voice muddled as he adjusted his mask. "But the rumors, the others breaking through—"

"That's not our problem. We leave the others to border patrol. We've got to focus on getting these supplies to the other side. Come on."

The camion's engine rattled back on, and Adele pressed her face into the broken concrete, feeling the vibrations in her very bones.

When the ground stilled, she stood up and shook off the dead man and the cold of his body, which had leached into her like ice over a winter lake. Night was coming. Ahead stood a grassy knoll, startling green against the gray road, surrounded by woods. She climbed it. Better to take a stand on high ground at night and anyway, she was hungry.

She built a fire and began to cook up the roadkill. Then she skinned the fox tails and braided them. They were soft like a baby's downy head, the meat stringy and tough. She tied some of it in strips, using the tails to dry the meat down to jerky.

The stars came out one by one. Others joined her one by one too, slinking out of the darkness. She saw their eyes in the woods, between the trees, moving up the hill slowly as if the harsh light of her campfire frightened them. But they weren't afraid of her. They lingered outside her ring of light, a patch of brightness in the pitch black stretching as far as she could see. Only one stepped past the circle of light her fire cast.

The Lovers (Mandarin duck)

Test, important choice, *indecision within sentimental relationships, unfaithfulness.*

"Come back with us," Orson begged. Orson always began his old plea with no preamble, no *I missed you*. "Don't you miss the smell of the forest, not scrounging for human food on the sides of roads, being able to run naked?"

"Go away, Orson," Adele said. She spat a bit of bone at his furry feet. His toes splayed at strange angles, tufts of gray between them as he paced before her fire. He'd shrunk, or was he broadening out and at the same time crouching lower to the ground? His thick black fur shifted on his back, sensing the warmth of the fire. Yet his eyes still shone as blue as the sea, and she glimpsed the sensitive red of his mouth beneath the beardy fur of his face.

"I can't leave you yet, not till I know you're a lost cause." He prowled the fire's circle, sniffing the air, taking in the scent of cooking fox meat, the wind in the woods, his other tribe waiting in the trees, and the hint of caccia death on her from earlier. When others came close he waved them away and they wandered back into the woods, willing to let him do the talking. *Our tribe,* Adele thought.

Adele found it impossible to take in all of him at once. She refused to note how quickly his human parts were disappearing, shifting back beneath the skin of other. "Haven't I always been?"

"How do you do it?" Orson asked, sitting back on his haunches near the fire. "Ugh. It's disgusting cooked. Don't you remember the taste of fresh meat?"

Adele remembered a lot of things. After finding her family long dead, killed by the war that soon spread until it overtook the entire continent, Adele knew she should've gone home, back to safety across the border. But instead she took refuge in the woods. Human Orson was there too and together they fell into the wild, let the woods swallow them up. They went *other.* She remembered losing herself in the darkness, coming into the place where the trees circled and the sky was a shimmering jewel above their peaks, nights spent ambushing small animals under the stars and days spent running from the solodats on hot pavement, her tender pads bleeding for weeks, cracked and dry, and then—the small lake where she bathed in acid, losing, letting go of her furry skin, leaving it behind her for some other poor wanderer. She'd left Orson to go find the city of her childhood, her human skin smarting with the exfoliated feeling of nakedness. Lost and found, Adele was a creature and now she was human.

Which came first, the caccia crystals or the others? It was a riddle no one knew the answer to. It was a spell cast over the land no one knew how to reverse. Perhaps the solodats built the caccia to fight others. Perhaps others evolved to fight the caccia. All she knew was her other immunity to the disease grew thinner each day, and beyond the border was salvation, sweet other and caccia-free safety. A world without riddles or stories.

"I remember," she whispered.

"I miss you," Orson replied, so soft she barely made out the words. For a moment she let them hang there in the air while they both remembered better days. Other Adele had forgotten about finding her family, about her memories of playing in the winding streets of her hometown, about her life on the other side of the border too, as a teenager necking boys in wheat fields, tipping cows. All of her past fell away then as she sat in the woods with Orson at her side. He always found her again.

"You miss other Adele, Adele the creature, not me. Stop haunting me."

"I can't. I can't." Orson shook back and forth. He curled up on his paws and fell asleep at her feet. And she let him, fool girl. She let him.

The Magician (Fox)

Shrewdness, will to succeed, lack of prejudice, *errors, lies*.

Later Orson woke when the sun was a slim suggestion on the horizon and begged her to play the card game with him. But first he needed to hear the story of how she found the cards, as if the magic of the cards was the story within the stories, the matryoshka of her past.

"When I was a little girl, I lived not far from here in a town whose name means 'tiny castle'. It was a walled city with the most beautiful churches ever built. I used to play among the olive trees lining the streets. And my grandmother gave me a pack of cards to play with." Adele settled into this part of the game, her memories age-gray in her mind's vision. "But I was sent to the countryside during the war like all the other kids. When I went back to the city all grown up, my parents were gone and the house was leveled, but our basement was still there and at the bottom I found the cards my grandmother left me."

"And you used to play another game with them, the game your grandmother taught you," Orson finished for her. "But not the game we play."

"No. This is a different game. I can't remember the rules to the one she taught me." It was a lie. The lie was part of the story, part of the game.

Orson huffed as if he didn't believe her either. "Deal me a good story then Adie." He eyed the sky and the road below. Adele knew he watched for the hulking forms of the camion, listened for their guttural whine. But all was quiet, and the sun washed butter-gold over the trees. The moon was a ghost on the horizon refusing to give way to the morning.

"We only have time for one round, I'd say."

"Do it quick then."

Adele shuffled the cards. They were large and awkward in her hands, with white borders tinged with red blood, and black in places from soot and fire. She'd tried her best to clean them after she went into the basement, but they clung to the red. The images were old, older than she understood. Their paint was yellowed and faded, coated with a thin layer of clear. Each time they played she changed her mind about what they meant.

She dealt a card onto the grass before them. Bagatto.

Orson shuffled his hind quarters in anticipation. "Ladies first," he insisted.

"Bagatto. The fox, robin, and mouse." Was it luck the fox was the first card from her hand, while the fox furs she'd found yesterday lay braided across her pack, still smelling of animal sweetness? Adele pushed this coincidence away and began to make up a story in her head for the card. "The fox sells candy on the mushroom. He hides it at first to hide the smell of truffle chocolate, then he lifts up his silver cups for the woodland animals to see. They trade for it with little treasures they find."

Orson regarded the card with his half-human blue eyes, memorizing the intricate lines. "No," he argued, always changing the story she set forth. This was the game. To find the best story for the card. "They're in a maze. They're trying to get out. See the green shoots and vines curling around them?" Orson set a paw on the card, gently. Adele knew he wanted to point with his fingers but he couldn't. "The fox bargains with the mouse to let him out of the maze. The mouse can run and jump through the vines without being caught because he's so small."

"What of the robin then?" Adele asked, baiting him.

"The robin is the gatekeeper." Orson's eyes shone for a moment as the sun crested the hill. Then, his eyes turned other, a glint of jade and nightfall, a sinking cave opening behind them. "He keeps them trapped in their bodies forever."

Adele sat back on her heels. She reached for her bag and drew a long knife from the side where she'd tied it for safekeeping, always within reach.

Orson growled low in his throat. The tender promise of the moon slipped out of the sky and the sun overtook the last vestiges of night. Orson's fur went rigid on his back, the snarl growing in his voice. Adele felt the stir of others in the trees.

She scrambled back from Orson, her knife in her hand, struggling to get the pack over her shoulder. Then she was running down the hill, Orson on her heels, his hot breath licking at her skin, his chest heaving with hunger, growling and barking, his teeth coming together in a loud snap as she stumbled onto the road. A camion trundled up the road, belching black smoke and blaring its horn at her. She sprinted to the other side of the road as it barreled past, rolling into the ditch, her shins scraping pavement and her elbows tucked beneath her, her eyes squinched shut, her breath ragged in her chest, the cards clutched to her heart. When she opened her eyes she lay panting in the dust, and Orson was gone. The forest swayed in the morning breeze, whispering to her of a thousand love-lorn secrets, the voices of other dissipating as they merged back into wild green.

Eight of Swords (Mouse)

Agreement, economic stability, social achievement, *obstacles, dangers, problems.*

The little churches, parish halls, thatched cottages once picturesque, winding cobblestone paths and scenic outcroppings, green vistas, felt achingly familiar to Adele. And yet, they were off-kilter. Church steeples lay on their sides, their bells cracked and forever silent. Town gates wiped clean that once bore names like Cerese, Solara, Nolay, and Utelle. Trees encroached where caccia did not. Brambles or crystal. Death, or merely another kind of death.

Houses abandoned, tables set for some never-finished dinner. Adele imagined families sitting down to tell each other of the day—as hers once did, her father laughing over market squabbles, her mother sheltering some animal she'd found in the meadow at her breast, her Grandmere playing the cards.

"Tomorrow it will rain," she'd say, laying the cards one by one on the table with the lentils and greens.

The day before they sent Adele away, the day before the war started, Grandmere drew the black crow. Sometimes Adele pulled the card from the pack—fingered the black feathers, the green lizard on the rock, the skeleton at his feet, the dirty crown on its bony head, waiting for a king—she stared at the card as if waiting for the bird to lift the crown and place its gold circlet on his forehead.

One remaining family huddled in one of the last villages. Half the village was black with mold from an old fire, burnt wood and caccia merging to form new coral. Whole houses were submerged in it like little fish-tank sculptures. The look of them struck Adele with the smell of salt-water, a memory long dissolved in her mind. She couldn't place it. A mother, two children, one crystalized on a bunk in the loft in the stifled house. The mother gestured Adele into the house: she wanted help, but she wanted to help Adele too. She'd stopped Adele on the road, coming out of the chicken coop like a ghost, holding what looked like their last good chicken by the neck, its head cut off.

"Salut, traveler," the woman said. "Come in and rest a moment." The woman was too old for her years, her body a minefield of survival scars.

"I've got places to be," Adele demurred.

"You're about my daughter's size. I've some of her old clothes might fit you."

Adele saw the girl lingering in the doorway. "I'm a bit bigger than her."

"My other daughter." The woman's face went slack. She led Adele inside. The tang of caccia, the scent of deep pools of water below the ground, burned through the house, emanating from the loft above. Laid out as a shrine, the woman's daughter was all shards. Her body splintered, pieces of it fragile, linked together with chains, a necklace of a body. *She'd make a pretty piece of jewelry,* Adele thought. *They should have let her skin hold in the caccia.* She tried not to look at the girl's face, all hard and crystallized.

Adele gave the remaining daughter a piece of the jerky and one of the fox tails. The woman gave her some old clothing, good sturdy jeans and work shirts, a pair of boots that didn't fit, but Adele thanked her anyway.

"Stay a while," the woman said, her eyes grayer than desperation.

"I've got somewhere to be." Another lie. Adele was becoming an expert at them.

"Alright. The woman and her daughter watched from the edge of the village as Adele made her way down the road. Adele willed herself not to look back but couldn't bear it. She turned and waved to them.

Ten of Cups (Penguin)

Happiness, agreement within the family, successful union, *ingratitude, psychological suffering.*

Adele gathered dry wood. She coaxed flame from a tinder nest built out of little things: dried bark, a piece of wax she'd found in an abandoned church, pine pitch, dry leaves, coniferous needles. She built a tiny pyre and imagined her other self stretched across it, heated down to leathery softness.

"How many more games do we have before the border?" Orson asked, coming out of the darkness to taunt her.

"Why are you following me?" she chanted back in a sing-song voice.

"Come on, we know where you're going. What do you think you'll find on the other side?"

Adele said nothing.

"I'm sorry." Orson paced the fire. The tribe crept close to the light, closer than ever before. "I hoped I might convince you to come back and I'm only now realizing I can't convince you to do anything."

"Took you long enough," Adele snorted. She wanted to laugh with him, human him. She wanted him to curl up naked and vulnerable beside her, without the protection of his claws or fur, simply gutted with her. She'd done so many bad things with him. He kept haunting her but he didn't realize she'd moved on long ago.

She knew the exact moment she'd wanted to be human again. It was the night she found Orson with the solodat's caccia gun draped across his paws and flesh in his teeth. The pack ran the next morning, pursued by the solodat's troop. They'd run for miles into the woods, avoiding the roads. But the solodats found them anyway and tried to burn the woods. It was damp, that was the only safety. The woods fought back. She and her other pack-mates barely survived. She'd asked Orson why, over and over again, why had he stolen the gun? It's our nature, he'd said. Somewhere along the way he'd forgotten who he was and other took over. He was pure other now, she knew. But she let him curl up at her fire anyway.

Other is unfiltered wild. It's woods and fire and rot—darkness. Other clings to the night, veils itself. Other makes the woods grow faster, builds a home around itself. Deep in the forest where even the small squirrels and foxes daren't wander, other pulses, its heart seeking out, tendriling into the minds of man.

There are two types of man. Those who resist the call of the wild and carry the caccia for safety, exposed at the hip like a heart worn on the sleeve. They are men who join the solodats, men who don't question orders. They think the caccia keeps them safe, but it's just another kind of desolation, a man-made wilderness of death.

Then there are wanderers, lonely souls without a path to call their own, not tied to anyone or anything. They wander into the woods and turn other easily, leave behind their human skin for another. The wild destroys them from the inside out, turns skin to fur and lengthens fingernails to claws, noses to snouts, like Orson, like Adele once upon a time.

I'm so messed up, Adele thought. She pulled out the cards. She needed the ritual too, she supposed. She rock-skipped through the story of her past tonight, feeling closed-off. She kept thinking about the daughter of the woman in the village, the way her body shone and glittered in the afternoon light. She didn't want to have to keep exposing herself to him. Why did she keep letting him play the game?

"I've told you how I found the cards a thousand times," she said when he argued she'd skipped parts of the story. "Don't you have it memorized by now?"

"I just like the way you tell it." Orson picked at his wolfy teeth with a claw. He spit a small piece of sinew into the fire. Adele was afraid to ask who he'd killed today She dealt a card. Chalices. Twin black birds with white stripes across their soft heads, their wings stunted. A white egg at their feet. A rainbow in the distance, crumpled with ink.

"The twin sisters walked in the market together," Adele began. "It was a beautiful day. Rain had just fallen and the air smelled like crushed almonds. A rainbow played at the edges of the sky, frolicking from cloud to cloud. The sisters were princesses bewitched into the form of common sparrows. They were once quite lovely, and men came from all around to win their hand." Adele paused to catch her breath.

"This sounds like a story you heard as a child. You have to make it up, you know," Orson said, grinning a bit at his chops.

"It's entirely of my own making. Stop interrupting." Adele poked the fire, sending sparks into the darkness of the sky. "The twins' father lost a game of cards to a witch, and she placed a spell on them. Until one of them bore a child, the witch would never let them go free. But no man would marry a common sparrow. So they went to the market. The sisters bought cups and glasses and wine glasses and all the things for holding liquid they could find." Adele felt her voice ease into the story of the card despite herself. "Then they went home and filled them all with clear water. And one day, a single white egg hatched in one of the glasses. The sisters argued over what to do, over whose child was in the egg. But they were too afraid of the witch, so they brought the egg to the witch. The witch tried to crack the egg in a hot pan for her breakfast, but a beautiful bird escaped. It was made of clear glass and as sweet as fresh spring water, and when it sang its voice was of the sea, not of the sky."

"But was the spell broken?"

"No. The twin sisters lived as spinster sparrows with their glass daughter, happily ever after."

"That was a good one." Orson stared at the card, trying hard to think of a better story. He scratched himself with a back foot. He tilted his head left and right. "I can't think of a better story than that. You win."

"Ha," said Adele. She snatched the card from the grass. "I win."

Knight of Swords (Puma)

Soldier, pugnacious person, enthusiasm, *tough dispute, wrath, arrogance.*

A control post rose up on the horizon. Miles of fence on either side—a wall of straggling teeth tethered between the hills and sparkling with fragments—the bones of its victims. No way through the border except the gates of the post, a square building. Adele could make out solodats there—standing side by side. She might sneak through at weak points in the wall but faster to go straight through, to bear the indignity. Although she knew she was immune, she didn't want to let the solodats know this. They would capture her or burn her alive. Fire was the only other way to death.

She walked toward the gate. When the solodats spotted her, they raised their weapons. The caccia guns shone in the sun, metal depths radiating rainbows outward across the men's body armor. The solodats wore requisition gear, criss-crossed ammunition of small crystal caccia balls on their backs, deadly ammo that when dropped into the magazine would shelter in its metal casing until the hammer broke its sleep and the caccia hurtled toward their next victim.

As she approached, Adele named each of the crystals already snug in the caccia. She raised her hands, empty, to the sky, as she walked the long walk to the post.

"Stop. Hands in the air!" A solodat cried out when she'd nearly reached the post. The men marched forward to meet her. She began to speak, but one knocked down her outstretched hands. He turned her roughly, in a moment he ripped the pack off her back. The other kicked her legs out from beneath her. She was glad for the blue jeans as her knees hit gravel. The caccia gun was cold against her temple. Inside the blackness crystal death waited to burst inside her body, to make her insides shards of light. Would the caccia be able to penetrate her? Or was she still part-other?

"I want to pass through the wall," she said through gritted teeth, willing her aching arms to stay in the air.

"Shut up." The solodat who'd spoken earlier was pulling apart her pack.

"I don't have any weapons," she said. The man grunted, a half-laugh. The cards went sprawling across the gravel. The little items she'd collected along the way came out too, the music box that played a tinny tune when turned, a scrap of her mother's bones pulled from the rubble, little giocattolo she'd found along the way, a red racing car, a Raggedy Ann doll, an elephant made of pewter, the book she'd been teaching herself to read with so when she went back to the real world she'd fit in better—Paradise Lost.

"Look," said the other solodat, pointing even as he held the weapon to her head. He pointed at the fox tails.

"You been with others girl?" The solodat asked, his fat fingers leaving her pack. He stood up and kicked the pack aside.

"No," she said. Her voice sounded tiny in her ears.

"Why do you want to cross?"

"I just want to go home," she said. *I just want to get back to the place before this place, the real world on the other side. The countryside, where I was safe, far away from the others and the cities that aren't cities anymore.* She wondered if anyone would remember her there. All her memories seemed tied to this place and the last few years, the last few horrible decisions. Waiting behind her. If she went across the border she might be able to travel back in time.

"You got a clearance to pass?"

"Is that necessary?"

"New rules. Others have been crossing over. Hidden."

She dared to look up at the man to see if he lied. But despite his guise of power, the power of the weapon now shouldered on his back, his face was a blank canvas. Not lying. The other solodat was now cleaning his weapon, adjusting his armor. Adele leaned back on her heels. The sun beamed down on her face. She glanced at the woods. They were flat-green, wavering in the summer heat. Once as a girl she'd played in their coolness, the olive groves and valleys of sweetness. Now they seemed always so close to the road, always encroaching on civilization, if you could call it that, threatening to take back what was theirs.

"I never needed clearance to get in."

"That's different. If people want to feed others with their own deaths that's one thing. But these new reports say others are getting through somehow."

"Breaks in the wall?" She didn't need to ask but she asked anyway.

The solodat shook his head. "Hiding in the skins of people."

Adele closed her eyes. She pushed down the feeling rising in her gut, the churning need to get away. "That can't be," she said.

"Come back when you've got clearance," the solodat said. He walked away, leaving her possessions scattered across the road. A camion labored up the road in the distance. Adele listened to its rumble, felt the ground vibrate with its weight. She scrabbled in the dust for her things, shoving them back in her pack, her face burning. When the camion passed, the solodats resumed their posts to wave it past.

Knave of Wands (Wolf)

Companion, friendship, good news, *rivals in love, bad news, gossip.*

Fante de bastoni. Once it lay on the rock between Adele and Orson, she immediately regretted letting herself play this game with him. He regarded the card with his bushy brows down over his face, and she saw a smile play at his chops. But he asked her to tell the story again.

"When I was a little girl, my grandmother played these cards with the old ladies in their sewing circle. They'd do the laundry, hanging great white sheets up between the houses, and their bloomers out for everyone to see. Then they'd sit in the courtyard between the white sheets and play cards. My grandmother never wanted to teach me how to play the game they played. She said I was too young for it. But when I went back, the cards were in the basement, tucked into her hope chest, waiting for me. The chest was the most beautiful thing I'd ever seen. It was made of cedar. Despite the smell of caccia all around me I could still smell the cedar."

"Too bad you couldn't take the hope chest too," Orson said. "I'd like to have smelled it just once." He nosed the card, urging her to flip it.

"Fante de bastoni," Adele muttered. "The wolf hunter. The lizard at his feet is his best friend. At night they go out hunting for food. Small rabbits. Foxes. But only under the full moon do they sing together. They sing about how happy the woods make them. They sing to the moon." Adele felt the wind shift around her, the trees whisper. Others lingered at the edges of the fire, listening to her voice.

Orson regarded Adele. "Do you remember when we went on our first hunt? We found that couple down by the lake. We scared them off and then we caught frogs because you were too afraid to try your first meat. Then we hunted again the next day and ate possum, bones and all."

"What story do you see, Orson?" Adele asked. Orson tilted his head at her.

"Do you remember the way we used to curl up at night all in a group? We'd groom each other and you'd sing us songs. You were our Wendy."

"Do you want to play the game or not?"

Orson looked back at the cards. "The wolf is not a wolf but other. A solodat other. He's carrying a caccia because he's a wolf in sheep's clothing. He's going to get past the wall in disguise. Then the other side will be other too."

Adele looked at Orson. He met her eyes but guilt flickered behind his irises. Adele looked out beyond the circle of firelight. She saw the eyes of others there in the darkness watching her.

"You can come with us across the border or you can stay here and die," Orson said, his voice danger-soft. "We'd prefer if you picked up your old skin and wore it proudly."

"Orson, you can't do this," Adele pleaded. The cards fell from her hands, tortoises and swans and cats and lions scattering across the moonlit grass. "You'll bring others to the real world."

"Who's to say what's the real world, Adie?" Orson asked. He looked up at the moon. It was dwindling. "Do you remember the night we first made love? You singled me out in the pack, scrawny me. Now look at how far I've come, I'm leading others to greatness."

"I didn't pick you from the pack, Orson. You were human, remember? We met in the woods and we both went other together."

"That's not how the story goes," Orson replied, looking confused.

He doesn't remember anymore, Adele thought. "You're leading them to death," Adele said. She stood up, picking up the cards one by one. So many beautiful settings and landscapes, all the animals safe behind plastic. She threw the cards into the fire. Orson made a small noise in his throat, like sadness, or anger. Adele looked at them, crackling, burning. She used to believe they were magic cards, that somehow if she found the right story the cards would save her.

How long before the solodats decided the woods were too dangerous to keep? Before they sent the camions into the trees, to break them down, to burn them to the ground? How long before the caccia crystals would be buried along the road, sprouting their spiky crystal ferns, eating up the passersby with their death-locks? How long before the caccia spread to the others, or worse, the other spread to everyone else?

The sky turned red slowly like blood welling from a pricked finger. Adele shouldered her pack. She walked between others. They made a path for her.

She reached the road. Farther back she'd seen a command center. She might be granted clearance there. The little square buildings lined the road leading up to the wall, where the soldiers had refused her escape.

Orson let her go, not knowing she'd get to the command and tell the solodats where a group of others waited in the woods, waited for their real leader to return, waited to take the bodies of unsuspecting men, waited to take the wall and tear it down with their teeth, waited to other the world forever. The others didn't know Adele wanted to be human again so badly she'd see their world burn before she let them other her again.

Have you received the answer you were seeking? There are other ways, of course, if you don't like this interpretation. You can always carry a single card in your pocket, sleep with it under your pillow, or try a different variation. Three simple cards laid in a row. The celtic cross. Or else, simply shuffle the deck again.

About the Author

Holly Lyn Walrath is a writer of poetry and short fiction. Her work has appeared or is forthcoming in Strange Horizons, Fireside Fiction, Liminality, *and elsewhere. She is a freelance editor and volunteer with Writespace literary center in Houston, Texas. Her website is www.hlwalrath.com.*

AFTERWORD

Thank you for reading! We hope noblebright fantasy has captured your imagination as it has ours. You can find more noblebright fantasy at springsongpress.com and at noblebright.org.

C. J. Brightley
Spring Song Press

Made in the USA
Lexington, KY
09 October 2018